# TRAITORS' GATE

They strove for mastery with gritted teeth, straining their muscles to the utmost and jerking from side to side as they fought. Grauber managed to keep a firm grip on Gregory's windpipe. Only by keeping his chin well down could he save himself from complete strangulation, and his breath was now coming in short, sobbing gasps. Yet he knew that his vicious chops at the German's Adam's apple must be causing him exquisite agony, and he could see that one eye was growing misty. A few more strokes and the pain must render him unconscious.

# BY DENNIS WHEATLEY

## NOVELS

The Launching of Roger Brook
The Shadow of Tyburn Tree
The Rising Storm
The Man Who Killed the King
The Dark Secret of Josephine
The Rape of Venice
The Sultan's Daughter
The Wanton Princess
Evil in a Mask
The Ravishing of Lady
  Mary Ware

The Scarlet Impostor
Faked Passports
The Black Baroness
V for Vengeance
Come Into My Parlour
Traitors' Gate
They Used Dark Forces

The Prisoner in the Mask
The Second Seal
Vendetta in Spain
Three Inquisitive People
The Forbidden Territory
The Devil Rides Out
The Golden Spaniard
Strange Conflict
Codeword—Golden Fleece
Dangerous Inheritance
Gateway to Hell

The Quest of Julian Day
The Sword of Fate
Bill for the Use of a Body

Black August
Contraband
The Island Where Time Stands
  Still
The White Witch of the South
  Seas

To the Devil—a Daughter
The Satanist

The Eunuch of Stamboul
The Secret War
The Fabulous Valley
Sixty Days to Live
Such Power is Dangerous
Uncharted Seas
The Man Who Missed the War
The Haunting of Toby Jugg
Star of Ill-Omen
They Found Atlantis
The Ka of Gifford Hillary
Curtain of Fear
Mayhem in Greece
Unholy Crusade
The Strange Story of Linda Lee
The Irish Witch

## SHORT STORIES

Mediterranean Nights          Gunmen, Gallants and Ghosts

## HISTORICAL

A Private Life of Charles II (*Illustrated by Frank C. Papé*)
Red Eagle (*The Story of the Russian Revolution*)

## AUTOBIOGRAPHICAL

Stranger than Fiction (*War Papers for the Joint Planning Staff*)
Saturdays with Bricks

## SATANISM

The Devil and all his Works (*Illustrated in colour*)

*Dennis Wheatley*

# TRAITORS' GATE

**ARROW BOOKS**

**ARROW BOOKS LTD**
3 Fitzroy Square, London W1

An imprint of the Hutchinson Publishing Group

London Melbourne Sydney Auckland
Wellington Johannesburg Cape Town
and agencies throughout the world

First published by Hutchinson & Co (Publishers) Ltd 1958
Arrow edition 1961
Second edition 1966
Third edition 1970
Second impression 1971
This edition 1975

Made and printed in Great Britain
by The Anchor Press Ltd
Tiptree, Essex
ISBN 0 09 910480 6

# Contents

The following quotations are of interest in view of the background of the story.

'Secrecy can only be maintained by deception. For this purpose I am . . . Thus we shall keep the enemy in doubt until the last moment.' Letter from Prime Minister to President regarding preparations for TORCH; 27/7/42. *The Second World War* by Winston S. Churchill, Vol. IV, p. 405.

'Even the President helped out in this particular deception.' *Crusade in Europe* by General Eisenhower, p. 105.

'. . . still engaged in discussions with the Prime Minister in Cabinet and the Chiefs of Staff Committee about the expedition's build up and various deception and security measures for keeping the enemy guessing its destination.' *The Turn of the Tide* by Arthur Bryant, based on the War Diaries of Field Marshal the Viscount Alanbrooke.

# Author's Note

The sequence of the seven books which recount the war adventures of Gregory Sallust is as follows: *The Scarlet Impostor, Faked Passports, The Black Baroness, V for Vengeance, Come Into My Parlour, Traitors' Gate* and *They Used Dark Forces*. Each volume is a complete story in itself, but the series covers Gregory's activities from September, 1939, to May, 1945, against an unbroken background incorporating all the principal events of the Second World War.

Gregory Sallust also appears in four other books: *Black August,* a story set in an undated future; *Contraband,* an international smuggling story of 1937; *The Island Where Time Stands Still,* an adventure set in the South Seas and Communist China during the year 1954; and *The White Witch of the South Seas,* a modern tale of intrigue and suspense set in Brazil, Guatemala and the Fijis.

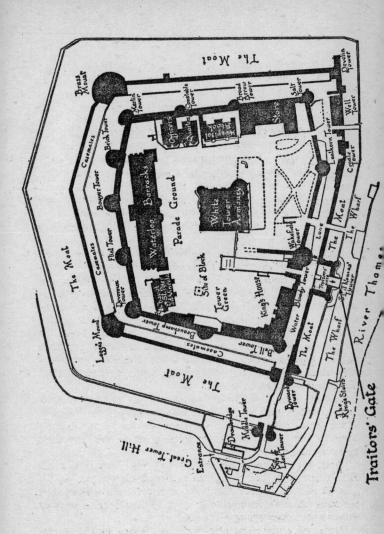

# 1

# A Small Buff Form for Gregory

Late on the night of July 25th 1942 a little group of senior staff-officers stood talking together in a small underground room. They all looked tired and a little pasty. That was hardly to be wondered at as they worked, on average, sixteen hours a day and seldom emerged from the fortress-basement in which, as members of the Joint Planning Staff of the War Cabinet, they had their quarters.

The semi-circular cellar in which they stood had been converted into a mess only as an emergency convenience during the worst air-raids of 1940. In its centre two card tables put together enabled six officers to sit down to a meal. One angle was curtained off and behind it a Royal Marine heated soup or knocked up an egg-dish as required; against the wall in the other stood a steel filing cabinet; but, instead of papers, its shelves carried an assortment of bottles and glasses. Crowded into the small space in front of it, the Planners were imbibing stiff whiskies and sodas before betaking themselves to their bunks in a still lower basement.

Usually their off-duty chatter was as light as that of other men, but they had just come from a midnight conference at which a momentous decision had been announced and instructions for intensive detailed planning given to them by their masters, the Chiefs of Staff.

'Well, Mr. Marlborough has got his way,' remarked a tall Air Commodore, 'but God alone knows how it will pan out.'

A Captain, R.N., nodded. 'Pity we couldn't have postponed the issue till 1943. Having to go over to the offensive so early means risking everything we've got.'

'Roosevelt's insistence that American troops should be employed against the Germans in 1942 left us no option,' shrugged a Gunner Colonel. 'Since the Washington Conference it has

11

only been a question of whether we did *Sledgehammer* or *Gymnast*.'

'The Cherbourg job would have been murder,' declared a Brigadier of Royal Marines. 'And, even if we could have established ourselves on the peninsula, we haven't got the weight of trained troops to break out. It would have become a wasting sore.'

The sailor nodded. 'At least we can console ourselves with the thought that we stopped Marshall and Harry Hopkins forcing that one on us, and have all along backed the P.M.'s preference for North Africa.'

'If it comes off it will pay tremendous dividends,' put in a Group Captain who always appeared to be a little sleepy, but was never quite as sleepy as he looked. 'With the whole of the south side of the Med. in our hands convoys will be able to go through again; and Malta, instead of being a drain on us, will become a dagger aimed at what the old man calls "the shoft underbelly of the Axchis".'

The tall Air Commodore took him up quickly. 'Now that Rommel has given the Auk such a bloody nose there can be no hope of the Eighth Army doing *Acrobat* this year; and it will be months before we can achieve a big enough build-up in Algeria to attempt an advance into Tripolitania. Any idea of a link-up in 1942 is now only wishful thinking.'

'We can't expect the Germans to take this show lying down either,' said the Colonel. 'I'd give pretty well any odds that the moment they learn that the Americans and ourselves have gone into Morocco and Algeria they'll scrap their agreement with the Vichy French and pour troops into Tunisia.'

'And put every aircraft they can spare into Sicily and Sardinia,' added the Air Commodore.

'It could be worse than that,' the Brigadier declared grimly. 'If there's a leak they'll take measures beforehand. Then our convoys will sail straight into a trap. Just think of it. Scores of transports crammed with troops coming through the Straits of Gib. with a submarine pack lying in wait for them. And Kesselring's dive-bombers thick as locusts coming in for the kill. It could be a massacre before we even had a chance to get ashore at all.'

At the awful picture he conjured up the others fell silent for a moment. All of them knew that shipping tonnage we could not possibly afford to lose, hundreds of escort vessels manned by the cream of the Navy, and many thousands of our best troops—in fact everything that Britain could scrape together short of sufficient squadrons of the R.A.F. to protect her from invasion—must be gambled in this great operation.

While they still stood silent a Lt.-Colonel, his fair hair slightly ruffled and his blue eyes a little blurred from having sat up till one in the morning reading staff papers, joined them. Smiling round, he said, 'Well, chaps; what's cooking?'

The Brigadier gave him a twisted smile. 'We've headed the Yanks off from getting themselves and us slaughtered on the French beaches; but *Gymnast* is on. That's definite. The P.M. has given it a new code name, though. In future it is to be know as "Operation *Torch*". At best, in about a year from now, we'll have the whole of North Africa. At worst, the chaps we got off from Dunkirk, and God knows how many thousands more, will be in Davy Jones's locker. Everything depends on the Germans being kept in the dark up till the very last moment. Even when our convoys are reported going through the Straits of Gib. the Boche must be led to believe that we intend to land the troops anywhere other than in Algeria. Thank God that's not my headache. It's yours, Johnny; so here's good luck to you!'

The Brigadier finished his whisky and added, 'You'll need it. This is about the toughest assignment any man has ever had.'

\*　　　\*　　　\*　　　\*　　　\*

At the time of the above conversation no one could possibly have foreseen that Fate had designated Gregory Sallust to play a key role in this tough assignment, and even less that his uninvited participation would make him liable to court-martial, imprisonment and disgrace.

To explain how this came about it is necessary to go back four months. To be precise, to the morning of Monday, March 30th, when at the breakfast table Gregory opened a buff envelope.

After one glance at the flimsy it contained, he sat back and roared with laughter. It was a 'call-up' paper, notifying him that he must report for a medical examination within fourteen days or become liable to grievous penalties.

His mirth was understandable seeing that for the past two and a half years he had been in closer and more constant con-

13

flict with the Nazis than had any member of our fighting Services. As a secret agent he had been parachuted into Germany in September 1939. Since then he had pitted his wits against *Herr Gruppenführer* Grauber—the dreaded chief of the Gestapo's Foreign Department—in Finland, Norway, Holland, Belgium, France and Russia.

On the other side of the breakfast table the Countess von Osterberg raised her tapering eyebrows. It was largely those eyebrows and her high cheekbones that gave her such a startling resemblance to Marlene Dietrich, and caused her still to be spoken of by those who had known her before her marriage as 'the beautiful Erika von Epp'.

In response to her look of interrogation, Gregory flicked the paper over to her and said, 'Early this month the Government extended the call-up to include men aged 41 to 45. It never crossed my mind that the measure would apply to me but, of course, it does.'

Having glanced at the paper, Erika smiled. 'But surely, darling, your name is on some special list; and all you need do is to let the people who sent this know that?'

'No. I'm privately employed by Sir Pellinore. For many years past the old boy has used a part of his millions to throw spanners in the works of the enemies of Britain, and on several occasions I have been the spanner. It was natural enough that when the war came he should ask me to carry on with the good work, and I've always preferred to play the part of a lone wolf. If one gets caught then it can only be through one's own ill-luck or stupidity.'

'Whenever you set off on a mission, though, the military authorities give you every assistance, and when you went to Russia you were accredited to the British Embassy.'

'Old Pellinore is persona grata with everyone who matters, from the King down, and he often pulls strings to get things done for the War Cabinet that they prefer not to appear in themselves; so it is easy for him to get me any help I require. But the fact remains that I am not even unofficially associated with any of our Intelligence Services.'

'Sir Pellinore could soon arrange that for you.'

'No doubt. But I don't want to be. I would be under orders then, and perhaps be roped in to play a part in some cloak and dagger job that I thought ill-conceived. When it is my life I am gambling with I prefer to make my own plans and keep them

14

to myself. Besides, twice in the past year old man Grauber has as near as damn it got me; so I don't feel inclined to give him another chance. At least, not yet, anyway.'

Erika needed no reminding how near a shave Gregory had had last time, for she had been with him,* and it still made her flesh creep to think of the sort of death that Grauber would have meted out to them. Yet, even so, death had reached out grisly fingers after their escape. That had taken place early in December and, as a result of exposure to the bitter cold, both of them had gone down with pneumonia while Gregory, in addition, was suffering from two cracked ribs.

Fortunately they had been met on the Swiss shore of Lake Constance by their devoted friend Stefan Kaporovitch, the ex-Bolshevik General with whom they had fled from Finland in April 1940. Stefan had secured prompt medical aid, stood by until they became convalescent, then arranged for them to be flown back to England.

Sir Pellinore had sent them up to Gwaine Meads, a great rambling mansion situated on the Welsh border, that had been in the possession of his family since the Wars of the Roses. The greater part of it was now an R.A.F. hospital maintained by him out of his private fortune; but he had retained one wing for his own use, although he never found time to stay in it himself. At the moment Erika and Gregory were its only occupants as there had been no newcomers since the end of February, when Sir Pellinore had arranged for Stefan to become a consultant to the Russian Section of the War Office; so he and his charming French wife, Marie, had gone to live in London.

By then Erika had sufficiently recovered to resume the duties she had undertaken at Gwaine Meads before she had been tricked into returning to the Continent. Technically she ranked as an enemy alien, but Sir Pellinore had saved her from internment by vouching for her, and she had since played a dual role, giving her able brain to the financial administration of the hospital and her ravishing presence to lightening the boredom of the convalescing officers.

Gregory, on the other hand, was lazy by nature and, in spite of the acute shortage of staff on the estate caused by the war, refused to be inveigled into any regular commitment. He knew little of mechanics and practically nothing about electricity; he had never used a spade, detested weeding, and con-

*See *Come into my Parlour.*

sidered that the only thing more soul-destroying than looking after horses was to look after cows, pigs or chickens. So he was useless in garage, stables, garden and farmyard. But he did spend a lot of his time yarning with the gallant young men who were knocking hell out of the Luftwaffe and, occasionally, he would labour furiously from dawn to dusk for several consecutive days on some suddenly self-imposed task, such as painting the summer house or reputtying the vinery.

It was now the end of March and, although for well over a month past he had again been reasonably fit, as he had just said to Erika, he felt no urge as yet to get back into the war.

Standing up, he walked over to the sideboard to pour himself a second cup of coffee. As he did so, Erika surveyed him critically. He was lean and loose-limbed; of medium height but actually somewhat taller than he looked from his habit of walking with his head thrust forward, which made him appear to have a permanent stoop. His lantern-jawed face had two deep laughter lines etched like brackets on either side of his thin-lipped, resolute mouth. His eyes were brown and his eyebrows slightly bushy. From the outer end of the left one a white scar ran up towards the dark smooth hair that made a 'widow's peak' in the centre of his forehead. On occasions such as the present, when something had occurred to worry him, he always reminded Erika of a very dangerous caged animal plotting to break free. After a moment she said:

'Each time you go abroad means months of agony for me, and the risks you have already run are far greater than most men have to take in a war. You would have nothing with which to reproach yourself if you decided against ever going again on a secret mission. Why not accept this as a kindly decree by Fate that, for the rest of the war, your chances of coming through should be no worse than those of any other Army Officer?'

'Officer, eh!' Gregory gave a cynical laugh. 'My sweet, you don't understand. This is not like the old war in which chaps such as myself could volunteer at the age of seventeen and were commissioned straight from our Public Schools. Now, people are called up in batches as required—the gallant, the cowards, the intelligent and the morons—and pushed through the military machine like so many sausages. Under this crazy system it takes a year at least for even the most promising young man to become a Second Lieutenant.'

Erica was descended from a long line of Generals and in Germany the 'officer caste' was still more sharply divided from the rank and file than it had ever been in Britain. Her big blue eyes wide, she stared at Gregory and exclaimed:

'You don't . . . you can't mean that they would put a man like you in the ranks?'

'They certainly would. Having held a commission in the last war counts for nothing in this one. And, as I am over forty, I'd probably find myself employed as a grave digger, or as an orderly in the Sanitary Corps. But I won't have it! I'm damned if I will! I don't mind danger but I've always loathed drudgery and discomfort.'

For a moment he glowered down at the small buff form, then he tapped it angrily with his forefinger. 'Still, I can't ignore this. Old Pellinore must get me out of it somehow. I'd better pack a bag and take the first train to London.'

## 2

## Dark Days for Britain

Sir Pellinore Gwaine-Cust was one of those remarkable products which seem peculiar to Britain. In his youth he had been a subaltern in a crack cavalry regiment and during the Boer War he had won a well-deserved V.C. A few years later, his ill-luck at some of the little baccarat parties that friends of his gave for King Edward VII, and his generosity towards certain ladies of the Gaiety chorus, made it necessary for him to leave the Army and he accepted a seat on the Board of a small private Bank which operated mainly in the Near East.

His acquaintances thought of him as a handsome fellow with an eye for a horse or a pretty woman, and an infinite capacity for vintage port, but very little brain—an illusion which he still did his utmost to maintain—so the Directorship had been offered to him solely on account of his social connexions. To the surprise of those concerned he took to business like a duck to water.

Under his bluff, jovial manner there lurked a most subtle

mind, and his transparent honesty seemed to have such an hypnotic effect on Orientals and Levantines that they usually failed to realise that he had got the best of the deal until they were well on their way home. Other Directorships had followed. By 1914 he was already a power in the City; after the war he had refused a peerage on the grounds that there had been a Gwaine-Cust at Gwaine Meads for so many centuries that if he changed his name his tenants would think he had sold the place; foresight had enabled him to bring his companies safely through the slump of the early 1930's and he had emerged from it immensely rich.

Although his name was hardly known to the general public, it had long been respected in Government circles. To his great mansion in Carlton House Terrace, Diplomats, Generals, Colonial Governors and Cabinet Ministers often came to consult him privately on their problems and they rarely left without having drawn new strength from his boundless vitality and shrewd common sense.

He was well over seventy, but the only indication of his age was the snowy whiteness of his hair, his bushy eyebrows and luxuriant cavalry moustache. His startlingly blue eyes were as bright as ever, he stood six feet four in his socks and could still have thrown most men of forty down his staircase.

When Gregory arrived at Carlton House Terrace he was told that Sir Pellinore was at a meeting in the City; but, knowing that he would be expected to stay the night, he had his bag carried up to the room he usually occupied, then went into the library to await his host's return.

It was a fine lofty room at the back of the house with a splendid view across St. James's Park to the Admiralty, the Horse Guards and the other massive buildings in which throbbed the heart of Britain's war machine. For a few minutes he stood looking out at the tender green of the young leaves now breaking on the trees of the park, then he took from one of the shelves a copy of James Hilton's *Lost Horizon* and became immersed once more in that wonderful story until heavy footfalls sounded on the landing and Sir Pellinore came marching in.

'Hello, young feller! Glad to see you!' he boomed, grasping Gregory's hand in his leg-of-mutton fist. 'So you're fed up already with kickin' your heels in the country, eh? Well, I'd hoped you'd continue to take it easy for a bit, but we're a long way from having won the damn war yet; so if you're spoilin' to have another crack at the Nazis it's not for me to stop you.'

Gregory gave a wry grin. 'You're off the mark for once. I didn't come here to ask about another mission and I do want another few months of idleness. But, unless you can pull a fast one for me, I'm not going to get them. I've been called-up.'

'Well, I'll be jiggered!' Sir Pellinore slapped a mighty thigh encased in pin-striped trousers. 'What a lark! Strap me, but this is the funniest thing I've heard for years.'

'It struck me as funny too, to begin with. But it is no laughing matter. D'you realise that they would bung me in the ranks and perhaps make me a mess-waiter?'

'Not to start with! That's promotion!' The elderly Baronet's bright blue eyes glinted merrily, and he gave a great guffaw of laughter. 'At least it was in my day. Job given to steady chaps who could be trusted not to pinch the sherry or pour the soup down one's neck. After one glance at that truculent jaw of yours, any Sergeant-Major who knows his business would put you on to cleaning out the latrines. That's about what you can expect!'

'But seriously, you must get me out of this.'

The under-butler had followed Sir Pellinore into the room with a tray of drinks. Turning, his master waved a hand towards them. 'What'll you have? I keep most of this muck for visitors who haven't the sense to respect their guts. Stick to good wine topped off with a spot of old brandy and you'll still be chasin' the gels round the gooseberry bush when you're as old as I am.' As he spoke he poured himself out a tumbler full of Manzanilla, then drank half of it off in a couple of gulps.

Having annexed a slightly more modest ration, Gregory asked, 'Now, what about it?'

Sir Pellinore carried his glass over to an arm-chair, sat down, stretched out his long legs and muttered: 'Damned if I know. If you were a Colonel and wanted to be a Brigadier, I don't doubt I could get you transferred to a job that carries that rank. If you wanted to shift a quarter of a million in gold from Arabia to Peru, I could fix it for you. If you had a yen for an O.B.E. I'd have your name pushed in well up in the next Honours List. But this is a very different kettle of fish. You have received a summons under an order decreed by Parliament, and even Cabinet Ministers can't monkey with the law.'

'Oh come! Miners, factory workers, agricultural labourers, and all sorts of other people get exemption; but their bosses have to make the application for them, and you are mine.'

'What would you have me put you down as? Olga Petrovsky, my beautiful spy? Be your age, boy! We couldn't let the little office wallahs who handle these sort of things get even an inkling of the truth.'

'You could say that I was your confidential secretary.'

'No damn fear. Too many people are aware that you are not.'

'Well; what's to be done, then?'

'The obvious thing is for me to get you put on the strength of one of the cloak and dagger outfits; then a chit would be sent from the War House putting you in the clear. Of course, these shows are under bureaucratic control just like all the rest, as far as their establishments are concerned; so you'd be graded, paid accordingly and expected to earn the money.'

'Then I'd probably have to work in an office sifting other people's reports for hours on end every day, or find myself bundled off abroad to some place that I have already made too hot to hold me. No, thank you.'

Sir Pellinore took another gulp of sherry. 'Does that mean you've had your fill of spying? Be a thunderin' pity—seeing you're so good at it. Still, after all the *coups* you've pulled off no one could blame you if you decided to swallow your vest pocket camera—or whatever is a spy's equivalent for a sailor's anchor.'

'No. It's the most exciting game in the world; and any time that you want me to undertake another mission I'll go back into Germany for you. But I've got *some* common sense, and I'd like still to be alive at the end of the war. If I let myself be made into a small time operator and make a regular job of sticking my neck in the noose, all the odds are that I shan't be.'

'That's fair enough. Trouble is though that you're now in an age group in which every man jack has to have a regular job of some kind. No evading that—unless you want to end up in a police court. It really would be best for you to go into one of the Services. I'd have no trouble about hoiking you out then, when required.'

'Most convenient for you, dear master. Just drop me a

postcard whenever you next wish me to risk being castrated by Grauber and Co. In the meantime, I'll be in the seventh heaven alternately swabbing dishes and lavatory seats.'

'Insolent young devil,' rumbled Sir Pellinore, brushing up his white moustache. 'It won't be as bad as all that, though. I'll get you fixed up in some white-collar occupation. Pay Corps perhaps, or interviewing cooks for the Army Caterin' Service.'

'Either would drive me off my rocker within a month; and I've already told you that I flatly refuse to serve in the ranks.'

'Very understandable in a man of your attainments. I'd feel the same myself. Glad I did my service while old Vickie was on the Throne. When I joined I took my own chargers, valet and groom, and they gave me a trumpeter to ride behind me. Now if the trumpeter has been in longer it's you who have to ride behind him—even if he couldn't get ten per cent marks in an average general knowledge paper. That's democracy; but there's another name for it—race suicide. Mark my words, Gregory; Hitler will never smash the British Empire, but our socialist-minded bureaucracy will.'

Gregory nodded, refilled his glass from the decanter, and muttered, 'Let's stick to my personal problem. You know that I wouldn't ask for a commission unless I felt justified in doing so. Damn it, I held one for two years in the last war and a score of times led men into battle. Surely there is some way you can fix it for me.'

'I know of none. Anyhow, as far as the Army is concerned. Still, I'm dining with the Castletowns tonight. Old Maudie told me that Pug Ismay will be there, if he can get away. Hope he is. Great fun listening to Pug at a mixed party. Everyone hangs on his words while he talks about the high direction of the war and gives away the most deadly secrets. At least, that's the impression he conveys. He's a genius at it. But later, of course, if one takes the trouble to analyse it all, one realises that he hasn't said a damn thing that anyone couldn't have read in the previous morning's paper. If he turns up I'll have a word with him about you.'

'Thanks. What is the latest low-down on the war?'

'The St. Nazaire raid proved a winner.'

'Good; that's fine.'

'Full details only just been issued. Complete surprise achieved. Navy broke the boom, then ran in an old U.S.

21

destroyer packed full of T.N.T. and blew the dock gates with her. Meanwhile the Commandos got ashore and gave the wurst-eaters bloody hell.'

'That's spendid news. The very thing the Navy needed to set its stock up again after that shocking business last month.'

'You mean *Scharnhorst, Gneisenau* and *Prinz Eugen* breaking out of Brest and cocking a snook at Dover as they sailed up Channel?'

'Yes. I wonder Nelson didn't rise from his grave at the very idea of an enemy squadron being allowed to pass the Straits without a battle.'

Sir Pellinore shrugged. 'The Boche were both patient and lucky. Waited for the worst possible weather, and it happened to coincide with a breakdown in our air-reconnaissance. They weren't spotted till they were off the Kent coast, and Dover is too vulnerable these days for us to keep any war-craft there. The real blunder was our attempt to retrieve the situation by attacking with aircraft so late on a February afternoon. The planes had to go in low down and practically blind. The hits they scored were at the price of suicide.'

'Surely there was still time to despatch some units of the Home Fleet, from farther north, to intercept the Germans before they reached their ports?'

'They were covered by successive wings of Luftwaffe the whole way up the coast. After the loss of *Prince of Wales* and *Repulse* last December we dared not expose any more of our capital ships to possible annihilation.'

Gregory nodded glumly. 'The news from the Far East continues to be pretty shattering, doesn't it?'

'Lord, yes! Hong Kong, Malaya, Java, Sumatra, Borneo—all gone in little more than three months. And we haven't seen the end of it by a long chalk. The Yanks have made a great stand in the Philippines, but they're now at the end of their tether. Same applies to our chaps in Burma. It's going to be a toss up if we can even save India.'

'If things are as bad as that it's a comfort to know that its defence now rests with General Sir Harold Alexander.'

'True! It couldn't be in better hands. Trouble is, it's barely a fortnight since they sent him out there; and there can't have been much for him to take over—only a tangle of broken units composed of poor devils half dead from having fought their way back right up the peninsula. Still, there's a sporting

22

chance that those little yellow apes may be sufficiently extended for Alex to hold them by the time they get to the Chin river.'

'And how about Australia?' Gregory enquired. 'That should be our worst worry at the moment.'

'It would be, if the U.S. were not prepared to take Australia under her wing. There's some reason, too, to believe that the Jap effort down in that direction is petering out. The United States Navy made them pay a very heavy price for their landings in New Guinea; and Australia is too big a mouthful for them to try to swallow. That is, unless they're prepared to go over to the defensive on all their other fronts.'

'The Australians don't seem to see things that way.'

'They would if it wasn't for that Socialist feller Curtin that they've saddled themselves with as Prime Minister. He's usin' the crisis as a political weapon—telling them all that Churchill and his Tory pals would rather not risk the skin off a little finger than raise a hand to save Australia from the Japs. It's a thunderin' lie, of course. All their troops have been released from the Middle East; and when Churchill was in Washington he secured a positive assurance from the President that, if need be, American troops should be sent to Australia instead of to Europe, and would defend the country to the last ditch. The lies that are being put out are Australian Labour's cover-up for their party's criminal negligence in having refused to introduce National Service, although it was clear that the Japs might enter the war against us at any time.'

Gregory nodded. 'It's good to think that our folk down under are in no real danger. Now; what's the latest low-down about Russia?'

'Oh, they never stop yellin' that they'll have to chuck their hand in unless we can take the pressure off them by openin' a Second Front.'

'Our new commitments against the Japs must have ruled that out for the time being.'

'Lord, yes. Having to make good the gaps left in the Middle East by the withdrawal of the Australian divisions, and putting some teeth into the defence of India, forced us to scrape the bottom of the bucket.'

'Still, the Russians must know that American troops have been arriving in Northern Ireland for the past two months; so it's very understandable that they should be calling for an

Anglo-American landing on the Continent. And I suppose the build-up might become big enough to justify that some time this summer?'

'Not a hope. It takes more than a lot of bodies to launch a great amphibious operation. You ought to know that. They've got to be specially trained. Then there's the Q side. Think of all the millions of tons of ammunition and stores required.'

'Now the huge industrial plants in the United States are fully geared for war, surely they can take care of all material requirements?'

'Ah, that's what the public think. Fact is we've more head-aches about equipment and supplies than we had last year. Before the Yanks came in they were giving us everything they'd got. Now they are having to think of themselves as well, and the war they're fightin' in the Pacific. It's meant that we'll not have anything like the numbers of aircraft and tanks we had hoped to have by the summer. Then there's the question of all these new-fangled landin'-craft. Hundreds would be required, and as yet we've got 'em only in dozens. That and shipping are the worst snags. Even if the Yanks could let us have the goods it's doubtful now if we could get them over.'

'Is the shipping situation really all that desperate?'

'Desperate's the word—or will be if sinkings continue at their present rate.'

'I thought the convoy system had taken the worst sting out of the U-boats.'

'So it has, in British controlled waters. But we haven't yet persuaded our friends on the other side of the wisdom of adopting it. Doenitz is cashin' in on that. Since Christmas his U-boat packs have been operating almost within sight of New York harbour. In January he was getting three ships a day; now it's up to nine. This month he's made a record killing. Eight hundred thousand tons sunk already. If he can keep that up God knows if we'll ever be able to launch an assault against Hitler's Europe. Anyhow, you can count it out for 1942.'

Getting to his feet, Sir Pellinore added in a more cheerful tone, 'Only comforting thought is that the British people are running true to form. We always have won the last battle in every war. That's what really matters. Can't stop gossiping here all night with you, though. Got to have a bath and freshen myself up. Sorry I've got to go out; but if you like to dine

24

here I'll tell Crawshay to get up a bottle of the Roederer '28 for you to drink with your dinner.'

'Thanks; that's a temptation to stay in,' Gregory grinned. 'But after our chat I feel I need a little cheering up; so I'll see if I can find a few blissfully ignorant and optimistic types at my club. It would be nice, though, if we could split that bottle in the morning.'

'Good idea. Eleven o'clock, eh? I often take a pint at that hour. Learnt the habit from my Colonel when I was a youngster. He used to call it "a little eleven o'clock", and always asked one of his subalterns to join him. Stuff cost only six bob a bottle in those days. Well, don't break your neck in the blackout. Poor sort of endin' for a feller like you.'

On the following morning, knowing that his host liked to have a clear hour in which to deal with his most urgent affairs, Gregory tactfully refrained from going to the library until eleven o'clock. On his entering it Sir Pellinore told his secretary to go and get on with the letters, then pointed to the bottle which already reposed in an ice-bucket on the drinks table. Gregory opened it, and for a few minutes, while enjoying the first fragrance of the wine, they exchanged pleasant platitudes; then, no longer able to restrain his impatience, he asked:

'Well; was General Ismay there last night?'

'What, Pug?' Sir Pellinore's voice was casual. 'Oh yes, he was in great form. I had a word with him about you. As I supposed, direct Commissions into the Army are absolutely out. Still, steps are being taken to fix you up right away on most favoured nation terms.'

'What exactly does that mean?' Gregory asked, a shade suspiciously.

Sir Pellinore's slightly protuberant bright blue eyes regarded him with faintly cynical amusement. 'Pug and I decided that, as you had been called up, the sooner you got through doing your stuff on the barrack square the better, so this time next week you'll be jumpin' around to the orders of a Sergeant-Major.'

# 3

# The Leopard Does Not Change His Spots

Gregory came slowly to his feet. His brown eyes were hard and the scar on his forehead showed white with anger as he exclaimed, 'I would never have believed that you, of all people, would have sold me down the river. Surely you could have got me into the Interpreters Corps, or some sort of half-way-house which did not call for me to be shouted at to form fours at my age.'

Sir Pellinore allowed himself a suggestion of a smile. 'R.A.F. never form fours. They use the old cavalry drill. Of course, if, as an ex-Army Officer, you have any prejudice against taking a commission in the R.A.F. . . .'

'You old devil!' Gregory's anger had evaporated in an instant. 'Any man would be honoured to wear that uniform. But how does a commission square with being ordered around by an N.C.O.?'

'The R.A.F. is the only service which is still granting direct commissions to applicants with certain qualifications—technicians, paymasters, schoolmasters, legal wallahs, and so on. They go in as officers but have to do a fortnight's Intake Course before being posted. There's a long waiting list, but if you sign your application this afternoon the Director of Plans, Air, will have it pushed in at the top; then you can start getting through this inescapable spell of square-bashing next week.'

'And what is to happen to me when I'm through it?'

'I felt you wouldn't mind becoming a Staff Officer in the War Room at the Cabinet Offices.'

Gregory's mouth fell slightly open. 'You . . . you're not fooling?'

'I never fool,' replied Sir Pellinore with mock severity. 'But you must thank General Ismay when you see him, not me. Of course, I've told him from time to time of the very valuable services you have rendered; so he knows of you already. After Maudie Castletown's dinner party I went back to his office with him. We had a word with Ian Jacob. Son of the old Field Marshal. Known him since he was a boy. He's a bright young man. Colonel now, and in charge of War Cabinet communications. War Room is a three service show and comes under him. At Pug's request Jacob agreed to get the D. of Plans, Air, to take you nominally on his staff.'

'But this is terrific! In my wildest dreams I would never have hoped for anything so thrilling.'

'Ah, well,' Sir Pellinore took a good swig of the Roederer, 'since you have to be in regular employment there are many worse jobs. It is a Wing Commander's post, but they have some fool regulation now that no one can be put up by more than one rank a month; so you'll have to go in as a Pilot Officer. Still, your promotion will be automatic and you'll be a *Colonel de l'Air* before the autumn.'

'I can't ever thank you enough.'

'Never mind that. Be at the Great George Street entrance to the War Cabinet Offices at three o'clock this afternoon and send your name up to Colonel Jacob.'

A few hours later Gregory was sitting on a bench in a dim hallway of the great block which forms the north side of Parliament Square. Seeing the special importance of the offices in this corner of the building, he had been surprised to find that the only obvious security precautions were that the Home Guards checking passes on the door wore revolvers, and that, compared with the constant bustle in great headquarters which he had entered when on the Continent, they seemed almost deserted.

After a wait of a few minutes an elderly messenger took him up in an old-fashioned lift to the second floor, then along a lofty corridor. It was here, well above the noise of the traffic, and with fine views over the lake in St. James's Park, that the principal offices were situated. Among the names on their doors Gregory noticed that of General Sir Hastings Ismay and Brigadier L. C. Hollis, then he was shown in to a secretary who took him through to Colonel Jacob.

The Colonel—dark, round-faced, young-looking—gave him a cigarette and at once disclosed that he knew all about his mission to Russia in the previous summer. After they had talked for a few minutes, he said with a smile:

'In view of your previous activities, I'm afraid you may find life here rather dull. Are you quite sure that you wouldn't prefer me to give you a chit passing you on to the chief of our Secret Operations Executive?'

'No, thank you,' Gregory replied promptly. 'I've had enough

27

excitement to last me for quite a time.'

'Very well, then.' The Colonel stood up. 'I had a word with the D. of Plans, Air, about you this morning, and he is expecting us; so we'll go over and see him.'

The Operational Departments of the Air Ministry were in the same vast building, on its far side overlooking King Charles Street. After walking through seemingly interminable and almost deserted corridors they reached the Director of Plans' office. There the Colonel introduced Gregory to a short, broad-shouldered Air Commodore who received them with cheerful briskness.

'I'm sorry we have to send you to Uxbridge,' he said. 'As you had a commission in the last war it's an absurd waste of time to lecture you on the elementary stuff that every subaltern picks up in a couple of months; but it's a hard and fast regulation that there is now no escaping. Just sign these papers I have had prepared and they will attend to the rest of the formalities at Adastral House.'

Half-an-hour later Gregory arrived at the big corner building in Kingsway which housed the Administrative Departments of the Air Ministry. He had a brief interview with a Group Captain, signed some more papers, was medically examined and passed fit. A little before five o'clock he was out in the Strand again and, short of being officially gazetted, was now Pilot Officer Sallust, R.A.F.V.R., under orders to report at the R.A.F. Intake Depot at Uxbridge on the coming Saturday afternoon.

When he reflected that at eleven o'clock that morning he had not even remotely contemplated such a step, it was borne in on him how swiftly the people at the top could get things done if they had a mind to it.

He was just in time to reach his tailor's before they closed and they promised, by hook or by crook, to get two sets of uniform and a greatcoat made for him by Saturday morning. Then he telephoned to Erika to tell her what had happened to him and asked her to take a few days off, so that they could hit it up in London for the last half of the week before he went into uniform.

She arrived next day and for once was able to enjoy a hectic time with him unmarred by secret nagging thoughts that this was the prelude to his going on another mission and these might be the last nights they would ever spend together.

28

On the Saturday afternoon she drove out with him to Uxbridge and was much amused to find that he showed a nervousness he would never have displayed had he been going to make a parachute drop into Hitler's Europe. The fact was that, although he rather liked himself in his smart new uniform, he was uncomfortably aware that, when putting it on, he had said good-bye to his independence. For the next fortnight, anyhow, his actions would be governed by bugle calls; he would, too, be given orders by numerous masters, some of whom might be fools or malicious, yet he would have to suppress the desire to tell them to go to the devil.

At the gate of the camp Erika had a twinge of conscience at her mirth, for his long face suddenly made her feel like a mother seeing her small boy off for his first term at a prep. school. But her belated display of sympathy did little to lighten his gloom and, his mind filled with pessimistic thoughts, he followed the airman who took his baggage through into the wired enclosure.

Uxbridge proved in some respects far worse, and in others much better, than he had expected. The accommodation left much to be desired. It consisted of old dormitories built to hold forty airmen, but with only eight basins and two bathrooms to each, and an antiquated hot-water system the vagaries of which were unpredictable. However, the food served in the big mess was hot, varied and of an excellence far beyond anything that Gregory had hoped for. On the other hand, it was announced by an Instructor on the first night that officers were strictly forbidden to keep any form of alcoholic liquor in the barrack rooms.

As drink had already become far from easy to obtain, Gregory had brought a suitcase full with him. He was quite prepared to share his drink with others, but not to forgo it. Greatly as he respected and admired King George VI he would even have defied the Monarch on this issue, as he considered the order a most unwarrantable infringement of the liberty of a Briton. No sooner had the Instructor left the room than, producing a bottle of brandy, Gregory invited his neighbours to join him in a night-cap.

This, and the fact that he was one of only six, out of the several hundred who formed the intake, wearing First War medal ribbons, led to his new companions regarding him with mingled awe and respect. By far the greater part of them had never worn a uniform of any kind before, so they crowded round him asking questions and automatically giving him the unofficial status which might have been accorded to a prefect. Knowing, too, the manner in which N.C.O.s expected to be treated by an officer, and being capable himself of drilling a squad at a distance of a quarter of a mile, he soon also had the drill-sergeants exactly where he wanted them.

His flagrant disregard of the regulation about drink apart, he considered that, as an ex-officer, it was his duty to set an exampled to the mostly younger men in whose company he marched, slept, fed and listened to lectures; so, in spite of his natural inclination to laziness, he performed his drill and kept his notes conscientiously.

After hours of marching up and down, and listening to talks, many of which he could have given better himself, he was by turns stiff, bored, relaxed, amused and resigned. The fact that his habitual stoop disappeared overnight meant nothing, as his life had more than once depended on its doing so when he had disguised himself in a black Gestapo uniform or that of a German Army Officer. All the same, he had to admit to himself that he felt considerably fitter when at the end of the fortnight he left Uxbridge for a little world as remote from it as Mars.

There, his companions had on average been ten years younger than himself and a good cross-section of the middle classes; some, coming from quite poor homes, had done well in their trades, others came from the rank and file of the professions. After the first night or two they had mentally shed their years; so that the atmosphere had become the friendly, somewhat boisterous, one of boys doing a last term at school.

Now, overnight, he exchanged four hours a day of vigorous exercise for a chair in a large basement room shored up with great beams, between which the walls were covered with maps made brilliant by neon lighting; for, although he had not realised it, the War Room in the Cabinet Offices was actually its Map Room. Here, there was no ragging or inconsequent chatter of girls, movies and binges, but quiet war talk occasionally spiced with sophisticated wit, and plans for fishing or shooting when a next leave came along.

The dozen or so men who ran it were Lt.-Colonels or of equivalent rank in the other two services, and most of them were considerably older than Gregory. The majority had reached their present rank in the First World War and, anxious to serve again, had been put in to carry on this most secret work on the recommendation of some old friend now high up in their own service.

They were much too discreet to question the sudden addition to their number of a Pilot Officer and, having accepted Gregory in a most friendly way, soon initiated him into his duties. These consisted of receiving reports from all the Intelligence centres, either in locked boxes or over an array of scrambler telephones ranged on a long table in the middle of the room, and making the adjustments necessary to the maps, or recording the information for inclusion in the daily 'Most Secret' War report which went to the King, the War Cabinet and the Chiefs of Staff Organisation.

As Gregory soon learned, the latter consisted in the main of some twenty officers who formed the Joint Planning Staff. The majority of them were also of Lt.-Colonel's rank, but they were a generation younger than those in the War Room and, with one curious exception, had all been hand-picked from among the most promising graduates of the three Staff Colleges. The exception, as it so happened, had been a Cadet in H.M.S. *Worcester* with Gregory when they were in their teens and, from time to time since, they had seen one another. He had been brought in some months earlier, like Gregory, by way of Uxbridge, but to do some special planning with a one-legged Colonel who had previously been Chief Instructor at the Intelligence College at Matlock.

Although the Planners and the War Room Staff worked in the same basement and shared a small mess, the former never discussed future operations in the presence of the latter, as it was an accepted rule that no one should ever be given information which his work did not make it necessary for him to have. But, all the same, Gregory and his colleagues usually had a pretty shrewd idea what was in the wind from the movements of forces and other indications that inevitably came their way.

The basement was a honeycomb of corridors and rooms of varying sizes. In addition to the ones where the routine work was carried on there were those in which the War Cabinet and Chiefs of Staff Committee held their meetings on nights when air raids were taking place, others allocated to individual Ministers who at times slept there, and others again which were slept in regularly by the senior War Cabinet personnel and members of the Prime Minister's Staff. There was, too, a complete suite for him in case an emergency should necessitate a retreat below stairs from the flat immediately above, known as 10 Downing Street annexe, which was his permanent wartime quarters.

Although Gregory had not at first realised it, the place was in fact an underground fortress. The Brigade of Guards supplied a guard for its entrances, which were further protected by armed Home Guards and Special Police; and inside it a body of Royal Marines could be turned swiftly from officers' servants into a garrison. It was bomb-proof, gas-proof and stocked with enough food and medical supplies to stand a prolonged siege. In it was situated the terminal of the Atlantic telephone and an exchange with direct underground lines to every principal city in Britain. So, had a German Airborne Division descended on Whitehall, the Prime Minister and all his advisers could have shut themselves in there and, from it, continued the High Direction of the war without interruption.

Successive teams of duty-officers kept the War Room operating night and day, but their hours were staggered so that each had different days and nights off duty every week; and they were at liberty to swap watches when that suited their individual plans. Finding that between dinner and midnight was the most popular time for Ministers and other V.I.P.s to look into the War Room for the latest news and a chat, Gregory was always willing to take over from any of his colleagues who wished to dine out, as he found the speculations of such big-wigs on the future course of the war intensely interesting and, now that Erika had returned to the north, nights out in wartime London had little appeal for him.

On his return from Uxbridge he had again settled into his old quarters in Gloucester Road. Soon after the First World War he had gone to live there because his Cockney batman, Rudd, had inherited a long lease of No. 272, which consisted of a grocer's shop with three floors above it of rooms to let. Gregory had had the rooms at the back on the first floor converted into a small flat and, although he could long since have afforded to move to a better address, he had always retained them because he was very fond of Rudd, and nowhere could he have found a more cheerful, willing and devoted servant. But he found evenings spent alone there hung heavily on his hands and most of his best friends had war jobs which had taken them out of London.

It was, no doubt, lack of occupation in his off-duty hours which, after a few weeks, first began to ferment in him a sense of restlessness. Once, too, he had fallen into the routine of the War Room, there ceased to be anything stimulating about it. The job carried little responsibility other than its extreme secrecy, and called for no initiative. Day after day he pinned little cards, giving the operative strengths of various types of aircraft at each airfield, on to a great map of Britain, while his naval and military colleagues moved pins denoting warships, or divisions and brigades, across oceans and deserts. Lunch or dinner at his club, or at another as the guest of one of them, provided the only break in the monotony and, when experience gradually showed him that few of the V.I.P.s were any better at predicting the next moves of the enemy than he was himself, he began to lose much of his interest in his chats with them.

Had the war been going well he might have been more contented but, as spring advanced into summer, one catastrophe after another befell the Allies.

While he was at Uxbridge the Japanese had driven the Americans from the Bataan peninsula, bombed Ceylon and sunk *Hermes*—one of our precious aircraft-carriers—and the cruisers *Dorchester* and *Cornwall,* in the Indian Ocean. During the latter part of April he watched the Japs climbing up the map of Burma, until they had driven the Chinese out of Lashio —the southern terminal of China's life line, the Burma Road —and pushed General Alexander back across the Chindwin river. By mid-May the Americans had lost Corregidor Island —their last foothold in the Philippines—Mandalay had fallen, and the British were being hard-pressed on the frontier of India.

Our relations with the French had further deteriorated as Marshal Pétain, although remaining nominally head of the Vichy Government, had now given Laval a free hand and full collaboration with the Germans was the new order of the day.

The U-boats continued to take a toll of Allied shipping that far outran new construction. The cost in sinkings of sending convoys to the Arctic with arms for Russia, and through the Mediterranean with help for Malta, was appalling; and it looked as if the garrison of the little island would soon be bombed out of existence.

Towards the end of May, Rommel attacked in Libya. For about a fortnight there was most desperate fighting but the reports put out by General Auchinleck's spokesmen in Cairo were full of optimism. Then, from the second week in June, things suddenly went wrong. After several days of heroic resistance at Bir Hakeim the Free French were withdrawn. Next day the Knightsbridge Box, which had been equally stubbornly defended by the British, was overrun. El Adam, Belhamed and Acroma were swiftly captured and our 4th Armoured Brigade was heavily defeated at Sidi Rezegh.

Tobruk was now cut off but no one imagined for one moment that it would fall. In the previous year, gamely defended by the Australians, it had successfully withstood a siege, and this time its prospects of doing so should have been much better. Its garrison commander, the South African General Klopper, had under him 25,000 fighting troops and a further 10,000 administrative details all capable of using a rifle at a pinch, while the fortress contained ammunition and supplies sufficient for ninety days. Yet, after only one day of heavy bombardment and a single determined assault by the enemy, the General ordered his troops to lay down their arms.

This terrible disgrace to British Arms was lightened only by one episode enshrined in words which equal the most glorious in our history. On receiving the order to surrender, Captain Sainthill, Coldstream Guards, sent back the reply, 'Surrender is a manœuvre that the Guards have never practised in peace so they do not know how to carry it out in war.' He then led his company to the attack and, together with 188 South Africans who were equally determined to save the honour of their country, succeeded in fighting his way through to the main body of the Eighth Army.

The conduct of Klopper, coupled with General Ritchie's apparent loss of control over the general situation, soon placed Egypt itself in jeopardy. Day after day Gregory glumly watched his military colleagues move the red-topped pins in the map of North Africa as they plotted another British Army in retreat. The Libyan frontier was abandoned; so, too, were the strong positions at Mersa Matruh. On the Prime Minister's insistence General Auchinleck all too belatedly relieved Ritchie and took over the battle himself; but by the end of the month the Army was back at El Daba, only ninety miles from Alexandria.

Churchill had received the shattering blow of Tobruk's surrender while in Washington. On his return it was known in the War Room that the Americans had shown the most generous sympathy and promised all possible aid to the Eighth Army; but it must take weeks before tank replacements could reach it from the United States. In the meantime no one could say where the retreat would end, and at the Auk's headquarters in Cairo the secret papers were being burnt as a precaution against Rommel's making a lightning thrust which would carry his armour to the capital.

July opened with a motion in the House of Commons declaring lack of confidence in the Prime Minister's direction of the war. The vast majority of the people rejoiced when it was defeated by 475 votes to 25; but the fate of the Nile Valley and our whole position in the Middle East still hung in the balance.

In July, too, the situation on the Russian front began to give cause for grave anxiety. During the winter months, owing to lack of suitable clothes and equipment, the German armies had suffered appallingly. But once the thaw was sufficiently advanced to permit rapid movement they had renewed their efforts to achieve a decisive victory. Colossal battles had raged for weeks in the Kharkov and Kursk sectors, in which Marshal Timoshenko had managed to hold his own; but the Germans had launched another all-out offensive farther south. Regardless of losses, they had stormed the Kerch peninsula and battered their way into Sevastopol. By mid-July they had broken through on a six-hundred-mile-wide front, reached Rostov, crossed the Lower Don and now threatened both Stalingrad and the Caucasus.

Such was the situation on the night of Sunday, July 26th; and as was the case on most Sundays, after a cold supper together, Gregory and Sir Pellinore were up in the big library giving free rein to their hopes and fears. For an hour or more their talk roved over the battle fronts, then Gregory summed up.

'So there we are; Alexander hanging on by the skin of his teeth along the Indian frontier, the Auk hanging on by the skin of his outside Cairo, and the Ruskies being chivvied a hundred miles a day towards their oil-wells without which they would have to chuck their hand in. It may be silly, but for the first time since the war started I'm beginning to lie awake at nights and wonder if we may not lose it.'

'What's that!' boomed Sir Pellinore, suddenly sitting bolt upright. 'Don't talk nonsense, boy! This is not like you. I can tell what's wrong though. It's having your nose so close to a lot of small maps all the time that's got you down. As Wellington said, "Always use the big ones".'

'There is no comfort to be got from doing that in this case. If the armies of Alex and the Auk both crack, within three months the Germans and the Japs will join up in Persia. Then we would about have had it.'

'I'd give long odds against the Axis pulling off a double. Besides, we wouldn't be sitting on our bottoms while the Nazis overran the whole Middle East.'

'It doesn't seem to me that there's much we could do to stop them.'

'We could launch a new campaign nearer home. That would force 'em to commit all the troops they had to spare.'

The decision taken only the night before, to do Operation *Torch* and occupy French North Africa, was still known only to a very limited number of people, and not even a rumour of it had yet reached the War Room; so Gregory shook his head and replied pessimistically:

'Everyone agrees that it is out of the question for us to open up a Second Front in 1942.'

'We might, and probably should, if driven to it by such an emergency. You are ignoring the brighter side, too, my boy. Think of the hell we have been knockin' out of Germany.'

'Oh, the R.A.F. is magnificent, I know. That 1,000 bomber raid on Cologne at the end of May, and the others since— Lubeck, Hamburg, Essen, Bremen. Not to mention the Desert Air Force. If it hadn't been for those lads Rommel would already be in Cairo.'

'United States Air Force is showin' well too now. Fine feat their bombing of Tokyo; and every week more of their heavies are being flown here to increase the weight of bombs we can put down on the wurst-eaters.'

'That's all very well; but as we've seen both in Burma and the Desert, a determined air force can delay, but cannot halt, a victorious army. Even if it is possible to bomb Germany into submission that would take years; and, in the meantime, the

German and Jap armies may have conquered half the world.'

Sir Pellinore made a gesture of protest. 'It's true that we've struck a bad patch; but whatever may happen in the next few months, 1943 will see us on top again. Once the great new American armies are fully equipped and begin to roll forward the house-painter will find that he's bitten off more than he can chew.'

'Not necessarily. Not if the Russians are forced to give in before an Allied army is able to come to their rescue.'

'Why should they? You went to Russia yourself. Like the wizard you are, you got the low-down from Marshal Voroshilov. He told you that their plan was to use their masses to make the Germans exhaust themselves, and that they were holding their best troops until the time came for them to go over to the offensive—or in the last event if Stalingrad was threatened.'

'That was ten months ago and their losses since have been immense. Stalingrad is only vital to them because, if they lost it, they could no longer get the oil from the Caucasus up the Volga to their central and northern fronts. But now the Caucasus itself is threatened; so they may already have had to throw in the crack Reserve Army that the Marshal told me about.'

'I see. Yes. You fear that there may be no stopping this great break through in the south. Of course, you're right about the oil wells. If they lose those their goose will be cooked.'

'And so will ours. Hitler now wields a whip over a dozen nations. He has coerced millions of men into both working and fighting for him. If the Soviets collapse he will be able to bring 180 divisions back into Western Europe. All hope of opening a Second Front would be gone for good then. For the Allies to attempt a landing on the Continent in the face of even half that number, in addition to the forces he has there already, would be plain suicide. We could only sit and watch him—just as we are doing now—while he sent forty or fifty divisions crashing down through Turkey and Persia into India.'

'Damn it, Gregory! You're giving even me the willies. Mind, I don't believe it will happen. But one must admit that it's just possible.'

'It could easily happen if we do nothing but twiddle our thumbs for the rest of the year. Just now you told me to use large maps, and I am using them. The armies of Alex, the Auk, and the Soviet army defending the Caucasus may be thousands of miles apart, but strategically all three are fighting back to back. The collapse of either of the first two would be a major calamity and prolong the war for years; if the Russians collapse, then I see no end to it.'

Sir Pellinore held out his glass. 'For God's sake give me a drink. Some of the high-ups who bring me their troubles have been pretty pessimistic lately; but none of them has painted as black a picture as this.'

Gregory poured them both another ration of old brandy, and remarked:

'That's probably because they are all worried stiff with their personal responsibilities; whereas I'm only a looker-on. And lookers-on get the best view of the game.'

'Well, what would you have us do?'

'Don't ask me; I'm not a planner. I only stick pins in maps.'

'Exactly. And it's that which has given you the time to do a bit of thinkin'. Come on now. What's the remedy?'

'There is only the obvious one. It is to stop burying our heads in the sand. You could at least try prodding your high-up friends into facing the situation and deciding on some definite action.'

'What sort of action?'

'Anything which would take a bit of weight off the Russians. Keeping them in the war is the thing that matters above all else; and, apart from sending them arms, we are doing nothing. Absolutely nothing! We are just calmly waiting for 1943. By then it may be too late, whereas some audacious move now could be the premium which would insure us against an eventual stale-mate, or something far worse.'

'Nothing short of a full-scale landing in France or Norway would force the Germans to withdraw troops from the Russian front; and I'm certain that a major operation of that kind is not possible.'

Gregory shrugged. 'To reject it is being penny wise and pound foolish. The withdrawal of ten or twelve divisions from the Russian front this summer might change the whole course of history. I don't think you would say that I'm normally a pessimist. But, if the Russians pack up before we can get into Europe, I don't believe we'll ever defeat Hitler.'

For a moment Sir Pellinore remained silent. Then he said, 'If ten or twelve divisions would do the trick, there is one possibility by which it might be brought about.'

'How?' Gregory asked, suddenly sitting forward.

'The Nazis are stretched to the limit already; so they'd have to recall that number if one of the countries they are holding down blew up behind them.'

'Surely there is very little chance of that. After being crushed between the German and Russian millstones, the poor old Poles can't have much kick left in them. And, since the Czechs assassinated Heydrich in May, I gather they are liable to be shot if they so much as lift a finger.'

'I wasn't thinking of the occupied countries. Germany's official allies were the birds I had in mind. Italy and Finland are no good—both too deeply involved. But there are Hungary and Rumania. They were dragged in against their wills, and such contributions as they have made to Hitler's war have been prised out of 'em by blackmail. Hungary is the best bet. I know a lot of Hungarians. They all loathe the Germans' guts. I'd bet a monkey to a rotten apple that they have some sort of league pledged to break away from Hitler as soon as they see a chance.'

'Even if you are right, I can't imagine that while things are going so well for Germany they would risk his wrath by ratting on him.'

'I don't know so much,' Sir Pellinore replied thoughtfully. 'After the last war the Allies treated Hungary pretty savagely. Under the Treaty of Trianon they gave more than half her territories away. Since then she's got most of them back. In March '39, when Hitler cut Czechoslovakia into three bits, he annexed Bohemia, made Slovakia a vassal state and let the Hungarians reoccupy Ruthenia. Then, in the summer of '40, the Axis made the Rumanians return Transylvania. But the Hungarians must fear that if the Allies win they'll be made to give these territories up again. For a promise that they should retain them and, perhaps, get back some of the other lands of which they were robbed in 1920, I believe they might consider ratting on the Nazis now.'

For a long moment Gregory did not reply. Then he said: 'On every front, except in the air over Europe, the Germans and the Japs are getting the best of us. In battle after battle the Allies are being driven back. To my mind it is imperative that somehow, somewhere, we should launch a new thrust at the enemy within the next few months. If we don't, it may be

too late, and we'll lose the war altogether. So, if you think there
is even a sporting chance that we could persuade the Hungarians to stick a knife in Hitler's back, you had better arrange
for me to go to Budapest.'

# 4

# Seconded for Special Service

It was not often that Sir Pellinore started anything uninten-
tionally; but he knew he had started something now, and he
was far from happy about it. His only son had been killed in
the First World War and it was Gregory who, as a very young
subaltern, had carried him back out of the hell of Thiepval
Wood after he had been mortally wounded. Since then
Gregory had gradually taken the place of that son in the old
man's affections.

Although it would have been against his principles to persuade anyone of whom he was fond against risking their life
for their country in time of war, he had been extremely glad
when the threat of the call-up had enabled him to plant
Gregory in a safe job; and he had hoped that he would come
to feel that honour had been satisfied by his previous exploits.
As this was no question of an urgent mission, and the whole
idea was drawing a bow at a venture, Sir Pellinore decided that
he was justified in trying to retrieve the situation; so he said
with apparent casualness:

'Not much good you goin' to Budapest. You don't speak
Hungarian.'

'What has that to do with it?' Gregory brushed the objection
aside. 'I have worked in Norway, Finland, Russia, Holland
without a word of the language of those countries. Anyhow,
everyone in Budapest speaks German, and that's my second
tongue.'

'The Hungarians wouldn't budge without a pretty strong
inducement. It would mean getting the War Cabinet, and
Roosevelt too, to agree that they should keep Transylvania and
Ruthenia after the war, and probably be given a port on the

Adriatic into the bargain. Our top chaps might not be willing to promise that.'

'I can't believe it! Statesmen don't usually boggle at giving away territory which isn't theirs to give. And if there is a chance that, given this promise, the Hungarians will do all that a Second Front would do for us, Britain and America would be mad not to make it.'

'True enough. But there's no call for you to get out your automatics and buy a Tyrolean hat. This is a job for the F.O. I'll put the idea up to someone there tomorrow morning.'

Gregory shook his head. 'Judging by the Foreign Office form in this war so far, that wouldn't get us anywhere. They would take a year to think it over; then go cap in hand to the wrong chap in Budapest. What's needed is someone to go there and find out what is cooking and who is the cook.'

'I hardly like to ask for you to be released from your job to go off in what may prove a wild goose chase.'

'Nonsense! The whole idea of putting me into the War Room was that my leaving it at short notice would not affect its efficient running for even a day. It would be another matter if I were a Planner, or doing an "I" job in some headquarters. General Ismay told me himself that he had suggested it as the most convenient way of keeping me on ice for you, and the time has come when I want you to take me off it.'

'All right, then,' Sir Pellinore conceded reluctantly. 'Have it your own way.'

'Fine!' Gregory grinned. In the last few minutes he seemed to have become a different man. His fretful despondency had completely disappeared and he voiced his racing thoughts. 'Those damn maps have been getting me down. A chance to use my wits again without taking on a suicide gamble was the very thing I needed. Budapest is a lovely city, the Hungarians are charming people, and there will be none of those blond beasts in black uniforms who might claim me at the end of a pistol as an old acquaintance. This, as the R.A.F. say, is a piece of cake. When can I start?'

'Bad policy to rush your fences. You'll do better if I first collect all the information I can for you to work on. That will take a little time. Then there are the arrangements for your journey. Say in about ten days.'

'Couldn't suit me better. I'm due for some leave and I can fix up to take it at forty-eight hours' notice. That will give me a clear week with Erika. Naturally I shan't tell the chaps in the War Room that I may not be coming back for a month or two. I'll leave you to arrange that with Colonel Jacob.'

Sir Pellinore nodded. 'I'll suggest that, when he puts in a replacement, he should say that you've been injured in a car-smash, or something. Anyhow, that's his affair. Will you go down to Gwaine Meads or have Erika up to London?'

'I'll speak to her on the telephone now, if I may, and see which she'd prefer.'

It was the sort of call that Erika had been dreading for some time past, as she knew her Gregory far too well to have any hope of his remaining in a safe job for the rest of the war.

After he had told her in guarded terms that he was going abroad again, she decided that she could better support the strain of his coming departure in the country than in the restaurants and night-clubs of war-worn London, which now offered so little and had become so tatty; so he told her to expect him on the coming Wednesday.

Gregory had started a spell of duty at six o'clock that evening and, in order that he might dine with Sir Pellinore, a colleague who owed him a turn had taken over from him at half-past seven; but he had promised to be back by eleven. As it was now close on that hour, he took leave of his host and, with a much more jaunty step than he had come, made his way through the black-out along the edge of the park till he found the gap in the barbed wire leading to the tall bronze doors in the basement beyond which lay his office.

The following morning he arranged about his leave and at ten o'clock went off duty. As he was leaving the building he found himself alongside the old friend who had once been a Cadet with him in *H.M.S. Worcester*. Together they turned left and, as they passed the bottom of Clive Steps, Gregory asked:

'What brings you out at this hour of the morning?'

'My daily jaunt to the War Office,' replied the other. 'It's part of my job to attend the meetings of the I.S.S.B.'

'And what may that be? Or shouldn't one ask?'

'Oh, there's no secret about what the initials stand for. It's the Inter-Services Security Board. They are the boys who check up on any leakages of information, and devise all the regulations for preventing news of what we're up to from reaching the enemy.'

A hundred yards further on they parted. The other airman crossed the Horse Guards Parade, went through the arch, over to the War Office and up to a room on the third floor, in which half-a-dozen officers were already seated round a table.

It was one of the Board's principal functions to scrutinise all troop movements and see to it that the public knew as little as possible about them; so, soon after any new operation had been definitely decided upon, the Board was automatically informed. That morning, Operation *Torch* was one of the items on the agenda, and was to remain so for many weeks to come; for the problems entailed in covering the movement of ships, men and aircraft, in preparation for the great expedition, were innumerable.

As yet they had only the outline plan, since 'Eps'—as the Executive Planning Staffs in the three Service Ministries were called—were still working on the nuts and bolts which would turn the plan from a broad stategic conception into a practical operation of war with the forces and supplies needed to carry it out nominated down to the last detail.

A middle-aged Major of the Royal Scots who had among his ribbons an M.C. with bar, and who was Secretary to the Board, read out particulars in clear incisive tones; the 'Cardinal' Colonel, who was Chairman, made some comments, then the Admiralty representative looked across at the airman from the War Cabinet Offices and said in a high-pitched, rather nasal, voice:

'Now we shall see if amateurs like you and your new Colonel can really produce the goods.'

The airman was junior to the sailor so he replied with chill politeness, 'Given a continuance of the help always so generously afforded us by I.S.S.B., sir, I think we may manage.'

The sailor was far from popular; so a large man in civilian clothes, who was Chief of counter-espionage in Britain and affectionately known to the rest of the party as 'Himmler', tittered.

The Major with the double M.C. gave the airman a friendly smile. 'Unlike our naval member, this old horse feels no pain and grief that such headaches are no longer ours. But this little affair is going to be quite something; and naturally the Board will be right behind you.'

A youngish, good-looking Captain who was on the secretariat looked up from the notes he had been making with his left hand, and added, 'It's going to be murder if things go wrong. The Jerries can hardly fail to spot a convoy of this size and what might happen if the U-boat packs got into it does not bear thinking about.'

'That's not our worst worry,' replied the airman. 'There would be losses, of course, but not serious enough to cripple the operation if the naval escorts do their stuff. Besides, there is at least some hope that we'll be able to get them down to Gib. undetected. The real trouble will start as soon as they turn in to go through the Straits. Then any cover we have managed to give their initial sailing must be blown. Once in the Med. the whole of the Axis air force will be alerted; and, if the object of the operation leaks out, the Vichy French may prove hostile into the bargain. If the landings are seriously opposed it could be a massacre. I only hope to God we'll be able to think up some way of foxing the enemy about our ultimate objectives.'

The Major nodded. 'I'd say that your new master will produce a better rabbit than we would have got from old one-leg Dumbo; but the two of you have certainly been given one hell of an assignment. This could be worse than Tobruk. The Order of Battle will include the best of everything the Army's got, and they'll be two thousand miles from home. There will be no getting the remnants off in small boats as we did at Dunkirk. Well, let us know how we can help, and keep your chin up.'

Had Gregory been at this meeting he would have been equally worried about the outcome of the expedition to North Africa, but at least he would have been disabused of his idea that the British and Americans intended to do nothing in 1942 which might force the enemy to withdraw a certain number of divisions from Russia. Such knowledge, had he had it the evening before, would certainly have caused his conversation with Sir Pellinore to take an entirely different turn; so it is most unlikely that the project of his going to Budapest would ever have arisen.

As it was, while the I.S.S.B. was discussing the first tentative arrangements for the security of Operation *Torch*, he was lying in his bath thinking of that lovely city, so justly termed 'The Queen of the Danube'. Or, to be more accurate, he was thinking of a wonderful three weeks that he had spent there three years before the war in the company of a very lovely young woman.

In the summer of 1936*, on behalf of Sir Pellinore, he had been engaged in investigating international smuggling operations which had assumed large and dangerous proportions; for, in addition to big consignments of contraband goods, a number of Communist agitators were being flown in by night to secret landing grounds in lonely parts of Kent. His painstaking enquiries on the French coast had got him nowhere until one midnight in the Casino at Deauville his curiosity had been aroused by the sight of a beautiful dark-haired girl and, quite incidentally, the fact that she was in the company of an elderly man whom he knew to be a crooked financier.

She had proved to be a Hungarian named Sabine Szenty, and it was through having got to know her later that night in unusually dramatic cricumstances that he secured his first clue to the problem which had so far defeated him. Unwillingly to begin with, then in rebellion against her crooked chief, she had eventually helped him to unmask the smugglers' organisation. It had very nearly cost both of them their lives and, even when the job was done, her own participation in their criminal activities left her liable to prosecution and a prison sentence. To save her from that he had performed a highly illegal act himself; but he had had no cause to regret it, for after their arrival in Budapest she had rewarded him in an entirely suitable manner.

He wondered now what had happened to her, and if she was still living in the Hungarian capital. It was probable that by this time she had married; but she had never sought to conceal the fact that she was by nature an adventuress, and believed in taking all the good things of life that offered with both hands; so he thought it unlikely that she would as yet have settled down to respectable domesticity. She could still be only about twenty-eight, and with beauty such as hers she would be able for years yet, should she wish, to change one rich husband for another.

Sabine, he decided, compared favourably with any of the numerous women whom for a season he had loved and who had returned his love. Erika was, of course, the great exception, and he was not being consciously unfaithful to her when he thought of those laughing carefree sunny days and hectic

*See *Contraband* (Published by Hutchinson & Co.)

45

nights that he had spent with Sabine beside the Danube, and wished that he had some magic formula for setting time back so that he might enjoy them all over again.

Later in the day, he told Rudd that on Wednesday morning he would be going north on a week's leave and that shortly after his return he expected to be away from London for quite a time.

Rudd pushed the greasy cap he always wore, both indoors and out, on to the back of his head, scratched in his yellowish hair above the right ear and said in a wheedling tone:

'See 'ere Mr. Gregory, sir; that's Dutch for you goin' abroad again, an' you don't 'ave to tell me no different. Can't yer take me wiv yer, sime as you done now an' again in the old days? I'd pull me weight. You know that. An' the 'ome Guard's become a farce now, wiv not a 'ope o' any of us old sweats wot's in it gettin' a crack at the Jerries.'

'Sorry, old friend,' Gregory replied with real sympathy. 'I wish I could; but this time it's right out of the question. I won't forget you, though, when another chance does occur to use the sort of help you have always given me so willingly.'

'Thanks, sir,' Rudd grinned, showing teeth that badly needed the attention of a dentist. 'Well, good luck then; an' should you be seein' little ol 'itler, give 'im an extra one from me right on the kisser.'

Up in Wales, Gregory was favoured with July sunshine, but even in the private wing of the big house there was little real privacy, and it was difficult for Erika to free herself from the work of administration as long as she remained under the same roof as the hospital. Earlier in the year, while he had been a permanent resident, he had not minded that, but now it irked him; so they decided to spend the weekend at Llandudno.

The trip was not a success. Owing to petrol rationing they had to go by train and were then tied to the town. At the hotel in which they stayed the war-time food was abominable, and even indifferent drink obtainable only at extortionate prices. To add insult to injury a bottle of champagne that Gregory bought from a wine merchant on the Saturday morning, for them to drink up in their bedroom that night, proved when opened—as happens occasionally for no known reason with the best of brands—to be badly corked.

They were both glad to get back to Gwaine Meads; but there their only out-of-doors escape from patients and nurses was to take picnics in the woods, and the weather suddenly went bad on them. As Gregory was now looking forward with cheerful anticipation to his mission, all this increased his impatience to be on his way to Budapest. About that he endeavoured to conceal his feelings from Erika; but she knew him so well that she sensed and resented it, with the result that they had few really happy hours during their last days together.

On Tuesday August 4th, he took the last train back to London. First thing the following morning he rang up Sir Pellinore, who told him to pack a bag and come to Carlton House Terrace. On his arrival in the library there shortly after eleven o'clock, the elderly Baronet told him to open a quart of champagne that was standing ready in an ice bucket. As soon as they had taken their first swig out of the silver tankards, Sir Pellinore said:

'Your terms of reference are simply to spy out the land— find out if the anti-German feeling in Hungary is strong enough for us to make practical use of it. There would be no point in your trying to act as a go-between with any anti-Nazi elements you may come across until the F.O. and the State Department have fully considered the whole question. But if the report you bring back is favourable, you may be sent out again to open secret negotiations.' Having taken another good swig at his champagne, Sir Pellinore went on: 'You'll be leavin' on Friday by the weekly diplomatic plane that serves our Embassy in Berne; so I thought you might as well spend your last two nights here. From Switzerland you'll proceed under your own steam by whatever route you think best. I've got devilish little information for you to go on, though. The fellers I've talked to all say their Hungarian files are hopelessly out of date.'

'Our spies can't be up to much then,' Gregory remarked, lighting a Sullivan.

'That's not the trouble. We haven't got any there.'

'Why on earth not?'

'One of the results of the MacDonald, Baldwin and Chamberlain Governments, all cheese-paring so idiotically on the Secret Service funds in the years before the war. What little money there was all had to go on the highest priorities— Germany and Russia. Funds were so short that, as we had an alliance with the French, we left it to them to keep tabs on Nazi activities in North Africa; so when the French ratted on us we hadn't even got a skeleton set-up there.'

'Chamberlain's shortcomings are ancient history now, though; and the M.I. shows have been on a war footing for close on three years.'

'Oh, they haven't lacked money since September '39. I was only explaining why we had no organ-grinders in Budapest. And we haven't been at war with Hungary that long, you know. We didn't declare war on Hungary, Finland and Rumania until last December.'

'Even so, I should have thought seven months was time enough to get something going.'

Sir Pellinore shrugged his great shoulders. 'I doubt if we should ever have declared war against these Nazi satellites at all unless Joe Stalin had pressed us to—and trained spies can't be got just by putting an advertisement in *The Times*. We've still probably only about one to every dozen employed by Himmler. With so much ground to cover, it would be a waste to send good men to places where the odds are all against our ever undertaking military operations. Anyway, I've drawn a blank about what's going on there apart from a digest of the stuff that has appeared in the newspapers'

'How about an identity and a passport?'

'That's all fixed up. I didn't do it through the old firm, though. I'm told that they perform miracles to keep us in the know about the enemy's Order of Battle, but in other ways it's far from being the show it was when the little Admiral ran it. There's a new firm that specialises in sabotage, but its people bring home a lot of stuff, and its Chief is much more of a live wire. Been parachuted into Hitler's Europe himself at least half-a-dozen times. You're to report to him at ten-thirty tomorrow morning.'

'Good. I must say I would have liked to have someone reliable whom I could contact, just to get the lie of the land; but if Hungary is now like darkest Africa to the professionals, I must go native and hope for the best.'

'Oh, I can give you a few names to start the ball rollin'. Old friends of mine. Now that our countries are at war they may not be willing to give you their active help. But they'll still observe the decencies. If you say you're a friend of mine they wouldn't dream of turning you over to the police. There's István Lujza. He was a Cabinet Minister in the last years of the old Emperor. And Prince György Hunyadi. He owns the finest

48

partridge shoot in Hungary; probably in the world. Then there's Mihály Zapolya. Never forget one night when we got tight together and shot out half the lights on the Franz-Joseph Embankment. What a lark! That's years ago, of course; but wars don't make any difference to friendship between people with whom you've done that sort of thing.'

Next morning Gregory took a taxi to a big block of offices a quarter of a mile north of Oxford Street. It was a hive of activity and, judging from its entrance, passageways and lift, it appeared to be staffed almost entirely with pretty girls. Most of them were in the uniform of the F.A.N.Y. but quite a number wore smart civilian clothes. When they addressed each other they spoke with the accent of Mayfair but, as they passed Gregory in short stages from the door up to the General's office, they were none the less brisk and efficient for that.

The General proved to be a small, dark, wiry man. Instead of the slacks usually worn by officers in London, or the ugly battle-dress which had been brought in only with the object of making officers less conspicuous in the field, he was turned out with the impeccable correctness of a staff-officer in the First World War. The sight of his beautifully cut riding breeches and highly polished field boots—in combination with the parachute badge on his arm—made Gregory's heart warm towards him, and within a few minutes they were talking together like old friends.

When they got down to business, the General said, 'Sir Pellinore tells me that you speak both German and French well enough to pass as a native of either country. As you must know, owing to centuries of Austrian domination the Magyars have an hereditary hatred for everything German; so I think you would stand a much better chance of winning their confidence if you clocked in as a Frenchman. Diplomatic relations between France and Hungary have never been severed. With a Vichy passport you should be able to go in and out freely whenever you wish.'

'Excellent,' Gregory nodded. 'I like that idea. There must be plenty of Frenchmen carrying Vichy passports who are de Gaullists at heart; so nobody will think it particularly odd if, when sounding them out, I express views uncomplimentary to the Nazis.'

'That is just what I thought; and we have an identity for you which should fill the bill. It is that of a Free French Officer who was an Interpreter with the Commandos and was killed in the St. Nazaire raid. Your story will be that you were fed up with serving under General de Gaulle, so during the confusion of the fighting you took the opportunity to desert; and that, as you had no time for Pétain either, instead of remaining in France you went to Switzerland. Why, after a few months, you should have decided to go to Hungary, I leave to you.'

'It depends rather on this chap's circumstances, doesn't it?'

'To some extent; but I don't think they will help you very much. His name was Etienne Tavenier. He retired from the Army with the rank of Major a few years before the war. Presumably he did so because at about that time he inherited from his father a pleasant property in Périgord. That suggests that he was fairly well off, so could have afforded to travel, and might some time have been to Budapest on a holiday. But they will give you such particulars as we have of him downstairs. Your passport is ready for you there too, and various other papers. Among them is a draft on a Swiss bank in Berne for £500. They will give you the lot in cash or open a credit for you as Commandant Tavenier in Budapest, just as you wish.'

Gregory smiled. 'That seems quite a generous allowance, as I am going there only to try to find out the form; and that should not take me more than a couple of weeks.'

'The amount is in accordance with Sir Pellinore's request,' the General smiled back. 'This being a private enterprise, he is footing the bill. If your report proves hopeful, no doubt you will be going out again to stir up some trouble. If not, and you have left some of the money in a Budapest bank, we can arrange for our Swiss friends to reclaim it. And now, I'm due at a conference; so I'll wish you luck and pass you on to the section that has been arranging about your papers.'

The General's beautiful secretary took Gregory to a room on a lower floor, and said to a girl seated behind a desk there, 'Oh, Diana, here is your customer for Budapest.' Then with a ravishing smile she left them.

Diana was another lovely—small, thin-faced, with the sort of golden hair that cannot be got out of a bottle, and a slightly arched nose. She looked only about twenty-two, so Gregory expected her to show him through to someone more senior; but she casually waved him to a chair, offered him a Lucky

Strike, then took one herself and, after surveying him for a moment from beneath her long lashes, said with a smile:

'It's a good thing you are only taking Tavenier's name and not attempting to pass as him. He was quite a lot older and going bald.'

'Did you know him, then?' Gregory enquired.

'No. But I got a description of him from C.C.O., H.Q., so that if you do run into trouble you could anyhow say that they are confusing you with a cousin of the same name, and be able to describe him correctly.'

'That was thoughtful of you.'

'Oh, it's just part of the Austin Reed Service.' Producing a folder from a drawer she tipped its contents out on to the desk and passed them to him one by one, methodically checking them off on a list as she did so.

In addition to the Vichy passport—which contained an up-to-date photograph of himself that he had had taken at Sir Pellinore's suggestion before going up to Wales—and the draft on the Swiss bank, there were a partly used Vichy ration card, two faked bills and several letters to support his false identity. When she had done, she said:

'As Tavenier lived over here from the time of his evacuation with other French troops from Dunkirk until the St. Nazaire raid last March, it would be quite in order for him to be wearing British underclothes; but you should remove any initials you may have on yours and, I suggest, buy yourself a French style suit and shoes when you get to Berne.'

Such advice to Gregory was very much 'teaching one's grandmother to suck eggs'; but he thanked her gravely, and she went on:

'Now this is off the record. I have one contact for you. But you must memorise his name and address; not write it down. It is Leon Levianski, wholesale furrier, 158 Kertész Utcza, Pest.'

'Thanks.' He repeated what she had said three times, then asked, 'How does this chap come into our picture?'

'He doesn't.' She lit another cigarette and looked down at her desk, her long lashes veiling her eyes. 'I happen to have an American boy-friend who is in O.S.S. Naturally we are terribly cagey with one another, but I told him the other night that we badly wanted a contact in Budapest and asked if he could help. He got me the name of this Jewish merchant. You see, it is still possible for the Hungarians to write to the U.S.

via Scandinavia or Turkey, and ever since America came into the war this man has been writing a monthly letter to a cousin of his in New York. Instead of his letters just being waffles, they are factual reports of what goes on inside Hitler's Europe—at least the old Austria-Hungarian part of it—as far as this man can assess it on all he hears by way of the Jewish grape-vine. After a while the cousin in New York thought they might interest the State Department; so now he sends them on regularly to Washington. Their writer might be able to help a bit. Anyhow, I think you would be quite safe in approaching him.'

Gregory repeated the name and address again, and nodded. 'I'm very grateful to you.' Then he read through the particulars of Etienne Tavenier. They were distinctly scanty. The Frenchman had entered the 14th Regiment of Tirailleurs in 1912, and served as a subaltern in the First World War. Afterwards he had spent several years in North Africa, then in 1926 married Mademoiselle Phoebe Constant (father's occupation unknown), and transferred to the 110th Infantry. It was believed that there were no children of the marriage, and that the wife's death (about the time of Munich) had been due to ptomaine poisoning. A year or so earlier Tavenier had come into his inheritance, a small château at Razac, not far from Périgueux. In 1939 he had been recalled to the colours, and in May, 1940, his battalion had been a part of General Blanchard's army, which had made a gallant stand beside the British. After being taken off from Dunkirk he had opted to remain in Britain as a member of the Free French Forces.

Having digested this, Gregory looked up and remarked, 'Not exactly a world-shaking career; but that is all to the good for my purpose. It is going to take quite a lot of thinking, though, to provide a plausible reason for a chap like that taking a holiday in Budapest in the middle of a war. If he was a sufferer from arthritis he might seek relief in a course of the famous mud baths; but it wouldn't be easy to bluff the doctors that I was afflicted in that way. Of course, the Hungarians are a romantic lot, so I might put it across discreetly that I had formed an attachment there before the war and had come back in the hope of being able to find the girl again.'

The goddess behind the desk shook her head. 'I don't like it. Middle-class Frenchmen are the most unromantic people in the world. But I have been thinking quite a lot about a story for you to tell. How about using foie gras?'

'Foie gras?' Gregory echoed in a puzzled voice.

'Yes; it's a national industry in Hungary. My mother and stepfather were there in 1938 and they brought back tins and tins of it.'

He nodded. 'You're quite right. One can't look out of the train anywhere in Hungary without seeing a flock of geese. But what is your idea?'

'Well, this foie gras was awfully good. The biggest tins had whole livers in them and they were that lovely shade of rich pink. There was only one thing lacking; there were no truffles to bring out the flavour.'

Gregory sat forward and thumped the desk. 'By jove! And I am supposed to own a place in Périgord, where the truffles come from. Of course, my object in going to Budapest is to get in touch with the foie gras makers and see if I can't fix up to supply them with truffles after the war.'

With the unselfconsciousness which is so often a by-product of beauty, the girl scratched her head with the blunt end of her pencil as she said, 'That's it. And my parents tell me that Budapest is an enchanting city. I do hope you'll have a pleasant stay there and a safe return.'

Ten minutes later Gregory left her office. He had never subscribed to the theory that blondes were necessarily dumb, and he knew from experience that beauty or the lack of it had no relation whatever to women's brains; but he did marvel somewhat that beings so young and glamorous as those in that secret headquarters should now be conducting affairs as efficiently as well-travelled men. He decided that he would bring Diana back the biggest foie gras he could find in Hungary as a reward for her excellent idea.

He could not know that before the month ended he would be counting himself lucky if he could get out of Budapest without bag or baggage, but alive to tell the tale.

# 5

# The Scene is Set

Gregory arrived in Budapest on Thursday, August 13th. On the previous Friday, after flying at a great height over France, the weekly diplomatic plane had landed him safely at Berne. Next morning he had presented his special letter of introduction at the bank and been shown into a private office. There he had made his arrangements about money and handed over both his British and French passports—the former for safe keeping until he reclaimed it, the latter so that the bank could get him a visa for Hungary, which they promised to have done for him by Monday, or Tuesday morning at the latest. He had then bought his tickets for the journey, a second-hand suitcase with several French labels on it, and some clothes of decidedly French cut.

On the Tuesday he had left Berne as Mr. Sallust and arrived in Lausanne as Commandant Tavenier. From there he had caught the Simplon-Orient Express down to Zagreb, where he changed trains and did the last lap north to the Hungarian capital.

He could have gone by air, but dismissed the idea because he knew that passengers who arrived in planes from foreign countries during wartime were much more closely scrutinised than the far greater numbers who crossed frontiers in trains; and he naturally wished to keep himself as inconspicuous as possible. Again he could have taken the quicker, direct route via Innsbruck and Vienna, but those cities now lay within Hitler's Greater Germany. The odds against his coming face to face during the short space of half a day's train journey with a Gestapo man who might recognise him were extremely long, but they were infinitely longer against his doing so on the stretch of railway which ran through Italy and Yugoslavia; and it was because he never took the smallest unnecessary risk that he had survived so many dangerous missions.

The same caution had decided his choice of an hotel. The Donau Palota was the most frequented by rich and influential Hungarians; so to stay at it would have given him his best chance of scraping acquaintance with the sort of people whose views on the future of Hungary he wished to find out. But it was there that in 1936 he had occupied a suite while having his affaire with the beautiful Sabine, and hotel servants have long memories. In consequence, on his arrival in Berne he had sent a telegram to the Vadászkürt, hoping that with five days' notice they would have a room for him. In that he was lucky, as when he was booking-in the clerk told him that, like those in most other capitals during wartime, the hotels in Budapest were now packed to capacity in season and out.

Having surrendered his passport for registration by the police he was shown up to a room on the third floor. Instead of opening into a passageway it was entered from a broad balcony that overlooked a huge oblong courtyard formed by the interior walls of the four sides of the hotel. Large trees were growing in the courtyard and beneath their leafy branches were several score of tables, as during the summer months it was used as the hotel's restaurant.

That night Gregory dined down there, and one glance at the menu showed him that Budapest was very far from being reduced to the scant choice of indifferent food which was all that could be offered by restaurants in London. Hungary, as he knew, had few industries, and from her vast farmlands had for centuries fed a great part of the Austro-Hungarian Empire; but he had expected to find at least fairly strict rationing owing to the voracious demands of a Germany that had now been at war for nearly three years. This first evidence that the Hungarians were by no means altogether under the thumb of their mighty ally was encouraging. He cheerfully ordered trout with melted butter, roast goose and green peas; then lingered over a fresh peach and a bottle of Tokay while listening to one of those gypsy orchestras for which Hungary is famous.

Next morning he did not go at once to seek out Leon Levianski or any of Sir Pellinore's old friends. He wanted first to get the feel of the capital; so he set off on what, for him, was a long walk.

Budapest is only one eighth the size of London and its centre is proportionately smaller; so during a stroll of two hours or so a sightseer may pass along most of its principal streets. It is, however, divided into two sharply contrasting parts. Buda, which is the older of the twin cities, is almost entirely residential, and consists of tier upon tier of ancient buildings, churches and palaces rising steeply to crown a ridge of hills on the west bank of the Danube. Pest, much larger and the centre of all commercial activities, is entirely flat. From just east of the river, where the smart shopping district is situated, it stretches away divided by the magnificent two-mile-long Andràssy Avenue, until its new factories and suburbs merge into the distant plain.

The Vadászkürt and other principal hotels are all in Pest, and only a stone's throw from the Vorasmarty Tér, out of which runs Vaczi Utcza, the equivalent of Bond Street; so Gregory turned in that direction. When he reached the square he saw that the windows of Gerbaud's, the famous patisserie, were, as of old, filled with rich cream cakes, crystallised fruits and sweets; and, on entering the Utcza, found that most of the other shops showed equally little sign of depleted stocks.

Strolling southwards he reached the great Market and spent a quarter of an hour there. Its stalls held an abundance of meat, game, fish and groceries, and the people in it were mainly well-clad. He found that less surprising when he suddenly recalled that Hungary had not become seriously involved in the war until Hitler had attacked Russia in the preceding summer; so, apart from a shortage of some manufactured goods, she would hardly have yet been reduced to such stringencies as clothes rationing.

There were quite a few soldiers about in drab wartime uniform, and a number of much smarter girls dressed as nurses and army drivers. In half an hour he had seen only two German officers, and confirmed his earlier impression that, after those of Vienna, the girls of Budapest were the prettiest of any city he had ever visited.

On emerging from the Market he had his first view of the Danube. It was a broad, turgid, fast-flowing stream, and far from blue; but it sparkled prettily in the August sunshine. To his right lay a broad mile-long embankment which was termed the 'Corso' for, in front of its many cafés, lay Budapest's most fashionable promenade. Turning along it he now had a fine view of Buda. Across the river it rose upon its hills, a miracle of beauty, its turrets and spires seeming to pierce the almost cloudless blue sky.

By Erzsébet Bridge he crossed the river. Slowly he made his way up past the Royal Palace, which was now the residence of the Regent, Admiral Horthy, and so into Buda's twisting cobbled streets where for a thousand years there had lived men and women who had played a part in Europe's history. Six years before, from a first-floor window in one of the ancient houses there, he had witnessed the annual celebration which embodied Hungary's great traditions, and it was a sight that he had never forgotten.

At some time in the Dark Ages the tomb of Stephen, the first King of Hungary who had accepted Christianity, had been opened, and it had been found that, although his body had fallen into dust, his right hand lay there unwithered. It had henceforth become the custom for this miraculous hand to be exposed to the veneration of the multitude by being carried through the streets of the city on the fifteenth of each September.

Gregory had seen many processions, but nothing to equal this in medieval pageantry. There had been the Palace Guards wearing silver pointed Saxon helmets, eighteen inches high, and carrying flashing halberds serrated like the prow of a Venetian gondola. The gold and crystal casket containing the sacred relic was surrounded by chanting priests. Behind it walked the Prince Archbishop, the Metropolitan of the Greek Church and the Papal Legate, resplendent in robes of purple, white and crimson, their trains held up by small boys in lace-bordered surplices. Then had come the Corps Diplomatique, brave in its orders and gold embroidered uniforms. The black clad Deputies of the Hungarian Parliament had next struck an incongruous note, but after them had come the handsome Regent Horthy in Admiral's uniform and, following him, the body of men who made the ceremony unique.

They were some three score of the Magnates of Hungary; all nobles who could trace their ancestry back to the times when their forebears had held Hungary as the bastion of Christian Europe against the Infidel. Their costumes were those worn in Napoleonic times, or earlier, and marvellously varied; gold tasselled Hessian boots, silver braided doublets of green, blue, black and cerise, half-cloaks trimmed with sable, astrakhan, ermine or sea-otter, flat busbies surmounted by plumes and aigrets, dolmans, sabretaches, and great jewel-hilted scimitars all jostled together forming a sea of colour, so that the eye was quite incapable of taking in the details of so splendid a spectacle.

As Gregory thought of it again, he thought too of Sabine, who had stood beside him in the window that they had hired,

57

holding his hand and telling him with low-voiced but passionate enthusiasm, as the procession moved below them, of the past glories of her country.

From the small square dominated by the Coronation Church, in which reposed the Sacred Hand of St. Stephen, he walked through to the open space behind the church where a great equestrian statue of the Royal Saint looked out over the river and the city.

This lofty emplacement was called the Fisher bastion and from it there was a truly marvellous view. To either side the red roofed houses of Buda seemed to be tumbling away down the steep slope on which the ramparts stood as though at any moment they might fall into the Danube. Seen from here the river looked even broader, and much more tranquil, as it wound its way between the twin cities. To the north it divided into two arms which embraced the mile-long *Margereten-Insel*.

This lovely wooded island had been made into a private park by the Archduke Joseph; now it had on it Budapest's latest luxury hotel—the Palatinos—an enormous open air bathing pool, and several café restaurants which after dark become night-clubs offering glamorous floor shows. In the opposite direction the river disappeared behind the lofty Citadel on its way towards distant Belgrade and Rumania. Far below, the famous Suspension Bridge linked Buda's hill with central Pest, along the shore of which stood the Parliament House with its many graceful spires, the Donau Palota and numerous other fine modern buildings. Beyond them rose the three hundred feet high dome of the Leopold Church from a sea of office and apartment blocks stretched away into the blue distance.

As Gregory sat there for a while he recalled that it was on one of these slopes that St. Gellért had met his fate. He was the Bishop who had converted King Stephen to Christianity; but certain full-blooded types had not approved the change, so they had put Gellért in a barrel and sent him rolling down the hill. As the barrel had spikes in it the unfortunate missionary could have been little more than a lacerated corpse by the time it bounced into the Danube.

Not a very pleasant death, Gregory reflected; but, after all, perhaps not so bad, as it must have been quite quick, and easily a hundred times less prolonged and painful than that which he might himself expect should he ever have the ill-luck to fall alive into the hands of *Herr Gruppenführer* Grauber.

Descending through the steep narrow streets, he recrossed the river, walked along to the Corso and, sitting down at a table outside one of the cafés, ordered himself a *baratsch*. This golden liquor is distilled from apricots and is the Hungarian national drink. It is made in every farmhouse in the country, and varies with quality and age from a fiery breath-taking spirit to a smooth and delectable liqueur. As it is unsweetened it is equally suitable for an aperitif or a digestive, and is drunk by all classes at all hours. While renewing his acquaintance with this invigorating tipple, Gregory considered the results of his morning's ramble.

Except perhaps for coffee, and other such items which came from distant lands, Hungarian larders were clearly not yet subject to the stress of war and, although prices had evidently risen considerably, there seemed no reason to suppose that for meat, bread, butter and other basic foods they were beyond the means of the workers.

Petrol was evidently short, as there were many fewer cars on the streets than he had seen there in peace time. On the other hand, there were many more horse-drawn vehicles, including quite a number of private carriages which must have been dug out by rich people from old coach-houses. Hungary had been slower to adopt the motor than most nations as her roads were bad and horses cheap and plentiful. Horse breeding was one of her national industries and the great herds reared on the plain of the Hortobágy made it certain that however long the war lasted the supply would never fail; so the Hungarians had no need to worry about local transport. In the matter of fuel, too, they could have no great anxieties, as most of the houses and offices were still heated in winter by old-fashioned wood-burning stoves which could be kept going from their own forests.

By the time Gregory finished his drink he had reached the conclusion that the chances of his mission being successful were far from good. Had he found a state of shortages and aggravating restrictions approaching those in Britain and Germany, there would have been reason to assume that a good part of the Hungarian people were war-weary and, not being so deeply committed as those of the two great powers to fight on to the end, might give ready backing to a movement for a separate peace. But that was not the case. So far, too, Budapest had not suffered a single air-raid; so, apart from the comparatively few walking wounded to be seen in the streets, there had been little really to bring the war home to the people of the capital. In short, the horrors and privations of Hitler's war were still unknown to it, and in its continued plenty and gaiety, its state was very similar to that which had prevailed in London for the greater part of the First World War.

Having lunched off a *gulyás* of venison, washed down with a carafe of the rich Hungarian red wine known as Bulls-blood of Badascony, he took an aged open carriage along to the nearest end of Kertész Utcza, where he paid it off, then strolled along to No. 158.

It proved to be a double-fronted shop in a rather dreary block, and the furs in the windows looked distinctly shoddy. Pushing open the door Gregory walked in. The shop ran back some way and was a much larger place than might have been supposed from the street; but it was three parts empty. Less than a quarter of the rows of hangers held coats, there were a few bundles of skins thrown carelessly on the floor, and the only person in it was a stout red-headed Jewess who was checking over raw pelts behind a long narrow counter.

Going up to the counter Gregory told her in French that he wished to buy a fur that could be made up as a collar for his winter travelling coat.

She replied first in Magyar, then in bad German, that she did not understand French.

Ignoring the fact that she did understand German, he repeated his statement in deliberately poor English.

As he had hoped, she again shook her head but, making a sign that he should wait, went to the back of the shop and through a glass door. A moment later she emerged again with a man of about forty. He was short, had a round face, curly black hair and a bluish chin, but he did not look particularly like a Jew.

Gregory was wondering if this was Mr. Leon Levianski. However, he had no intention of asking, as the approach had to be made with the greatest circumspection. It was a possibility that one of Levianski's more recent letters to his cousin in New York had fallen into wrong hands. If so, it was quite on the cards that he would have been arrested for conveying useful information to the enemy. Any stranger enquiring for him thereafter would at once be suspect; and the last thing

Gregory wanted was to have a description of himself in such a connexion turned in to the police.

The dark man came forward and said in passably good English: 'If you please, sir, I have no French. Speak with me please in English and tell me what you wish.'

In broken English Gregory once more enquired for fur which would make a warm collar to a travelling coat.

The furrier shrugged his broad shoulders and spread wide his hands, 'I regret. I have little to offer, sir. This time last year, yes. I could have given you choice of a dozen Sea Otter. Smartest and best wearing fur for gentleman's coat. But now, some odd pieces of Persian Lamb which we could make up; otherwise nothing.'

'Why have you become so short of stock?' Gregory enquired.

'Russia,' came the prompt reply. 'Our Hungarian troops, they go properly clothed for the war we fight. But the Germans, no. Hitler is everyone say a very clever man. Perhaps, but his judgment is not good when he expects to conquer Russia in one summer campaign. Winter comes and many thousand Germans they shiver, get frost-bite, die. Their Fraus and Fräuleins make sacrifice of vanity and send them fur coats. But it is not enough. Our Government orders that we hold nothing back from the German Mission that comes to purchase.' After an almost imperceptible pause he added, 'And as they are our Allies it is right that we should give best help. But it has left us deplete, very deplete.'

'I quite understand,' Gregory replied, 'It was a Sea Otter that I wanted though; so I think I had better try elsewhere. Still, I'm sorry, as furs are tricky things; and I was assured by a Mr. Levianski of New York that your firm was a reliable one.'

'You know my cousin, then!' exclaimed the furrier. 'But this is different. For you I will enquire of my friends in the trade, and somehow a Sea Otter find for you.'

'Would you, perhaps, be Mr. Leon Levianski?' Gregory now felt it safe to ask.

'Why, yes. And that you should know my cousin is of much interest. Has it been long, please, since you see him in New York?'

Gregory held the dark eyes only a few feet from his own with a steady glance, and said in a low voice. 'I have never met your cousin; but I know about the letters that you write to him.'

Levianski's face blanched slightly, then he essayed a not very convincing laugh. 'My letters! I am surprise that he should think it worth while to show to anyone. They are gossips only of things here which I think might interest him.'

'Your gossip has been found interesting by good friends of his who wish well to Hungary,' Gregory swiftly sought to reassure him. 'And I would greatly like to talk to you about this. Could you meet me for a drink somewhere this evening?'

'Yes, I could do that,' Levianski agreed after a moment's hesitation. 'Where have you to suggest?'

Gregory smiled. 'It is always safer to discuss this sort of business in a crowd. Would six o'clock at the Café Mignon on the Corso suit you?'

'Thank you. Yes, please. I am happy to make acquaintance.' Returning his smile, the furrier bowed him out of the door.

As it was a heavenly afternoon, Gregory decided to have a bathe. The Hungarians have a passion for bathing and, it is said, there are no less than one hundred and sixty public baths in Budapest to choose from. But he had no hesitation in having himself driven in another old fiacre across the bridge to the *Margareten-Insel*.

The oblong pool there was as large as a small lake. Its sides, for twenty feet out, sloped very gradually so that hundreds of children could splash about along them without danger; yet there was still ample room in the middle of the pool and at its deep end for an equal number of good swimmers to enjoy themselves without undue crowding.

Gregory dived and swam for about half-an-hour, then came out and lay sunning himself on the sand which had been brought from the shores of Lake Balaton as a surround for the pool. It was delightful there in the warm windless air, with the faint hum of conversation and occasional laughter coming from the groups nearby. The fact that millions of men, from the Arctic to the deserts of Egypt and the remotest islands of the Pacific, were at that moment desperately endeavouring to kill each other, when they might be enjoying something similar to this, struck him as both tragic and crazy.

Yet his bliss was not entirely unalloyed, for he was subconsciously a little lonely. He would have given a lot to have had Erika there—or Sabine. A mental picture of the latter, as she had once sat beside him not many yards from where he was lying now, flashed into his mind. Only the more intimate parts of her slender golden-brown body had been encased in a white satin swim-suit, and she had been sitting with her hands clasped round her bent knees, from time to time shaking the dark hair which fell to her shoulders, because its ends had got a little wet under the bathing cap she had just taken off.

As he thought idly of the fun they had had together he wondered where she was now, and if he would run into her. Then, with a little shock, he realised that such a meeting could prove highly dangerous. She knew him to be an Englishman, and her country was at war with Britain. She knew, too, that he had acted as Sir Pellinore's secret agent in getting to the bottom of at least one conspiracy to sabotage British interests; so she would immediately jump to the conclusion that he had come to Budapest as a spy. Women who have parted with their lovers as good friends are, he knew, more prone to be ruled by pleasant memories than patriotic considerations; so he thought the odds were that she would not turn him over to the police, but one could never tell. There was, too, the nasty possibility that should they suddenly come face to face in the presence of other people she might, from astonishment at seeing him, give him away inadvertently.

Much as he would have liked to spend a few hours with her again and hear from her what she had made of her life, he decided that he must keep a sharp look-out for her and, should he see her, beat a quick retreat before she had a chance to recognise him.

While in the pool he had seen that there were many more women than men bathing and among them quite a number of pretty girls, some of whom had looked at him more than once with the sort of glance which invites conversation. But he had no intention of becoming involved in anything of that kind, even temporarily. It was just such dalliance with young women about whom one knew nothing which could have the most unexpected repercussions and, at times, lead men employed on his sort of work to an extremely sticky end.

In due course he dressed, drank a *baratsch* at the pool bar, then had himself driven to the Corso. Sitting down at one of the tables in front of the Café Mignon, he ordered himself a stein of dark lager, and soon afterwards saw Levianski coming towards him.

With a wave of his hand and a smile he called out as if to an old acquaintance, *'Wie geht es Ihnen? Was wollen Sie trinken?'*

The broad-shouldered little Jew returned his greeting, said that he too would like a dark lager, then, sitting down, added in a lower voice, 'So you do speak German?'

Gregory answered in an equally low tone, 'My pretending not to was only a ruse aimed at getting your assistant to fetch someone who spoke French or English. I hoped it might be you; and I was lucky. But we will speak German together from now on, so as not to draw unnecessary attention to ourselves.'

Nodding agreement, Levianski said, 'Now tell me, please, how you came to see my letters, and what you want with me.'

That he could not be expected to talk freely, unless he was trusted to some extent, was obvious. But Gregory did not mean to reveal his true identity. With disarming candour he replied:

'My name is Etienne Tavenier, and I am a retired Major of the French Army. For some time I have been living in Switzerland. I am not a de Gaullist but my sympathies are with the Allies. Naturally they have an information centre there. I have an English friend who works in it, and he asked me if I would make this visit to Budapest. I agreed, but I do not come as a spy, to pry into military matters. I assure you of that. Although I have been a soldier I am at heart a man of peace; and my one wish is to help in any way I can to stop this terrible war before it destroys all Europe.'

Having paused to light a cigarette, he went on, 'Evidently the letters you wrote to your cousin were passed on by him, as I feel sure you must have intended them to be. Anyhow, copies of them were sent to the Middle Europe Section of the Allies' information centre in Switzerland. That is how your name came to be given to me as a man I could trust, and one who might be able to help me with the answers to certain questions that I have come here to investigate.'

Levianski's dark eyes were quite expressionless as he asked, 'What are those questions?'

'They can really all be embodied in one. What is the attitude of the Hungarian people towards the war?'

'That is not simple to answer. The fact that I am a Jew does not make me any the less a Hungarian; but my attitude is very

64

different from that of the average Catholic priest, big land-owner or peasant.'

'Naturally. But what I mean is, do you believe that the bulk of the people are convinced of the rightness of the cause for which they are fighting?'

'I can only repeat that the views of the main elements which make up our population vary greatly. You see, Hungary is quite different from most other nations. Her classes are not integrated in the same way. By that I do not mean that we are torn by class warfare. In fact, in peace time, we suffer very little from labour troubles, and in all classes there is a high degree of patriotism. But, where international relations are concerned, there is no unity of opinion to bind us together; as, for example, the mutual hatred of the French and the Germans which is common to all classes in both countries.'

'Please go on, and tell me about these conflicting interests.'

'Well, to start with, Hungary has not yet really emerged from feudalism. The greater part of the land is still divided into vast estates which are owned by a hundred or so families. They lost them after the First World War, but the Bolshevik revolution led here by Bela Khun lasted only six months. That was not long enough to destroy the attitude of mind of the peasants, which had been engrained into them through many centuries. When the magnates returned from temporary exile, their peasants received them joyfully, restored their lands and went back to work for them.

'By the Treaty of Trianon the size of Hungary was reduced by half. In that way many of these great magnates lost some of their estates; but most of them retained enough land and wealth for their way of life to remain almost unaltered. In their great country houses they keep staffs of up to fifty servants, and as many more outside to run their stables and their shooting parties. Up there, opposite to us, on the hill of Buda the great stone buildings that you can see are their town palaces. All of them hold priceless art treasures and fine libraries, for the Hungarian aristocracy is a highly cultured one; but it has the faults as well as the virtues of all feudal aristocracies.

'The Magyar nobility is brave, open handed and casually kind to those who are dependent upon it, but it is also proud, cynical and immoral. They despised the Austrian aristocracy because in most cases Austrian family trees do not go back, by several hundred years, as far as theirs. They regard Hitler and his Nazi *Gauleiters* as the scum of the gutters. Yet, for their own ends, they received the Austrians as equals and treat these jumped-up Germans with most considerate politeness. As for their morals, those of cats are better. The tittle-tattle of their servants on that aspect of their lives is so consistent that it cannot be doubted. Within their own small circle husbands, wives and even unmarried girls take and exchange paramours with a freedom which would be considered utterly shameful did they occupy a less exalted station.

'You will appreciate, therefore, that they are concerned only to maintain their privileged position. But naturally they also have a heavy bias towards any policy which, while protecting their present sources of wealth, might lead to their getting back the estates which they lost in 1920 by the creation of Poland, Czechoslovakia and a greatly enlarged Rumania.'

Levianski took a long pull at his lager, then went on. 'You will now expect me to speak of the middle-classes. Well, there are none. At least not as there are in other countries. The noble Magyars would not soil their hands with commerce, or allow even their remotest relatives to do so. That is, until 1920. After the revolution some of the younger ones who had become impoverished through it became motor-salesmen, travel agents and so on; also the general spread of education qualified a few thousand of the younger peasants to move into the towns and replace the Austrians who had previously acted as our petty officials, but neither group is sufficiently numerous to form a class. It was the void between lord and peasant which attracted my people to Hungary. That was many centuries ago, of course, but the Jews gradually established themselves here and by their industry made themselves indispensable.

'Today in Pest there are three hundred thousand of us— nearly a third of the population of the capital. Many of our families have grown rich on the proceeds of doing the things that the aristocracy was too proud or too lazy to do; but we have served Hungary well. We are the doctors, the lawyers, the industrialists, the importers of the things that Hungary must have and the exporters of the things she has to sell. Without us the country would fall into a state of chaos overnight. The Magyar lords have always recognised that; therefore they have not only given us their protection through the centuries, but

treated us generously. Whether they would be strong enough
to continue to do so with Europe at peace and Hitler its overlord is a very different question.

'We watch with awful fear what is happening in the lands
where Hitler has only to give an order for it to be obeyed.
Himmler is, if possible, even more demented in his racial
theories than his master. From the Germanic part of Poland
he deported a million Jews, and to fill the void he has been
dragging from all parts of Europe people, many of whom
cannot even speak German, just because they are of German
blood. For them it means loss of homes, properties, friends
and occupation; but these Nazis are too fanatical to care even
for the welfare of their own race.

'For my people, of course, matters are infinitely worse. They
are despoiled of everything except the clothes in which they
stand up. Last winter thousands of the women, children and
old folk who were despatched to East Prussia, packed into cattle
trucks, did not survive the journey. They were frozen stiff
hours before they reached their destination.

'In Austria things are no better. Within a week of the
Anschluss, at the order of Heydrich, Karl Adolf Eichmann set
up in Vienna his "Office for Jewish Emigration". A very few,
like Mr. Louis de Rothschild who ransomed himself by signing away his steel rolling-mills, were allowed to emigrate;
180,000 others were not so fortunate. Most of them are dead;
the rest tortured skeletons in huge concentration camps, like
Dachau and Mauthausen.

'Eichmann's "Office" already has a branch in Budapest. It
has been spending enormous sums in stirring up anti-Jewish
feeling here. As the Government would find it almost impossible to carry on its war industries without us, we are still
protected. But if Hitler and Himmler were freed from their
war commitments . . .'

'You would not have a hope,' Gregory cut in. 'They would
send in their Germans to take over your businesses; and it
could only be a matter of time before you suffered the same
terrible fate as the Jews in Germany, Poland and Austria.
Now, what about the peasants?'

'The Germans and the Russians are both hereditary enemies
of the Hungarian people,' Levianski replied, 'but they dislike
the Germans more because for so long they were bullied by
the German-speaking Austrian petty officials and tax gatherers.

In their case, though, there is a more important factor than race prejudice; it is religion. Roman Catholicism still has a firm hold on Hungarians both rich and poor. The country people are devout and their village priests are looked up to by them. They are told from the pulpits that Stalin is anti-Christ and that they must think of the war against the godless hordes of Russia as a crusade. Therefore, much as they dislike the Germans, they are fighting beside them, for the most part, willingly.'

'To sum up, then,' said Gregory, 'the nobility will continue to support Germany because they fear that a Russian victory would lead to their losing everything, and the peasants will fight on in defence of their religious beliefs; but your people would rather see the Russians win, as the lesser evil.'

Levianski pulled a face. 'It would be only a lesser evil. Things were bad enough during the Bela Khun revolution. The Soviet-isation of Hungary would mean the loss of our businesses and private fortunes. But at least our lives would be spared; and that is more than we could hope for under a Nazi controlled government.'

'I think you are right that the Russians would plunder Jewish and Christian capitalists alike, if Hungary fought on to the end and Germany is defeated. But it would be a very different state of affairs if she decided to make a separate peace now. I feel sure that, pressed as they are at the moment, the Russians would be only too glad to guarantee Hungary's independ-ence, and that the other allies would underwrite that guaran-tee.'

'Ah, yes,' Levianski sighed. 'If only that could be brought about how happy we should all be. But I see no prospect of it. Besides, if Hungary deserted her allies, it is quite on the cards that the Nazis would march in, and we would then be at the mercy of their Gestapo murder squads.'

'I don't think that would happen. Hitler has his hands full in Russia. He couldn't spare the divisions to open up another front; and that is what he would have to do if he were opposed by the Hungarian army.'

'Perhaps you are right.'

'I'm sure I am; and think what such a move could lead to. If Hungary made a separate peace and withdrew her troops from the Russian front, that might be the beginning of the end. Hitler is in a relatively strong position now, but he must know that he will have to face up to America next year. He might very well decide that he could get a better peace by opening negotiations in 1942 than if he continues the struggle in '43 or '44. As I have told you, my one desire is to see peace restored before Europe becomes a shambles. But I am convinced that neither Britain nor Germany will make a first move; so the only hope is that one of the smaller countries will do so and set the ball rolling. It was for that I came to Hungary; to find out if there was any chance of her Government entering into a secret understanding should it be approached by the British.'

'I am in no position to say,' Levianski spread out his hands, 'but I should think it most unlikely.'

'For the Jews of Hungary it could mean not only life, but future security and prosperity,' said Gregory earnestly. 'The fact that they control Hungary's industry and commerce must give them considerable power. Surely there are ways in which they could exert their influence on the Government to consider a separate peace?'

Levianski shook his head. 'You do not understand. The Jews have been well treated here because for hundreds of years they have performed many useful services. But never, never, have they sought to interfere in politics. To have done so would have been to invite an end to the tolerance with which they are regarded. It is true that we have come to think of ourselves as Hungarians, and that financially we run the country. But the fact remains that the Hungarians still look on us only as guests here. And the guest in a man's house does not presume to tell him how to run it.'

They talked on for another half-hour; but it was already clear to Gregory that the Jews of Pest were unlikely to contribute anything worth while towards the downfall of Hitler. Despite their numbers, and immense financial resources, the fatalism which was tied like a millstone round the neck of their race weighed them down so heavily that they were incapable of standing up in defence of their rights as human beings; or even of using such power as they had in an organised attempt to protect themselves from future massacre. The best that could be hoped from them was that in devious ways they would hamper the Hungarian war effort and, should a movement for an independent peace arise, give it their backing.

Nevertheless, Leon Levianski showed himself personally to be a courageous man; for he said to Gregory before they parted: 'These endeavours of yours to find a way to bring about peace are most praiseworthy; the more so as making them may easily bring you into danger. I am sure you would not willingly involve me in trouble with the police. But, if they get after you and you can evade them for a few hours, come to my apartment over the shop. I could hide you there for a time, until you could make a plan for getting safely out of the country.'

Gregory thanked him for his generous offer. They then shook hands firmly and went their separate ways through the August dusk. As Gregory walked back to the Vadászkürt he decided rather glumly that there now seemed little hope of his being able to take a favourable report back to London. His talk with Levianski had reinforced his own opinion formed that morning, that the Hungarian people were as yet by no means war-weary, and also revealed the fact that even if they had been it would not have made much difference, as the issue of Hungary's continuing in the war lay entirely with the aristocracy. Naturally, he intended to see and sound Sir Pellinore's friends, but since the governing classes were not subject to pressure from the masses it seemed unlikely that they would be willing to abandon the pro-Nazi policy which they had evidently decided offered the best prospect of preserving their wealth and estates. And during the past fortnight the Russian situation, worry over which had been the origin of his mission, had been going from bad to worse.

He could only console himself a little with the thought that, anyhow, a fortnight's holiday in Budapest with good food and good cheer to be had for the asking would be a most pleasant change after the dreariness of London. As he entered the hall of the hotel, he was thinking that for dinner he would order that famous Hungarian dish, chicken stewed with rice and red peppers. He was not expecting any letters so would have walked straight through had not one of the porters called to him from behind the desk, 'Excuse me, sir!'

When he crossed to the desk the man handed him back his passport and with it a cheap looking envelope addressed to M. le Commandant Tavenier. Tearing the envelope open, he gave a swift glance at the single sheet of paper that it contained. It was a typed note from the French Consul General to the effect that information having been received from the police of M. le Commandant Tavenier's arrival in Budapest, it was requested that within twenty-four hours he would attend at 17. Fö-utca in order that his stay in the Hungarian capital might be regularised.

This was something for which Gregory had not bargained. No doubt it was only a routine matter; but all the same he had an uneasy feeling that having to make his number with the Vichy authorities might, sooner or later, land him in just the sort of tricky situation he was very anxious to avoid.


# 6

# A Sinister Figure

On the following morning Gregory took a cab across the river to 17. Fö-utca and handed the porter at the door the summons he had received. The porter was a Hungarian and after a glance at the letter announced its bearer in bad French over a house telephone to some invisible person. He then showed Gregory into a small sunless room. It was furnished with the sparse economy typical of French officialdom, and occupied only by a dark-haired middle-aged woman. With a cigarette dangling from her lower lip she was thumbing through some dog-eared papers on the narrow desk before her. As he came into the room she gestured towards a wooden bench against one wall, then took no further notice of him.

After sitting there for ten minutes his patience began to wear thin, and he was just about to demand that she did something about him, when a door behind her opened and over her head a tall man gave him a swift scrutiny.

Returning the glance, Gregory was far from favourably impressed by the man's appearance. He was wearing a dark blue suit with a stiff white collar, out of which arose a scrawny neck, surmounted by a hollow-cheeked face, a long narrow nose, eyes with liverish pouches beneath them and an almost bald head, that together gave him some resemblance to a vulture. With a slight inclination of his bony skull, this sinister looking individual said:

71

'Monsieur le Commandant, my name is Cochefert. I regret to have had to trouble you to come here, but there are just a few formalities. . . . Please to come in.'

Gregory followed him into a somewhat larger but equally bleak room. Monsieur Cochefert gave him a hard chair and sat down in another behind a bare table piled high with bundles of documents. Drawing a printed form towards him and picking up an old fashioned steel-nibbed pen, he asked:

'May I have the object of your visit to Budapest?'

Had Gregory been less experienced in such matters he would have been tempted to reply, 'We are not on French soil, so you have no authority here. My business has nothing to do with you, and you can go to the devil.' But he was much too old a hand needlessly to antagonise any official; so, with pleasant memories of the charming and helpful Diana, he said quite amiably:

'I own a truffle farm in Périgord and I have come here to investigate the possibility of supplying Hungarian foie-gras makers with truffles after the war.'

'Indeed!' Cochefert raised eyebrows having so few hairs in them that they were only just perceptible. 'That sounds a good idea. The paté made here is excellent, but could be much improved by the introduction of truffles.' As he made a note on the form, Gregory saw that it already had on it Tavenier's home address and other particulars; so the Hungarian police must have given the French Consulate a sight of his passport. To give substance to his cover story he said:

'As a matter of fact, even if I had not had the note asking me to call here I should have done so to ask if I could be supplied with a list of the names and addresses of the principal foie-gras manufacturers.'

'Strictly speaking, that is a matter for our Commercial Attaché at the Embassy,' the Frenchman replied, 'but I will telephone him and ask for a list to be sent to you.'

Gregory made a little bow. 'Monsieur is most kind.'

'It is a pleasure. May I ask how long you intend to stay in Budapest?'

'For about a fortnight.'

'Good. I see that you obtained your visa for Hungary in Switzerland; so I take it you broke your journey there?'

'I have been living there for the past three months. Fortunately I am fairly well off and investments that I have

72

there enable me to do so in reasonable comfort. I find it much more congenial than France, now that our poor country has fallen into a such a sad state.'

'That is very understandable. I, too, am glad to escape the annoyances and privations suffered by everyone in France these days, and I hope to retain my post here until the end of the war. Talking of the war, Monsieur le Commandant, at your age you must have been with your regiment in 1939. I would be interested to hear how you fared?'

'My battalion formed part of General Blanchard's Army of the North,' replied Gregory promptly. 'As you will know, it was trapped with the British in Belgium and the greater part of it was killed or captured. But several thousand troops of General de la Laurencie's IIIrd Corps were taken off from Dunkirk, and I was lucky enough to be among them.'

'I see, and you opted to return to France?'

Gregory shook his head. 'No; I was one of those who favoured fighting on. Later, like many others, I realised the futility of doing so. Most of them are still stuck in England, but I had the good fortune to get away. I was posted as an Interpreter to one of the Commando units that took part in the St. Nazaire raid last March. Soon after I got ashore I took advantage of the smoke and confusion to slip away and look for a good hiding place. I went to earth in a grain warehouse on the docks and I had brought sufficient iron rations in my haversack to last me several days. When the excitement had died down I took a chance with a dock-foreman. He brought me a suit of civilian clothes and I had enough francs for my railway fare; so four days after the raid I was back at Razac—the village in Périgord where I own the château.'

Cochefert nodded his vulture-like head, and sighed. 'Ah, Monsieur le Commandant, this war is not like other wars. It has set brother against brother; and often left gallant officers such as yourself no alternative but to adopt such means as you describe to save their honour—and the honour of France.'

'Yes; the honour of France,' Gregory repeated piously.

It was the sanctimonious phrase which sprang to the lips of many Frenchmen in those days; in most cases to disguise from themselves the fact that they had been led by their military idol, old Marshal Pétain, into deserting their ally and entering into a pact with Hitler.

On this they both stood up, remained silent for a moment as

though paying tribue to the memory of some highly respected friend who had recently died, then shook hands. It seemed then that Monsieur Cochefert had no further questions to ask for, after exchanging punctilious salutations with his visitor, he showed him out to the front door.

Back in the sunlit street, Gregory felt that he had dealt with a possibly dangerous business very successfully. The line that he had at first thrown in his lot with the Free French but later 'seen the light' was, he thought, a nice artistic touch; and the foie-gras story could not have gone down better. Cochefert might lack most of those physical attributes which would have made him the answer to a maiden's prayer, but he had fulfilled his tiresome function in a friendly spirit and appeared to be entirely satisfied.

The next item on Gregory's agenda was to get in touch with Sir Pellinore's old friends. Just in case he ran into any trouble, he thought it wiser not to do so from his own hotel; so he walked along to the Bristol. Going up to the hall-porter's desk he asked the man to get him Count István Lujza's telephone number.

The porter looked at him in surprise and said, 'If you mean the ex-Minister, sir, he has been dead for two years or more.'

Murmuring that he had not been in Budapest since before the war, Gregory asked him to try Count Mihály Zapolya. This time the porter held a short telephone conversation in Hungarian, then reported:

'I have spoken with the doorman at the palace in the Illona Utcza, and he says that as usual in the summer months His Excellency the Count is living on his estate at Nagykáta.'

Hoping that he would prove luckier with the third string to his bow, Gregory asked for Prince György Hunyadi. The porter gave a dubious shake of his head and replied:

'I feel almost certain that His Highness is still abroad, sir; but I will ring up the Foreign Office.' Another telephone conversation followed, and it emerged that the Prince was in Buenos Aires as Hungarian Ambassador to the Argentine.

That left only Count Zapolya as a possible contact; so Gregory enquired where Nagykáta was. He learned to his relief that it was only about thirty miles from Budapest; but the station which served it was no more than a village halt, and there were only two trains that stopped there each day. As it was not yet half-past ten, by hiring a two-horse carriage and promising its driver a liberal tip, he just managed to catch the morning one, which got him there by half-past eleven.

When he jumped down from the train he could see no sign of a village or a large country house, and there was no conveyance of any kind available. But he had taken the precaution of writing the Count's name in block letters on an envelope and, on showing this to the solitary porter, the man grinned and pointed up the road towards a slight eminence, crowned by trees, that stood out from the flat plain.

After a half-mile walk he found that beyond the trees lay the village, and that it was a replica of a dozen others that he had seen from the train. To one side of a broad uneven open space stood a small onion-spired church; the rest of the buildings varied little except in size. They were thatched and squat, the eaves of their roofs coming very low down; nearly all of them were whitewashed and had semi-circular arches leading to inner yards. There were no motor vehicles in the street, but a number of huge hay-wains each drawn by a team of four slow-moving white oxen, and flocks of cackling geese straggled in all directions. Not one of the villagers was in any kind of uniform; there were no notices with arrows pointing to air-raid shelters or Red Cross huts and, in fact, it made the war seem so immeasurably remote that the bombings, the sinkings and the barrages that were killing thousands every day might have been taking place on another planet.

At the village inn he found a man who could speak German and, while he drank his first *baratsch* of the day, a horse was harnessed for him in leisurely fashion to an ancient carriage. There followed a two-mile drive between the endless fields of rich black earth, which had no boundary banks or hedges and were broken only by an occasional low farm-house with a few barns clustering about it. More trees at length indicated an entrance to a private park. In it, grassy meadows with fine herds of cattle grazing in them sloped down to a long lake, partly covered by bulrushes and with a few swans gracefully sailing about its open spaces.

The house was hideous. Except for one much older wing, the main building was a product of Victorian times and even the green-painted wooden colonial style shutters that flanked its many windows could not redeem it architecturally. Yet in eighty years its lemon-yellow brick had mellowed sufficiently to give it a not unfriendly appearance, and fine magnolia trees, the flowers of which gave out a heavenly scent, broke up the flatness of its barrack-like walls.

When the carriage pulled up in front of the porch, Gregory got out, signed to the coachman to wait for him, then took an envelope from his pocket. It contained a note that he had thought out during his journey and written in the village inn while the carriage was being got ready for him. It was in French, addressed to Count Zapolya, and read:

*I have recently arrived in Hungary, and Sir Pellinore Gwaine-Cust particularly asked me while here to seek an opportunity of conveying his kindest remembrances to Your Excellency. Owing to the unhappy events which have disturbed so many social relationships in Europe during the past three years, it is possible that Your Excellency may prefer not to receive me; but I trust this will not be the case, as I have proposals to make which might prove to Hungary's advantage.*

He had written it in French only because that was the *lingua franca* of Sir Pellinore's generation; he had all but said that he was in Hungary on a secret mission as the agent of an enemy power, and he had signed the note with his own name. His reason for this unusual rashness was his instinct that, should he introduce himself to the Count as a Frenchman, then later have to admit that he was an Englishman, it might so offend the susceptibilities of an old-school Central European nobleman at not having been trusted in the first place that he would refuse to play any further part in the matter.

A servant in livery had hurried out of the house as the carriage drove up. He ushered Gregory into a hall panelled in pine and hung with ibex antlers and other trophies of the chase, bowed him to one of half-a-dozen big ebony elbow chairs, then put the note on a silver salver and hurried away with it.

Five minutes later he returned to lead Gregory through an even larger hall in which there were some fine suits of armour and several very beautiful Ming vases on tall carved stands, then down a long dim corridor to a pleasant sunny room at the south-west corner of the house. As Gregory was shown in an elderly man stood up, moved out from behind a desk, bowed slightly and said:

'Zapolya.'

Returning the Continental greeting by saying his own name,

Gregory took swift stock of Sir Pellinore's old friend. The Count's hair was still thick and dark, except for white feathers just above his ears, but his lined face gave the impression that he must be seventy or more. He still held himself very upright and, from his prominent nose, chin and dark velvety eyes, it was apparent that as a young man he must have been very good-looking. Another legacy of his youth that he retained was the fashion of wearing short side-whiskers and an upturned waxed moustache. He smelt faintly of eau-de-Cologne and fine Havana cigars, and was wearing country tweeds that had the cut of Savile Row. Having offered Gregory a chair, he sat back in his own and said in French:

'It is now quite a few years since I have seen Sir Pellinore, but I am always delighted to have news of him. I trust that he is well, and that even the war has not robbed him of his remarkable capacity for enjoying life?'

'When I left London ten days ago he was in excellent health and spirits,' Gregory smiled. 'And over our last dinner together he told me with tremendous zest of some of the marvellous times he had had with you here in Hungary.'

'Ah, we were both younger then,' the Count smiled back, 'but such memories keep the heart young even in old age. So you have come from London, eh? May I ask your nationality?'

'I am an Englishman; but I came here from Switzerland on a French passport.'

'You are, then, a member of the British Secret Service?'

'No. If I were caught I should expect to be treated as a spy, and shot. But I give you my word that I have not come here to ferret out Hungary's military secrets. I am the personal emissary of Sir Pellinore, and my object is to find out if there is any chance of detaching Hungary from her alliance with Nazi Germany.'

Gregory expected the Count to shrug and shake his head; but instead, changing to English which he spoke as fluently as he did French, he said, 'This is most interesting. Nothing would please myself and most people of my class better than to break with that horrible man Hitler, if it could be done with reliable safeguards for Hungary's future. Please tell me your proposals.'

For a moment Gregory remained silent. It would not do to show his surprise, or the sudden excitement which rose in him at the thought that, after all, he might succeed in sticking a

77

knife in Hitler's back and reducing the pressure on the Russian front by a dozen divisions. Leaning a little forward, he said earnestly:

'Your Excellency will appreciate that I am not authorised to enter into negotiations. I am here only on behalf of Sir Pellinore to explore possibilities. But, as you may know, Sir Pellinore is very close to His Majesty's Government; so you may take it that his ideas, as brought to you by me, would certainly receive very serious consideration and, probably, official endorsement. His suggestion is that Hungary should enter into a separate peace with the Allies and withdraw her Army from Russia. In return Russia, Britain and the United States would jointly guarantee Hungary's frontiers after the collapse of Hitler and thus she would save herself from occupation and imposition of a heavy war indemnity.'

'You speak with great confidence of the collapse of Hitler; but in all the three years the war has lasted, he has never been in a stronger position, and the territory he controls is still increasing every day.'

'His new gains might well be compared to a swollen stomach,' Gregory smiled. 'It is my belief that the chunks of Russia that he is swallowing will give him a frightful belly-ache before he is through.'

'Perhaps; but if he succeeds in biting the heart out of Russia it is she who must collapse.'

'That would not save him. He would have to leave half his army to occupy these vast areas of enemy territory, and he would still have Britain and America building up to leap upon his back. The Allied Air Forces are already pounding hell out of the German cities; and air-power is the dominant factor in modern war. As the months go by we shall be putting two, three, five, seven, ten aircraft into the air for every one of his. When the time is ripe the Allied armies will land in Europe and, with German industry in ruins, the Nazis will no longer be able to maintain their army in the field. That is why Hitler must ultimately be beaten.'

Zapolya nodded thoughtfully. 'Personally, I believe that with regard to the final outcome you are right; but Hitler is a very long way from being beaten yet. Germany might exact an extremely heavy penalty from Hungary should she attempt to insure her future with the Allies in the way you suggest.'

'That is a risk which must be run if Hungary is to sit among

78

the victor nations at the Peace Table. She would find no seat there if she waited to act until Germany was on her last legs. Now is the time when Hungary's help would be of real value to the Allied cause, and so worth their agreeing to pay for in solemn undertakings which would ensure her future well-being.'

'You implied only that she would not be treated as a defeated enemy. That is not enough. You may recall what happened in the First World War, when Rumania decided to throw in her lot with the Allies. General Von Mackensen and his Germans overran her in a few weeks. The same thing might happen here.'

Gregory countered that suggestion with the arguments he had used to Levianski, but the Count waved a slender hand in a gesture of rebuttal. 'It is true that the Germans are very heavily engaged in Russia, but they still have several armoured divisions in the West. I can hardly imagine that sufficient trained American troops have yet arrived in Britain for the Allies to be contemplating an assault on the Continent; so those armoured divisions could be used to subdue Hungary. Our people are brave and most of them hate the Germans, but nearly the whole of our own army has been sent to the Russian front. It could not get back in time to defend our cities, and their garrisons of reservists would be practically helpless in the face of several hundred German tanks.'

After a moment's thought, Gregory said, 'Even if the Allies are not yet ready to attempt the liberation of the Continent, I think they are quite capable of making a landing in force strong enough to pin down the German armour in the West. Again, I speak only as a private individual; but Mr. Churchill has always used large maps. I think it quite possible that he would press the Americans to agree to such an Allied landing, if Hungary definitely undertook to break with Hitler, as Italy might then follow suit, and that would bring a complete Allied victory within measurable distance.'

'It would.' Zapoyla drew slowly on his fine Havana. 'And if such a landing succeeded Hungary would have little to fear. But what if it failed? What if the Germans drove the Allies back into the sea? Their Panzers would then face about and come dashing across Europe to destroy us.'

'I have already agreed that some risk must be taken if Hungary is not to suffer the fate of a vanquished nation when the Allies finally defeat Hitler.'

'And I have already said that merely to be guaranteed her present frontiers is not enough. If she is to risk being overrun and forcibly held down, perhaps for several years, while many of her leading citizens are murdered by the Gestapo or thrown into concentration camps, her people must have something more than that to look forward to.'

'You mean a revision of the Treaty of Trianon?'

'Yes. By that iniquitous settlement forced on us after the last war, Hungary was robbed of over half her population and nearly two-thirds of her ancient territories. The Allies would have to give a solemn undertaking to repair permanently this monstrous injustice.'

Gregory had known that if he could get any Hungarian to enter on a serious discussion of his mission that demand would be made, but he had deliberately refrained from leading off with any proposal smacking of bribery. Now he smiled, and said:

'Sir Pellinore raised that matter with me. Few English people realised the way in which Hungary was being torn to pieces by the Allied statesmen who dictated the Peace Treaty; and those of us who have since considered the facts feel that she was greatly wronged. Proposals for revision would, Sir Pellinore assured me, be most sympathetically considered by His Majesty's Government if informal talks such as we are having now develop into actual negotiations. I think, too, we can look even further than that. Quite apart from the question of old wrongs being righted, there is another side to it. A few minutes ago you referred to Rumania's having been overrun in the First World War because she sided with the Allies. It was largely to compensate her for her sufferings in the Allied cause that she was given Transylvania at Hungary's expense. In this case the position would be reversed. General Antonescu brought Rumania in on the side of the Germans, so the Allies owe her nothing; whereas, if Hungary now exposes herself to the possibility of repression by the Nazis, she would be able to put forward claims at the Peace Conference which could not decently be rejected.'

'You are right! Yes; you are right,' Count Zapolya nodded vigorously. 'But we should need an undertaking signed by Churchill, the President and Stalin, so that we could proclaim it to the people. Given that I believe that the Hungarian nation to a man would favour defying the Nazis.'

This enthusiastic declaration swept away the last traces of the pessimism that had weighed on Gregory's spirits since his talk with Levianski. In fact, to arouse a united Hungary against Germany was far more than he had hoped to do when leaving London. Striving to suppress the excitement that had risen in him at the entirely unexpected change in his prospects of succeeding in his mission, he asked as calmly as he could:

'What does Your Excellency suggest should be my next step?'

'We must consult with certain of my friends. Like yourself, I am only a private individual and have no power to enter into actual negotiations. It would, in fact, be futile for anyone here to do so without having the approval of the Regent. But Admiral Horthy could not fail to be swayed by the opinion of a powerful group of his brother magnates. From frequent conversations I know the views of most of them are similar to my own; but we must get them together so that a committee of them can set about exploring the conditions on which Hungary might enter into a separate peace with the Allies. The first, of course, would be that the Allies should make a landing and do their utmost to contain the German armoured divisions in France and the Low Countries. Everything else hangs upon your being able to obtain for us a firm understanding from the Allied Governments that they will do that.'

'In that case,' Gregory suggested, 'I think it would be best if I returned and reported to Sir Pellinore right away.'

'No, no; I wish you first to discuss the whole matter with some of my friends.'

'Surely that could come later? An Allied landing on the Continent in sufficient strength to be effective would, I imagine, necessitate drastic changes in Allied strategy. Given that Mr. Churchill and President Roosevelt both favoured it, they would still ask the advice of their Chiefs of Staff, and they in turn would not give an opinion until the question of forces available, and all sorts of other matters, had been thoroughly gone into. The decision is such a momentous one that they could not be expected to take it without prolonged discussion. Therefore, the sooner I set the ball rolling the better, and in the meantime you could be preparing the ground among your friends; so that there would be less delay on this side in the event of my coming back with a favourable answer.'

The Count shook his head. 'I appreciate your arguments; but, all the same, I am opposed to your leaving Hungary for another week or so. I consider it important that you should first meet a few of the leading personalities in our Upper House and talk to them as you have to me.'

Feeling that it would be tactless to oppose the Count's wishes, Gregory agreed. But all his instincts warned him against discussing these highly dangerous matters with a number of people; and, before he was very much older, he had cause to regret bitterly that he had allowed himself to be persuaded.

## 7

## The Magnates of Hungary

Barely a moment after it had been settled that Gregory should not yet return with his now promising report to London, the door was opened by a footman. Bowing to Count Zapolya, he uttered a short phrase in Magyar.

Standing up, the Count smiled at Gregory. 'Luncheon is about to be served. My wife and relatives will be most interested to hear news of London, and a first-hand account of the air-raids which the Nazis claim caused such devasation.'

As Gregory's freedom, and possibly his life, depended upon particulars about himself being kept secret, his host's casualness filled him with alarm. But he took some comfort from the thought that Etienne Tavenier had been in England between his evacuation from Dunkirk and the St. Nazaire raid as he said quickly:

'I will tell them about London with pleasure. However, Your Excellency will recall my mentioning that I entered Hungary on a French passport. I am sure all the members of your family are entirely trustworthy, but I feel that it might spare them grave embarrassment, should they meet me again later outside your family circle, if you introduce me to them now as Commandant Tavenier.'

'Tavenier, eh! Yes, that would be wise,' the Count agreed.

Then he led Gregory down a wide corridor, the walls of which were hung with great dark oil paintings of male and female Zapolyas through the centuries, to a large bay-windowed room the dominant motif of which was rich yellow brocade. There were nine or ten people in it and Gregory soon found that the pale amber liquid in the glasses most of them were holding was not *baratsch,* but Dry Martini.

He found, too, that, except for a Bishop and one walrus-moustached old gentleman who was a Baron in his own right, they were all either Counts or Countesses, as the Magyars followed a widespread Continental custom that all children took the title of their parents, distinguishing themselves by the use of their Christian names. All of them spoke German, French, English and Italian with almost equal fluency and, apparently, as the spirit moved them at the moment; so the conversation was a veritable Babel.

Zapolya's wife, the Countess Dorottya, was plump and grey-haired, but appeared to be still on the right side of fifty, so a good twenty years younger than himself. As she extended a beautifully kept hand to Gregory he remembered just in time not to kiss it, as a chance remark he had heard in the bar of the Zur Krone two nights before had informed him that the Hungarian aristocracy now regarded the custom as bourgeois. That she was the Count's second wife emerged a few minutes later when a tall man with Tartar features, also about fifty, was introduced to him as the Count's eldest son, Count Rudolph.

There was a beautiful black-haired Italian, the Countess Marcella, who was the wife of a much younger son, not present, and a bronze-haired Countess Erzébet, who was a daughter of the house; a handsome young man named Count István, and a hunchback with a clever, amusing face named Count László. But before Gregory could gather more than a vague idea of their relationships they all went in to lunch.

They were using, as Gregory learned later, the smaller dining room; but it could easily have seated twenty. Standing in it near the far end of the table were a sandy-haired young man with thick-lensed glasses, whom Gregory thought looked suspiciously like a German, a mousey looking woman in a white blouse and black skirt, a boy of about nine and a pretty little dark girl of about eleven. The children, Count Sityi and Countess Teresa, belonged to the Countess Marcella, and the grown-ups were their Austrian tutor and French governess.

Throughout the meal a major-domo stood behind Count Zapolya's chair while elderly footmen handed dishes that had nothing Hungarian about their cooking, but were obviously the productions of an excellent French chef. Nevertheless, it proved a jolly, informal, family party with everyone laughing and talking at once. But for the medley of tongues it might have been a luncheon in one of the stately homes of England for, like the English, and unlike the Germans, Austrians and French, these Magyar aristocrats regarded the fact that they had been born noble as so natural that they made no effort whatever to impress, or to protect their dignity behind a cold, formal manner.

In the rôle of the French major who had got away from Dunkirk, Gregory gave an account of wartime life in England, and described the blitz. Most of them knew London well, and while the burning of a large part of the City meant little to them, they pressed him for further details when he spoke of the great raid on the West End.

On that Saturday night he had been dining with friends at Hatchett's when a stick of bombs crashed along Piccadilly and scores more fell in the neighbourhood. An hour or so later, when they left the restaurant, fires along the wide thoroughfare had made it as bright as day from the Circus to the Ritz, and from pavement to roof every window in 'Burtons the Tailors' building was belching great tongues of flame.

Most of the men among Gregory's listeners had pleasant memories of being entertained at the famous clubs in Pall Mall and St. James's Street, so were distressed to hear that many of them had been severely damaged; yet, having no experience of air raids, it was the after effects which struck them most forcibly. No doubt they would have faced the dangers of the blitz with commendable bravery, but they were quite shocked when Gregory told them that, after he had made a tour of the area the following morning to see the worst for himself, owing to the electric and gas mains having been wrecked the Berkeley could provide him only with a cold lunch.

With fruit and dessert wines the luncheon continued in leisurely fashion till past three o'clock, then the Count told Gregory that it was the custom of the house-party to go for a drive in the afternoon. Thereupon Gregory remarked that his poor driver must be wondering how much longer he meant to stay, and that in any case it was time for him to be starting back for Budapest; but Zapolya would not hear of his doing so.

'Nonsense, my dear fellow,' he declared. 'My people will have seen to it that the man was given a meal then paid off. If you must return to Budapest tonight, I'll have you driven to the station at any hour, and the Station Master will flag the first train that comes along to stop and pick you up. But unless you have engagements that you cannot possibly cancel by telephone, I suggest that you should spend the next few days here. We shall then have an opportunity to discuss matters in more detail.'

Gregory said that he would have been delighted to accept but had not with him even a tooth-brush, let alone a change of clothes. The Count waved the objection aside. He would send his valet in on the next train to collect Gregory's things from the Vadászkürt, and the man would be back by nightfall. He would also arrange with the management that Gregory's room at the hotel should be reserved so that he could return to it whenever he wished.

In consequence, Gregory drove out with the family, and on his return was equipped for dinner, by the charming Countess Elizabeth, with an Hungarian costume, selected from the great store of finery kept in the house for amateur theatricals and dressing up. To put him at his ease several of the other men also wore the national dress that night and the women all congratulated him on the fine figure he cut. When, at two o'clock in the morning, he eventually went up to bed he found that all his own things had been arranged in his room as though he had already occupied it for a week.

On waking the following morning between the fine lawn sheets he found it difficult to believe that he was not still dreaming. Twenty-four hours earlier he had been convinced that he had come to Hungary on a wild goose chase; now there seemed a definite possibility that he might succeed in engineering a break between the Hungarians and the Nazis. The half-waking thought was made all the more unreal by kaleidoscopic memories of having the previous day walked into a world of luxurious, cultured leisure that he had believed to have become extinct for two years or more all over war-torn Europe. Yet his transitory doubts were dissipated by the arrival of a French-speaking man-servant who brought him a breakfast which could not have been surpassed in pre-war days, and asked him at what temperature he liked his bath.

For the next three days he remained at Nagykáta, enjoying to the full a gracious hospitality, and much laughter; but the secret reason for his presence there was kept well in mind by his elderly host. Unostentatiously the Count called several conferences in his own room. Before the first he explained to Gregory that his eldest son, Count Rudolph, was interested only in agricultural problems, so would be of little use in their deliberations; but the Baron Alacy—who was also a retired General—the Bishop, and the merry-eyed hunchback, Count László, were called in. All three agreed that, short of some unforeseeable circumstance, the combination of the United States, the British Empire and Soviet Russia must in the end defeat Germany and Japan; so that Hungary's best hope for the future lay in going over to the Allies. But there was a considerable divergence of opinion on the question of the conditions to be stipulated in any secret pact and the timing of this exceedingly dangerous volte-face.

In the meantime, Zapolya had written guardedly to a number of his other relations and most intimate friends, and convened a meeting at the Nobles Club in Budapest for Thursday the 20th.

From the time of Gregory's arrival in Budapest up to the morning of that day, the news had been far from favourable to his mission. Lieutenant-General Gott, who he had heard was the most promising of our younger Generals in the Middle East, was reported killed while over Libya in an aircraft. The British had arrested the leaders of Congress on evidence that they were preparing to sell out India to the Japs, which had led to serious rioting in Bombay. Another attempt to relieve besieged Malta had been carried out at heavy cost, the cruiser *Manchester* and the aircraft-carrier *Eagle* both being sunk as well as many other ships. And, worst of all for the Allied cause as a whole, the German offensive in Russia was meeting with spectacular success. Von Bock was still being held outside Stalingrad, but further south the Germans had penetrated the foothills of the Caucasian mountains and were threatening Krasnodar. The hope that these claims might be exaggerated had been nullified by an admission from the Soviet High Command that they had evacuated Maikop, the oil centre north of the Caucasus, and were destroying many oil wells in the threatened area.

Then, on the morning of the 20th, came the first news of the British and Canadian landings at Dieppe. The German communiqué stated that, although many thousands of men and considerable numbers of tanks had got ashore on six beaches the preceding day, after nine hours of severe fighting, the invaders had been driven back into the sea with great loss in killed and prisoners.

Having no source but the German to go on, Gregory could only hope that the action had not proved as costly as reported. But he was certain in his own mind that it could have been only a reconnaissance in force, with no intention of trying for a permanent foothold. In any case, despite the victory claimed by the Germans, it strengthened his hand enormously, as it showed that the British had both the will and the ability to make such descents on the Continent; and, that being so, the Germans would not now dare risk withdrawing any considerable part of their forces which were holding the European coastline from Northern Norway to the Pyrenees.

In consequence, he was in excellent heart when, after breakfast, with the Count and the others who were in the plot, he left for the capital, the intention being that all of them should lunch at the Zapolya Palace on the Illona Utcza before the meeting.

Although termed a 'Palace', it was actually one of a hundred or more similar mansions that crowned the slopes of Buda and was no larger than the fine London houses of the British aristocracy; but, unlike them, it was built round a courtyard entered through a big semi-circular arch and, from the terrace on its north-east side, had a magnificent view over the river. The Count pressed Gregory to stay there but he was anxious not to compromise Sir Pellinore's old friend more than was absolutely necessary, just in case one of the numerous people who were soon to be told about his mission gave him away; so he tactfully declined the offer and had his bags sent on to the Vadászkürt.

After lunch they drove to the Nobles Club, or the Casino as it was often termed owing to the heavy gambling to which many of its members were addicted. As they went up the broad staircase Gregory was surprised to see in the place of honour at its top a large portrait in oils of King Edward VII.

Catching his glance Zapolya smiled at him and said:

'When Edward VII was Prince of Wales he came many times to Budapest and, as an honorary member of the Club, he made himself so popular that the Committee decided to have his portrait painted. During the First World War several German nobles who were sent here as liaison officers were also made honorary members, and they objected most strongly to our continuing to display the portrait of the late King of a country with which we were at war. But we told them that wars should not be allowed to interfere with private relationships, that it was our Club, and that if they did not like our way of conducting its affairs they need not come to it. That is still the case, and nothing would induce us to take it down.'

'How I admire that spirit,' Gregory replied. 'It is the greatest tragedy of modern times that wars are no longer fought with chivalry, and that whole populations are made to hate one another. The killing which cannot be avoided entails misery enough without the destruction of personal bonds built up over long years of friendship and respect.'

The Count nodded. 'That at least is one way in which we Hungarians need feel no shame at the accusation that our country is behind the times. We still do all we can to ameliorate the hardships that war brings to enemy civilians. The professional at our golf club is a case in point. He is, like nearly all of them, a Scotsman; so, when Britain declared war on us, he was arrested and interned. But we decided that to keep him behind barbed wire for months, or perhaps years, through no fault of his own was both harsh on him and stupid as far as we were concerned. So within a week we had him released on parole and back at the Club.'

In a large room on the first floor some twenty men were assembled. Gregory was introduced to each of them in turn as Commandant Tavenier; then they all sat down round a big baize-covered gaming table and the meeting began. The Count informed them of his reason for calling them together; Gregory followed with a statement in general terms of the object of his mission, and when he had done a long discussion took place.

It was clear from the beginning that no one present had any love for the Nazis, or for the Germans as a people; but they regarded them as a lesser evil than the Russians, and feared that an Allied victory might lead to Communism's spreading southward into Hungary,

Gregory contended that, if Hungary came over to the Allies, when the war ended she would be preserved from an occupation by Russian forces and her Government be in a strong position to take adequate measures against the spread of Communism. Whereas, should she stand by Germany to the end, her defeat would lead to bankruptcy and social upheavals which must make the triumph of Communism inevitable.

As the latter alternative was exactly what had occurred in 1919, his contention met with general agreement but, as several people were quick to point out, it would not apply if Hitler won, as he would crush Communism once and for all.

The question of which side would win was then argued and opinion upon it was sharply divided. Most of the older men believed that time was on the side of the Allies and that their almost limitless resources would enable them to overcome Hitler in the long run; but many of the younger ones were convinced that if he could once put Russia out of the war Britain and America would never be able to break him.

The view of these younger men being that which was held in secret by Gregory himself and, in fact, the very fear which had led to his coming to Budapest, he had all his work cut out to argue convincingly against it; so, as soon as he could, he sidetracked the discussion to what was likely to happen in Hungary should the war end in a German victory.

For him this was a much better wicket, because National Socialism was no friend to any aristocracy. The Hungarian Nazis, who sported the Arrow-Cross as their symbol, were mostly disgruntled intellectuals, minor officials of Austrian descent and hot-headed students, and so far the magnates had managed to keep them very much in their place. Whereas in Germany no noble could now hope to hold a position of influence unless he accepted such people as equals by becoming a member of the *Partei*, the great landowners were ordered about by the *Partei Gauleiters* and the rich were both heavily taxed and blackmailed into making big special contributions to the *Partei* funds. With Hitler as undisputed Lord of Europe it could not be long before these Hungarian magnates found themselves either dancing to the tune of the Arrow-Cross boys or having to put only one foot wrong to find themselves in a concentration camp.

These purely class interests were reinforced by the intense concern, common to all Hungarians, that Hungary should retain such provinces as she had succeeded in getting back since the Treaty of Trianon, and have the others she had lost restored to her. These 'Lost Provinces' had, under the Treaty, gone to Italy, Rumania, Austria and the newly created sovereign states of Czechoslovakia and Yugoslavia. Hitler, having occupied the last two against opposition, had penalised them by making them disgorge to Hungary much of the territory she had been forced to cede to them in 1920; but the question was, would the United States and Britain allow them to keep these lands that for twenty years had been a part of the newly created countries which had recently become the victims of Hitler. Above all they were concerned to retain their beloved Transylvania and get back Croatia with the old Hungarian port of Fiume on the Adriatic. They had little hope that Hitler would ever coerce Mussolini into giving up the latter, whereas, although the Allies might insist that the two new States should retain their pre-war frontiers, Rumania and Italy had played the part of enemies who could be despoiled in favour of a Hungary which had taken a hand in Hitler's defeat.

Eventually it was agreed that as a long-term policy it would be in Hungary's best interests to go over to the Allies; but soon several voices were raised with fearsome warnings of the brutal treatment that the country might receive at Hitler's hands before help from the Allies could reach her. Gregory spoke of the landings at Dieppe on the previous day and asserted with confidence that others in greater strength would hold the German armour; but again controversy raged on whether such measures would prove successful.

He was bombarded with scores of questions on these various aspects of the problem and could only say that he was in no position to answer for the British Government, but that if the meeting could give him an idea of the terms likely to be acceptable he would return to London and come back in a few weeks' time better qualified to enter into negotiations.

The upshot was the appointment of a Committee to discuss matters further with him and determine the Heads of Agreement under which a secret pact might be formulated. Count Zapolya was asked to serve but declined on the grounds that he had done his part by bringing them together, and that he now wished younger men to formulate the policy upon which the future of their country might depend. However, as the retired General—Baron Alacy—the Bishop and the hunchback

Count László Zapolya had all participated in the early conversations with Gregory at Nagykáta, they were elected. To them were added a youngish Colonel named János Orczy, who had lost his left arm early in the war and was now serving in the War Office, and a Count Zsigmond Szegényház who held a post in the Foreign Office.

It was six o'clock before the meeting broke up, and after several drinks in the big *salle* downstairs Gregory took leave of Count Zapolya and his other new friends with very mixed feelings.

On the one hand he was extraordinarily elated by the thought that, whereas only five days earlier he had been prepared to write off his mission as a total failure, there was now a body of the most influential men in Hungary actually preparing to negotiate on his proposals.

On the other he was horrified and alarmed by their complete disregard for security. It had been bad enough at Nagykáta, as he had found that within twenty-four hours the whole house party had become aware of the reason for his presence there; but at least they were an isolated group with only the Austrian tutor—whom he hoped was still in the dark —as a possible immediate danger. Here, in Budapest, matters were infinitely worse.

When opening the meeting, Count Zapolya had not asked his friends for any pledge of secrecy, or even warned them to refrain from mentioning the matter under discussion to anyone who had not been invited. Then, after the meeting broke up, several groups had dispersed about the Club still debating the subject in tones loud enough for members who had not been present to hear what they were talking about. No doubt the Count took it for granted that the high sense of honour traditional among the Hungarian nobility was guarantee enough of secrecy. But Gregory was well aware that many men, however discreet in other respects, confided everything to their wives, and that quite a number of women had the deplorable habit of treating their hairdressers as father confessors; so, one way or another, there seemed a quite frightening possibility that, before many days had passed, the news that a conspiracy to break with Hitler was brewing would reach the ears of some fanatical pro-Nazi.

At the Vadászkürt a clerk behind the reception desk told him that his old room had been kept for him and that his luggage had been sent up. As he took the key he got the idea the man had given him a rather queer look; but he thought no more of it until he stepped out of the lift on the third floor. The chambermaid who had done his room during his first visit was there sorting out some dirty linen. Stopping her work she bobbed him the usual curtsy and murmured, '*Küss die Hand*'; but no smile accompanied the greeting and she stared at him with an unhappy expression in her round blue eyes.

Gregory was liked by servants because he not only always had a pleasant word for them and never showed ill temper, but was tidy by nature and took some pains to save them as much work as possible. Now, it did not occur to him that this plain strong-limbed peasant girl might be concerned on his account, but thinking something had upset her he smiled and asked:

'What's the trouble, Tina?'

In her halting German she stuttered out, 'Perhaps, sir, I should not tell. But there are men in your room. The Manager, he bring them up an hour ago. They wait for you. I think they are the police.'

The smile froze on Gregory's lips. His spine stiffened slightly and he had the sensation that his feet had suddenly turned to lead. But his brain raced from thought to thought with the swiftness of a prairie fire.

Could someone who had been at the meeting have inadvertently betrayed him already? No; that was hardly possible —quite impossible, in fact, if the police had been waiting in his room for him for the past hour. Could one of the women at Nagykáta have blabbed about his talks with Zapolya and the others? That was unlikely as they were still all in the country and would hardly have been so wantonly indiscreet as to give particulars about him and his mission to anyone in a letter or during a telephone conversation. But what of the Austrian tutor? Surely no one in the house party would have been so imbecile as to confide in him? He might have overheard something to rouse his suspicions, though, then deliberately played the part of a snooper and sent the results of his spying to the police.

As Gregory released the breath he had unconsciously been holding, the thought flashed across his mind that the police might wish to see him only on a routine matter. But he instantly dismissed it. If they were concerned with some regulation to do with foreign visitors, which he had failed to observe, they would simply have left a message for him to call at the police station, or sent a man round to catch him in the entrance of the hotel as he came in. There would not be two of them—and Tina had made it quite clear that there was more than one. And they would not be waiting to confront him without warning in the privacy of his room.

The question now was what course to take. Should he face the music or cut and run for it?

It was certain that the police would be armed and, although he was carrying a small automatic that he had smuggled through the customs, a shooting match at close quarters was not a thing to enter upon lightly. Anyhow, they would be two to one and, even if he succeeded in rendering them both *hors de combat,* once the sound of shooting had raised a general alarm he would not be able to get out of the hotel without encountering further trouble. Yet if they did know about his secret mission and he entered his room but did not shoot it out with them, in another few minutes he would be walking back along the corridor with his wrists locked into a pair of handcuffs.

Fate, in the form of Tina's warning, had given him an alternative. He need not go on. Instead, he could step back into the lift and make a bolt for it. But what then? How much grace could he expect? The men in his room might wait there for another hour or more without suspecting that he had slipped out of their clutches. But no! The desk clerk would probably have telephoned up to let them know that he had just come in. Anyway, the clerk would telephone when he saw the man they were after going out again. Possibly, even, the clerk would call on the porters to hold him till the police could be fetched down. That would mean a fight in the hall. He could put a couple of shots over their heads to scare them into letting him pass; but they would all shout 'Stop thief!' and start a hue and cry in the street. Even if he got clear away, within a few hours he would have the whole police force of Budapest on the look-out for him. Fortunately in another hour or so it would be dark. But he would have to leave the city that night, or go into hiding with Levianski. The risk of recognition and capture would be much too great for him to go about openly any more. Such a handicap could make it almost impossible to continue with his mission. The Hungarian nobility were not the sort of people who would take kindly to furtive meetings in obscure cafés—and for him to be able to make contact with them again at all depended on whether he could keep his freedom for the next half-hour.

While Tina stood there staring at him, and nervously clasping and unclasping her hands, he strove to weigh the chances. If he turned tail immediately he would become a hunted man. If he went into his room and, should the police attempt to arrest him, fought his way free, he would likewise become a hunted man. And, as a hunted man, there could be little hope of his completing the talks that had developed in such a promising way that afternoon. Only one possibility remained of his being able to do that. It was to face the police and do his damnedest to bluff his way out of any charge they might have against him.

Next moment his mind was made up. Since there was just a chance that he might be able to carry through his mission he must take it. With a smile he said to Tina:

'Thank you very much for the warning, but I think I know what it is that the police want to see me about in private.'

Then he walked past her on his way to his room.

8

Thin Ice

As soon as Gregory was round the corner of the landing, out of Tina's sight, he transferred his small but deadly automatic from his hip pocket to the right-hand pocket of his jacket. Walking on down the long balcony-corridor he did not look ahead but over its open side down towards the restaurant, scrutinising with new intentness the tall trees that grew among the tables in the courtyard.

It had occurred to him that should he have to make a bolt it he would stand a better chance of getting out of the hotel quickly if, instead of dashing for the lift or stairs, he jumped into the branches of the nearest tree and shinned down it to the ground. At the moment there were only a few groups of people drinking aperitifs at widely separated tables, and there

94

was an hour or more to go before the courtyard would become crowded with diners and waiters; so the odds were good against his being tripped or caught by grabbing hands as he ran across it.

Having decided on the branch at which he would take a flying leap, he took out the key to his room and inserted it in the lock with his left hand. His right closed about the butt of the automatic in his jacket pocket, he turned the key and pushed the door open.

Monsieur Cochefert of the French Consulate was sitting in the armchair near the window and a plump red-faced young man in the uniform of the Hungarian State Police was perched on the end of the bed. At a glance Gregory also took in the fact that the lids of both his suitcases were a little raised, evidently owing to their contents having been taken out and thrust back into them without the least care. The two men were smoking and looked bored, but a pistol lay ready to Cochefert's hand on the broad arm of the chair in which he was sitting.

The sight of the weapon and the contemptuous lack of any attempt to conceal the fact that his suitcases had been searched confirmed Gregory beyond all doubt in his belief that this was not a routine visit. Having already decided that his best hope lay in attempting to bluff his way through any trouble he raised his eyebrows in feigned astonishment at finding people in his room, then demanded sharply of Cochefert:

'Monsieur! Kindly inform me what you are doing here!'

The Frenchman picked up his gun and came slowly to his feet. His nearly bald head, thin beak of a nose and long scraggy neck protruding from the stiff white collar made Gregory again think of a vulture. With an ironical bow he replied:

'When we met before I neglected to introduce myself fully. I am Captain Jules Cochefert of the Vichy *Deuxième Bureau*. My companion, here, is Lieutenant Puttony, of the Hungarian Security Service. He does not speak French, and I understand that you talk quite fluent German with the staff in this hotel; so we will use that language.'

Gregory could feel his heart beating slightly faster, as it always did when he was in a dangerous situation; but his brain swiftly registered the implications of the disclosure. Cochefert was not just a minor Civil Servant but an officer of the French 'Quisling' police, who were hand in glove with the

Nazis. Evidently something had aroused his suspicions that Commandant Etienne Tavenier might be working against his paymasters. Next moment, with a sardonic grin which displayed two rows of yellowish teeth, he led Gregory to suppose that he was putting the grounds for those suspicions into words by asking:

'How are you progressing with your arrangements for selling truffles to the foie-gras factories?'

The sigh of relief that Gregory heaved was internal, but none the less heart-felt. So that was it! The Vadászkürt had forwarded on to him at Nagykáta a list of foie-gras firms from the French Commercial Attaché's office. As he knew nothing of the technicalities of truffle growing and foie-gras tinning, he would probably have decided that it was wiser not to expose his ignorance of the subject by calling on any of these people even if he had had the opportunity; but his having been at Nagykáta for the past five days had put the matter outside his jurisdiction. Evidently this Paul Pry had learned of his commercial remissness and had assumed that to be evidence that he was engaged in some nefarious activity.

Since entering the room he had kept his hand on his gun; so that at any moment he could have shot through the cloth of his coat before either of his visitors could level a weapon at him. Now, feeling that he had little to fear, he took his hand out of his pocket and said affably:

'Oh, I decided that before I got down to work here I'd take ...'

He got no further. His hand had hardly left his pocket when Cochefert raised his pistol and snapped:

'Thank you! Shooting through a pocket is rarely accurate but can be dangerous to others. I have been waiting only to relieve you of the temptation to experiment. Put your hands up! The *Herr Leutnant* will oblige by securing your weapon.'

Mentally cursing at having allowed himself to be tricked, Gregory obliged. The stolid looking Hungarian police officer stepped forward, fished the little automatic out of Gregory's pocket, frisked him quickly to make sure that he was not carrying another, then plumped himself back on the edge of the bed.

'Now!' said the Frenchman, 'I have introduced myself to you. Be good enough to reciprocate.'

Pretending a lack of concern about his situation that he was far from feeling, Gregory replied, '*M. le Capitaine,* I fail to understand the reason for all this drama. I come into my room, upon which you jump up grasping a pistol. As I carry one myself I naturally put my hand on it. There is nothing strange in that. Regarding the truffle business, I was about to tell you that I decided to take a few days holiday before calling on any of the foie-gras merchants. As for introducing myself, you know already that I am Commandant Etienne Tavenier.'

'That is a lie!' snapped Cochefert with sudden venom.

'What causes you to think so? You have seen my passport.'

'It is a stolen one.'

'Nonsense! The photograph in it could be of no one but myself.'

'Of course. I meant stolen, then tampered with; or perhaps a complete fake made by the British.'

This was really dangerous ground. Gregory could only pray that they had no proof that he had come from London. He launched a violent protest:

'Your suspicions are absurd! There is nothing whatever wrong with the passport. Besides, I can prove my identity in other ways. I have letters, bills . . .'

Cochefert made an impatient gesture. 'They too will be fakes. It is useless to go on like this. I know beyond all doubt that you are not Commandant Tavenier.'

'What makes you so certain?'

'The fact that for the last two months the Commandant has been living at his own home, at Razac in Périgord.'

These words, spoken with conviction, struck Gregory like a bolt from the blue. It was the very last thing he had expected, and at one stroke destroyed the whole foundation upon which his false identity had been built. Yet, after a moment, he managed to think up a forlorn hope which might save him until further enquiries had been made. With an angry shake of the head, he exclaimed:

'This man must be an impostor! Someone who resembles me, perhaps. But no! I have it! He is a rascally cousin of mine who was also christened Etienne. I have no wife or children to protect my property. The swine would know that I have been missing since May 1940, and after two years he must have decided to go and live at Razac.'

Lowering the hooded lids of his dark eyes a little, Cochefert appeared to consider this. Gregory continued to look indignant; and he had ample cause as he thought of how he had been let down by someone in London. He might have to pay with his life for their blunder in stating that Tavenier was dead when he was not only very much alive but living at his old home, and so could be traced without the least difficulty by the Vichy police. After a moment the Frenchman said:

'But you have not been missing since May 1940. At least, the story you told me was that you got back to France by coming with the British on the St. Nazaire raid; that was towards the end of March this year.'

'True. And that is how I got back.'

'You said, too, that you arrived at Razac early in April. If so your cousin must have known that you were alive and free. How then do you account for his having illegally occupied your property only a few weeks later?'

Gregory saw now that his 'cousin' theory was not going to provide even a temporary loophole. Swiftly changing his ground, he said:

'All right. Since that does not seem to make sense there must be some other explanation. Perhaps you have been misinformed. Yes; that must be it. Police forces are not infallible. I suggest that we postpone this discussion for twenty-four hours while you have fresh enquiries made. I'll bet you a hundred *pengos* the result will be that there is no one calling himself Etienne Tavenier living at Razac after all.'

'Then you would lose your bet.' Cochefert's vulture head nodded and his yellowish teeth showed in a cynical smile. 'I will tell you now how we know the truth. My first enquiry was only our normal check up with Vichy on all Frenchmen arriving in this country. Vichy reported back that the name Etienne Tavenier was not on the list of those to whom passports had been issued this year, but that there was a retired Commandant of that name. The real Commandant Tavenier was sought out and interviewed. It is true that he returned to France last March with the British when they made their raid on St. Nazaire. He was not only shot and severely wounded but afterwards thrown into the dock by a German corporal; so it is not at all surprising that anyone who witnessed the incident should have reported him as among the killed. But he was hauled out while still alive and put into hospital where he remained for two months. When discharged he was crippled for life; so, although a de Gaullist, instead of being interned he was allowed, on compassionate grounds, to go to his home.'

After pausing for a moment, Cochefert went on. 'So, you see, I was only amusing myself when I let you produce that poor hare about a cousin of the same name. It is useless for you to flounder like a fish in a net any more. Whatever game you have been playing it is finished now; and, no doubt, after a little persuasion you will tell us all about it.'

The game of bluff was so clearly up that Gregory only shrugged and asked, 'What do you intend to do with me?'

'To enter any country on a false passport is an offence. Under Hungarian law you are liable to a term of imprisonment, then to deportation. But for the duration of the war we have somewhat different arrangements. The Hungarian State Police have the right to detain you indefinitely but should they have no particular grounds for doing so they will, on an application for your extradition, hand you over to me. I shall then send you under escort to France, and my colleagues there will extract from you any information you may possess which would help us to defeat those who, by continuing to oppose Herr Hitler, are preventing the restoration of World Peace.'

Gregory knew that there was little to choose between the uniformed thugs whose reign of terror kept the Pétain government in power and the Gestapo. They had no more scruples than the Nazis about torturing the leaders of resistance groups, or agents of the Allies parachuted into France—including women—who had the ill-luck to fall into their hands. He was terribly tempted to tell Cochefert just what he thought of the senile old Marshal and the gang of unscrupulous politicians with which he surrounded himself.

But this was no time to air his true feelings. Russia was being hammered to pieces. If she broke it might take twenty years of war before Europe could be liberated—just as it had in Napoleon's day. And he, Gregory, held the threads of a move that would hamstring the German advance into the Caucasus, put Hitler in the devil's own mess, and bring his defeat very much nearer. The fact that the real Commandant Tavenier had had the good luck to survive the St. Nazaire raid now threatened to render any chance of that move abortive. For Gregory to pretend any longer that he was the Commandant was obviously futile; yet an issue of enormous consequence hung upon his keeping his freedom.

Even had he still had his gun and succeeded in shooting his way out that, as he realised more fully now, would have been no real solution; for, as a fugitive, it would be next to impossible for him to complete his mission.

There was only one chance left to him. He still had a last card up his sleeve, and he must play it. It could prove an ace, but might well be regarded as just as phony as his passport was now known to be. If so, there could be no escape from being marched off to prison and turned over as a de Gaullist agent to the tender mercies of the Vichy secret police. In any case, he was most reluctant to produce this fraudulent trump because it would tie him up with the Gestapo and, even should Cochefert accept it at its face value, unless he could get out of Hungary quickly it might have most disastrous repercussions. But there it was. It was that or the absolute certainty of being marched off to prison there and then.

He took the plunge artistically. No one hearing him could have suspected for one moment that he regarded the men of Vichy as a bunch of treacherous self-seeking swine. Drawing himself erect he clicked his heels together, bowed sharply from the waist and said to Cochefert with a genial smile:

'My congratulations, *Herr Hauptmann*. I have done my utmost to preserve my incognito; but you have got me in a corner from which I see no escape. Since you supposed me to be an enemy agent, such work is most commendable, and I shall not fail to see that you get a good mark for it in the right quarter.'

Staring at him with a puzzled frown, Cochefert muttered, 'What the devil are you talking about?'

Gregory had been fingering the left lapel of his jacket. With the one word, 'This,' he drew from a secret pocket he had had made under it a small square of cardboard, and laid it on the dressing-table. On a dark night in the previous December he had taken it from a man whom he had first shot twice in the stomach. He had then, for his own good reasons, hacked off with a chopper the man's right hand and thrown his body into Lake Geneva. It was the card issued by the *Geheime Staatspolizei* to *Obersturmbannführer* Fritz Einholtz, and signed Reinhard Heydrich.

For a minute that seemed an age Gregory's eyes were riveted on Cochefert's carrion-crow features, striving to assess the movement of every tiny muscle and judge whether he would accept it or declare it, too, to be a fake.

As the Frenchman read the card his eyes widened. When he spoke his voice had lost its cocksure sneering tone. It was lower and held an unmistakably servile note:

'I had no idea. . . . The last thing I would wish is to interfere with the operations of the Gestapo.'

Taking the tide of fortune at the flood, Gregory instantly reacted. As though set in motion by the sudden pressing of an electric switch, he stamped hard with his right foot on the wooden floor, jerked his body erect, threw back his head, shot out his right arm at a steep angle and cried:

'*Heil Hitler!*'

Taken by surprise, his two visitors hesitated only a second. The Hungarian got swiftly to his feet, then both in chorus responded with the Nazi salute.

'Now,' said Gregory, 'you, *Herr Hauptmann,* are clearly a man to be trusted; so I propose to take you into my confidence.' His whole manner had undergone a complete change. He spoke in a sharp official voice, and as a superior who was about to do an inferior a favour. Giving a quick glance towards the Lieutenant, he added in French, 'But what of our friend here. Can he be relied upon to keep his mouth shut?'

'Yes, Colonel,' Cochefert replied in the same language. 'He is an Arrow-Cross Party member.'

'Good!' Gregory reverted to German, and turned to Puttony. '*Herr Leutnant,* I shall also confide in you. All that I say must be regarded as of the highest secrecy. You will report to your superiors that you are fully satisfied about the bona fides of Commandant Tavenier, and not even hint at the work I have been sent to Budapest to do. Is that understood?'

The plump, lethargic looking Lieutenant, who had so far been a silent spectator of the scene, was now standing stiffly to attention and regarding Gregory with the veneration of an athletic-minded schoolboy for a Rugby Blue. Tensing his muscles, he snapped out, '*Ja, Herr Oberst.*'

'Very well, then.' Gregory took out his cigarette case and, without offering it to either of the others, lit a cigarette. He then perched himself on the arm of the easy chair that Cochefert had been occupying and went on:

'Reports have reached the *Führer* that certain elements in Hungary are not putting their full weight behind the war effort.

This applies particularly to the magnates. Many are still leading lives of luxury and pleasure highly discreditable to them at a time when the whole German people are making the utmost sacrifices to achieve victory. Allies should share their burdens. In Germany thousands are being rendered homeless by the bombing of our cities and the people submit cheerfully to strict rationing, while here, in Hungary, it is as though a state of war hardly existed. That is very wrong. But I should make it clear that we do not blame the Hungarian people. It is only natural that they should continue to enjoy the good things of life as long as they are encouraged to do so by the example of the nobility. It is those who set this example who must be disciplined; and I have been instructed to list the worst offenders so that the *Führer* can insist that the Regent should take action against them.'

Gregory paused for a moment, then went on. 'But there is a still more serious matter. It is reported that some of the senior officers in the Hungarian Army are adopting a most reprehensible attitude. One cannot say they are defeatist. To do so would be absurd when it has been obvious to everybody from the beginning that the *Führer* will triumph over all his enemies. But they are putting obstacles in the way of sending further divisions to the Russian front. They are deliberately conserving Hungarian man-power at the expense of Germany. They do their best to arrange that the spoils Hungary will claim after our victory shall have been paid for in German blood. Worse, much worse, it is even said that some of them question the wisdom of Germany having gone to war with the Soviets, and speak slightingly of our glorious *Führer*.'

Cochefert and Puttony both shook their heads and made murmurs which could be taken as expressing amazement and horror at such blasphemy. Having given time for this little demonstration of loyalty, Gregory continued.

'Such men are traitors. They must be identified and routed out. I have come here for that purpose. Naturally they would not be quite such fools as to air their subversive views in front of a German; but it was thought that they might do so before a Frenchman, particularly if that Frenchman pretended to get drunk at some of their parties and showed himself to be at heart a de Gaullist.

'A fortnight ago I was summoned by Herr Himmler to his Headquarters in the *Albrecht Strasse* and charged with this mission. The appropriate department then provided me with the identity of Commandant Tavenier. They thought it important that I should be able to talk as though I had been evacuated from Dunkirk and had imbibed the British point of view while in London. We have good contacts in the Free French Headquarters there, who had reported Tavenier as having been killed at St. Nazaire; so his identity seemed very suitable. In failing to check with Vichy, which would have disclosed the fact that Tavenier was still alive, the *Albrecht Strasse* slipped up badly. Had I been in an enemy country it could have cost me my life. I am fortunate to have been found out only by collaborators. No harm is done; but you will both appreciate my reluctance to admit that I was not Tavenier. If that got out it would completely ruin my mission.'

'Of course, Colonel. You may rely on us.' Cochefert gave a quick bow. 'It may even prove that we can be of some assistance to you.'

'Yes, sir,' Puttony added quickly. 'If you want a watch kept on certain people, please don't hesitate to let me know. Apart from being an officer in the Security Police I am also the commander of an Arrow-Cross Youth Section; and my lads will do just as I tell them without asking questions.'

Standing up, Gregory replied, 'I thank you both. Should an occasion arise when I need the help of either of you, I will certainly avail myself of it. Now, let us go downstairs and, without ostentation, drink a *baratsch* to the health of our glorious *Führer*.'

Taking their agreement for granted, he strode towards the door. But just inside it he turned suddenly and said to Puttony, 'By the by, you still have my pistol.' With a murmured apology, the Lieutenant handed it over. Hiding a smile, Gregory pocketed it and, with the arrogance in keeping with his new rôle, marched on, leaving his 'collaborators' to tag along behind him.

Down in the courtyard, at a small table across which the leafy branches above now cast long shadows, he became genial and talkative, while maintaining the sort of condescending charm suited to a lordly representative of the *Herrenvolk* who wished to make himself pleasant.

Over the drinks he learnt that he had got nearer to the mark than he knew when inventing a mission for Himmler to give him. Puttony disclosed that the Hungarian Nazis were worried and angry because their country was not pulling its weight in the war. They had already made representations to the *Führer* about it, with the recommendation that he should summon Regent Horthy to Berchtesgaden and insist on his purging both his Cabinet and Government offices of their lukewarm elements.

Gregory guessed that the move was an attempt by the Arrow-Cross leaders to secure a number of the key jobs for themselves, with the hope that this would later enable them to get control of the country. But he thought it unlikely that it would come off. Whatever the Regent might be bullied into promising, the magnates were too firmly entrenched and the Hungarian Nazis still too few and lacking in influence for it to come to anything in practice. Nevertheless he regarded the information as a windfall, since it would make an excellent lever for exerting pressure on the Committee appointed to discuss terms with the Allies.

As soon as his visitors had gone he took stock of his situation. Upstairs in his room he had had to skate on the thinnest possible ice, and there had been several nasty moments when he had thought that nothing could save him from going through it. Even Einholtz's Gestapo card had been a doubtful asset as, although it was genuine after all that had gone before, and the fact that Heydrich had now been dead for three months, he had half expected it to be declared a forgery, or Cochefert to accuse him of stealing it. That it had instantly been accepted at its face value had saved his bacon. But, all the same, he was far from happy at having had to produce it.

On the credit side, doing so had completely cleared him in Cochefert's eyes, and Puttony could now be counted on to stall off tactfully any unwelcome interest that the State Security Police might begin to take in his activities. In addition, with the subtlety and swiftness which made him such a brilliant secret agent, he had improvised a reason for his imaginary orders from Himmler which would give him better cover for his own mission. Not only was he now free of any necessity to implement his old cover by calling on several foie-gras merchants, but he could hob-nob with the Hungarian aristocracy as often as he pleased without it being thought strange that a truffle farmer should do so.

But on the debit side Cochefert and Puttony now both believed him to be a fairly senior official of the Gestapo and that might prove his complete undoing. It was a sure thing that the Gestapo would have Liaison Officers in Budapest with their own headquarters, and that the normal drill would have been for him to report there on his arrival. Should Puttony, after all, prove indiscreet and a mention of 'Commandant Tavenier's' mission reach the ears of one of those Liaison Officers, the fat would be in the fire with a vengeance. The thought of such a possibility quite spoilt Gregory's dinner.

He was uncomfortably aware that his only really safe course was to leave Budapest next morning but, now that his mission showed such promise of developing from a tentative reconnaissance into a concrete hope of bringing Hungary over to the Allies in the comparatively near future, he felt that he could not possibly throw his hand in prematurely. He knew that opportunity did not often knock twice on the same door, and that some hazard of war might soon change the outlook of the Hungarian nobles. He had them well warmed up now, so must remain in Budapest until they had completed their 'Heads of Agreement' for him to take back to London. Then the Foreign Office would have the chance to strike while the iron was hot.

He endeavoured to comfort himself with the thought that Puttony must have had security training; so it was really very long odds against his gossiping. Anyhow, it was a risk that must be taken, and the only way to minimise it was to urge the Committee to complete their deliberations as swiftly as possible.

The Committee met the following afternoon in a small private room at the Nobles Club. Count Zsigmond Szegény-ház, a tall thin man with the delicate features of a dilettante intellectual, was the second oldest member of it. He was also the head of a department in the Hungarian Foreign Office; so obviously the best choice for Chairman, and he was duly elected. After the preliminary of drafting their own 'Terms of Reference' had been completed, Gregory asked leave to speak and addressed the Committee at some length on the question of Security.

He pointed out that while the work the Committee was engaged upon was inspired by the highest patriotism it could be classed as treason, and that if its activities came to the ears of pro-Germans in the State Security Police the Government would be compelled to take notice of it. Should that happen, however anxious the Regent might be to protect friends and relations of his who were involved, Hitler would be certain to demand that drastic steps should be taken against them. Therefore, if for no other reason than to save the Regent from grave embarrassment, it was only right that they should take all possible precautions to keep their proceedings secret.

The sound sense of this was admitted and as a move in the right direction it was agreed that, instead of future meetings being held at the Club, they should take place at the home of each member in turn.

Gregory then went on to give an account of his narrow escape from arrest the preceding evening, and ended by repeating Lieutenant Puttony's statement to the effect that the leaders of the Arrow-Cross Party had recently made representations to Hitler that he should summon the Regent to Berchtesgaden and insist that Hungarian affairs should be brought more into line with Nazi interests.

Count Zsigmond nodded. 'What he said is true. But the Regent has consistently refused to kow-tow to Hitler, and I am glad to say that he has refused to go to Berchtesgaden. However, the Germans' case for Hungary's bearing a greater share of the war-burden could not be ignored; so it has been agreed that Ribbentrop should come here for discussions. He is due to arrive early next week.'

'Do you know the form his demands will take?' enquired the Bishop.

'Only in general. It is certain that he will ask for further reinforcements for the Russian front, and for much greater supplies of food than we are sending to Germany at present. He will probably also ask us to receive considerable numbers of refugees from the bombed cities. They would be useless mouths, of course: old people and young children who cannot be employed in the German factories.'

'That,' said the Bishop, 'is a burden we should accept on humanitarian grounds. What else?'

'He may ask us to issue another loan, or even suggest a capital levy to be devoted to a common war chest.'

A grin spread over the handsome face of the one-armed Colonel János Orczy. 'We can rely on the Baroness to get us out of that one.'

Gregory gave him an enquiring look, but it was Count László who satisfied his curiosity. 'Ribbentrop's mistress, the Baroness

Tuzolto. She is a Hungarian, and a very beautiful one. Of course she is a Nazi, but she naturally protects the interests of her country as far as she can. On more than one occasion already she has acted as the secret intermediary between him and our magnates. He is completely venal and if the bribe is big enough will agree to anything provided that he can see his course clear to explain it away to his master. No doubt we'll have to find more men and food, and perhaps float a new loan. But she always travels with him and, if there is any suggestion of a levy affecting the great estates, she will buy him off for us.'

They then began to discuss the Heads of Agreement, but their views were so divergent that although they talked for another hour-and-a-half they did not get very far. When it came to fixing their next meeting, it transpired that all of them except Colonel Orczy had arranged to spend the weekend in the country; so Monday was the earliest day they would all be available. Gregory pleaded the urgency of getting matters settled, but in vain. The Bishop said that he could not neglect his spiritual duties in his diocese, old General Baron Alacy had his annual tenants' party on his estate, and the others said it would be pointless to continue the discussions without them.

The casual postponement of deliberations on which so much hung, and the additional danger to himself of remaining in Budapest even two days longer than was strictly necessary, filled Gregory with annoyance and frustration, and he made no great effort to conceal his feelings. Seeing his long face, János Orczy slapped him on the shoulder and cried cheerfully:

'Don't look so glum, my friend. Even should that Police Lieutenant speak of you to the Germans, we will find some way to get you safely out of the country. And there are worse places than Budapest for a little relaxation. Come out to dinner with me tonight and we will forget this wretched war for —a while.' Then Count László added, 'I am returning to Nagykáta for Saturday and Sunday nights. Why not come with me? Mihály Zapolya would, I know, be delighted to see you. I'll call for you at your hotel tomorrow morning at eleven o'clock.'

Gregory gratefully accepted both invitations, and a few hours later the young Colonel took him to a restaurant in a back street of Buda. It had low vaulted ceilings, all the furniture was bright red painted with Hungarian flowers, and the waitresses were dressed in gaily embroidered national costume.

For their main course they had goose. The whole bird was cut into joints and served on a low revolving wooden dish placed in the centre of the table, so that by swivelling it round they could help themselves to any joint that took their fancy. A feature of the place was its famous Tzigane band which played alternately gay and soulful music. The gypsies too wore brilliant costumes embellished with bunches of many-coloured ribbons. A bald old man with a face like a wrinkled walnut performed prodigies on the Tzimberlum, and the leader, walking among the tables, drew marvellous melodies from his fiddle. Later in the evening their music grew wild and passionate, and gypsy girls with flashing eyes, their dark hair streaming out behind them, whirled madly in ancient dances.

The sight and sound of so much revelry made Gregory feel that the war and its cares were more remote than ever, and when, after a session in a night-club that did not end until five in the morning, he got back to his hotel, he was in fuller agreement than ever with his charming host that there were worse places than Budapest for a little relaxation.

Six hours later Count László called for him as arranged and he spent a pleasant but uneventful weekend at Nagykáta. On the Monday they received bad news which plunged the household into gloom. The Regent's eldest son, Stephen Horthy, had been killed in an aircraft disaster. As he had been nominated heir-apparent this was a sad blow; for it once more put Hungary's future in the melting pot, and raised the not altogether welcome possibility of an Italian Prince being invited to mount the throne.

In the afternoon Gregory and Count László returned to the capital to find black streamers hanging from the windows of most of the houses and a general air of depression; but they did not feel called upon to postpone the next meeting of the Committee and drove straight to an apartment owned by the Count in which it was to be held.

This was situated in a suburb of Buda, and with a twinkle in his merry dark eyes the hunchback took Gregory from a sitting room that had a dining alcove through into a bedroom almost entirely filled by an enormous low bed. He then opened a wardrobe and displayed to him a collection of some twenty women's dressing-gowns of varying colours and rich materials.

On Gregory's raising an enquiring eyebrow, the Count laughed and said: 'You did not think I lived here, did you? Nearly everybody who is anybody in Budapest has a little place like this in which to receive his girl-friends discreetly. You might perhaps suppose that my unfortunate deformity makes success in that direction difficult for me, but I can assure you it is quite the contrary. Women are my passion and their greatest weakness is their curiosity. Few of them can resist the temptation to find out if I am as good a lover as other men, and God has kindly compensated me by giving me quite unusual virility. There is hardly a pretty Countess in Budapest who has not been tumbled on that bed, and then come back to be tumbled again.'

Recalling what Levianski had said about the morals of the Hungarian aristocracy, Gregory thought it unlikely that the Count was boasting. Moreover he was not altogether without evidence of their lighthearted ways himself. While at Nagykáta the charming bronze-haired Countess Elizabeth had made it unmistakably plain that she would have liked to enter on an affaire with him, and had even gone to the lengths late one night of coming along to his bedroom with a book which she said she thought he might like to read.

The meeting went quite well until it came to the question of the territories lost by Hungary under the Treaty of Trianon being retained or restored to her. At first the Committee were set on demanding every square inch of land that had ever been Hungarian soil; but Gregory said they must be reasonable, as the Allies could not be expected to penalise all Hungary's neighbours on her account. Then, each member stood out for the permanent absorption of lands in which his own family had once owned estates.

After a long wrangle to which Gregory listened in silence, he put it to them that he thought they would be well advised to confine their terms to the retention of Transylvania and the granting of a port on the Adriatic, as those were reasonable requests, whereas it was unlikely that the Allied Governments would consent to any alteration of the frontiers of pre-1939 Czechoslovakia.

On the question of Austria, the old General proved the nigger in the wood pile as up till 1919 an uncle of his had owned a local railway in a strip of country that had been given to the Austrians, and its loss had considerably reduced the fortune of that side of his family. At their meetings he had so far done little but mumble through his walrus moustache, but on this matter he became angrily loquacious and the meeting broke up without having got any further.

Next day they met again at the Bishop's quarters, which were a sumptuous private suite looking on to a charming cloister garden in a monastery situated in the oldest part of Pest. Gregory's opinion of the prelate as a man of God was not a high one. He was only in his early thirties but very fat and very lazy. At Nagykáta Mass had been celebrated every morning by Count Zapolya's private chaplain in the ornate chapel of the house. The servants all attended as part of their daily routine and a good sprinkling of the family; but, according to the Countess Elizabeth, the Bishop never did so. When telling Gregory this, she had added with a smile that he *said* that he preferred to perform his devotions in the private oratory adjacent to his bedroom, but she was sure that was only an excuse for him to lie abed.

Nevertheless, he was an intelligent man and a fluent talker; and he succeeded in arguing the General round about Austria. But when they went on to discuss Czechoslovakia all five of them united to declare that not only would they retain Ruthenia but they must have back the far larger Slovakia.

The Czechs were to the Hungarians as a red rag to a bull; and Gregory knew enough of European history to be aware of the reason. For many centuries the two great Kingdoms of Hungary and Bohemia had been deadly rivals, until Austria absorbed them both. Bohemia had fared worst as, after a crushing defeat in the seventeenth century, nearly the whole of her nobility had been barbarously executed and every vestige of independent power taken from her. Hungary, on the other hand, had remained a Kingdom, and her magnates had been strong enough to exact terms from the Austrians by which they preserved their ancient rights and their own Diet and refused to acknowledge the Emperor except by the title of King of Hungary. Yet the destruction of the Czech nobility had resulted in the rise of a powerful middle class which had developed trade and industry in a way that left Hungary far behind. In consequence, to the ancient hatred of the Hungarians for their neighbours in the north had been added a sour jealousy, coupled with contempt for them as a nation of bourgeois. To have had to surrender Slovakia and Ruthenia to them in 1920 had therefore been the bitterest pill of all and having got these back in 1940 they were determined to keep them.

When it became clear that the Committee would not budge without many hours of further persuasion, the exasperated Gregory suggested that this one question should be left open for the time being, so that he need no longer delay his departure. It then transpired that Colonel Orczy had sent a message to General Lakatos, one of the principal commanders of the Hungarian forces on the Russian front, asking him to return to Budapest for consultation on an urgent matter. The General was known to be violently anti-Nazi, so was entirely to be trusted, and they wanted his professional opinion upon the number of Anglo-American divisions it would be necessary to land on the Continent in order to hold the German armour in the West. But the General was not arriving until Friday and Gregory had to agree with the Committee that his report would be of little practical value if he left before he could include in it their stipulations on this highly important point; so it was now obvious that he would not be able to get away until the weekend.

Had he been left to himself except for these meetings he would have been driven nearly mad by frustration, but the members of the Committee made up for their dilatoriness in business by lavish hospitality; for they were all intensely proud of their beautiful city and delighted to do the honours of it.

He had, of course, known that Buda had once been the most important bastion of the Roman world against the savage hordes that inhabited the lands north of the Danube; but he had not realised, until Count Szegényház told him, that the Romans had brought civilisation to Hungary long before they had to Britain, and five hundred years before the Germans were slowly emerging from a state of barbarism. The Count, who was a learned antiquarian, had a fine collection of ancient pottery and weapons and, as Gregory showed much interest in them, took him on a fascinating tour of the National Museum. They also visited the Roman baths at Aquincum, and the thermal establishment at which for close on two thousand years countless sufferers had received relief by being packed in radio-active mud.

The Bishop took him to the Matthias Church to see the sacred relics and to the Bergberg where he had the Coronation regalia in the treasury specially brought out for Gregory to examine. Colonel Orczy motored him up to the Fortress of Ofen and the heights of the Bocksberg, then took him to dine with the Officers of the Guard at the Royal Palace. The old General invited him to lunch at the Houses of Parliament and afterwards to witness a session in the Hall of the Magnates, as the Upper Chamber was called.

On Wednesday 27th the Committee did not meet, as on that day the funeral of Stephen Horthy took place. He had been in his middle forties and neither brilliant nor particularly popular, but as the Regent's heir he was given a State funeral. Although the soldiers lining the streets were in their drab wartime uniforms the magnates gave the procession a touch of semi-oriental splendour, and Ribbentrop and Count Ciano walked side by side at the head of the group of notables representing Axis and neutral countries. Out of sympathy for the mother and father every shop in Budapest was closed and all acitivities for either pleasure or profit suspended; but on the following day the black streamers had disappeared from the windows and the city returned to normal.

That night Count László gave Gregory dinner and afterwards they went to the Piccadilly, which had the most glamorous cabaret of the luxury night-clubs on the *Margareten-Insel*. They had been there for about an hour, drinking champagne and watching the lively singing and dancing of a bevy of near naked beauties, when there was a sudden hush and many heads were turned towards one of the entrances.

A party of six people was being obsequiously bowed by the maître d'hôtel to a reserved table on the edge of the dance floor. The leading couple were a tall man with a high bald forehead and a strikingly beautiful dark-haired girl.

'There's Ribbentrop,' remarked Count László, 'and his pretty Baroness.'

Gregory turned to look, then caught his breath in surprise and consternation. The girl was his old flame Sabine.

Next moment she glanced in his direction. Their eyes met. Her arched eyebrows went up and her scarlet lips opened a trifle. He knew then that she had recognised him. It was too late to slip away. The danger he had foreseen from an unex-

112

pected meeting, when he had thought about her after his bathe on his first afternoon in Budapest, re-entered his mind like the shrilling of an alarm bell.

# 9

# Playing With Fire

Gregory had hoped that if he did run into Sabine she would be alone and that, by hinting at the reason for his being in Budapest, he might ensure her sympathetic silence. Anyway he had felt confident that he would be able to overcome any feeling she might have that it was her duty to hand him over to the police.

Even had she had friends with her of her own nationality, and from surprise at seeing him had greeted him with an exclamation in English, dangerous as such a situation would have been he might, with luck, have put up a bluff of some kind which would have stalled off any immediate action.

But to come across her in the company of a Nazi, let alone Hitler's Foreign Minister, was a thing that he had never remotely contemplated. Still worse, from what he had heard she made no concealment of the fact that she was Ribbentrop's mistress, and a convinced Nazi herself.

As they stared at one another from fifteen paces' distance he kept his face completely immobile. For her English lover to turn up in Budapest during the war was so unlikely that, if he showed no signs of recognition, he thought there was just a chance she might decide that she had been misled by a resemblance. But instead of looking away, while Ribbentrop was motioning the rest of his party to the places at the table where he wished them to sit she touched the maître d'hôtel on the arm and pointed át Gregory.

His heart missed a beat. For a second he thought she was telling the man to have him watched, so that he did not slip away, while sending for the police. But the Maître d'hôtel only shook his head, showing that she had simply asked if he knew who Gregory was.

Count László turned to him with a smile. 'The Baroness seems to be interested in you.'

'Unfortunately, yes,' Gregory replied in a low voice. 'It is several years since I've seen her; so her present name conveyed nothing to me. But she turns out to be an old friend of mine; and as she is now a friend of Nazi No. 4, that may have extremely unpleasant results for me before I am much older.'

The laughter died in the hunchback's merry brown eyes. 'You mean she knows you to be an Englishman?'

'That's it. And the moment she looked in this direction she recognised me. By keeping a poker face I hope I've sown doubt in her mind; but if she tells her new boy-friend her suspicions my goose will be properly cooked. For me to make a hurried exit might precipitate catastrophe; but I want to get out of here as soon as I can without appearing to be making a bolt for it. Would you send for the bill, so that the waiter won't come running after us if we get up to go in about fifteen minutes.'

Ribbentrop's table was now empty. After a thick-set man in the uniform of the Arrow-Cross Party, who was apparently playing host, had ordered wine, all three couples moved out on to the dance floor. But each time the dancing brought Sabine in view of Gregory her wide dark eyes became riveted, over Ribbentrop's shoulder, on him. He gave the impression that he was unconscious of her glance, keeping his own in another direction; but he was watching her out of the corner of his eye, and wondering with acute anxiety at what precise moment she might decide to tell her partner that she thought she had recognised a man who must be a British spy.

Under his breath Gregory murmured to Count László, 'For God's sake tell me some funny stories to make me laugh. The only hope I have of foxing this woman is to sit on here for a bit appearing unconcerned and natural.' Then he began quite openly to ogle a pretty blonde who was sitting at a nearby table. She looked a little surprised by these sudden attentions, but having taken stock of Gregory's lean good looks she responded, at intervals when her companion was not looking at her, with sly half-smiles.

Getting up, Gregory went over to her table, made a formal bow to the man who was with her, and asked if he might ask her for a dance. Her companion looked far from pleased but, taken by surprise and seeing the smile with which she greeted the invitation, he mumbled his consent. Gregory led the blonde on to the floor, grasped her firmly and began to tell her how, as a visitor to Budapest, he found the city enchanting and her the loveliest thing in it. Her name was Terézia and she was a model in a smart dress shop. He secured her address and telephone number, and said he would ring her up next day; a promise that he had no intention of keeping. Then he took her back to her table and returned to his own hoping that Sabine, who must have observed the incident, would conclude from it that no spy who had been detected would have the nerve to remain within call acting the rôle of a play-boy.

Ribbentrop's party had now re-sorted themselves. He was dancing with a statuesque red-headed woman and Sabine, who had evidently declined further dancing for the moment, was back at the table with the Arrow-Cross man. As Gregory gave her an anxious sidelong glance, he saw that her dark head was bent over the table. Count László had paid the bill, and ogling the blonde then dancing with her had occupied a good quarter of an hour; so he murmured to the Count, 'I think we might go now.'

As they stood up, he saw that Sabine was bending over the table because she was writing a note. At that moment she lifted her head, saw that he was about to leave, and made a gesture with her hand that he should stay where he was. He responded with a look of blank surprise appropriate to receiving a signal from a complete stranger; but she beckoned up a waiter, folded her note and pointing out Gregory sent the man over with it.

It was impossible for him to ignore the approaching waiter. Another few moments and he might have been out of the place, but now he had been caught. Cursing under his breath, he sat down, then took the note from the plate the waiter held out to him. Unfolding it he read the single line in her well-remembered spidery writing:

*You can't fool me. What are you doing in Budapest?*

So much for his bluff that he was not who she thought him. It was clearly futile to attempt to maintain it any longer. And there was now no escape from giving her some explanation. All he could hope to do was temporarily to stall her off from

115

telling her friends that he was English by inducing her to play up to one of his cover stories until they could talk together alone.

For him to pretend to be Fritz Einholtz with Ribbentrop in the offing would be a suicidal risk, as the Foreign Minister might have known the Gestapo Colonel. On the other hand, if he posed as Tavenier there was just a chance that the Arrow-Cross man might be Puttony's chief, and that the Lieutenant had confided to him that Tavenier was really only a cover name for *Obersturmbannführer* Einholtz.

Ribbentrop was just returning to the table, so would see Sabine receive the reply to her note. It was certain that he would question her about it, and if she said Gregory was a Frenchman of her acquaintance the Arrow-Cross man might try to show how well-informed he was by telling her that she was mistaken and revealing what he believed to be the truth. For a moment Gregory contemplated fabricating an entirely new identity for himself. But that would not do either, as scores of people in Budapest now knew him as Commandant Tavenier and it was quite possible that one of the other women at the table had been at some party he had attended and heard him addressed by that name.

His mind turning over like a dynamo, he decided that the lesser risk was to continue to pose as Tavenier; so he picked up a menu and wrote on the back of it in French:

*My dear Baroness,*
*Only the fact that you are in such illustrious company prevented me from reclaiming your acquaintance. I still treasure the memory of Paris when you were staying there as the guest of my aunt in 1936. Permit me, I beg, to call upon you tomorrow morning, so that I may tell you of my adventures after my recall to the army and how, after being evacuated from Dunkirk, I succeeded in getting back to France. I rejoice to see that these few years have made you more ravishingly beautiful than ever.*
*With my most distinguished compliments,*
*Etienne Tavenier.*

Folding the menu over, he gave it to the hovering waiter to take to her. Then he said in a low voice to Count László, 'I only hope to God that will do the trick. If her memories of

116

our affaire are as delightful as mine, it should—unless that Arrow-Cross chap knows that the real Tavenier is still living in France.'

The Count smiled. 'You are most fortunate to have had an affaire with her. Not only is she very beautiful, but she is one of the most intelligent and amusing women I have ever counted among my friends.'

'You know her well, then?'

'Oh yes. I have known her since shortly after she left her Convent. In fact, I might even claim to have contributed a little to her education; although that came a year or two later when she had become bored with the limited conversation of handsome young officers.'

Into Gregory's mind there flashed a picture of the enormous bed at Count László's discreet apartment in the suburbs. But his gaze was riveted on Sabine. She had read the note and was talking to Ribbentrop; then she spoke to the Arrow-Cross man. Gregory was on tenterhooks for what seemed an age while he watched them conferring together, but actually it was only two minutes before she beckoned to the waiter again and sent him over with a message. Hurrying between the tables he bowed and delivered it:

'Gentlemen, the *Herr Reichsaussenminister* presents his compliments and asks that you will join his party.'

Count László half covered his mouth with a hand that held a cigarette, and murmured quickly behind it in French, 'This is Hungary, not Germany; so you do not have to go. Walk out if you like. I will express your regrets and tell them you had to leave because you have a date with a lady.'

'No,' Gregory replied in the same language, as he stood up. 'If she has given me away they'd have the police after me in ten minutes. Better to face the music and hope things will turn out all right. If not, please don't involve yourself. Say you hardly know me—that we met in the bar and as we were both alone decided to share a table.'

A few moments later they were bowing in turn over Sabine's hand. To Gregory's great relief she greeted him in French. Then she introduced them to the others at her table, explaining that the Arrow-Cross man was their host. He proved to be Major Szalasi, the leader of the Hungarian Nazi Party, and the red-haired woman was his wife. The third man, a tall blond fellow, was Ribbentrop's aide-de-camp, Captain

Von Trott, and his companion, a girl whose looks were a little marred by a mouth as wide as a letterbox, was a Fräulein Weiss.

The bull-necked Szalasi had shown no dangerous reaction when Sabine, having asked Gregory's present rank, had presented him as Commandant Tavenier; so, this second hurdle being behind him, he took one of the extra chairs that had been brought up, accepted the glass of champagne Szalasi poured for him, and entered with zest into his part.

For the first minute or two Sabine regarded him with a coolly detached expression, but with truly Gallic exuberance he launched into an invented account of how he had taken her boating on the lake at Vincennes and fallen in, and she had nearly brained him with an oar while trying to help him out, upon which her dark eyes began to brim with merriment. Mischievously she enquired after his mythical aunt and was hard put to it to maintain a suitable expression of sorrow when he told her in a tragic voice that in the first year of the war the poor lady had had the tip of her nose bitten off by her pet poodle, and that as a result she had died of sepsis.

For the benefit of the others he changed from French to heavily accented German, as he described his agony of indecision as to whether it was his duty to shoot the poodle as the murderer of his aunt. Then, breaking off abruptly, he declared that this was no place in which to talk of death, and soon he and Sabine were outbidding one another in absurd, entirely fictitious, stories beginning, 'Do you remember,' and everyone at the table was laughing with them.

It was Ribbentrop who turned the conversation to more serious matters by saying, 'I understand, *Herr Major,* that you were evacuated from Dunkirk and spent some time in England. It would be interesting to have an eye witness's account of that operation as the enemy saw it, and to have your impressions of London under war conditions.'

About Dunkirk Gregory had no need to call on his powers of invention, as for the best part of twenty-four hours he had sat on the beach watching the troops taken off; although, his own mission being uncompleted, instead of going home with them he had then got into an abandoned tank and driven off in the direction of Paris.

About London he exaggerated both the bad and the good with the intent of depressing his audience. He described the

results of the bombing as frightful beyond belief, which delighted the Germans; but then went on to say how, all the
unreliable elements having fled from the capital, those who
remained had displayed the pig-headedness for which those
accursed islanders were notorious. They had suddenly begun
talking to their neighbours in buses and trains and sung a silly
song about rolling out a barrel and—'pardon, but you will
understand I speak of the filthy British'—gone about greeting
one another with laughing cries of 'To hell with Hitler!'

Having despatched this barbed arrow, he swiftly returned
to his own adventures, telling how he had skilfully managed to
desert from a British Commando at St. Nazaire and that as,
alas, France had not yet actively entered the war against the
perfidious English he had come to Budapest in the hope of
selling truffles.

He then paused to await with some curiosity their reaction
to this admission of his pseudo-commercial acitivities. Ribbentrop had been widely sneered at by the world Press because
in pre-Nazi days he had earned his living as a champagne
salesman. Why, Gregory had never been able to understand,
for it seemed to him that few trades could be more civilised
and pleasant than selling wines; and, although he had no right
to the 'von' he claimed, as only his mother's family had been
noble, he came of respectable people. Moreover, he had been
no ordinary commercial traveller, as he had married Anneliese Henkel, the heiress of the great German Sparkling-Wine
House. But nobody made any comment on Gregory's commercial activities, and a moment later the band started up a
new number.

Standing up, Sabine smiled at Ribbentrop, then said to
Gregory, 'Come and show me if you still dance as well as you
used to when we were in Paris.'

'With the utmost pleasure,' he replied gaily, and led her out
on to the floor. But as they moved smoothly off among the
throng of dancers, her manner changed and she asked abruptly:

'Now! What are you really up to here?'

'Surely you can guess,' he replied lightly. 'I am assessing the
weight of bombs it will take to blow Budapest off the map;
and how many Hungarian girls we can hope to save from the
ruins to supply the brothels we maintain for the coloured
troops of the Empire.'

119

'The Allied bombers will never get as far as Budapest, and . . .'

'I wouldn't be too certain of that,' he cut in with sudden seriousness.

Her voice was low and soft but held no note of friendliness as she replied, 'That, as I was about to add, is beside the point. I want a sensible answer to my question.'

'Let's say then that, my poor old bones now being racked with arthritis, I have come to do the cure at your famous mud baths.'

'Gregory!' She gave the back of his hand a sharp dig with her nails. 'Stop fooling! You are as fit and lithe as ever you were. And anyway . . .'

'Softly, my sweet, softly,' he chided her. 'Please remember that my name is now Etienne.'

'You will have exchanged your name for a number in a cell if you exasperate me much further. And I am not your sweet!'

Ignoring the threat, he smiled down at her. 'Alas, no. I fear that your taste has deteriorated since the wonderful time we had together—in Paris, of course. About that you played up marvellously, and I am most grateful to you.'

Without returning his smile, she replied, 'Yes, it was all very amusing; but I am no longer in the mood for comedy. For the sake of old times I refrained from denouncing you, and I am now giving you an opportunity to explain yourself. Take it, or I shall get Major Szalasi to send for a policeman.'

He gave her a look of shocked surprise. 'Surely you wouldn't do that?'

'Why not? Our countries are at war and I run into you here posing as a Frenchman. It is obvious that you are an enemy secret agent.'

'Then why not snatch up a champagne bottle from the next table we pass and bash my head in with it?'

A slight shudder ran through her slender body, and she exclaimed, 'What a horrible idea!'

'I suppose it is rather—particularly when you remember that you used to enjoy running those slim fingers of yours through my hair. Yet the effect of a real good crack from a bottle would be precisely the same as if my head were smashed in by the bullets from a firing party; and that would probably be my fate if you gave me away. So you see you would simply be getting somebody else to do your dirty work.'

Her skin was flawless, with the matt texture of magnolia petals, but a worried frown creased her broad low forehead, and a warmer note crept into her voice as she said, 'God knows, I would hate to bring about your death. But don't you see that meeting you like this has placed me in an impossible position?'

By first making light of his own situation then just touching on the grimmer side of it, Gregory had played his cards skilfully. Few women can resist the appeal of a man who is in great danger yet instead of asking help talks gay nonsense about it: and he judged from Sabine's softened expression that he now had her patriotic scruples on the run. Stooping his head a little he murmured in her ear:

'I would not say impossible, but exciting. How could it be anything else when you recall the last time we danced together here. I find it incredibly thrilling that fate should have brought us together again like this. You have no idea how often I have thought of you.'

'Oh come!' she protested. 'Please don't pretend that you are still in love with me.'

'I wasn't an hour ago. Now I'm not so certain. Anyhow, I very soon can be.'

'You are saying that because you hope to persuade me to let you get away with whatever you are up to.'

'I'm not. You must know that you are lovely enough to turn any man's head—especially one who has such memories of you as I have.'

She gave a quick sigh. 'Yes; it was wonderful while it lasted.'

'It ended all too soon; only because I had to go back to England and it was impossible for you to go with me.'

'I . . . I know,' her voice faltered a little.

As they swayed to the music he drew her closer. 'Being with you here again like this makes it seem as if the years between have been no more than a one-night's dream.'

'But they haven't been a dream!' Her words came faster now and she looked up into his face with troubled eyes. 'It is common knowledge that I'm Ribb's mistress, and even if I were not we couldn't pretend they have. Our countries are at war, and you have as good as admitted that you are here as a spy. How can you expect me to ignore that and continue to lie to people about your being a Frenchman I met in Paris?'

'Listen, Sabine. This is the truth. I am not a spy; but I am here on a secret mission.'

'Well, that's much the same thing, isn't it?'

'Not necessarily; and not in this case. If I can succeed in my mission I honestly believe that it will be a good thing for Hungary.'

'In that case there is nothing to stop your telling me about it.'

'Nothing except time. This dance must be nearly over and, anyhow, to go properly into the matter I'd need an hour at least. What are you doing tomorrow?'

'I don't really know. Ribb will be up at the Palace most of the day, having conferences with Admiral Horthy; and probably in the evening too. I expect I shall do some shopping, lunch with friends and bathe in the afternoon. But that has nothing to do with it. This thing has got to be settled tonight.'

'Why? Are you afraid I'll run away?'

'You might. Perhaps it would be the best solution if you did. That is, if I could be certain that you had left the country.'

He smiled down at her again and stuck his chin out. 'Well, I'm not going to. There is too much at stake. So if you are really set on getting me off your conscience tonight, there's only one way you can do it. You'll have to call in the police.'

'Oh, Gregory, you are a brute! You haven't changed a bit. You're just as dictatorial as ever.'

'You haven't changed, either. But I'm not a brute. You know jolly well that I am the easiest, softest creature in the world, and that you never had the least difficulty in twisting me round your little finger. Look, why not cut out your shopping and all that tomorrow and spend the day with me?'

She closed her eyes and shook her head. 'No, no. Get thee behind me, Satan.'

'Why should I when it's such a joy to look at your face, Angel?'

Her eyes remained closed, their long dark lashes making fans upon her cheeks; but her lips broke into a smile, as she murmured, 'We're being absolutely crazy.'

'What is there crazy about trying to snatch a little happiness from life. If we can't put the clock back altogether we could for a dozen hours tomorrow.'

'Oh, you're incorrigible!'

'No; just human. I'll tell you about this mission of mine;

then we'll forget the damn war and enjoy ourselves.'

Suddenly she opened her eyes. They were bright as stars and brimming with laughter. 'All right,' she nodded, 'you win. Where shall we meet?'

At that moment the band stopped. Under cover of the clapping he said, as he took his arm from about her, 'Let's start the day just as we used to, with a swim at the Gellért. I'll meet you there at eleven o'clock.'

She pressed his hand before letting it go, and whispered, 'That would be lovely, darling. Now we must think up some more funny stories about our time in Paris to keep Ribb in a good temper. Be careful how you look at me, though, because sometimes he gets jealous.'

Gregory was much too old a bird not to heed her warning; so he did not ask her to dance again, although he danced with Madame Szalasi and twice with Fräulein Weiss. Between-whiles he played the part of a cultured Frenchman who is something of a buffoon, and amused the party with cynical stories illustrating the hypocrisy and stupidity of the English. He found Ribbentrop somewhat conceited and very self-opinionated but, apart from that, congenial company.

It was the Nazi Foreign Minister's easy affability that had first opened to him the road to fame. On Anneliese's money they had lived in a comfortable villa in the rich Berlin suburb of Dahlam, and made themselves a popular host and hostess. To their parties had come Von Papen, Himmler and then Hitler. The latter found Ribbentrop useful to him in giving colloquial translations of leading articles in the British and French press and then the villa at Dahlam made an excellent rendezvous for holding secret meetings. In it, during January 1933, had been hatched the conspiracy which led to the aged Hindenburg's giving his agreement to a Von Papen-Hitler coalition government, and from then on the genial host of the conspirators had never looked back. Many of his fellow party chiefs resented his arrogance and doubted his abilities, but the ex-house-painter, Hitler, was so abysmally ignorant of all foreign affairs that he could never be persuaded that Ribbentrop was not a second Bismarck.

Even conceding that to be an absurd exaggeration, by comparison Gregory found the Hungarian Nazi a dull dog, the A.D.C. only a moderately intelligent yes-man, and the two women of very limited mentality; but that was a good, rather than a bad, thing as it left him free to concentrate on the two principal members of the party.

Soon after two o'clock it broke up. Ribbentrop and Szalasi both had large cars waiting for them, and from the point of the island their ways lay in opposite directions across the two halves of the bridge which joined it to the opposite banks. As the Germans and Sabine were staying in Buda they offered Count Lászlo a lift, and the Szalasis, who lived in Pest, said they would drop Gregory at the Vadászkürt. But before they parted he managed to get a brief word with the Count.

'It was a near thing,' he confided, 'but I'll only have myself to blame now if she gives me away. I'm spending all tomorrow with her; so please let the others know why I shall not be able to turn up at our meeting. I can't make any further contribution, anyhow, so I'd be only a listener. But do press them to get something definite from General Lakatos. It is more urgent than ever now that I should get away from Budapest. I want to leave on Saturday.'

Count Lászlo had proved himself the most reasonable and helpful member of the Committee, and he promised to do his best; so Gregory took such comfort from that as he could, but he knew that during the next day or two he would be faced with a most tricky piece of tight-rope walking.

In spite of his light-hearted fooling with Sabine during the first part of their dance together, he had soon realised that the only way to prevent her from turning him over to the police was to invoke her happy memories of their love affaire. That had not proved difficult; but, with her slender body pressed to his and her lovely face so close, his own memories had flooded back to him with most unsettling clarity.

He wondered now just how much that had influenced him in suggesting that they should spend the whole day together —when an hour's talk over a drink before lunch would probably have been sufficient to satisfy her curiosity and secure her silence—but he decided that, although it had been an added incentive, he would have done the same with any woman in similar circumstances, solely because she was Ribbentrop's mistress. It was certain that a conceited man like the *Reichsminister* talked freely with his intimates, so Sabine must be privy to many Nazi secrets. She might prove as close as an oyster but such a chance to pick up red-hot inside information about the enemy was one nothing would have induced him to miss, and to make the utmost of that chance necessitated his getting her to himself for as long as he could.

The disturbing fact was that when he had proposed this long session he had had in mind no more than a day spent together as old friends, whereas she seemed to have read into it more than that. Recalling the words he had used to win her over, he could not blame her; but just before they left the floor she had called him 'darling', and she had said it in a tone which implied her expectation that, if only for a few hours, when next they met they would resume their old relationship.

Such a prospect had no strings to it—provided that it was only for a few hours. But later, in conversation at the table, it had emerged that, while Ribbentrop was returning to Berlin on Saturday afternoon, Sabine was staying on in Budapest to attend the wedding of an old friend the following Tuesday before driving back to Berlin in her own car. That meant that from Saturday evening she would be her own mistress; and Gregory foresaw that if he had not left Budapest by then, a situation was likely to develop which would put him in a fix.

He did not want to be unfaithful to Erika, but he knew his Sabine; and one of her attractions for him had been the frank joy she took in giving rein to her passions. He knew, too, the truth of the old saying that 'hell hath no fury like a woman scorned'. After a long day spent together, and with Ribbentrop out of the way, it was a certainty that she would expect matters to reach their logical conclusion. And if, after having again aroused her passion for him, he refused to play . . . ?

It was that he had had in mind when he had told Count László that, if she gave him away, he would have only himself to blame. If he was not out of Budapest by Saturday he would be safe only if he put his scruples behind him. And even that was not the final issue. If he did find that Sabine was inclined to be indiscreet about Nazi affairs, and that with patience he could wheedle really valuable information out of her, to make the utmost of such a marvellous opportunity he would feel it his duty to stay on in Budapest as long as she did. Then there could be no escape from becoming her lover again.

He was honest enough with himself to admit that should that happen one side of him was going thoroughly to enjoy it; but the other side was his private conscience, and as far as that was concerned, Sabine was no longer just an old flame. She had become fire—and he was playing with it.

## 10

## Divided Loyalties

The St. Gellért Baths were, perhaps, the nearest thing of their kind in the modern world to those palatial establishments for health, social intercourse and sensual pleasure that had been such a prominent feature of Roman civilisation. The great building stood facing the Danube on the slope of the Gellért hill at the southern end of Buda.

In its lower floor there were marble halls and corridors leading to scores of rooms in which patients consulted their doctors and every variety of treatment could be given. On the next level there was a true replica of a Roman swimming bath. Towering columns flanked its sides, on its broad paved surround stone seats, where the bathers could rest awhile, were interspersed with larger-than-life-size statues of the gods and goddesses, and the water in it bubbled; for it was known as the 'champagne bath', from being aerated by pipes set in its bottom so that swimmers should enjoy additional friction as they passed through these aerial fountains. On the same floor there were long corridors of rooms in which dozens of male and female attendants plied their trade as masseurs.

Above, and set still further back into the slope of the hill, was another swimming pool open to the skies. The tiles with which it was lined gave the effect of the water in it being blue, and at regular intervals a mechanism connected with it created artificial waves, so that bathers could take their choice of going in either when it was rough or smooth. The pool was set in a horse-shoe shaped arena, the base of which was occupied by a restaurant. Outside it there were tables shaded by gaily coloured umbrellas. Round the rim of the horse-shoe there was every type of well-sprung lie-low, swing-seat and basket chair, and the whole was protected from the wind by a sixty-foot high bank planted with flowering shrubs and flowers.

At a few minutes before eleven Gregory was waiting for Sabine on the broad flight of steps outside the entrance. She arrived shortly afterwards, driving herself, in a pale blue and silver Mercedes. When she had parked the car she greeted him without a smile and a shade hesitantly.

'I can't think what got into me last night. I behaved like a sentimental schoolgirl. This morning I was in half a mind not to come: but I couldn't quite bring myself to have you arrested without first having heard what you have to say.'

'I'm glad of that,' Gregory replied with becoming seriousness, 'because if you had I am quite sure that for ages to come you would have suffered the most terrible remorse from having sent me to my death.'

'You seem to be more concerned for me than about yourself.'

'Naturally.' He grinned suddenly. 'Once dead I wouldn't have anything to worry about.'

She gave him a reluctant half-smile. 'Aren't you even a little bit afraid that I might put my duty before sentiment, and tell the police I know you to be a British secret agent?'

From the higher step on which he stood he smiled down on her, then shook his head. 'No, not even a little bit. You are far too nice a person to betray an old friend; and, anyhow, you're quite wrong about me being here as a spy.'

'I wish I could believe that; but knowing the sort of man you are, how can I?'

'What's come over you this morning? I suppose it must be that having me on you conscience gave you a bad night. Come on; let's go inside and bathe. Then we'll have our talk and, if you really feel you must, you can put the police on to me afterwards.'

'I'm not going to bathe with you. And you're right about my having had a bad night. I've been worrying myself silly over this thing, and I want to get it settled right away.'

Gregory saw now that he would have to go all out to win her round again, otherwise she might prove a really serious danger to him; so he said earnestly: 'Listen, Sabine. I may have been exaggerating a bit when I said that if you denounce me I will be shot. You must know that I'm not the sort of man to allow myself to be arrested while there is fighting chance of keeping my freedom. But I might quite well be caught before I could get across the frontier. If I were, there would be nothing you could do about it afterwards. Like it or not, you would be compelled to give evidence that I am an Englishman and that, coupled with the fact that I am here under a false identity, would certainly lead to my being condemned as a spy; and in wartime spies *are* shot. So for both of us this is a really

127

serious matter, and you will feel much more capable of taking a right decision about it after you have freshened yourself up with a swim.'

'I haven't brought a swim-suit.'

'That's no difficulty. I'll hire one for you.'

'I . . . I don't like wearing things other people have used.'

'Nonsense! You know perfectly well that in a place like this they are thoroughly sterilised. What you really mean is you would prefer to display that lovely figure of yours to me in a swim-suit chosen by yourself. That is quite unnecessary when I remember so well all the hidden charms beneath anything you wear—including that tiny mole on the left side of your tummy.'

A faint blush coloured her magnolia cheeks for a moment and she stamped a small well-shod foot. 'Really, Gregory! It's not fair to rake up the past; and I didn't mean to let you talk to me about that sort of thing.'

'Am I to take it, then, that you neglected to say your prayer this morning?'

Her eyes widened. 'My prayer? What d'you mean? I have no special prayer.'

'Oh yes, you have. At least, you used to say one in the old days. It went: "Holy Mary, I believe, that without Sin Thou didst conceive. And now I pray, in Thee believing, that I may Sin without conceiving".'

Too late he realised that, by implying that she might have said that prayer before coming to meet him, he had fully committed himself as aspiring again to become her lover. But the merry little rhyme did the trick. Throwing back her head she suddenly burst out laughing. Then she cried:

'Of course I remember. And every morning you used to buy flowers to set before my little statue of the Virgin, just to show that we didn't really mean to take her name in vain. What fun it was.'

Taking her gently by the arm he led her unresisting up the steps into the baths; and she made no further protest while he bought their tickets.

It was the last Friday in August and a day of brilliant sunshine; so there were far fewer people in the Roman bath than up round the Blue Pool on the higher level, yet the horse-shoe terrace there was by no means as crowded as Gregory remembered it in peacetime. To bathe there was as expensive as

128

to swim from the Excelsior on the Lido or the Bar du Soleil at Deauville, and although Budapest's hotels were full it was not with wealthy holiday-makers from other countries; but the terrace was a favourite haunt of those in the capital's smart set who remained in it for a part of the summer, so as Sabine came out to the Pool several acquaintances waved greetings to her.

Gregory took note of these salutations with silent satisfaction. She had already compromised herself the night before at the Piccadilly by accepting him as a friend, and she was doing so again. It could now be pointed out to her that, should conscience drive her to the police, she might explain away her failure to act the previous night as being due to reluctance to create a scene in public, but it would not be easy to laugh off having come swimming with him the following morning. That, coupled with a disclosure that he had formerly been her lover, might make things decidedly awkward for her with Ribbentrop. He was in good hopes now that she would not force him to resort to such shifts in defence of his safety; but he knew from the past that she was, like so many Hungarians, fanatically patriotic and, as a woman, distinctly unpredictable; so he got down to the work of setting the clock back by every means he could think of.

It was work that entailed little effort and no hardship. There she was with her golden-brown body made the more striking from having chosen a white elastic swim-suit, and looking more like a million dollars than most things one sees in *Vogue*. She could swim like a fish and dive like a heron. In the great bath there were rubber seahorses, dolphins and a huge coloured ball to play with. As a background there were a score of other bathers and two score more lounging round the pool, with a lot of pretty women among them; but they served only to throw her up as their superior. Laughing and romping they went in and out until after half-an-hour they had just pleasantly tired themselves. Then Gregory piloted her to a rubber mattress that was out of earshot from other people and, as she stretched herself on it, sat down on a cushion beside her. Signalling a waiter he sent for two champagne cocktails, and as the man went off said to Sabine:

'Now, tell me about yourself.'

'It's for you to tell me about yourself,' she replied with a sudden return to gravity.

He shook his head. 'Not just yet. I don't think we are going to quarrel, but we might; and I'm much too fond of you to run the least risk of that before I've learnt what has been happening to you these past few years.'

'If you were all that interested you could have written to find out.'

'No. You know as well as I do that we agreed we wouldn't write because letters would only make our craving for one another greater.'

'That's true. And they probably wouldn't have found me anyway; because after our brief romance I travelled quite a lot—mostly in Italy.'

'Tell me about your marriage.'

'That was in the autumn of nineteen thirty-eight. Kelemen Tuzolto was a nice person. He was cultured, intelligent and very distinguished looking. I can't honestly tell you that I worshipped the ground he walked on, but he was a man a woman could respect, and I had a great fondness for him.'

'It sounds as if he was a good bit older than yourself.'

'He was.'

'For that matter, I am. You can't be much more than twenty-eight, and I'm over forty.'

She gave him a contemplative look from under her long lashes. 'I think you will still be attractive to women when you are sixty. It's not your lean face and muscular body so much as your mental vitality. No one would ever be bored while in your company. Anyhow, twelve years or so isn't much between a man and a woman, and personally I've always hated being pawed by empty-headed children who think they are irresistible because they have just put on their first uniform. No, Kelemen wasn't terribly exciting and he was a little on the wrong side of fifty, but he was one of the nicest people I've ever known.'

'From the way you speak of him I take it that he is dead?'

'Yes. He died about eighteen months ago from a heart attack. It was an awful shock, and I've been terribly restless ever since.'

'Poor you. But why the restlessness? Did he leave you badly off?'

'Oh no. I receive quite a big income from our stud-farm down on the Hortabágy, and as Kelemen had no legitimate children I have the life tenancy of the Tuzolto palace on the

130

Szinháy Utcza. It is one of the smaller ones, but a very pleasant house. And I've a villa on Lake Balaton.'

'Your making a wealthy marriage must have been a great relief to your mother after the difficult time she had in making two ends meet while you were a girl. Is she still alive?'

'Yes, when I married, Kelemen insisted that she should come to live with us, and she has her rooms in my three houses. But for most of the year she lives down on the Hortabágy, and we don't see much of one another these days.'

'Why? Don't you get on together?'

Sabine sat up, shrugged, turned over and lay down again on her tummy. 'I wasn't very clever about my early life, as I think I once told you. My morals were no worse than those of other girls of my class, but the trouble was that they were rich and I was not. They could afford to have their affaires and still make good marriages. My only asset was my looks, so I ought to have made them the bargaining price of marriage, but I didn't; and by the time I met you I had got myself the sort of reputation that doesn't induce a rich young man of good family to lead a girl to the altar for her looks alone. It was that which caused the breach between mother and myself.

'I met Kelemen in Italy, and being older he did not have to have his family's approval to marry me; and, of course, when I returned like a sheep to the fold as a Baroness, mother was delighted. Kelemen's having made an honest woman of me, she naturally expected that after his death I would make another good marriage, but I disappointed her by becoming Ribb's mistress instead. She wouldn't have minded so much if I had gone back to having brief affaires with anyone who took my fancy, but a permanent liaison with such a prominent statesman is impossible to conceal, and she is such a hypocrite that she refuses to recognise that living out of wedlock with one man is much less reprehensible than going to bed with half-a-dozen in the course of a year. So, once again, my name with her is mud.'

As Sabine lay face down on the mattress her chin was resting on her crossed arms. She had taken off her bathing-cap and her dark hair fell on either side of her face leaving a central parting down the back of her head. Where the parting ended there was one small curl about the size of a farthing on the nape of her neck. Looking down on her Gregory felt an almost irresistible desire to bend forward and kiss it; but, forcing the thought from his mind, he said:

'Tell me, why did you enter on this affaire with Ribbentrop?'

'Because I prefer it to playing hole in the corner games with men that I don't really love.'

'Surely you can't love him. Even decent Germans consider him an awful blackguard.'

'I don't love him; but he has something else to offer. He provides me with an intensely interesting life. He is not much of a lover, but he is clever, amusing, tolerant and a charming companion; so I like him quite a lot. As for being a blackguard, that is a matter of opinion. Most men who climb to such a high position in the world have to put the end before the means at times; and when he was Ambassador to Britain there were plenty of people among the English aristocracy who did not regard him as too much of a blackguard to court his friendship. He became a great favourite with the Cliveden set.'

'That's true,' Gregory admitted thoughtfully. 'And I can quite understand how fascinating you find it to be on the inside of all that's going on. Have you ever met Hitler?'

'Oh yes. I have twice stayed at Bertchesgaden.'

'Do tell me about it.'

Suddenly she turned over and sat up. 'No. That's the sort of thing I don't talk about to anyone—and you are the very last person to whom I'd risk giving something away. Anyway, now I've told you all about myself it's quite time you came clean with me.'

It was now half-past twelve, and the terrace was much more crowded than when they had first come out on to it. Two groups of sun-bathers had settled themselves quite near enough to overhear anything Gregory and Sabine said unless they kept their voices very low, so he said:

'Look. I'm not trying to stall on you, and we'll stay here if you like. But we don't want to run the risk of anyone reporting this conversation; so don't you think it would be wiser if we went somewhere a bit more private?'

She considered for a moment. 'Well, perhaps you're right. But where?'

'Let's go up to the Hármashatárhegy.'

'It's quite a long way.'

'What matter? You have a car, and I imagine that you are immune from such annoyances as petrol rationing. The shortage makes it all the more likely that it will be almost deserted. Anyhow, the tables in the garden are set far enough apart for us to talk freely.'

'When we have dressed we could go down and talk in the car.'

'What I have to say will take quite a long time. It will be close on one before we're dressed, and by the time I'm through we are going to be jolly hungry. It would be much more sensible to have our talk while we lunch.'

'But I didn't mean to lunch with you.'

'You've got to lunch somewhere, and this is just the day to lunch up on the mountainside among the birchwoods. Come along!' She was already sitting up; taking one of her hands, he stood up himself and pulled her to her feet. Then he added, with a grin, 'If we were alone in a sandy cove I'd give you a good spanking for being so obstreperous.'

She smiled at that. It called up another memory. They had gone for the weekend to a small hotel on a little frequented part of Lake Balaton. A good-looking American had been staying there on his own and had tried to get off with her. Gregory had told her that he did not want to have to take the fellow outside and give him a lesson; so she must not encourage him by returning his glances, and that if she did he would give her a spanking. She was not the least interested in the American, but out of devilment she had smiled at him that night as they were leaving the dining-room. Gregory had not appeared to notice, but he had suggested a walk in the moonlight and taken her down to the little cove a good half mile away from the hotel. There, after a brief struggle, he had got her in a wrestler's lock with his left knee under her stomach and his right leg crooked over her calves to keep her legs down. Then he had torn off her drawers and spanked her until she had yelled for mercy. It had really hurt, but all the same she had loved it; and when, with tears still wet on her cheeks, he had made love to her afterwards that had been absolutely marvellous.

In the pale blue and silver Mercedes they roared along the bank of the Danube, turned into the valley between the St. Gellért and main Buda hills and out into the country. The way wound up through woods that at times formed cool tunnels and at others dappled the road with sunlight. Moving at such speed along an almost empty road, the drive did not take long, and by half-past one they were seated at a table in the garden of the inn.

Only half-a-dozen tables were occupied so they were able to get one between two others that were empty, but adjacent to the rustic railing that ran round the little plateau which had been made into an out-door restaurant. The ground dropped away below them and from where they sat they could see for many miles. In the distance the capital, with its innumerable domes and spires, looked like a fairy city, and to either side of it the Danube wound away to disappear in the faint haze of the summer heat.

Gregory ordered a cup, made half from sparkling and half from still wine with pricked fresh peaches in it, and they ate cold Fogas, the most delicious of the Lake Balaton fish, garnished with fresh-water prawns. But while the waiter took their order and served them they kept off the subject they had come there to talk about.

He asked her if she had again run across Lord Gavin Fortescue—the dwarf with the distorted body and mind who had very nearly had both of them murdered—and she replied that she thanked all her gods that she had not. He told her then that he had heard rumours that for some years past Lord Gavin had been living in South America.

She enquired affectionately after Sir Pellinore—who had been very kind to her during the difficult time she had spent in England—and he was able to tell her that the elderly Baronet was as hale and hearty as ever. Then, for a good part of the meal, they talked about the extrordinary adventure that had first brought them together.

With their wood-strawberries they drank Tokay. It was not Imperial, as that had left the Imperial cellars only as a personal gift of the Emperor to other crowned heads on their birthdays, or to Ambassadors on their departure after many years *en post* in Vienna. But the wine-waiter dug out for them a little bottle of 1874 from the vineyards of the Duke of Windezgratz. Its grade of Five *Puttanos* indicated that five small barrels—the maximum number—of grapes that had been left on the vines until they were almost raisins had gone into the big cask of earlier-vintaged wine; and age had taken off its original cloying sweetness. This nearest thing to bottled sunshine had the flavour of honey diluted with fine dry sherry, and it provided the perfect complement to their two heaped plates of little red, highly perfumed *Fraises-des-Bois*.

When they were halfway through them Gregory said, 'Now for the awful truth about my nefarious activities.' Then he told her the object of his mission, but he made no mention of how he had progressed with it.

She listened to him with grave wide eyes, and when he had done asked:

'What conclusion have you come to as a result of your enquiries?'

'That I have been wasting my time,' he lied, returning her gaze without the tremor of an eyelid. 'Of course, there are a certain number of people in every country who would like peace at any price; but from those I've talked to there doesn't seem to be much hope of getting Hungary out of the war.'

'Whom have you talked to?'

'A number of chaps that I've picked up in bars. Count László was one, of course; but naturally I dared do no more than sound them while playing my rôle of a Frenchman who is inclined to be a bit pro-de Gaulle. There was only one exception. After three years of war London is hopelessly out of touch with what goes on here, as we have no permanent agents stationed in Hungary at all. But they gave me the name of one man to whom I could come clean with safety. He is a Jewish merchant and he gave me a far from encouraging general idea of what I should hear from other people later, although naturally he and all his race would like to see Hungary go over to the Allies.'

'Naturally. And no one can blame these wretched Jews for hating the Nazis.'

'Well!' he smiled. 'That's all there is to it, and I hope I've convinced you now that I am not a spy.'

'No.' She drew hard on her cigarette. 'You are not a spy but, by God, you are a saboteur. Blowing up all the bridges on the Danube *and* the Arsenal would be just nothing to what you are attempting to do.'

'That depends on how you look at it,' he replied quietly.

'There is only one way I can look at it. You came here with the idea of trying to get Hungary to desert her allies. If she did Germany might lose the war.'

He nodded. 'She will lose it anyway. It's only a matter of time.'

'I don't agree. Hitler now has a firm grip on Europe from Northern Norway to the Pyrenees, and from Crete to the Gulf of Finland. He can do what he likes with Vichy France, which gives him North Africa from Casablanca to the Egyptian frontier, and the few remaining neutrals—Sweden, Spain, Portugal—dare not lift a finger against him. He has only to finish off Russia and, to use your own phrase, it will then "be only a matter of time" before the British and Americans have to agree a peace on such terms as he cares to give them.'

'My dear, you are making the same mistake of under-estimating the British as your friend Ribb did when he was Ambassador and told his master that we hadn't got the guts to fight. Nothing short of invasion and conquest could enable Hitler to impose a peace on Britain; and he missed his chance of that in 1940.'

'It will come again. Once he has put Russia out of the war, he will be able to send two hundred divisions to do the job.'

'That won't help him. They would still have to cross the Channel, and the R.A.F. is now infinitely stronger than it was in the Battle of Britain. An attempt to invade now could lead only to a massacre in which hundreds of thousands of Germans would be drowned.'

After a moment she said, 'You may be right about that; but one thing is certain. Even with their air superiority the British could not invade the Continent. And if they did refuse Hitler's terms that would not just lead to a stalemate. He would send armies down through Turkey and Egypt into Asia and Africa. Within a year he would have conquered India and all Africa down to the Cape, while bigger than ever U-boat fleets got a stranglehold on Britain and starved her into surrender.'

'You are forgetting the United States.'

She shrugged. 'And you are forgetting the big German and Italian populations over there. America's heart is not in the war in Europe. It is the Japs she is so mad against; and they are going to take a lot of beating. They will keep the U.S. busy for two years at least, and that will be quite long enough for Hitler to have forced Britain to her knees.'

Gregory naturally refrained from telling her that America was already pouring men and aircraft into Britain with the intention of attempting the liberation of the Continent as soon as the build up was big enough. Instead he said:

'I quite understand your point of view, but you must admit

136

that you are counting your chickens before they are hatched. All this depends on Russia's being defeated, and she is very far from that yet.'

'On the contrary. Russia is on her last legs. She can't carry on without oil.'

'I know that, but the Germans will find the Caucasus a hard nut to crack. It is much easier to defend than the great open steppes further north. They will be held up in the mountains and get bogged down there for another winter.'

Sabine gave a superior little smile. 'The German General Staff aren't fools; they know that, and they'll do no more than pin large Russian forces down there. Stalingrad is the key to the situation, and that is why the Russians are fighting so hard to hang on to it. Once Stalingrad falls the Volga will be cut. The supplies of oil which are sent up it will cease and the whole of the Russian front north of Stalingrad must collapse.'

With a rather gloomy nod Gregory admitted, 'I suppose you are right about that.' But inwardly he was smiling. The friend of his who had been with him in the *Worcester* had said to him a few weeks previously over lunch, 'The one snag about being on the Joint Planning Staff is that one simply dare not discuss the war with people outside the set-up; and for that reason I've had to give up seeing nearly all my old friends. You see, however careful one is, it is practically impossible to talk about what is going on without the risk of giving something away—not actual plans, of course, but while making some general statement.'

And that was precisely what Sabine had done. She had spoken with such assurance all through their conversation that her opinions were clearly those she had heard expressed by Ribbentrop and his friends, and now she had as good as said that the Germans meant only to maintain heavy pressure in the Caucasus while throwing everything else they could possibly rake up against Stalingrad. Coming from such a source it was a piece of information of inestimable value. For it meant that, there being no threat to the Russians' immensely long front to the north of Stalingrad, they could safely denude it of reserves and use them to stem the German advance in the vital sector.

Gregory felt that if, in all other respects, his journey to Budapest had proved a failure, this plum alone would have made it more than worth while. It strengthened his feeling that, come what might, he must contrive to spend as long as possible in Sabine's company, on the off-chance that from her full scarlet lips there might drop other pearls of strategic knowledge.

'So you see,' she was going on, 'the Russians haven't a hope. With two months still to go before the winter closes in, the Germans have ample time to mount another all out offensive. The army defending Stalingrad will be overwhelmed by sheer weight of numbers, and by Christmas Stalin will have been compelled to throw his hand in.'

That was, of course, the very thing Gregory feared himself, and it was in the hope of saving the Russians by taking pressure off them that he had come to Budapest. In the circumstances, he could produce no sound arguments against her contentions; so he tried another tack:

'Very well, let's concede that, and look at the broader picture. It still leaves Britain and America in; and the Americans may not take as long as you think to finish off the Japs. Meanwhile, I give you my word that the British would sooner eat cats and rats than accept a dictated peace, and they will keep on bombing hell out of the German cities. It might go on for years and years. Think of the untold misery that will be suffered by millions of people on both sides. Surely it's up to all of us to try to find some way to prevent that happening?'

'Naturally,' she agreed at once. 'Nobody but a lunatic would want this awful slaughter to go on for a day longer than it is necessary. But your proposal is no solution. If the Hungarian army withdrew from the Russian front the Germans would have to fill the gap. That would leave them without sufficient reserves to make their break-through. Then the war there would drag on indefinitely; so you would have brought about the very thing you say you are trying to prevent.'

'No. Once Hitler realised that he could not finish the Russians off in the foreseeable future, he would have to think again. Given time to train and equip their huge manpower, the Russians will be able to go over to the offensive, and with every month the United States is growing stronger. Hitler would see the red light and put out peace feelers before the tide started to turn against him. If he did so this winter I think there is an excellent chance that an arrangement could be reached by which both sides might save their faces.'

Gregory did not really believe that either side would now stop fighting short of complete victory, but he thought the possibility worth holding out. It proved quite the contrary, for Sabine shook her head and promptly declared:

'If there were a patched up peace, it would be a bad day for Hungary.'

'Why do you think that?' he enquired.

'Because Bolshevik Russia would have survived, and would continue indefinitely to be a menace to Christian Hungary.'

'That is an old bogey. You put down your own revolution here in 1919 and for the twenty years that followed Hungary was never threatened by Russia; so I don't see why you should think that she might be in the future.'

'You would if you had watched the Soviets' five-year plans going forward through those years, and realised the overwhelming strength Russia would have attained, given another ten years of peace to develop her resources. And, remember, Hungary is very differently situated from England. We had a common frontier with Russia and if those ruthless swine ever get back to it they could mass their huge armies within a hundred-and-fifty miles of Budapest.'

'True. But the Bolshevik revolution is long since over, and there is at least some reason to hope that this war will bring Russia back into lasting friendly relations with the democracies. Anyhow, if Hungary had made peace possible by withdrawing her support from Germany, I am certain that the Allies would guarantee the integrity of her frontiers at the Peace Conference.'

'The Allies!' Sabine exclaimed, her dark eyes going almost black with anger. 'Would you place your life in the hands of a known murderer? Look what the Allies did to Hungary after the last war. That filthy, double-crossing little Welsh lawyer, Lloyd George, the dyed-in-the-wool socialist, Clemenceau, and that idiot American schoolmaster Woodrow Wilson between them stripped Hungary bare, put her on the rack then drew a knife across her throat. It is a miracle, and only by God's grace, that she survived. They stole the lands we have enjoyed for centuries and gave them to anyone who cared to ask. Chunks of Hungary's living body were hacked off and thrown to the Rumanians, Czechs, Italians, Austrians, Croats and Serbians, then what remained of her carcass was left a prey to its own lice—Bela Kun and his bloody revolutionaries.'

Gregory held up a hand in protest. 'I know; I know! But that occurred when the whole world had been turned upside down by its first major catastrophe, and it is admitted now that, while trying to sort things out, the Allied statesmen made all sorts of stupid blunders. Every thinking person has since recognised that the Treaty of Trianon was an iniquitous injustice.'

'Well!' Sabine's voice was intensely bitter. 'What did they ever do about it? Nothing. Take my own case. It so happened that all the estates of my family were in Sclavonia. We were practically beggared and, if we had not had a few things in Budapest that we could sell, we should have starved. But we were lucky. Do you know that no less than one million five hundred thousand Hungarians were handed over to their old enemies? They were deprived of their nationality and treated as if they were serfs or cattle. That we have since got Transylvania, the Banat and Ruthenia back we owe entirely to Hitler. The British and French preferred to make friends of those awful Czechs, then sold them out to their enemies. Trust the Allies! No, thank you. I'd sooner rely on the word of the Devil.'

'I can well understand your feelings; but try not to let them obscure your judgment in taking a long-term view of matters. If Hungary stands by Germany to the end she will almost certainly be deprived of Transylvania and Ruthenia again; whereas if she came over to the Allies now, when her help would be of real value, she would be certain of keeping them and, in addition, probably be given a port on the Adriatic. That is, assuming that the Allies win. But say you are right and Hitler wins, it would be a poor look-out for Hungary. That's why she should help us, otherwise within a couples of years she would be reduced to the state of a German province.'

'Worse things than that could happen to her.'

'Does that mean that you have become a Nazi?'

'No. They go too far. I have no love for the Jews, but this wholesale massacre of them simply does not bear thinking about. Neither do the things that go on in the concentration camps. Of course, putting cranks and trouble-makers behind the bars until they come to their senses is entirely justified, because it is for the good of the majority. It is the only way to nip in the bud riots and disturbances which might otherwise bring injury, loss and hardship to thousands of people. But that can be done the way the Fascists did it in Italy. As I told you, I lived there for quite a time, and I became a great admirer of Mussolini.'

'So was I,' Gregory admitted frankly. 'There is no doubt about it, he saved Italy from going Communist and afterwards did a fine job of work in cleaning the country up. There was a good case too for his going into Abyssinia. The trade in slaves that was carried on from there across the Red Sea to Arabia was nobody's business, and conditions were still so barbarous that in the prisons men and women convicted of petty theft were chained to big logs. No one else wanted the place, so why we couldn't let Musso bring a little daylight into it and colonise it with some of his surplus population goodness only knows.'

'If you thought that, it seems you differed from most of your countrymen.'

Gregory shrugged. 'Oh, we aren't all woolly-minded idealists. Quite a lot of us, and myself included, were all for Franco in the Spanish War. If he had lost, Madrid would be controlled from Moscow by now. Franco has proved a cleverer man than Musso, though, in keeping out of the present struggle. By remaining neutral the Duce had all to gain and nothing to lose. He could have turned Italy from a poor into a rich country by putting his whole population on to manufacturing the goods and growing the food that they could have sold to both sides for pretty well any price Italy liked to ask; whereas he is now committed to maintaining armed forces which will bankrupt his country, and when the end comes he'll be lucky if he gets away with his life.'

'There you go again with your absurd idea that the Allies are going to win.' Sabine gave him a slightly pitying smile. 'It really is only wishful thinking, and Mussolini knew quite well what he was doing when he threw in his lot with Hitler. He couldn't expect to get something for nothing, but now he will get Malta as a stepping stone across the Mediterranean, and Egypt, the Sudan and Kenya; so he'll have the whole of North East Africa from Tripoli to Zanzibar as a new Roman Empire.'

'He won't while Churchill has a kick left in him,' Gregory declared firmly. 'But we are getting away from the point.'

'At least we are agreed that Communism is the great Evil.'

'Yes, I'm with you there. But Hitler is nearly as bad.'

'The devil you know is better than the devil you don't know;

141

and Hitler is by no means all devil. About many things he is a great idealist. Anyhow, much as we Hungarians would like to enjoy complete independence, Hungary will be a paradise with Hitler as her nominal overlord compared to what she would be under the Soviets. That is why we must stick to Germany and do every mortal thing we can to speed her victory. Only one thing matters. The complete and utter destruction of Communist Russia. If we fail in that it will be the end, not only for us here in Central Europe, but sooner or later for you in Britain too.'

Gregory had always been intensely anti-Communist, and he had a horrible feeling that she might be right. But it was not for him to question whether Britain would not ultimately find Russia a more deadly enemy than the Nazis. It was a case of first things first and Hitler represented an evil which must be destroyed. But he felt that he had no further arguments by which he might hope to win Sabine's approval of his mission; so he said:

'Well, there it is. We must agree to differ about immediate ends. However, I hope I have convinced you that, as my mission has met with no success, I am doing no harm here.'

'No.' She shook her head. 'I am not convinced of that. You are an enemy agent and a would-be saboteur. You are an intelligent and resourceful man; so highly dangerous. And I have only your word for it that you are not ferreting out all sorts of secrets which might be helpful to the Allies—and to Russia. It is impossible for me to refrain from taking any action about you.'

He suddenly sat forward. 'Sabine! You can't really mean that you intend to have me arrested?'

'I would, without hesitation, if you were anyone else,' she replied seriously. 'I may have to, and I certainly will if you refuse to accept the way out for you that I have thought of to square matters with my conscience. From here we are going straight back to the Vadászkürt. There you will pack your bags under my supervision. Then I intend to see you off on this evening's non-stop express to Vienna.'

# 11

## The Devil Pulls a Fast One

Gregory smiled, but only to cover his inward consternation. Since she had allowed him to persuade her to come up to the Hármashatárhegy he had been 'counting his chickens; but this showed her to be a much tougher proposition than he had bargained for. If he agreed, he would not be able to attend the Committee meeting fixed for next day, and would have to go home without learning their final decision after hearing General Lakatos's opinion about the number of Allied divisions needed to hold the Nazis in the West. He would be able to report nothing more than that prospects of getting the Hungarian magnates to force their government into breaking with Germany seemed good, instead of bringing back, as he had excellent reason to hope, cut and dried terms. After having stayed on for the past week, and by great tact during the long wrangles of the Committee got them so near agreement, he did not mean to be robbed of his triumph if he could possibly help it. Realising that his only chance now lay in temporising, he said lightly:

'As I have already learned that my mission has no prospect of success, I've nothing against leaving Budapest—except . . .' His smile deepened and his brown eyes looked straight into hers. 'Well, you can guess that one.'

'I take it you mean me.' She gave him a half-smile then quickly looked down and stubbed out her cigarette. 'Thanks for the compliment, but I accept it with reserve. I'm not quite such a fool as to fail to realise that you chose this place for lunch because I brought you here on our first evening together in Budapest.'

'Of course,' he admitted, 'and what a wonderful night that was. We stood hand in hand by the railing, here, watching the million twinkling lights in the city, and the blue-black vault above it sprinkled with a million stars. Then we were driven down the hill back to the Donau Palota to become lovers.'

'You needn't go on. As I was just going to say, I realised at once that by arousing such memories you were hoping to overcome my scruples about you. But it hasn't worked; and it won't.'

'That's not quite fair. On my word of honour those memories are very precious to me; and I have already accepted your decision that I must leave Budapest. I was only expressing how greatly I regret that it must be tonight, as that robs us of the chance to put back the clock for a day or two.'

'Yes, I do believe you about that,' she admitted in a softer voice. 'And I feel the same. Terrible as it is to know that as we sit here in the sunshine thousands of Englishmen and Hungarians are being killed and wounded fighting on opposite sides in this terrible war, that doesn't make any difference to personal relationships. I would have loved to revisit with you all the places where we had such happy times together. But it just can't be done. I made up my mind in the small hours of this morning about how I must handle this, and I'm not going to change it.'

Her frank admission that she was still drawn to him gave him a gleam of hope. If only he could persuade her not to insist on his departure until the next day, he would somehow manage to see Count László that night and learn from him the all-important final decision of the Committee. But for the moment he refrained from pressing her, and said instead:

'I quite understand; but why do you wish me to go to Vienna?'

'Because it is the quickest way out of the country.'

'Maybe; but I have no visa for Germany.'

'I can fix that. It is only half-past three so there's plenty of time and I'll go with you to the Passport Office.'

'They'll take twenty-four hours at least to get a visa from the Germans.'

She shook her head. 'Not if I go with you. There are advantages, you know, in being Ribb's special friend. There are very few things that I couldn't get done in any of the Ministries. We'll have it back in a couple of hours.'

He grinned. 'It's nice to have a pull like that; but I'd very much rather not go to Vienna. The Gestapo are a pretty bright lot, and heaven help me if I slipped up while in their home territory. I would much rather go out through Yugoslavia, as I came in that way. Surely you've no objection to my leaving via Zagreb?'

'Yes, there is a snag to that. The Vienna express stops only at the frontier. I intend to get the Passport Control people to telephone and have you met there, and seen across it. I don't mean as an undesirable, but with special courtesies as a V.I.P. That will ensure you really leave Hungary. The train down to Zagreb makes several stops on the way; so you might get out at one of them and come back.'

'Why should I? As I have already satisfied myself that I can do no good here, there would be no point in my returning.'

She smiled at him quizzically. 'I have only your word for that. Apart from the mission you told me of you may be collecting all sorts of valuable information.'

'I promise you, I'm not. And even if I were, as I have already been here a fortnight, what could another night or two matter?'

'It wouldn't,' she said slowly. 'That is, if I could keep an eye on you.'

'Darling, that is the very thing I am asking you to do.' At that sign of her weakening his response had been immediate; although in making it he set a course that if followed up would put an end to his hope of being able to remain faithful to Erika. Somehow he had got to remain in Budapest overnight —so as to see Count László before leaving—and he could think of only two ways in which he might manage to do that.

One was to get tough with Sabine. He had few scruples, but his sense of what one could or could not do with a clear conscience forbade him luring her into the woods then binding and gagging her, and leaving her there until he put through an anonymous call to the police next morning telling them where they could find her. Gags had an annoying way of being either too loose or too tight. If the former, after a quarter of an hour's hard jaw-working the victim could shout for help; if the latter, within an hour or two the victim died a most painful death from slow suffocation—and he certainly was not prepared to gag Sabine in a way which would cause her more than temporary discomfort. But he could either leave her sitting here while he drove off in her car, or put her out of it on the way back. The snag was that if he used any of these ways of freeing himself from her, within an hour she would have every policeman in Budapest hunting for him, and several hours must elapse before it was any good going to see Count László; so he would have to run a high risk of arrest in order to do that and a still greater one before he could get out of the city and across the frontier.

The other possibility of pulling his chestnuts out of the fire was to persuade Sabine that he was in earnest about wanting to remain in Budapest solely on her account. If he could do that, he felt confident that a chance would occur for him to slip away from her for an hour or two and get his business settled. It was unquestionably the sounder plan and now that he was launched upon it he went on quickly:

'Listen! There is an alternative route to Zagreb which runs along the south shore of Lake Balaton. Why not let's go down for the weekend to that little hotel where we stayed before? That is two-thirds of the way to the frontier; so after we've had a lovely reunion it would mean only an hour in the train for you to come down and see me over it yourself.'

'You have forgotten about Ribb.'

'But I thought you said that he was going back to Berlin tomorrow afternoon. We could still get down to that little hotel in time for dinner; and we'd have all Sunday—or a whole week there together if you liked.'

'That is out of the question. I must leave for Berlin on Wednesday in any case; but it is really tonight that I was thinking of.'

It was 'tonight' that he was thinking of too; but the fact that she was now giving serious consideration to his proposal made his heart beat a little faster, as he said: 'You told me that you expected Ribb to be tied up with Admiral Horthy this evening, and you as good as promised to dine with me; so why shouldn't you?'

'He will be, and I could.' She pulled hard on a newly-lit cigarette. 'But I won't be entirely free to do as I like until he is on the train for Berlin. He is staying with the Regent at the Palace, of course; and all these top men work themselves so desperately hard that it is unlikely that he will come to my house in the Szinháy Utcza to say good-bye to me until lunch-time tomorrow. But one never knows.'

'Damn him!' Gregory muttered, with a scowl. But actually he was thinking 'This could not suit my book better. If I can get the hours between midnight and dawn to work in there will be no excuse for me to stay on and go down with Sabine to Balaton.' At the same time a small devil was telling him insistently that he would be behaving like a lunatic and always regret it if he left her in the lurch and ran away from this lovely gift the gods were now offering him. Quickly he quieted

146

the devil with the thought that he was not forced to decide either way as yet, then he said:

'Anyhow, there is nothing to stop us dining and dancing together, and meeting again tomorrow afternoon after Ribb has gone.'

'Oh, but there is!' came her quick rejoinder. 'I had made up my mind not to lose sight of you until I saw you on to the train for Vienna. After all, I can't ignore the possibility that you have made useful contacts during your fortnight here, and that a last talk with them before you go might enable you to take valuable information back to London.'

She had now come so perilously near the truth that he could only look innocent, shrug and say, 'If you think that, I'll agree to any precautions that you like to suggest against my meeting people.'

After a moment's thought, she said, 'I'll have to make you my prisoner. We will collect your things from the Vadászkürt and you must come to my house. My servants are fully trustworthy as far as not letting on to Ribb is concerned; and they will see to it that you don't go out at any time that I am otherwise occupied.'

He laughed then. 'What an amazing situation. There can never have been another like it. Think of it as a headline— "From patriotic motives famous beauty keeps her lover prisoner." But, joking apart, I surrender willingly. Bless you, my sweet, for giving us this chance to recapture past joys.'

Sabine gave herself a little shake, then laughed back at him. 'After all the good resolutions I made this morning I must be crazy to do this. But the moment I set eyes on you last night I felt certain something of the kind was bound to happen.'

Laying his hand gently on hers he murmured, 'It won't be my fault if you regret it.' And at the time he meant what he said; although at the same moment he was thinking that, in spite of her servants, short of her locking him up in a cellar he would have lost his cunning if he could not find some way of leaving her house undetected in the early hours of the morning.

Now that their long battle of wits was over and a decision had been taken, they made no further reference to the subject, to the war, to Ribbentrop or to anything which had a bearing on the strangeness of their situation. Like two knights of the same companionship who have thrown off their armour after having had to joust against one another, they suddenly became completely relaxed, free of all strain and able to talk and laugh together without further thought of the hidden implications of what they might be saying.

The waiter had already cleared away but they sat on there in the now almost deserted garden through the long sunny afternoon. She told him of her life in Italy and later of when she was married to the Baron, and he told her of some of the intriguing jobs he had done for Sir Pellinore before the war. But again and again they came back to their own affaire with the words 'Do you remember . . .' Later they ordered Café Viennoise, which was served iced in tall glasses with thick cream, straws and long thin spoons. By the time they got up to go their minds were as well attuned as if they had never parted, and as they strolled slowly across to the car park they were holding hands.

It was nearly six o'clock when she dropped him near the Vadászkürt, as they had already agreed that it would be better that she should not be seen picking him up from it with his luggage. She had no fear now that he might run out on her and disappear underground, and he had no intention of doing so; because now that she had consented to his staying on in Budapest he felt confident that he could complete his business without the risk he would have had to run had he let her down.

After asking at the desk for his bill, he went upstairs to his room and put through a telephone call. He knew that the Committee would already have met at Count Szegényház's house, but as the meeting had been called for half-past-five he thought it unlikely that they would have yet reached their final decision, and in that he proved correct. Count Lászlo, to whom he spoke, could only tell him that the proceedings had opened well. He then explained to the Count in guarded language that he had become involved with the Baroness and was no longer a free agent. He added that he would be staying at her house for the night, but hoped to get away some time during it and, if he could, would come to Lászlo's house; then he arranged that should he fail to do so the Count would call at Sabine's the following morning at nine o'clock, and insist on seeing him on a private matter.

Having insured in this way that he would get the vital information, even if Sabine did lock him up for the night, he quickly

148

packed his things, paid his bill and took a carriage to her house.

He found her small 'palace' to be similarly constructed to the Zapolya's much larger one. There was a lodge for the gate-keeper at one side of a big semi-circular arch, and beyond the arch a square courtyard. Along its sides were garages, stables, laundry, brew-house, etc., with accommodation for the servants above them. At its far end a glass-roofed vestibule led to the main hall which was evidently also used as a sitting-room; for, although August was not yet out, wood fires were burning in big fireplaces on either side of it, and in front of both of these were a settee, easy chairs and occasional tables. In the centre of the hall a broad shallow staircase led up to a balustraded gallery at either end of which were suits of Turkish armour, then corridors leading to the first floor rooms and to narrower staircases running up to a second storey. The rooms were all low for their size; so the vaulted ceiling of the double-tier hall was not too high for comfort, and the upper surfaces of its cream stone walls being broken up with tapestries of the chase prevented it from being cold in appearance.

After Gregory had waited there for a few minutes Sabine came down the staircase. She had changed out of her day things into a house-coat of crimson velvet. The colour threw up both her pale magnolia skin and the dark beauty of her eyes and hair. As she came smiling towards him, he caught his breath; for, seen against this background, she might well have been a princess who had stepped straight out of a Ruritanian romance.

He told her so, and she raised a well-arched eyebrow.

'Thanks for the charming thought; but perhaps it's as well that I'm not. No doubt they looked lovely enough, but they had nothing under their clothes but solid pink ice cream. I imagine you would be quite peeved if I sent you back to England with no more exciting memory of me than a half-dead rose thrust into your hand at parting.'

'I certainly should,' he laughed, and took a quick step towards her. But she put up her hand with a swift glance of warning. A butler had just come through a side door carrying a bottle in an ice bucket and a tray with glasses. Opening the wine, he poured it and brought two glasses over to them. As Sabine took hers, she said:

'I thought you would prefer champagne to a cocktail.'

Raising his glass he replied, 'Any time, anywhere; but never more so than here with you.'

Sitting down they began to discuss how they should spend the evening. In gay Budapest, both in peace and war, it was not unusual for couples to dine at one place then put in an hour or two at each of three or four others afterwards, and there were several of their old haunts that they would have liked to revisit; but Gregory knew that he had now burnt his boats and, without any mention being made of the matter, it was common ground that from after dinner onwards they could provide better entertainment for one another than any night-club had to offer; so their choice had to be restricted to one place in which to dine.

Eventually they decided on the Arizona, which was strictly speaking a night-club; but its floor-shows were the most original in Budapest, and a first performance was given for people who dined there, so the choice would enable them to kill two birds with one stone.

When they had finished their wine Sabine said, 'I'd better show you your room, so that you can bathe and change. I've had my bath already so if half an hour is enough for you I'll be down again by then.'

At the head of the staircase she turned left along the gallery, threw open a door at the far end of the corridor, and said, 'This is my room. Do you like it?'

Gregory followed her inside. The room was spacious but low ceilinged, furnished in excellent taste, and there hung about it the subtle perfume which, even had Sabine not been there, conjured up the image of a lovely and fastidious woman. At its far end there was a wide semi-circular window and, walking over to it, she drew aside two of the curtains. Dark had fallen but it was still light enough to see the graceful Swing Bridge two hundred feet below them, the Danube and beyond it the spires of Pest merging into the coming night.

For a full moment they stood side by side in silence. Suddenly her hand clutched his and she turned towards him. Next moment she was in his arms. His mouth came down on her eagerly parted lips in a long rich kiss. They broke it only to gasp for breath then their mouths locked again in another. Her arms tightened round his neck and he could feel her small breasts crushed against his chest. The muscles of her body grew rigid and she began to quiver as though shaken by a fit of ague. Throwing back her head she exclaimed in a hoarse whisper:

'Darling! Oh, darling; I want you so badly. I can hardly wait.'

Although they were alone his voice too came in a whisper, as he strained her to him and replied, 'Wait! My sweet; why should we wait?'

'No!' With sudden resolution she jerked her arms from across his shoulders, put her hands against them and forced him away. 'No! Not yet! It would spoil things for us . . . later.'

Reluctantly he released her and muttered, 'I suppose you're right. But with you in my arms time has no meaning any more.'

'It hasn't for me either. But we've all night before us, and the moon will not be up for two hours yet. I want you first to love me in the moonlight, just as you did on our first night together. Do you remember?'

'God alive! As though I could ever forget!' He grasped her arm and gave her a slight shake. 'You had better show me my room now, though; otherwise you won't get your wish.'

Drawing a quick breath, she murmured, 'You're right. I ought never to have brought you in here. Your room is immediately above this. Come; I'll show you.'

Out in the corridor she pulled aside a velvet curtain that masked a narrow flight of stairs, and led him up them to the room above. Still speaking in a conspiratorial whisper, she said, 'Half-an-hour. No longer.' Then, blowing him a kiss, she turned away, and ran down the stairs.

His heart still pounding heavily, Gregory looked about him. It was a double guest room and his bags had already been unpacked. To the right an open door showed a bathroom dimly lit; at the far end of the room there was a deep bay window similar to that in Sabine's. Walking over, he pulled aside a curtain, opened a section of the window and peered out.

Immediately below him was a balcony on to which Sabine's room opened. Below that, on the courtyard level, projected a wide terrace, and from it a steep retaining wall sloped down to a street on a lower level. That, he decided, was the way he must go when he left the house in the early hours of the morning. It would be much simpler than fumbling his way downstairs in the dark and making his way out by the vestibule. The drops to Sabine's balcony and from there to the terrace looked quite easy; and by then she should be sunk in the deep dreamless sleep that follows satisfied passion, so there would be little chance of her hearing him outside her window.

He was much relieved at finding his way clear to paying a call round about dawn on Count László. That would ensure them an uninterrupted private talk; whereas, had he had to rely on the sheet anchor he had thrown out of the Count's coming to Sabine's, it was possible that she might have smelt a rat and refused to allow them to remain alone together.

Now, thrusting from his mind all thoughts but those of joyous anticipation in the evening that lay before him, he went into the bathroom. Finding that a bath had already been run and scented for him, he sniffed appreciatively, pulled off his clothes and got into it. After a quick shave he dressed in his evening things and was back down in the hall just under the half-hour that Sabine had stipulated.

She joined him a few minutes later, now dressed in a light bodice and long full skirt of yellow silk brocade, and with diamond pendants sparkling below her ears. He helped her on with her sable coat, then they went out to the car.

The Arizona lay across the river in Pest, but it took them only ten minutes to get there. Having parked the car in a side-street nearby, they walked the last hundred yards through the still, warm night to the entrance of the Club, while Gregory recalled to Sabine the last time they had been there. The place had then been owned by a huge fat woman possessed of a most ingenious imagination and a passion for dressing up. She always appeared at least once in her own cabarets, and on that occasion the high spot of the performance had been a tableau inspired by ancient Rome. Her mountainous body draped in a toga, and a laurel wreath perched on her sparse hair, she had lain upon a couch depicting one of the more decadent Caesars, while a giant negro held a feather fan above her head, and a bevy of her beautiful young girls posed nearly nude around her, offering fruit, wine, a peacock pie and other delights.

As Sabine assured him that this jolly old trollop was still the proprietress of the Arizona, they entered the Club, then separated while Sabine went into the cloakroom to leave her furs. Gregory had come hatless and coatless; so he had nothing to leave, but he took the opportunity to pay a visit to the 'gents'.

Just inside the door, he found himself looking straight into the vulture-like face of Captain Cochefert. The Vichy security man recognised him at once, and exclaimed with a toothy smile:

'Why, *Monsieur le Commandant!*' Then his voice sank to a lower note and he added, 'I have brought a guest here this evening whom I am sure you will know.'

At that moment the door of one of the cabinets opened, and out minced a plumpish man with hair cut *en brosse,* a heavy jowl and a thin sharp nose. In utter consternation Gregory found himself staring at his most deadly enemy—the chief of the Foreign Department of the Gestapo, *Herr Gruppenführer* Grauber.

# 12

# No Holds Barred

Grauber was in his middle forties. His pasty complexion and a quite noticeable paunch gave the impression that physically he was not formidable, but they were deceptive; his broad shoulders gave him the strength of a bull, his long arms the grip of an orang-outang and, in spite of the smallness of his feet, he could move with the swiftness of a cat. Uusually, however, for strong arm measures he relied on a member of his harem—a selection of blond young S.S. men as brutal and perverted as himself—one or more of whom generally travelled with him.

His small, light eyes had been set close together, but since November '39 he had had only one. Gregory had bashed out the other with the butt of a pistol. Its socket now held a glass imitation and, as it did not swivel with the other, the unnerving thought leapt to the mind that the Gestapo Chief was capable of looking two ways at once.

Through his Department, U.A.-1, he controlled by far the greater part of Germany's secret agents outside the Fatherland—the exceptions being the old military organisation under Admiral Canaris and a small service run by the Foreign Office to provide Ribbentrop with special information. His rank was equivalent to that of a Lieutenant-General and he was responsible only to Himmler. He spoke many languages and was an adept at disguise. Frequently he went about dressed in women's clothes, as he had a flair for playing feminine parts, much aided by a naturally effeminate voice. But tonight he was dressed in a well-cut dinner jacket.

Gregory had first come up against him quite early in the war, at his secret headquarters in Hampstead. He had had an acid bath there for disposing of inconvenient corpses, but first induced his helpless victims to give him useful information by applying the lighted end of his cigar to their eyeballs. When in Finland, a few months later, he had beaten Erika for twenty minutes every morning on the muscles of her arms and legs with a thin steel rod. It was that which had determined Gregory, if he ever got the chance, to kill him very, very, slowly.

That this was not the chance Gregory needed no telling. In fact the odds were all the other way, and if he fell alive into Grauber's hands he could expect to die even more slowly.

As it was still early, few people had as yet arrived at the Arizona. In the wash-room there were only Gregory, Cochefert, Grauber and the Hungarian attendant. The latter, unaware of the dramatic situation that had so suddenly developed within a few feet of him, was cheerfully swishing out the basin that Cochefert had just used. Gregory, his mouth a little open from stricken amazement, had his eyes riveted on the unhealthy face of the *Gruppenführer*. Grauber, equally astonished at this unexpected meeting, returned his stare without moving a muscle. Both were for a few moments like birds that have suddenly become paralysed from meeting the hypnotic glance of a snake. Of the three, Cochefert alone retained a normal manner. Still smiling at Gregory, he waved a hand behind him, then said in French, and too low for the attendant to catch his words:

'You see, Colonel, I am honoured tonight by the presence of your Chief.'

As though the sound of his voice had released two springs, the other two sprang to life. Grauber was no coward, and such was his hatred of Gregory that to secure him for the torture

154

chamber he would have risked his other eye. Gregory knew that if once he allowed himself to be arrested he would be better dead. His one hope was that he might render both men *hors de combat* before they could call in the police. Sabine's car was little more than a hundred yards away. If he could only reach it he would be able to get clear of Budapest before a serious hunt for him could be set going.

His right hand jumped to his hip pocket. It was there that he always carried his little automatic. His adrenalin glands suddenly began to function overtime, and beads of sweat started out on his forehead. The pocket was empty. While he had been changing, his thoughts had been so full of Sabine that he had forgotten to transfer the pistol from his day clothes. If either Grauber or Cochefert was carrying a weapon he was now at their mercy.

Grauber was not. At Gregory's swift gesture a flicker of fear had shown in his eyes. Then he caught Gregory's expression of dismay and saw his hand come away from his hip empty. With a cry of triumph, he thrust the astonished Cochefert aside and hurled himself forward.

There was not much room to manœuvre. To get past Cochefert the *Gruppenführer* had had to step up on to the raised strip of floor on which stood the line of half-a-dozen white porcelain *pissoirs*. Doing so threw him slightly off his balance. Seizing on this advantage, Gregory rushed in, ducked beneath the long arm thrust out to grab him and landed a blow on his enemy's body. With a howl of fury Grauber went over sideways, striking his head against one of the *pissoirs* and collapsing into it.

Barely ten seconds had elapsed since Gregory walked in through the door. The clash had occurred so swiftly that Cochefert had had no chance to speculate upon the reason for it. He still believed that Gregory was *Obersturmbannführer* Einholtz of the Gestapo, so was taken completely by surprise when he and Grauber rushed upon one another. But Grauber was unquestionably the senior. As he went over sideways and crashed into the porcelain gutter, discipline decided the Frenchman that he must side with him. Stepping a pace back from Gregory, which brought him up against the opposite wall, he pulled a small revolver from his pocket.

Gregory had already swung round towards him. Lifting his right foot he gave Cochefert a swift kick on the shin. The

Frenchman's reaction was to lift his injured leg with a gasp of pain and, as his stomach contracted, the upper part of his body jerked forward. Instantly Gregory chopped with the flat of his hand at the forearm of the hand that held the gun. With a second gasp Cochefert dropped the little weapon. It clattered on the tile floor.

Both stooped to make a grab for it. Their heads came together with a crack. They staggered back; but Cochefert was quick enough to give it a swift sideways kick. It slithered away out of Gregory's reach before he could make another dive at it.

Meanwhile, with a spate of blasphemous curses, Grauber had picked himself up and was now yelling, 'Seize him! Seize him! Call the police! He must not escape!'

But there was no exit to the room other than the one Gregory was blocking; so the attendant could not get out to call anyone. He was entirely unaware of the implications of the fray, and was naturally anxious to keep out of it. His only contribution was to snatch up the gun, which slid to a halt at his feet and, with laudable eagerness to prevent its being used, throw it into the dirty towel basket.

As Gregory was still at the door end of the room he could, at any moment, have swung round, wrenched it open and fled. But unless he could prevent Cochefert and Grauber dashing out on his heels, he knew that he would never reach Sabine's car. With shouts of 'Murder!' and 'Stop thief!' they would secure the aid of the Club door-porter and various other people, one of whom would be certain to catch hold of, or trip, him. In another attempt to render them *hors de combat,* so that he could get at least a flying start, he first feinted at Cochefert then landed a terrific blow on the Frenchman's thin curved beak. Swinging round on Grauber, he tried the same tactics, but the more skilful German ducked the blow and closed with him.

Half blinded by the pain, and with blood dripping from his nose, Cochefert staggered aside. The other two went down in a heap with Gregory on top. Both of them knew every dirty trick worth knowing and neither had the slightest scruple about using them.

The German got one hand on Gregory's throat and with the thumb of the other attempted to jab out his nearest eye. Gregory tried to knee his antagonist in the groin, but failed in that. Then striving with one hand to break Grauber's grip on his throat, he struck savagely with the other, using the hard side of the palm, down on his adversary's Adam's apple.

They strove for mastery with gritted teeth, straining their muscles to the utmost and jerking from side to side as they fought. Grauber managed to keep a firm grip on Gregory's windpipe. Only by keeping his chin well down could he save himself from complete strangulation, and his breath was now coming in short, sobbing gasps. Yet he knew that his vicious chops at the German's Adam's apple must be causing him exquisite agony, and he could see that his one eye was growing misty. A few more strokes and pain must render him unconscious.

But there was still Cochefert. For a moment or two the Frenchman stood swaying drunkenly as the result of the terrible blow which had broken the bone in his nose. Then, lurching to the row of washbasins, he snatched up a large bottle of hair-oil, turned, raised it aloft and brought it down on the top of Gregory's head. The bottle smashed; the scented oil streamed down over his face. With stars and circles flashing in sudden blackness before his eyes, it was he who then slid into unconsciousness, falling sideways across the body of his groaning enemy.

He was not out for long. By the time they had carried him to a car and thrown him on to its back seat he was again aware of his surroundings, if only vaguely. For a good two minutes he lay slumped in his corner wondering why he had such a pain in his head, how he had got where he was, and where he was being taken. Then his having run slap into Grauber in the men's toilet room at the Arizona suddenly came back to him.

Instantly everything else connected. His heart seemed to contract as the full knowledge of his position flooded in upon him. If Sabine had proved adamant, that would have been bad enough. But before she could have had him arrested he would anyhow have had a flying start; and if he had had the ill luck to be caught there would still have been a chance that, with the help of his Hungarian friends, he might have got away again. There would be no chance of that now that he had fallen into Grauber's hands. The *Gruppenführer* was not the man to let a prisoner communicate with anyone, or leave him the smallest loophole for even a forlorn hope of escape.

Still more shattering thought, Grauber's bitter personal hatred of him would undoubtedly lead to his being treated with the utmost brutality.

As he opened his eyes a new wave of pain shot through his head. In front of him a man in a chauffeur's cap was at the wheel; so it looked as if they were in a civilian car. Next to the driver sat a bareheaded man wearing a white jacket. Peering at him in the dim light, Gregory wondered who he could be; suddenly it flashed upon him that it was the wash-room attendant.

Turning his head very slightly, in order not to give away that he had come to, he looked sideways at the man beside him. The man's kepi showed that he was a Hungarian policeman. Beyond the policeman there was another figure, occupying the other corner of the back seat. After a few moments Gregory got a glimpse of him that confirmed his worst fears. It was Grauber.

The distance between the Arizona and the Police Station was quite short, and the still-dazed Gregory had hardly catalogued his fellow passengers before the car pulled up. He now had his senses about him sufficiently to feel dismay. Had the drive been twice the distance he might at its end have been recovered enough to attempt making a bolt for it as they got out, but he was still terribly shaky.

Grauber opened the rear door on his side and slid out on to the pavement. The policeman took Gregory by the shoulder and gave him a shake. Feeling that there was nothing to be gained by having himself carried, he pretended to rouse up and lurched after the policeman out of the car.

His brain kept on telling him that if he once allowed himself to be taken inside he was finished. Only death could follow; and death at Grauber's hands would be more painful than anyone who had not been inside a Gestapo torture chamber could imagine. Yet, as he struggled out of the car, his knees almost gave under him, and he realised that he could not have staggered a couple of paces before being set upon and dragged into the Station. In an agony of mind he allowed the policeman to put a hand under his arm and guide him up the steps into the building.

It was only when the little group, minus the chauffeur, stood facing a Sergeant across his desk in an office that Gregory realised that Grauber was also a prisoner. Apparently the two of them, and Cochefert as well, had all been arrested for causing a disturbance in a public place; but the Frenchman, owing to his nose having been broken, had been taken by another policeman to hospital.

Now that, in spite of the pain in his head, Gregory's brain was functioning again, he exerted it to its utmost capacity in striving to find a way in which he could turn this totally unexpected situation to his advantage. He had plenty of money on him; so if only he could induce the police to accept a cash deposit of any sum they liked to name as security that he would turn up to face a charge before a magistrate in the morning, he might yet wriggle out of Grauber's clutches.

Yet, even as he toyed with this exhilarating possibility, he knew in his heart that he would never get away with it. Grauber was one of the highest Police Chiefs of an allied power. He had only to produce his credentials and say that the fracas had occurred solely as the result of his recognising a British spy for him to have his enemy clapped into a cell, and walk out himself a free man.

And that, in effect, was what happened. The wash-room attendant made his statement about the fight he had witnessed. Grauber produced his Gestapo card and declared Gregory's passport as Commandant Tavenier to be a fake. The Sergeant telephoned to the Gestapo liaison office in Budapest and, having given a description of Grauber, satisfied himself about the German's identity. He then asked, at Grauber's request, that a car should be sent to collect the *Gruppenführer,* and declared his intention of holding Gregory on the charge preferred.

Grauber angrily protested that a civil charge of having created a disturbance was not good enough. He wanted Gregory to be held as a dangerous enemy agent awaiting examination; and, further, demanded the right to proceed forthwith to examine him himself.

At that the Sergeant demurred, arguing that some evidence must be brought to support such a charge; and that, anyhow, it would be time enough to produce it when Gregory was brought before a magistrate next day. He added that he could not allow the prisoner to be cross-questioned there and then, as it was against regulations.

At that Grauber flew into a rage. Thumping the desk with his fist he shrilled out falsetto threats of what he would do to the Sergeant unless he was given his way. The Sergeant, overawed by the high rank of the German Police Chief, decided that discretion was the better part of valour, so agreed to submit the matter to the Station Commandant.

While Gregory waited on tenterhooks a constable was sent to fetch the Commandant. Five minutes later he joined them: a square-shouldered tough-looking Captain of Police, with a slight cast in his left eye. After he had been given a brief résumé of what had occurred, he dismissed the wash-room attendant and took Gregory and Grauber into a small, barely furnished waiting-room.

The Captain's eyes were blue although his nose was flat and his cheekbones high, indicating Tartar descent. For a moment he stood sizing up the two men before him, then he said to Grauber:

'It seems there is little doubt about your identity, *Herr Gruppenführer*, so naturally I wish to be as helpful as I can. Although it is against all ordinary procedure to allow one of two people picked up on the same charge to question the other about something entirely different, since you say the matter is urgent you can go ahead.'

With a brief word of thanks, Grauber turned to Gregory and snapped: 'Now! What are you up to in Budapest?'

Gregory knew that he could not bluff Grauber; but he hoped that he might keep the mind of the Police Captain open by replying, 'I see no reason why I should submit to being questioned by you; but the sooner this matter is sorted out the better. It is evident that when you attacked me you mistook me for someone else. I am a Frenchman and I own a truffle farm in Périgord. I am here to sell my truffles.'

'A fine story!' Grauber sneered. 'And now I will tell you why I am here.'

'Thank you.' Gregory shrugged. 'But as I have never met you before I am not in the least interested.'

'Ah! But you will be! I am here because word reached my office a few days ago that a conspiracy is afoot in which a little clique of Hungarian magnates is plotting to bring pressure on their Government to sell out to the English.'

Gregory managed to keep his face expressionless; but Grauber's words were a sickening blow. His fears, that a leak to the Nazis would result from the casual disregard of security displayed by Count Zapolya's friends after the first big meeting at the Nobles Club, had proved well founded. He could only pray that so far Grauber had not secured any actual evidence against the members of the Committee, and hope for a chance to get a warning to them. Meanwhile the plump, pasty-faced German was going on:

'To run into you was a real stroke of fortune. On your past record as a secret agent, I would wager *Reichsmarschall* Goering's cellar against a bottle of sour claret that you are at the bottom of this plot.'

'You are completely wrong. I know nothing whatever about it.'

'Oh, yes, you do! There is no war activity in Budapest which would bring a man of your calibre here, but such big game as this is just your meat. Now; I want the names of everyone you have met since you arrived in Hungary.'

'If I had anything to hide I would not tell you; but during the fortnight I have been here I have met scores of people. My first few days were a little dull but I got into conversation with all sorts in the bars and at the swimming pools, and if you know how hospitable the Hungarians are you will appreciate that soon I had not a dull moment. There is hardly a night that I have not been to a party, and . . .'

'Enough!' Grauber cut him short. 'It is useless to try to fog the issue by giving me a list of names a yard long. I want those of the people who know you to be an Englishman.'

'There are none; for the simple reason that I am not one.'

At that moment there came an interruption. The Sergeant poked his head round the door and announced the arrival of the car sent to collect Grauber. Two his aides-de-camp had come in it, tall pink-cheeked young Gestapo men; as the Sergeant stood aside they entered the room, clicked their heels and saluted.

Grauber gave them a nod and waved a hand towards Gregory. '*Herrschaft*, we are in luck this evening. Allow me to present to you Mr. Gregory Sallust, the most skilful and dangerous of all British operatives. He has personally killed several of our colleagues and been responsible for the death of many more. It was to him that I owe the loss of my eye, and in due course I mean to pluck out both of his with my own hands. However, at the . . .'

Simulating intense anger, Gregory suddenly burst out, 'This is fantastic! Not a word of it is true! My name is Etienne

Tavenier, and I am a retired Major of the French Army. I have documents to prove it.'

'Documents!' sneered Grauber. 'Do you take me for a child? Of course you would have come provided with documents, but not one of them will be worth the paper it is written on.'

Gregory knew only too well that, as soon as Cochefert was sufficiently recovered to be brought in on the matter, to continue the pretence that he was Tavenier would be completely futile. Moreover, as it was from the Vadászkürt that his false passport had reached Lieutenant Puttony, and the Arizona was in the same district, it seemed highly probable that the Lieutenant was attached to this station. Should he come on the scene that would equally blow the Tavenier story. But Gregory had no other means of repudiating Grauber's charges; so the only course open to him was to stick to his guns in front of the Hungarian Police Captain, in the desperate hope that some chance to escape might offer if only he could gain a little time. In a further effort to maintain his bluff, he shouted at Grauber:

'My documents are in perfect order! They have been checked by the police and by that *Deuxième Bureau* Captain who was about to introduce me to you when you attacked me. If you don't believe me, ask him; or send a telegram to Vichy. They know all about me there.'

The Hungarian, obviously impressed, nodded. 'Yes. After all, it is quite possible that you are mistaken, *Herr Gruppenführer*. This man may be whom he says he is.'

'He is an English spy, I tell you!' Grauber's high-pitched voice rose almost to a scream.

'I am nothing of the kind!' Gregory yelled back with all the excitability of an angry and injured Frenchman. 'Telegraph to Vichy about me, and you will be made to eat your words.'

Again the Hungarian nodded. 'Why should we not do that? I will hold the prisoner until morning, and by then we should have a reply.'

White with fury, Grauber banged his clenched fist on the table. 'I need no telegram from Vichy. I know this man as well as I know my own face in a mirror. And the enquiry I am engaged upon is urgent. As soon as it gets out that he has been arrested the men he has been conspiring with will take fright. They will go into hiding, or try to leave the country.

That is why I have got to have the truth out of him here and now.'

'Since he maintains that he is not the man you think him, I don't see how you can.'

Grauber gave a short, sniggering laugh, and turned to leer at his two S.S. men. 'We'll get it all right, won't we, boys?'

They both grinned, and the taller said, 'Leave it to us, *Herr Gruppenführer.*'

Turning back to the Hungarian, Grauber said abruptly, 'Take us down to a cell and provide us with a piece of cord. We'll string him up by his thumbs to start with and see if that will make him open his mouth.'

The Hungarian hesitated a moment, then he said, 'I am anxious to oblige the *Herr Gruppenführer,* but I don't think I could do that.'

'And why not, if you please?' Grauber asked in a suddenly silky voice.

'For one thing, his identity is still uncertain.'

'You said that you are anxious to oblige me. You can do so by taking my word about that.'

'I have already stretched a point in allowing you to question him about a matter that has no connexion with the charge on which I am holding him.'

'*Teufel nochmal!*' Grauber exploded. 'Is Hungary Germany's ally, or is she not?'

'*Herr Gruppenführer,* the fact that our two countries are allied has no bearing on police procedure.'

'It has, *Herr Hauptmann.* Our Governments, our fighting services, our police and yours are all pledged to aid each other by every means in their power. I now formally request your help in the carrying out of my duties.'

Gregory was listening to the discussion with bated breath. He now had little enough to pin his hopes upon in any case, but the outcome of this swift exchange of words meant for him the difference between a few hours' respite and being put to the torture within the next few minutes. The palms of his hand were damp with apprehension as he watched the Hungarian's face. It was a strong face, but he feared very moment to see it weaken under the pressure that it was certain Grauber would bring to bear.

To the German's request he replied, 'I have no wish to withhold my co-operation; but the procedure of the two police

163

forces differ, and to do as you suggest would be contrary to our regulations here.'

'I suppose you mean that, when a prisoner refuses to talk, you are too squeamish to make him?' Grauber sneered.

'Let us put it that in Hungary we do not approve of torture.'

'Do you presume to criticise German methods?'

'I criticise nothing. I only obey the orders of my superiors.'

Grauber was seething with rage. His thin sandy eyebrows drew down in a scowl and his single eye gleamed with malice, as he said, 'Listen, my little Captain. My rank is far superior to yours and should you continue to oppose my wish I am quite powerful enough to insist on your own Chief disciplining you. Now! No more nonsense. Send for a piece of cord and lead us to a cell.'

To Gregory's intense relief the threat had the contrary effect to that he had feared. The Hungarian's chunky face went white but his blue eyes suddenly blazed with anger. Thrusting his chin forward, he snapped, 'This is not Germany! You can't yet ride rough-shod over everybody here! Say what you damn well like! I'm not afraid to be judged by my own people for having refused to let you turn my Station into a torture chamber. Now! Get out of here, and be quick about it.'

Beneath his breath Gregory murmured, 'Well done! Well done! May the gods reward you for your courage.' But a moment later he realised that he was not even temporarily free of Grauber yet. The *Gruppenführer* had not climbed to his eminence as a Gestapo Chief by bullying alone; he had an extraordinarily flexible mind, and much subtle cunning. Quite quietly he turned to his two aides and said:

'*Herrschaft*, I have often told you that you can learn much from the errors of your superiors. It is of great importance to us that I should get the truth out of this man Sallust without delay; but as I am placed at the moment I have not a free hand to do so. In my eagerness, I blundered. Observe, please, this Hungarian officer carefully. Look at his broad forehead, his frank expression and his well-developed jaw. These are the indications of an honest man, a humanitarian and one who has the courage to stick to his convictions. I should have taken stock of those myself, and realised that I could gain nothing by threatening him. We consider that our harsher methods of obtaining information swiftly are justified by the emergencies of war. But in this the Hungarians differ from us. By refusing to allow us to use our methods of persuasion in his Station, he was only carrying out his standing orders. For that we must admire him. Tomorrow, instead of a complaint, I shall now put in to his superiors a testimonial to his commendable adherence to his duties. To do otherwise would be dishonourable and tend to weaken, instead of strengthen, our ties with our Hungarian allies.'

After pausing for a moment, Grauber turned to the Hungarian and went on. 'But the *Herr Hauptmann* will appreciate that delay in examining this man may prove fatal to the success of my mission here. Therefore I cannot doubt that he will agree to a solution which will both enable me to do my duty, and save him from any feeling that he has failed in his. I should have thought of it before. It is so simple. I will sign a receipt for the prisoner and an undertaking that he shall be returned here tomorrow morning in time to face before a magistrate the charge of which he is accused. There can be no objection to that?'

Again Gregory's heart was in his mouth. The time was still only about ten o'clock. If Grauber were allowed to take him away and wreak his will on him for the next eight or ten hours, all the odds were that he would be returned to the Station a gibbering idiot. Little beads of sweat broke out on his forehead as he kept his eyes riveted on the Captain's face. But a moment later he could breathe again. The Hungarian shook his head:

'Thanks for the kind remarks, *Herr Gruppenführer*; but I can't do that. There is still this question of identity to be settled. And, anyhow, I couldn't hand a prisoner over to anyone without a formal authorisation.'

Stymied again, Grauber's small, pale eye darted swiftly from side to side. Gregory knew his mentality so well that he felt sure he could read the thoughts which were now flickering through that unscrupulous brain. He was assessing the chances of a snatch.

Many a time Gestapo agents had raided homes and hotels on foreign soil, dragged their victim from his bed, slugged him unconscious, carried him down to a car, and smuggled him back into Germany. In this case, counting out the victim, there were three of them to the one Hungarian. Going through the outer office they would have to deal with the Sergeant and the policeman on the door; but they had a car waiting outside.

The element of surprise and the use of brute force without scruple might well enable them to pull off a kidnapping and break out.

Gregory moistened his dry lips with his tongue. His thoughts were moving as swiftly as Grauber's. They might take the Captain by surprise, but not the object of the snatch. He was neither in bed, nor asleep. If they thought they were going to carry him out like a sack of potatoes, they had better think again. He already had his eye on a wooden chair. At his enemy's first move he meant to snatch it up and charge him with it—legs foremost. Tough as the pouchy German was, he must go down under such an assault. The two brawny thugs might then get the better of the battle in the room, but by the time they had there was a fair hope that the shindy would have brought half-a-dozen Hungarian policemen running to the outer office, and that the last word would remain with them.

Perhaps Grauber realised that too. Perhaps, even, he baulked at the idea of knocking out a Hungarian Police Captain and forcibly abducting a prisoner from his Station. That was very different from kidnapping some unsuspecting person, and might cause quite a lot of tiresome correspondence between the Chancelleries of Berlin and Budapest. After staring for a long moment at the Captain he switched his glance to Gregory, and said:

'Very well, I will leave you for the night in the custody of the *Herr Hauptmann*. But don't imagine you are going to get away with the story that you are a Frenchman. There are plenty of people in Germany who know you as Gregory Sallust, and if necessary I'll have witnesses flown in to support my identification of you.

'Anyway, when you are brought into court tomorrow morning, I mean to accuse you of the murder of *Obersturmbann-führer* Fritz Einholtz, and others, and to apply for a warrant for your extradition. When you have been handed over to me we'll talk again. First you'll tell me all about this conspiracy; then I'll take you back to Germany. In six months' time you will still be alive, but for five months and twenty-nine days you will have been wishing that you were dead.'

# 13

# A Night of Surprises

Even when Grauber and his two henchmen stamped angrily from the room Gregory could not be certain that the wily *Gruppenführer* would not suddenly turn on his heel and return to try some new trick for getting possession of him. But the sound of trampling feet across the outer office faded, and after a last minute of dreadful suspense he felt that temporarily, although only temporarily, by sticking to his bluff, he had got the better of his enemy. Turning to the Hungarian, he said in the heavily accented and faulty German that he had used since being brought into the Station:

'Captain, I cannot be sufficiently grateful to you for your protection from those thugs. It is appalling to think that in their own country they have the power to torture anyone they choose merely on suspicion. How good it is to find that here in Hungary you still maintain the same traditions of justice which we have for so long cherished in France.'

The Captain made a grimace. 'These Germans are beasts, but the Russians would be worse; so we must put up with them. Fortunately they are not our masters; so even if it were certain that you were an English spy I would not have allowed them to torture you. But make no mistake about it, if they can prove you to be the man they think, and demand your extradition for crimes committed in Germany, we shall have to hand you over to them.'

'God forbid that should happen! But it may.'

'Do you mean that you are, as they say, a British agent?' the Captain asked with a frown.

Gregory hated to have to deceive him, but in doing so lay his only chance to take advantage of the short respite that he had been granted. Throwing out his hands in a typically French gesture, he exclaimed:

'No! No! Do not think that, I beg. I meant only that I may have difficulty in persuading your magistrates that I am Commandant Tavenier. You have been more than a friend; so I will be frank with you. When I suggested that a telegram of enquiry about me should be sent to Vichy I was seeking only to gain time—to save myself from being tortured there and then. If one were sent it would do me no good. It would confirm that I am Tavenier but declare me to be an enemy. The truth is that I am a de Gaullist. I served with the Free French Forces in England, and landed with the British when they made their raid on St. Nazaire. I was wounded and left for dead. De Gaullist sympathisers hid me until I recovered, but I am listed by Vichy as a traitor. That is why I made my way secretly to Switzerland and then to Hungary. You see, I dare not appeal to the French Government; and how, otherwise, can I prove that I am Tavenier? The thought that I may fail to prove my identity fills me with terror; but it means that the Germans' word will be taken that I am this man Sallust.'

The Captain nodded. 'I see. In that case your situation is certainly a most dangerous one.'

'If these accursed Germans once get hold of me they will tear me into little bits.'

'I fear you are right.'

'Yet I am innocent. My only crime is that I believed, like many thousands of my countrymen, that, for the honour of France, all of us who were able to do so should fight on.'

'I appreciate that. It is tragic for you that a resemblance to another person should have landed you in this appalling mess.'

Having won the Hungarian's sympathy, Gregory felt that the time had now come to play a card that might just prove a trump. After a moment he asked, 'What exactly is the charge against me?'

'With having created a disturbance in a public place and inflicted bodily harm upon the *Gruppenführer* and a Captain Cochefert who was with him.'

'But it was the *Gruppenführer* who assaulted me.'

'That is a matter in dispute. It will be decided on the evidence of the wash-room attendant when the case comes up before a magistrate in the morning.'

'As I understand it, then, the *Gruppenführer* has been charged too, and will have to appear in the dock with me?'

'Yes; and Captain Cochefert also, if after treatment in hospital the doctors consider him well enough to do so.'

'Why, then, should you have released the *Gruppenführer* and detained me?'

The Hungarian shrugged. 'Your circumstances are very different. He is a high official in the police force of an allied

168

country. His word that he will appear when summoned is sufficient. You, on the other hand, are both a foreigner and a temporary resident here. If you were allowed to go free you might take the first train in the morning out of Budapest.'

'True, but the charge is only a civil one; surely your regulations enable you to release me against security for my appearance?'

'Yes; normally I could do so.'

Gregory tried to still the beating of his heart as his hopes rose. 'Then why should you not? Fortunately I have a considerable amount of money on me—in fact a very large sum, as I was too late to pay it into the bank today. I will willingly deposit the bulk of it with you as a recognisance.'

The Hungarian's face broke into a smile. 'You mean that, having made provision in advance against a probable fine, you would not turn up?'

'The sum would cover a fine *and* there would be a very handsome balance which could go to your police orphanage.' Gregory smiled back, in good hope now that his scheme for bribing the Captain to let him go was about to come off.

But the Hungarian shook his head. 'No. It can't be done. Ordinarily there would have been no difficulty about what you suggest; but you seem to have forgotten that the Germans believe you to be a spy.'

'That is the whole point,' Gregory countered. 'If I had nothing to fear from appearing in court tomorrow, I'd be a fool to offer several thousand *pengoes* to save myself a night in a cell; but my life may depend on my becoming a free man again tonight.'

'I realise that; but I cannot help it.'

On seeing his one chance slipping Gregory began to plead desperately. 'But you can! You can! I am not charged with spying. You have only to go by the letter of the law and treat me as though I were an ordinary stranger in Budapest who had created a row in a night-club. If it hadn't been for the *Gruppenführer* you wouldn't hold me. To do so is to associate yourself with his frightful error and, perhaps, bring about my death.'

'Not necessarily. You still have a way out.'

'Way out? If you've thought of one for God's sake tell me of it.'

169

'To come clean with the magistrate, as you have done with me.'

'But if I admit to having fought as one of the Free French I shall be counted an enemy and interned.'

'Well, that is not much to worry about compared to being carried off by the Gestapo.'

'That may be my fate just the same, unless I appeal to Vichy to substantiate my identity.'

'Then you must do so.'

'Admittedly that would knock the bottom out of the Germans' case, but Vichy in their turn would at once apply for my extradition.'

'Why should they bother? If you were interned here you could do them no further harm.'

Gregory had been aware of this weakness in the wholly academic argument he was putting up; but, short of saying that he was wanted for murder by the Vichy police—which it could be assumed would at once alienate the Hungarian's sympathy from him—he could see no way of making it appear that should he call on Vichy he would be jumping out of the frying pan into the fire. All he could do was to adopt a middle course, and say:

'As I have already told you, I am listed by Vichy as a traitor. You may be sure they would not be content to leave me here; and if I am sent back, God knows what will become of me. Some of these Pétainists are as bad as the Germans, and they delight in the chance to revenge themselves on officers who have shown them up to be cowards.'

'All the same, they won't torture you, as the Germans would.'

'No, but they might shoot me.'

'I see no reason why they should; unless you have done something to deserve it.'

'You do not know these Vichy traitors as I do. They stick at nothing to curry favour with the Germans.'

The Hungarian shook his head sadly. 'It is an evil day for any country when such things can happen in it. But it looks as if you must take your chance with Vichy as the only way of keeping out of the clutches of the *Gruppenführer*.'

'Either way the most terrible ordeals await me,' Gregory replied with great earnestness. 'Yet you have it in your power to save me from them. You alone can play the part of a good

170

angel. God would reward you for it. One word from you—the signing of a paper ...'

'No!' The Captain held up his hand to check the flow of pleading. 'It is useless for you to go on. I'm sorry for you, but I have to think of myself. I've a wife and two youngsters. I'd be only too willing to let you go if you could produce any concrete proof that you were not this English spy, Sallust. But as things are, I daren't risk it. I've already earned the animosity of that *Gruppenführer*, and he is too powerful a bird to be just laughed off. If I fail to produce you in court tomorrow he will create hell with my own Chiefs, and what possible excuse could I give? I'd be out of a job, or, at the very least, suffer a reduction in rank.'

Gregory saw now that his endeavours had been in vain. He could only nod gloomily, as the Captain went on: 'We've spent quite enough time in talking, and I have work to do. Come along now, and we'll put you in a cell for the night.'

As they left the waiting-room, Gregory caught sight of himself in a small mirror. Up till that moment he had been so desperately concerned with trying to save himself that he had paid little regard to his physical condition and none to his appearance. Now he saw that the hair-oil from the half-full bottle that Cochefert had broken over his head had wrought havoc with his collar, shirt and jacket, and he became newly conscious of its oily stickiness; so he asked if he might wash.

His request was granted. He was taken to a washroom where he succeeded in getting most of the surplus oil out of his hair and off his face and neck, but about his clothes nothing could be done short of sending them to a cleaners.

He was then taken to a cell and locked in. Only a dim blue pilot light was burning in it; but that was sufficient to show him that it was clean and reasonably comfortable. It contained an iron bed with three coarse blankets, a chamber-pot, a chair and a small table. On the table there had considerately been placed a mug of steaming coffee. Having sipped it he found it to be ersatz stuff, probably made from acorns, but he was none the less grateful and, sitting down on the bed, he slowly drank it while reviewing his situation.

Whichever way he looked at it he could see no ray of comfort. From a modern police station of this kind there could be no escape, and there was no reason at all to suppose that a chance to do so would occur when the routine drill was followed next morning of taking him from it in a black-maria to the court.

Once there, he would not have a leg to stand on. He hoped that the injury he had inflicted on Cochefert was proving extremely painful, but it could not have rendered him inarticulate. If the Frenchman had not already made a statement to the police, he would certainly do so next day. His statement would include irrefutable proof that Gregory was not Tavenier, and also disclose that he had passed himself off as Lt.-Colonel Einholtz of the S.D. If anything could add to Grauber's vindictive rage it would be that he had posed as this favourite disciple in frightfulness of whose services he had deprived the Gestapo for good and all.

The outcome must be that by afternoon he would be in a train under heavy guard on his way to Germany, to await the *Gruppenführer's* grim pleasure. It seemed that only one eventuality might prevent this—namely Grauber's failure to appear in court. Yet there was not the least reason to suppose that he would fail to do so.

There had been other occasions when Gregory had fallen into Grauber's clutches and been equally despondent about ever getting out of them. He had done so because, although the *Gruppenführer* was brave enough in other ways, he was terrified of high explosives. Once an air-raid alarm had scared him into abandoning his prisoner, and another time, when they were both in a submarine, depth charges had panicked him into abandoning ship prematurely. But Budapest was hundreds of miles outside the range of Allied aircraft, and there was not the remotest possibility that bombs, shells, showers of grenades or any other form of big bang was likely to keep Grauber cowering in a cellar next morning.

Taking off his still sticky jacket, collar and tie, and shoes, Gregory spread out the blankets and lay down on the bed. As the bottle of hair-oil had struck him neither on the temple nor the base of the skull, but a little to one side of the top of his head, it had caused him no serious injury. His head still ached but now only slightly, and not sufficiently to prevent his continuing to think coherently without undue effort, although there was no longer any desperate necessity for him to do so.

He began to wonder about Sabine, and if she had learned that he had fallen foul of a Gestapo man, or knew only that he had been run in for participating in a brawl. In any case,

172

his arrest was tough luck on her, because his efforts, during their long day together, to restrain her from wrecking his mission had succeeded only through their appeal to her emotions. There had been setbacks from time to time, but by evening she was clearly thinking of him again as a lover whose presence filled her with ardent desire; and when they had been together for those few minutes in her bedroom, she had made it plain that she was longing for the night of passion that she then believed lay before her.

She was going to be bitterly disappointed and so, for that matter, was he; although the loss of a night's pleasure with her was a microscopic infliction compared with what he had to expect from the cause of their enforced separation. With Grauber's threats in the forefront of his mind he was too much of a realist to take any comfort from the thought that the *Gruppenführer* had preserved his moral rectitude by forcing him to remain faithful to Erika. She, he knew, would have preferred that he should sleep with a dozen other women rather than that he should pass one night at the mercy of Grauber.

For some time he thought of her with that deep abiding warmth of affection which is the essence of real love. Then his thoughts turned again to Sabine. He hoped that she was not going to become involved in his disaster, and thought it unlikely that she would be. It was not as though they had been carrying on a long intrigue, as it was barely twenty-four hours since they had recognised one another at the Piccadilly. Her association with Ribbentrop would protect her from any prolonged cross-questioning about him; and if the worst came to the worst she could always explain having spent the day with him by saying that she had known all the time that he was an Englishman, and had decided to do a little counter-espionage work herself by trying to get out of him what he was up to in Budapest.

About Count László, Colonel János the others he felt there was much more cause for worry. Fortunately, his reply to Grauber about the people he had met while in Budapest had been only a slight exaggeration of the truth. In the past fortnight he had made many new acquaintances; so no investigation of his activities would pin-point the conspirators. Since the formation of the Committee he had, too, constantly impressed on its members the necessity for secrecy, and they had taken serious notice of his warnings. But there remained the danger to them from that first conference at the Nobles Club to which Count Zapolya had indiscreetly invited such a large number of his friends. It must have been through either someone who had been present at that meeting, or one of the Club servants, that Grauber had got wind of the affair, and if the former then that person, having witnessed the election of the Committee, might also give away the names of its members.

As there was no way in which Gregory could send them a warning, he could only hope that when Count László called at Sabine's as arranged, at nine o'clock next morning, on hearing of his arrest he would take fright, then swiftly warn the others, so that they could all go into hiding until the danger was past. But that they would do so on the bare information that he had been pulled in on account of a row in a night-club seemed unlikely, and by the time they learned more of the matter it might be too late.

Gregory was still speculating on the point when he heard a jingle of keys out in the corridor, the door of his cell was unlocked, and the warder signed to him to get up.

With an inward groan he obeyed. After Grauber's departure he had thought himself safe at least until after he had been taken before a magistrate, but only about an hour had elapsed since he had been brought to the station. There could be only one reason for rousing him up while the night was still young. Grauber must have gone straight to some higher authority and had now returned with an authorisation to collect him. He might have known that his old enemy was not the man tamely to accept defeat, or let the grass grow under his feet in rectifying a temporary setback. At the thought of what he might now have to suffer before morning, Gregory's hands grew damp, his mouth dry, and as he followed the warder down the corridor his feet seemed as though made of lead.

To his utter astonishment and boundless relief, as he stepped through the door of the waiting-room he saw that beside the Police Captain stood, not Grauber, but Sabine.

The chunky-faced Captain looked from him to her and asked, 'Baroness, do you definitely identify this man as Commandant Etienne Tavenier?'

'I do,' she replied with a smile at Gregory.

The Captain smiled at him too, and said, 'My friend, your

174

luck is in after all. This lady with whom you went to the Arizona has taken steps to secure your release. Please sign this declaration that nothing has been taken from you while in custody, and you are free to go.'

Almost in a daze, Gregory signed the paper, thanked the Captain, and followed Sabine out to the main office. A policeman politely opened the front door of the station for them and they stepped from the bright light into semi-darkness, nearly colliding with another officer who was about to enter. He stood aside then turned to stare after them for a moment before going in. Sabine's Mercedes was standing at the kerb in the narrow street, and as Gregory sank into the seat beside her he let out a great sigh of thankfulness.

Before driving off she lit a cigarette, then turned to him and said, 'You are looking terribly groggy, darling. Did you get badly hurt?'

'No,' he murmured. 'No. I'll be all right in a minute. I was hit over the head with a bottle of hair-oil; but I've got a thick enough skull to stand much worse things than that. I was unconscious for only a few minutes, and I've hardly a trace of a headache left. If I look queer it is from the pleasantest shock I've ever had. You can have no idea what you have saved me from. I'll be in your debt till my dying day.'

As she slipped in the clutch and the car moved off, she replied, 'I was right, then, in my surmise that you were arrested as a spy, and not just taken up, as they said at the Arizona, for getting mixed up in some silly fight.'

'Yes and no. I haven't been spying here. I told you the truth about that. And I was only charged with a breach of the peace. But I had the accursed ill-luck to run into one of the top boys of the Gestapo who knows me to be an Englishman. In the morning, when I was taken to court, he meant to charge me with espionage and secure my extradition to Germany.'

'Thank God I got you out then! Tomorrow morning would have been too late, and I wouldn't have been able to.'

'I marvel that they let me go tonight. That Captain was a decent chap; he protected me from the Germans and kept an open mind. But he knew they believed me to be an English agent named Sallust; so it really is surprising that he should have released me simply because you said that you knew me as Commandant Tavenier.'

'He didn't; and I don't suppose for a moment that he would

have in the ordinary way. He was only verifying that I was satisfied that you were the person referred to in the paper I had brought.'

'What paper?'

Sabine laughed. 'I told you this morning that I could get most things I wanted done for me in any of the Government Departments because, like it or not, they have to play along with the Germans. When I heard you had been run in, as the Ministry of Justice was closed I went to the house of Erdélyi, the Minister. He wasn't too pleased at being dragged from a game of bridge; but I told him what had happened, declared that it was not your fault because, being a foreigner, you had misunderstood some remark that was passed about me, and that I was determined you should not spend a night in jug through acting as my champion; so he must give me an order for your release. As a further inducement to make him play, I added that we were expecting Ribb to join us for supper and he would be terribly annoyed if you weren't there, as it was his last chance to see you before returning to Germany. Of course, I've known old Butyi Erdélyi for years, and there was no reason for him to suspect that there might be more behind your being detained than just a fist fight; so he wrote me out a note to take to the Police Station.'

'Bless you, my dear.' Gregory laid a hand on her knee. 'But I'm afraid you may get into bad trouble for having done this.'

'Why should I? No one can prove that I knew all the time that you were an Englishman. I gave the impression of being just a spoilt young woman who was furious because she had been deprived of the man who was taking her out to dinner, and meant to make trouble in high places if he was not restored to her. There is nothing criminal about that.'

'No; I suppose not. All the same I . . .' The car had turned out of the Zrinyi Utcza and was heading for the Swing Bridge. Gregory broke off to ask quickly, 'Where are you taking me?'

'Home, of course,' Sabine replied lightly.

'You mustn't!' he exclaimed. 'Please stop here so that I can get out.'

'What! And leave you to go off on your own in that state! Is it likely?'

'All right. But don't cross the river yet. Turn along the Corso and pull up under the trees. If we don't handle this thing carefully we will both land in the soup. We simply must talk things over before you commit yourself any further.'

With evident reluctance, she did as he suggested. Meanwhile his thoughts were running swiftly. 'She has been marvellous. What a fool I was ever to think that she might hand me over to the police. It looks as if she has managed to keep herself in the clear, and for me to involve her now would be the height of ingratitude. I must leave her, and the sooner the better. That Jewish furrier, Leon Levianski, said he would hide me if I was hard pressed. Best thing I can do is to take advantage of his sporting offer, anyhow for the night.'

As Sabine pulled the car up, he took her hand, kissed it and said, 'Listen, my sweet. I hate to say it, and more than ever after what you've done for me; but this is good-bye. I'm red-hot now. Or anyway I will be once the Germans hear that I'm a free man again. You'll have quite enough to answer for tomorrow, without having me still on your hands. This day with you has been wonderful, but it has to end like Cinderella's at the ball. My fairy trappings as Commandant Etienne Tavenier are already falling in rags about me, so I've got to run out on you.'

'Say I agree, what will you do?' she asked quickly.

'I think I told you that I had one contact here, a Jewish merchant. He offered to conceal me for a bit if I got into trouble, and could reach his place without being followed. There should be no difficulty about my doing that. Fortunately I've plenty of money on me. I'll get him to buy me some peasant clothes, and leave the city on foot after dark tomorrow.'

'You seem to forget that you can't speak Hungarian.'

'Yes; that is a snag. Still, lots of the better class country people speak German.'

'True, but they speak Hungarian as well, and you don't. You will come under suspicion in the first village you stop at for the night.'

'Then I'll have to sleep in hay-stacks until the hue and cry dies down. After a few days it should be safe for me to board a train going towards the frontier.'

'What about a passport? You can't use the one you've got.'

'No; I'll have to leave the train before it reaches the border, and get across in some lonely spot at night.'

'Darling, it's no good!' she cried in desperate protest. 'You'll never make it! Living like a vagabond, yet without a word of

Hungarian and no passport to produce if you're questioned, you are bound to run into trouble. Long before you reach the frontier you'll find yourself in some village lock-up. It is certain that a description of you will be issued to all police stations. Someone will recognise you from it. Then you'll be hauled back to Budapest and handed over to the Germans.'

'That is taking the blackest view. I have been in worse spots before. I'll manage somehow.'

'But why inflict such hardship on yourself and take such a prolonged risk when there is an easy and quick way out?'

'If you know one, tell me of it.'

'It's quite simple. I planned it while on my way to the police station. I have an Italian chauffeur who is fairly near your age and colouring. He has been with me ever since I married Kelemen, and I am sure he will let me have his passport. You can dress up in his uniform and we'll make an early start on Sunday morning—just as if I was setting off for Berlin three days earlier than I originally intended. We'll have ample time to reach a town on the Yugoslav frontier before nightfall, and you can drive me straight over it. Once you are safe you can put off the chauffeur's uniform and we can spend a little honeymoon together. Then . . . well, then I'll recross the frontier on my own at a different place and drive straight to Berlin.'

'Oh, my sweet!' he kissed her hand again. 'It is terribly gallant of you, and terribly tempting. It is a perfect plan, too; but I simply can't let you take such a risk.'

'Don't be silly. The risk is negligible. Ribb got me a diplomatic *laissez-passer*; so that I should never be put to any inconvenience when crossing frontiers. That frees us from having to fill up any forms, customs' examinations, and formalities about currency. No official would dream of holding us up and questioning us once I've shown him that; so we won't even have to worry about my chauffeur's passport photograph not being very like you.'

'I suppose you are right.' All against his instinct Gregory weakened. After the hour of dread he had just been through, he would not have been human had he rejected outright this alluring prospect of escaping all sorts of difficulties and dangers by driving straight out of the country.

'Of course I'm right,' Sabine insisted, and leaned forward to press the self-starter.

'No; wait!' he caught her hand. 'What is to happen in the meantime?'

'You are coming home with me. You'll be perfectly safe there.'

'I shan't, and neither would you be. As it was you who secured my release and I drove off with you in your car, your house is the first place they'll come to when the balloon goes up in the morning.'

'Really, darling! I think that whack on the head must have temporarily deprived you of your wits. Is it likely that I shouldn't have realised that? I shall say that I was driving you back to the house to change your clothes when you said that having been knocked out had made you feel sick. So I stopped the car for you to get out. Then, to my amazement, instead of being sick, you ran off down a side-turning; and I haven't the faintest idea what became of you afterwards. That is entirely in keeping with what would probably have happened if I had really believed you to be Tavenier.'

He nodded. 'Yes; that is just about what I should have done. Knowing that the Germans had got on to me, once you had got me out of prison I should have left you as quickly as I could. In fact, just as I meant to.'

'Exactly. And the very last place you would have let me take you to would have been my house; because they are certain to make enquiries there.'

'Yes, they probably would even if I had got out of prison by some other means. The odds are that they will find out that after I left the Vadászkürt this afternoon the driver of the carriage took me and my luggage to your palace. That is the sort of thing that worries me. What reason are you going to give them for having done that?'

'A perfectly straightforward one. I greeted you in front of a tableful of people last night as an old friend, and mentioned that I had stayed with your aunt in Paris. I wished to return her hospitality, so asked you to stay for a few days, and you accepted. There is nothing wrong about that.'

Gregory had a feeling that there was somewhere, but another thought struck him and he asked, 'What about Ribb? Won't he kick up rough when he hears that you invited your ex-boy friend, without his aunt, or a wife or chaperone of any kind, to come and stay with you?'

'No. That is one of Ribb's good points. At times he fools

around rather half-heartedly with little film-starlets and I never make scenes. But in return I assert my right to go about with whom I like, and he stands for that, because he enjoys my companionship more than anyone else's. Providing I am always on hand when he either wants to talk or show me off to his friends, and I don't let other men make up to me while he is present, he doesn't seem to mind much what I do when he is otherwise engaged.'

'You are a clever girl, and I give you full marks,' Gregory said with a smile. But he at once became serious again, and added, 'All the same, I can't possibly let you run any further risks on my account. At least, not as far as coming back to your house is concerned. I'll lie low in the city tonight and tomorrow; then, if you are really confident that you can get away with it, we'll do our trip to the frontier on Sunday.'

'No, Gregory; no!' She hit the wheel angrily with the palm of her hand. 'You are being stupid again. My whole plan hangs on your taking my chauffeur's place, and driving me off as though we were setting out for Berlin. How on earth can we do that if I have to pick you up somewhere? And if you came to the house early Sunday morning, you might be spotted entering it. All sorts of complications might crop up. The only certain way for us to pull it off is for you to come back with me to the house now.'

He sighed. 'There is an awful lot in what you say. But I'm so scared that something may go wrong when the police come along to question you about me in the morning. If you tell them that I bolted from you tonight, and after that they find that you are concealing me, you won't have a leg to stand on. You'll be in it up to the neck.'

'There's no reason why they shouldn't believe me.'

'You never can tell. Some little thing may make them suspicious; then they might insist on searching the house.'

'They wouldn't dare!'

'Wouldn't they? You don't know *Herr Gruppenführer* Grauber.'

'Is he the man who recognised you?'

'Yes; and he is the most ruthlessly efficient swine that ever wielded a rubber truncheon. What is more, he has personal reasons for wanting to take me into little pieces, so he'll stick at nothing to ferret out where I've got to.'

'Where did you come up against him before?'

'Oh, in lots of places. The first time was in England and the last in Russia. But Fate seems to take a special delight in throwing us together, and during the past three years we have done our best to kill one another in half-a-dozen countries.'

'You misled me, then, about your mission to Budapest being a special thing. From what you say, it's clear now that all through the war you have been working against the Germans as a secret agent.'

'No, I didn't mislead you. I simply refrained from telling you about my previous wartime activities because I didn't want to quarrel with you—and you had made it clear that you were on the Germans' side.'

'I am. Oh, Gregory!' Her voice held a sob of acute distress. 'Why are you English so blind? Can't you see that the Russians are the real enemy? If we don't destroy them now we have the chance, they'll destroy us later. They are evil, utterly evil; and given time they will grow so powerful that either by peaceful penetration or by war they will become the masters of the whole world.'

He sighed. 'You may be right. God knows. I've no illusions about Communism, and the way in which it turns all those who come under it into slaves. But first things must come first. Stalin is little worse than Hitler and . . .'

'That is not true! I know Hitler is a fanatic about some things, and that his persecution of the Jews is unforgivable, but . . .'

'No ruler who employs men like Grauber can be allowed to continue to enforce his will on millions of people. But this is not the time for us to wrangle about degrees of evil. What I was about to say was that Grauber is the head of the Gestapo Foreign Department; so, apart from Himmler, there is no German who has a bigger pull with your police, and they will stick at nothing to get me for him. That is why, if they have the least suspicion that you are lying, they will search your house.'

'I tell you they will not. This is not Germany, you know. First they would have to go away and get a search warrant; so you would have plenty of time to make yourself scarce.'

'They might bring one with them.'

'I should refuse to allow them to execute it until I had telephoned to the Palace. I would get on to Ribb and have him

181

speak to Admiral Horthy; and he would send an order that they were to leave me in peace.'

'If they were hunting for an English spy at the request of the Germans I don't see why Ribb should interfere.'

'Then I'll tell you. The top Nazis hate each other's guts. All of them are always trying to get hold of some piece of dirt that will discredit one of the others with the *Führer*; and Ribb and Himmler are at daggers drawn. Ribb would accept my version of what had happened and jump to the conclusion that one of Himmler's boys was trying to pull a fast one on him by seizing this excuse to search my house in the hope of finding something among my papers that could be used against him later.'

'If that is really so . . .' Gregory murmured. 'But wait a minute! Ribb is leaving tomorrow afternoon for Berlin and, according to your plan, we don't leave for the frontier until Sunday morning. If the police come back with a search warrant on Saturday night Ribb will no longer be here for you to appeal to.'

For a moment she considered that, then she said, 'I decided on Sunday morning because it is much more natural to set out on the first stage of a long journey with a whole day ahead of one; and anyway I couldn't leave till fairly late on Saturday afternoon because Ribb and I will be lunching together and he will expect me to see him off from the airport afterwards. But, if you like, we will start as soon as we can after he has gone.'

The temptation to leave himself in her hands was overwhelming. She was so completely confident that no harm would come to her through his doing so; and, as far as he was concerned, the alternative held all sorts of dangerous uncertainties. Levianski might be away from Budapest or get cold feet and, after all, refuse to hide him. He was unarmed, hatless and the clothes he was wearing were dirty and torn, showing that he had recently been involved in a fight. He had plenty of money but could not use it till the morning to buy other clothes, and a ruck-sack to carry essentials in for his journey. Even if he succeeded in getting safely out of Budapest, he would be faced with many hazards before he could reach the frontier; then he would have to run the gauntlet between two lots of guards in getting across it and, as Yugoslavia was controlled by the Germans, still be without a passport that he dared to show. Yet his instinctive caution against committing himself to an easy course made him continue to search his mind for possible holes in her alluring offer. After a moment, he said:

'My clothes. When the police learn tomorrow that I was going to stay with you, they will ask you for them on the chance that I have left something among them which would help to trace me.'

'Pipi, my butler, will pack them up and hand them over. I gave away most of Kelemen's things after he died, but there are still enough of them in various cupboards to fit you out; and he was only an inch or so taller than you are.'

'I gather, then, that Pipi is to be trusted. But what about your other servants? Surely there is a big risk that one of them might give away the fact that I am still in the house.'

'Apart from Mario, my chauffeur, only Pipi and his wife, Magda, need know. She used to be my personal maid until she married Pipi and I made her housekeeper, so that she could remain with him while I am away. When I come to Budapest I leave my new girl Lili in Berlin, and Magda still maids me. All three of them are devoted to me. You will have to stay up in your room, of course; but Pipi and Magda between them will look after you and bring you anything you want. Stop havering, darling. It's having been through such a horrid time that makes you so nervy. Really, you can leave everything to me.'

'It's only that I should never forgive myself if, through trying to save me, you found yourself charged with aiding and abetting an enemy agent.'

'Most men wouldn't give a damn if they saw a good chance of saving their own necks. Your scruples make me love you all the more. That's settled, then. Let's go!'

Gregory made no further effort to stop her. The car slid forward, along the Corso back to the bridge, crossed it and followed a zig-zag course up the slope of the Buda hill, until Sabine brought it to a halt in a dark, narrow street. On the right could be seen a row of small palaces; on the left only a stone wall sloping slightly inwards that reared up into the darkness. The section of wall alongside which Sabine pulled up was the great buttress in the hill-side which supported the east front of the row of palaces in which hers was one. Flush with it, like a ladder from the water to a ship's deck, was a steep narrow flight of stone stairs. Pointing to them Sabine said:

'That's the way in that lovers of the Tozolto ladies have used for centuries. At the top you will find a gate leading on to the terrace. Wait there until I have taken the car round to the courtyard, then I'll come and let you in.'

Five minutes later she unlocked the gate, led him across the terrace and through french windows into a dark salon. There she took his hand and guided him between the dimly seen furniture to a further door which opened into the vaulted hall. When they came out from under the broad staircase he saw the man-servant who had taken his things that evening standing by the outer door, and it was evident that Sabine had told him to wait there.

The butler was a middle-aged man, with a pleasant open, rather round, face and slightly greying hair. As he bowed to his mistress she said with a smile, 'Pipi, this is *Herr Kommandant* Tavenier, who came this afternoon to stay with us. Unfortunately there was a row at the Arizona tonight and he got into trouble with the police. It was a stupid business and will all blow over in a day or two, but it would be embarrassing for him if he had to appear in court. You can tell Magda what I've told you, but I don't want anyone else at all to know that the *Herr Kommandant* is here. Is that understood?'

'Yes, Lady Baroness,' the man replied with a frankness and lack of servility that impressed Gregory very favourably.

'Now,' Sabine went on, 'the police may call tomorrow morning to make enquiries and collect the *Herr Kommandant's* belongings. I want you to go up to his room, pack them all up and bring them downstairs ready to be handed over. Then take up to the room everything you can find of our Baron's things for him to use until this silly affair is cleared up. When you have done, come down and let us know.'

With a murmur of assent the butler left them, and Sabine went over to a trolley of drinks. On its lower shelf, under transparent covers, reposed the usual plates of sandwiches, biscuits and cake, in case she came in late and felt like nibbling something with a nightcap before going to bed.

'As we had no dinner, we had better eat something,' she said. 'Although I'm not really hungry; I had such a large lunch. How about you? If you would like something more solid Pipi could get it for us.'

'No, thanks; there is plenty here. A couple of sandwiches

and a brandy and soda will suit me.'

'Ought you to drink anything? Alcohol, I mean, after that blow on the head.'

He smiled. 'Don't worry. I've been knocked out too often not to know when I'm likely to get delayed concussion. All I need now to make me my own man again is a drink and a good hot bath to get this oily muck off my neck and chest.'

'All the same, your poor head ought to be seen to,' she said solicitously. 'Mix me a brandy and soda too, while I get things to bathe it.'

Having left him for a few minutes she returned with a basin of hot water, lint and ointment. Her examination confirmed that the blow had had no serious effect. Only the skin of his scalp was broken and there was very little clotted blood about the place. After cleaning the wound she applied the ointment, and they settled down to their alfresco supper, eating considerably more than they had at first expected.

They had not long finished when Pipi came back to report that he had carried out his orders. Greatly to Gregory's surprise Sabine stood up and said to him:

'You must still be feeling very groggy after that fight you got mixed up in. What you need is a hot bath and a nice long sleep; so I won't keep you up any longer.' Then she turned to Pipi and added, 'Please see the *Herr Kommandant* up to his room.'

Hardly believing that she could mean it, Gregory thanked her and bowed over her hand. But she confirmed the impression that she really intended him to go to bed by saying, 'Good night; I hope you will feel quite recovered in the morning. We'll have lots of time to talk tomorrow.'

Pipi escorted him up to his room and having ascertained that there was nothing else he wanted, left him.

Immediately he was alone he went over to the bedside telephone. To his relief he found that it was connected direct with the exchange and, since all the operators spoke German, he had no difficulty in getting Count László's number. As it was only just on eleven o'clock he feared that the Count might be out, but a moment later he came on the line.

Using French and phrases which would obscure his meaning to anyone who might be listening in, Gregory gave a swift résumé of the disaster that had overtaken him that evening, and warned the Count that he should get in touch with their other friends at once, so that on various pretexts they could all leave Budapest before the threatening investigation got properly under way. He then enquired anxiously about the result of that evening's Committee meeting.

In equally round-about parlance the Count told him that everything had been settled. The Hungarian magnates were prepared to force their Government to break with Germany on the following conditions:— An Anglo-American undertaking to guarantee Hungary from Russian aggression; allocation to Hungary after the war of the territories already stipulated by the Committee, being the greater part of those of which she had been deprived by the Treaty of Trianon; and that the Anglo-Americans should land a force of not less than fifteen divisions on the Continent, on a date to be agreed, and before the Hungarian Government declared against Hitler.

It was the size of the expeditionary force, which the Hungarians would demand should engage the German forces in the West, that had been in debate, and Gregory felt that fifteen divisions was not unreasonable; so when he put down the receiver he smiled his satisfaction.

Abusing Sabine's hospitality to get in touch with Count László on a matter that might lead to Germany's defeat had given him a sharp twinge of conscience. But it had been imperative that he should somehow or other warn the Committee of its danger and, if he possibly could, fulfil his duty to his own country by bringing back definite terms upon which the Hungarians would act. To have succeeded in the one and have a good prospect of doing the other took such a load off his mind that he hardly gave Grauber another thought, and became again as full of good spirits as he had been when he had changed to go out some three hours earlier.

Throwing off his soiled clothes, he got into the bath that Pipi had already prepared for him. The warm scented water soon relieved from stiffness those of his muscles he had strained during the struggle, just as the telephone conversation with Count László had relieved his mind of all immediate worries.

He lay there for quite a long time, acutely conscious that, but for God, the Hungarian Police Captain, Sabine and his lucky stars, he might by now be suffering agonies with Grauber glaring at him, and rendered thanks for his preservation. Then he got out, dried himself, put out the lights and drew back one of the curtains of the bedroom windows.

186

The moon had risen over Pest, and it brought sharply back to him what Sabine had said when they were kissing in her bedroom before going out. As he got into bed he marvelled at her restraint. Since she had made her feelings for him so plain, he could only suppose that she thought he needed a full night's sleep to recover from the ordeal he had been through, and had resigned herself to wait until the brief 'honeymoon' she had proposed that they should take when they were over the frontier.

Drowsily he wondered if that 'honeymoon' would come off, or if some unforeseen circumstance would arise to prevent it. Now, it almost seemed as if Fate had decreed that, whether he would or not, he should, after all, remain faithful to Erika. He could not make up his mind if he was sorry or not. Then, as thoughts of Sabine lying in bed in the room below him suddenly took possession of his mind, he knew that he was already regretting her having packed him off alone to bed.

It was at that moment that a slight sound made him turn his head. The door had opened and Sabine was closing it behind her. She had on a dressing gown, her face was pale as a magnolia blossom in the moonlight and her dark hair rippled down over her shoulders.

As she came towards him, and he quickly sat up, she said: 'Why didn't you come down to me? You know where my room is.'

'I thought . . .' he stammered. 'You said . . . You led me to suppose . . . Damn it! You packed me off to bed as though I was not up to . . .'

She gave a low laugh. 'You dear idiot! You told me you were feeling perfectly recovered, but I've always thought it only right to preserve the decencies as far as possible in front of the servants. I said good night to you like that simply to keep face with Pipi.'

Untying the belt of her dressing-gown, she let the garment slip from her shoulders. She had nothing on underneath it and for a moment stood there, her full beauty revealed in the moonlight. Then, with another low delighted laugh, she slipped into bed beside him.

Exactly nine and a half minutes later the sound of a musical klaxon horn came up to them through the open window.

'Holy Mary!' exclaimed Sabine, wrenching herself from

187

Gregory's embrace. 'That's Ribb. And he told me positively he didn't mean to come here tonight. Oh, God! How utterly damnable!'

## 14

## Battle of Wits

Sabine scrambled out of bed and Gregory after her. As he snatched up her dressing-gown from the floor and helped her on with it, he said, 'If you are so positive that Ribb did not mean to come and spend the night with you, it must be about me that he's come here.'

'Do you really think so?' She was nearly weeping with rage and frustration. 'It is unlike him to change his mind; but he might have done.'

'Perhaps; but I've a horrid feeling that Grauber has somehow found out that you secured my release, then got on to Ribb and asked him to come and question you.'

'That . . . that might be the explanation,' she sobbed. 'But oh, God, why couldn't the fool wait till morning!'

It was no laughing matter, but Gregory could not suppress a smile. 'We must give him the benefit of not knowing that you would be otherwise engaged. At least, I hope to goodness we can; if not, we'll both be for the high jump.'

She gave an angry shrug. 'Oh, my story is watertight enough. You go back to bed. When I've given him a drink and heard what he has to say, I'll get rid of him as soon as I can and come back to you.'

As she hurried towards the door, Gregory said quickly, 'I daren't stay here. It's quite on the cards that Grauber has come with him. If so they may search the house. It would be the end of you if they find me in it. I mean to make the bed, then climb out of the window and down into the street.'

She halted in her tracks. 'No! No! For heaven's sake don't do that! Ribb's car is down there. If his chauffeur sees you climbing out of the window he'll think you are a burglar and raise an alarm. I've told you Ribb would never let them search but, if you're really afraid they may, go up to the attics. There are half-a-dozen places there where they wouldn't find you if they hunted for hours. Promise me you won't leave the house. Promise me!'

Gregory was loath to give her his promise, but she was right about Ribbentrop's chauffeur, and this was no time to argue; so he said, 'All right; I'll first make the bed then hide somewhere. Maybe Ribb's only come . . . er, on a courtesy call, after all. Anyhow, good luck!'

As she ran from the room he was already starting on the bed. Immediately he had made it he pulled open the doors of a big old-fashioned wardrobe. In it was a strange assortment of the late Baron's clothes—presumably all that Pipi had been able to find for him. They were mostly dress or fancy garments for which, if given to them, poor people would have had little use, but he found a crested blazer to go with a pair of black velvet trousers. In a chest of drawers there were several silk shirts with a coronet and monogram embroidered on them, and a variety of ties to choose from.

While getting dressed at top speed he cursed himself for having allowed Sabine to persuade him to come back there. The past quarter of an hour had put it beyond all doubt that when doing so she had been largely influenced by the desire, which had been growing in her all day, to spend the night with him. But, to be fair, he had to admit that the arguments she had used were sound ones. If she was right about being able to get away with her story, he was much better off where he was than in Levianski's apartment with many days of unforeseen dangers in front of him. That he was out of prison at all he owed to her, and he suddenly decided that he was being extremely mean in setting against the risks she was running for him the fact that she had fallen harder than he had expected for his deliberate arousing of the memories that they shared.

The truth was that though he could find no concrete reason for rejecting her plan he had, all along, instinctively distrusted it. In consequence, Ribbentrop's surprise visit had at once seemed to justify his fears. All the same, they might be quite groundless. After all, Sabine was the Foreign Minister's mistress. As she was not supposed to be leaving until Wednesday and was motoring back to Berlin, it would be the best part of a week before she arrived there. If he had got through his business with the Regent earlier than he expected, there was nothing in the least strange about his deciding to sleep with her instead of at the Palace.

By the time Gregory had stowed in his pockets his money, papers and his little automatic—which Pipi had considerately left for him when removing his other things—he was feeling very much more optimistic. Nevertheless, he was not the man to take chances. Having stuffed his soiled clothes into the unlit stove, he swiftly tidied the bathroom and the bedroom so that, short of examining the bed and finding its sheets rumpled, no one would realise that the rooms had recently been occupied.

Stepping softly out into the corridor he closed the door behind him and listened intently. No sound disturbed the silence. Turning up the collar of the blazer, so that its lapels would hide the V of pale shirt, he moved like a ghost towards the staircase. He had already decided not to adopt Sabine's suggestion that he should hide up in the attics. If any serious searching was done that was the very place they would ransack for him. Instead he meant, if possible, to get down to the ground floor, and he hoped to find there a small room with a window either giving on to the courtyard or the terrace. Then, if the worst came to the worst, although he would have to break his promise to Sabine, he would at least be well-placed to make a bolt for it.

Sitting down on the top step of the stairs, and using his hands as levers, he went from step to step to the bottom swiftly and noiselessly. From beyond the curtain that masked them filtered a faint light. Standing up and peering round it, he saw that the light came from the open door of Sabine's bedroom. But there was still no sound of movement or voices. He guessed, rightly, that, while he had been hurrying into his clothes, Sabine had spent some minutes there touching up her face before going down to open the gate to Ribbentrop. She would have known that once he had seen the light in her room go on, showing that she was at home, he would not mind waiting for those few minutes while she made herself presentable.

Stepping out into the broad corridor, Gregory now saw that the lights were also on in the hall, throwing into sharp relief the balustrade of the gallery which, with the head of the main staircase, formed the central section of the corridor. On tiptoe he ran towards them, hoping that he might get down the stairs while the hall was still unoccupied.

In that he was thwarted. As he reached the head of the stairs, he heard a door close and the murmur of voices. Pulling up he looked quickly about him. At the ends of the gallery there hung two six-feet wide velvet curtains on semi-circular rails, their purpose being to form a background for the two suits of Turkish armour. With swift cat-like strides he reached the nearest curtain and slipped in front of it, then stationed himself behind the armour. The steel and leather shape of a man hid him from anyone who looked up in that direction from the hall, and if Sabine brought Ribbentrop up to her bedroom the curtain would conceal him while they passed behind his back.

He had hardly taken up his position when Sabine and her midnight visitor emerged from under the stairs into his field of vision. The Foreign Minister was wearing undress uniform: a naval type jacket of dark blue with aiguillettes of gold braid draped on his right shoulder, a long row of medals and four stars of various orders on his left breast. Gregory decided that he really was quite a good-looking fellow and took in with silent satisfaction the fact that he had not brought anyone with him.

That was a good omen, yet the atmosphere seemed slightly strained, for the couple crossed the hall without speaking. Sabine again had on her crimson housecoat, her glossy dark hair framed her pale face with no trace of disorder and, as she calmly lit a cigarette before sitting down in an arm-chair, no one could possibly have supposed that less than ten minutes earlier she had been in bed with a lover.

Ribbentrop walked straight over to the trolley and mixed himself a drink. As he did so Gregory was alarmed to see that on it there still stood two dirty glasses: his own and Sabine's. That might prove a give-away. But the tall Foreign Minister did not seem to have noticed. Having swallowed half his drink, he said:

'I'm sorry to have pulled you out of bed on account of such a stupid affair; but I must know what you have been up to with this man Tavenier.'

Gregory's upper teeth closed gently on his lower lip. So he had been right. Grauber *had* got on to Ribbentrop and asked him to question his mistress. Well, it was now up to Sabine.

Only a trained eye like Gregory's could have spotted any sign of agitation in her. She had her long legs crossed. From beneath the edge of her crimson housecoat the bare ankle of the upper one showed and from the forepart of her foot there dangled a marabou-trimmed silver mule. It began to swing back and forth, but her voice was perfectly calm as she answered.

'I told you last night, Joachim. He is an old friend of mine. I saw quite a lot of him before the war, when I was staying with his aunt in Paris. This morning I ran into him again at the Gellért Baths. He offered to give me lunch, and as I had nothing particular to do I accepted. You know how amusing a sophisticated Frenchman can be. But I needn't stress that point. You must have seen for yourself last night what good company Etienne is. As you were tied up with those eternal conferences, we decided to spend the rest of the day together. Then I had the idea that it would be fun to have him to stay for a night or two. I could hardly do less after all the time he had spent taking me round Paris. He collected his things from the Vadászkürt and came here to change. After a drink we went out to have dinner at the Arizona. You appear to know the rest.'

'I know about your having got him out of the lock-up; but what happened after that?'

'We got in the car to drive home . . .'

'He is here, then!' Ribbentrop's voice held a staccato sharpness.

'No. And that is the only strange part about it. Just before we reached the Swing Bridge he said he felt ill and wanted to be sick; so I stopped the car and he got out. To my amazement, without a word to me, he ran off into an alley. I shouted after him, but he took no notice. I can only suppose that the blow on the head he had had temporarily sent the poor fellow out of his mind. I drove home and waited for some time, hoping that he would get back his wits and remember that he was supposed to be staying here. But he hasn't put in an appearance or telephoned; so I haven't the faintest idea what has become of him.'

'There are grounds for believing him to be an English secret agent.'

'What!' Sabine exclaimed, her big eyes growing round with well-feigned astonishment. 'But that is absurd! I know him to be a Frenchman.'

Ribbentrop shrugged. 'Perhaps he is a de Gaullist who is

working for the British. Anyhow, after he had been questioned at the police station he knew that he had been recognised as a man wanted by the Gestapo. That would account for his leaving you like that. He knew that if he came back with you he would soon be followed here and re-arrested; so as soon as he could he seized on the chance to get away.'

'I can't believe it!'

'I was dubious myself—anyhow about his being an Englishman. But Grauber claims that he knows him well; and that he is an ace-high British spy named Sallust.'

'Who is Grauber?' Sabine asked with a puzzled frown.

'Have you never heard of him? He is one of Himmler's top men and is responsible for all Gestapo activities outside the *Reich*. He is in Budapest to investigate rumours that a little clique of anti-Nazi Hungarian notables is toying with the idea of entering into negotiations with the enemy. Purely by chance he ran into this man Tavenier, or Sallust, or whoever he is. As you know, they had a fight and were both taken off to the police station. Grauber showed his credentials and wanted to remove his catch to the Villa Petoefer—that is the Gestapo Headquarters here—but the Hungarians wouldn't let him. So he came up to the Palace, to ask me to get a special permit signed by Admiral Horthy. He was given it, but by the time he got back to the police station you had let the bird out of the cage. Back to the Palace came Grauber, in a fine rage, to demand that special measures should be taken to catch the bird again; and when I heard that you were responsible for the fellow's release I decided that I must see you at once to find out what was behind all this.'

'There is nothing behind it. I have not the least doubt that it is a case of mistaken identity. You had better go back to the Palace and tell this man Grauber so.'

'You will have a chance to tell him so yourself in a few minutes.'

Sabine suddenly sat forward and asked in a voice just a shade higher than usual, 'What do you mean by that?'

'He left me to collect some of his colleagues who have been mixed up in this thing; but he must be on his way here by now.'

Gregory, peering down from behind the suit of armour, stiffened where he stood. Those last words confirmed his worst fears of the way matters might develop. For a moment he contemplated slipping behind the curtain, hunting round till he found some back stairs, then trying to find a way out of the house; but instead of appearing perturbed Sabine displayed only calculated indifference.

'Am I to understand,' she enquired, raising her eyebrows, 'that you intend to stand quietly by while I am grilled by some Gestapo thug?'

'No! No! Of course not!' he protested quickly. 'But they are entitled to any reasonable help that I can give them. I take it that Pipi has gone to bed?'

'Yes. Why do you ask?'

'I was thinking about letting these people in. It would be better to keep the servants out of this.' As he spoke the Minister walked towards the vestibule, adding over his shoulder, 'It is so warm, it won't matter leaving the front door open; then they will not have to ring.'

Gregory was greatly tempted to step out from behind the armour, lean over the gallery and call softly down to Sabine, 'Quick! Get the glass I used out of the way.' But he decided that the risk of Ribbentrop's returning before he could regain his cover was too great. It was just as well, for the Minister was out of sight for barely a minute and, as he re-entered the room, there came the faint sounds of a car driving into the courtyard. Turning, he walked back to the door of the vestibule, returned a loud greeting of '*Heil Hitler*,' and led in the visitors. To Gregory's dismay, he saw that Grauber had with him Cochefert, Major Szalasi and Lieutenant Puttony.

Szalasi bowed over Sabine's hand. Grauber and Cochefert were presented to her. The whole middle section of the Frenchman's face was swathed in a great bandage. Only his hooded eyes showed above, and his chin below it. Evidently his nose had been plugged as, when he spoke, it was in a voice so distorted that it sounded as though he had a split palate or acute adenoids. He was so shaky from loss of blood that he was given a chair, but Grauber was not invited to sit, and the pink-cheeked Puttony remained modestly in the background. After these greetings, Ribbentrop said in a cold haughty tone:

'*Herr Gruppenführer*, the *gnädige Frau Baronin* has consented to answer any questions you care to put to her. Please be as brief as possible.'

Having bowed his respectful thanks, Grauber asked Sabine to tell them where she had first met the man calling himself

194

Commandant Tavenier, and all that she knew about him.

In a quiet, detached voice, Sabine repeated with a few minor embellishments what she had already told Ribbentrop: such as the address of the apartment at which she had stayed as his aunt's guest in Paris and approximately the date of her stay there. She gave as her reason for the visit that his aunt was a partner in a big French fashion house, and that she had been commissioned by a Hungarian shop to buy models from the firm—all of which was quite plausible as, in her poorer days, she had been for a while a professional model.

As Ribbentrop and Szalasi had both been present when she had again met Gregory the previous evening, they had no reason whatever to doubt her veracity, and both nodded confirmation as she went on to give Grauber an outline of what had happened. In the same rather bored manner, she continued with the rest of her story, ending with a positive assertion that, however much Tavenier might resemble the Englishman the Gestapo wanted to catch, he could not possibly be their man.

Having heard her out, Grauber gave her a queer little smile, and said in his high falsetto, 'It is the *gnädige Frau Baronin* who is mistaken.' Then he turned to Ribbentrop, and added: '*Herr Reichsaussenminister*, we have proof—incontrovertible proof. Listen, please, to what *M. le Capitaine* Cochefert of the *Deuxième Bureau* has to say.'

From the moment the Frenchman had entered the hall, Gregory had realised that Grauber must have gone to the hospital where Cochefert was being treated and, on hearing his revelations, have insisted that he should leave his bed to repeat them to Ribbentrop. While arguing with Sabine in her car he had failed to take into account that his two enemies might get together again so quickly, and it was only in the past few minutes that it had struck him how disastrous their collaborations must prove. His instinctive feeling that Sabine's story was not entirely watertight was now to prove only too well-founded and, for both their sakes, he cursed his folly in having allowed her to persuade him into coming back with her.

Snuffling his words, and obviously speaking only with considerable pain, Cochefert gave particulars of Vichy's reply to his routine enquiry and recounted how, when cornered, Gregory had admitted that he was not Tavenier.

Sabine rose splendidly to the occasion. She shrugged and said with a slightly malicious smile, 'In view of the damage that Commandant Tavenier has done to *M. le Capitaine's* face, I can understand his desire to be revenged; but I do not believe one word of his story. It is typical of what one hears of the low morality of the Vichy police, and their servile anxiety to curry favour at any price with the Germans.'

Ribbentrop grinned openly, and Gregory mentally took off his hat to her. But he knew that her broadside had been fired in vain. There was the stocky, wooden-faced Puttony standing at attention in the background, and at any moment Grauber could bring him into play.

Cochefert began to splutter with rage, but choked on his own blood, and had to turn away, coughing agonisingly into a big silk handkerchief. Ignoring him, Grauber kept his single eye on Sabine, pursed up his small cruel mouth, and said:

'The *gnädige Frau Baronin's* attack upon this officer is entirely unwarranted. Fortunately, we have a witness to his integrity. The Lieutenant of Police whom we have brought with us was present at the interview. He will confirm that your . . . er, friend confessed to being an impostor.'

'How much are you paying him to do that?' Sabine rapped back. 'Everyone knows that you Gestapo people will stick at nothing to get into your hands any person you suspect.'

'Whatever we do is done in the best interests of the *Reich*,' Grauber retorted sharply. 'But let me tell you something else. When this "suspect", as you call him, was arrested he secured a new lease of freedom by producing a Gestapo pass, and declaring himself to be *Obersturmbannführer* Einholtz. To my personal knowledge he murdered the *Obersturmbannführer* last December. And it is our word—and the word of all three of us—against yours, *gnädige Frau Baronin*.'

It was useless for Gregory to reproach himself for not having foreseen that, should Grauber and Cochefert compare notes, Sabine's story would be blown wide open. He could only strain his ears and eyes to learn how she would face the fatal breach in her defences.

Ribbentrop's swift brain had already summed up the implications. Swinging round on her, he said, 'One can no longer doubt that the *Herr Gruppenführer* is right. The man who has been passing here as Tavenier is the Englishman Sallust; and that makes nonsense of your assertions that he is a French‹

man with whose aunt you stayed in Paris. There must be some explanation. I can only assume that you knew him to be Sallust all the time, and have been playing some deep game. If this was so, please tell us?'

Sabine took the cue, smiled at him and said, 'How clever of you, Joachim. Of course I knew; but I kept his secret with the idea of finding out what he was up to here. If these fools had not butted in, I was hoping that he might return here, and that before you left tomorrow I would be able to report to you a really valuable piece of counter-espionage.'

Gregory heaved an inaudible sigh of relief, and the Minister, having his hopes that his mistress would be able to exonerate herself so swiftly confirmed, exclaimed to Grauber with a laugh, 'There you are, *Herr Gruppenführer!* And that, I think, puts an end to this annoying affair.'

But Grauber was not the man to be sent about his business so peremptorily. With no trace of sarcasm, but what sounded like genuine humility, he piped, 'I am abashed that I should have forced this disclosure from the *gnädige Frau Baronin.* My zeal for the *Führer's* service must be my excuse; and on that account I feel confident that she will not deny us the results of her endeavours?'

'On the contrary, you are welcome to them,' Sabine replied graciously. 'He came here to investigate the possibility of Hungary's being induced to make a separate peace with the Allies.'

'There!' Ribbentrop exclaimed again. 'That ties up with what you told me of your own mission.'

'Correct, *Herr Reichsaussenminister.*' Grauber gave a jerky little bow; then turned back to Sabine with a look of deferential interrogation.

She shook her head. 'I'm afraid I have little to add. He had been here a fortnight and was convinced that he was wasting his time.'

'Did he make no mention at all of his contacts?'

'He said that he had talked with one or two Jews, and a number of people of some standing with whom he had scraped acquaintance; but he did not disclose the names of any of them to me.'

'Then he was holding out on you, *gnädige Frau Baronin.* We have very good reason to believe that a group of magnates is conspiring against the regime. It would be too much of a coincidence if he were not in touch with them.'

'I may yet find out more if he does come back.' She glanced at Ribbentrop. 'It was with that object I invited him to stay here for a few nights.'

Gregory was feeling much easier now. It really looked as if Sabine's confidence in her ability to hold the fort whatever happened was about to be justified, and that Grauber must now retire with his tail between his legs. But almost casually he said:

'As the *gnädige Frau Baronin* has tacitly admitted that her story of staying with this man's aunt in Paris was no more than a temporary cover device, perhaps she would be graciously pleased to tell us where she did first meet him?'

Sabine lit a cigarette, and replied truthfully. 'It was in the summer of 1936 at Deauville. I was at that time in the employ of an international financier named Lord Gavin Fortescue. I did not realise it until later, but Lord Gavin was engaged in criminal activities. He had built up a formidable organisation for smuggling not only great quantities of dutiable goods, but also agitators, into England. Mr. Sallust had been given the task of investigating these secret landings by a Sir Pellinore Gwaine-Cust, and . . .'

'What!' Ribbentrop broke in. 'But he lived only a few doors from our Embassy in Carlton House Terrace. When I was Ambassador in London I knew him well by sight, and on several occasions I ran into him at official receptions. His was an unforgettable personality, and the stories about him were legion. He poses as a sort of damn-fool retired Guards Officer, but he has made an immense fortune for himself in the City. His influence is enormous and it is even said that more than once his hand has been behind changes in the Cabinet.'

Grauber gave a quick nod. 'Correct, *Herr Reichsaussenminister*. According to our records this old Sir Cust has a finger in every pie, and is privy to every secret. It should be added that after Churchill he is Germany's most inveterate enemy. In the past quarter of a century he has a score of times thwarted endeavours to increase the power of the Fatherland.'

Raising her eyebrows, Sabine remarked, 'You both surprise me. He seemed to me an unusually straightforward and very charming old gentleman.'

'You know him, then?' Grauber asked with quick interest.

'Yes; I met him through Mr. Sallust, and he could not have been kinder to me.'

'In what way?' enquired Ribbentrop.

'Well, through going to England and carrying out Lord Gavin's instructions I had made myself liable to arrest by the British Police. Sir Pellinore knew that, although he did not say so at the time. But he told me that if I got into difficulties with the authorities about anything I was not to hesitate to let him know. He also said that whenever I wished to stay in London his house and servants would always be at my disposal.'

'Why should he have taken such a special interest in you?'

'Because he was an old friend of my father's. Both of them were fine horsemen and they used to jump against one another at the Olympia Horse Shows in King Edward VII's time. Sir Pellinore had also stayed with my parents at our castle for the partridge shooting; but, of course, that was before I was born.'

'And did you escape arrest, or did Sir Pellinore use his lawyers to get you off on some technicality?'

'I escaped arrest, but that I owed to Mr. Sallust. At considerable risk to himself he got me out of the country, and probably saved me from a very unpleasant prison sentence.'

'So!' Grauber exclaimed. 'Then gratitude is the explanation for the *gnädige Frau Baronin's* concealing Sallust in her house.'

Gregory caught his breath. For the past few minutes he had been lulled into a false belief that the worst was over. He saw Sabine stiffen, and she asked sharply;

'What do you mean by that?'

Grauber gestured towards the drink trolley. 'That you brought him back with you and have concealed him somewhere. Otherwise why should there be two dirty glasses on that tray?'

'Really, *Herr Gruppenführer!*' she gave an impatient shrug. 'You may be a very clever policeman, but this time you are on a false scent. There are two dirty glasses because I had one drink before I went up to bed and another when I came down again.'

Ribbentrop was now looking extremely worried and Gregory wondered if it was because he realised that Sabine was lying. He should have if he cast his mind back over the past twenty minutes, for Sabine had not joined him in a drink when they had come in together. But he made no comment.

199

Grauber only smiled and walked across to the far side of the staircase where for a few seconds he was hidden from Gregory's view. When he came into it again his back was turned and he was carrying something in front of him. Holding it out to Sabine, he said:

'And this, *gnädige Frau Baronin*. How do you account for this?'

Having put the question he moved his arm sideways, so that Ribbentrop could get a better view of the thing he held. Gregory could now also see it. To his horror it was the small basin half-full of pinkish water, and with the bloodstained piece of lint in it, that Sabine had used to bathe the cut on his head.

Still undefeated, Sabine stalled again with a half-admission. 'I take back what I said just now, *Herr Gruppenführer*, about your being a poor detective. Mr. Sallust did not run away from me as I told you. He wanted to but I wouldn't let him. I still hoped to get more out of him if I could keep him with me. When we got in I did give him a drink, and I bathed his head. But I couldn't induce him to stay here. He was convinced that, when you learned that it was I who got him out of the police station, you would come here and demand to search the house. As soon as he had finished his drink he told me to give you his compliments and say that he would yet live to see you dangling from a hangman's rope. Then he didn't even stop to collect his things, but asked me to keep them for him till he came back after the war.'

It was so exactly what Gregory might have done that it sounded extremely plausible. But Grauber still had an ace up his sleeve. Shaking his bristly head, he said:

'*Gnädige Frau Baronin*, that will not do. We know that he is still here.' Then beckoning Puttony forward he said to him, 'Lieutenant, report the help you have given us to the *Herr Reichsaussenminister*.'

The stocky young Hungarian advanced a few quick paces, came stiffly to attention, then rattled off as though he were giving evidence before a magistrate, 'On completion of my tour of duty I returned to the Station. As I was about to go in I met the *gnädige Frau Baronin* and the man who has been passing as Tavenier coming out. He was dishevelled and his clothes were torn. The Station Captain had seen them to the door. I asked him what had been going on. He told me that the man had had a fight in the Arizona with Captain Cochefert and a *Gruppenführer* of the Gestapo. I had been present when the man had admitted to a Captain Cochefert that he was not Tavenier. He had then produced a Gestapo pass in the name of *Obersturmbannführer* Einholtz and said that he assumed the name of Tavenier only because he was in Budapest on an undercover mission. For him to have fought with a Gestapo Chief and Captain Cochefert made it clear to me that he could not after all be a Gestapo Colonel, and was probably an enemy agent. Without enquiring further I ran from the Station and jumped on my motor-cycle. I was in time to catch up the *gnädige Frau Baronin's* car as it was about to cross the Swing Bridge. She did not cross it but turned off down the Corso and there pulled up. For some time the car remained stationary. While I was keeping it under observation a motor-cyclist patrol passed and I called him to my assistance. When the car restarted we followed it here. I sent the patrol round to the lower road with orders to tail the man if he left by that side of the house. Not far from the courtyard entrance there is a telephone kiosk. While using it I was able to continue my watch on the archway. If I had waited to ask the Station Captain why he had just released a man who had attacked a *Gruppenführer* I should have lost the car; but the more I thought about his having done so the more it puzzled me. In the circumstances I decided not to ask help from him. Instead I telephoned Arrow-Cross Headquarters. Fortunately Major Szalasi was there. He volunteered to come himself and arrived a few minutes later with a truck-load of his young men. We posted them on both sides of the house and round the whole block. I then telephoned the Station and learned that Captain Cochefert had been taken to hospital. In order to find out exactly what had occurred I went there. With him I found *Herr Gruppenführer* Grauber, to whom he presented me. I returned here with them.'

With grim attention Gregory had followed each incisive sentence. He knew now why the outline of the officer they had almost run into on leaving the police station had seemed vaguely familiar, and that Puttony was far from being such a fool as he looked. But for his eagerness to ensure against his superior's having made a blunder, Sabine might have got away with it; but now it seemed that her last line of defence was breached. She had put up a splendid show, but the combination

of Grauber, Cochefert and Puttony had been too much for
her, and there was no way in which Gregory could give her
aid. With a sinking heart he watched the pack close in.

'*Gut, sehr gut, Herr Leutnant,*' Grauber nodded to Puttony.
'And now, *Herr Major,*' he turned with a gesture of invitation
to Szalasi.

The Arrow-Cross leader had not so far uttered a word.
Now he looked a little uneasily at Ribbentrop, then said half-
apologetically, 'As far as I am concerned the Lieutenant's
report is accurate. He asked me urgently for help to catch a
spy. I collected my Headquarters' Staff and rushed them here
in a wagon. We surrounded the block and I can vouch for it
that nobody answering the wanted man's description has left it
since our arrival.'

With a smirk of triumph Grauber turned back to Sabine.
'You see, *gnädige Frau Baronin.* There is no room for doubt.
Sallust is somewhere here in your palace, and I mean to have
him. Be good enough to spare us any unpleasantness by
giving him up.'

Stubbornly she shook her head. 'You are wrong, *Herr
Gruppenführer.* He left, just as I told you, after I had
bathed his head. That would have been about the time that
your friend the Lieutenant was telephoning from the kiosk.
By remaining in the shadow thrown by the houses on this
side of the street it would not have been difficult to slip away
unobserved.'

'*Nein!*' Grauber's shrill negative cut the tense atmosphere
like a knife. 'I have been patient. You abuse your privileged
position too far. I will be trifled with no longer. We have
plenty of men outside. Give up this man, or I will order the
house to be searched.'

Gregory took the little automatic from his pocket, so that
there should be no delay in clicking a bullet up into its chamber. He knew that once a search started he could give up all
hope of escape. But he did not mean to be caught alive. And
he meant to take Grauber with him. This was not the first time
that he had had the chance to kill him out of hand; but on those
previous occasions, although he had known them to be absurd,
scruples had restrained him from shooting down his enemy
unawares. Now, he had no such feeling. The circumstances
were different, and this was the last throw. If he had to die he
could at least rid the world of a monster before he choked

out his last breath. With not a ripple of doubt ruffling his con-science about the rightness of the act, he decided that when the moment came he would put no less and no more than three bullets through Grauber's stomach.

He wondered then if he ought to shoot Ribbentrop as well. After all, Ribbentrop was Nazi No. 4 and, even if indirectly, had been responsible for an incalculable number of deaths and tidal waves of misery. Yet, unlike Grauber, there was nothing positively evil about him. He was rather a pleasant person; an exceptionally gifted play-boy whom a strange fate had given the opportunity of jumping on to the biggest of all band-wagons. There was another thing. While he remained alive there was a chance that he might protect Sabine. As Gregory was himself impotent to do so, he decided that, after the gallant fight she had put up on his behalf, the least he could do was to leave her the one man who was powerful enough, and might have the inclination, to save her from the Gestapo.

While these thoughts had been rushing through Gregory's head, Ribbentrop had come to a decision. Turning on Grauber he said sharply, *'Herr Gruppenführer,* you forget yourself! The initiation of any action to be taken here rests with me.'

*'Herr Reichsaussenminister,'* Grauber piped aggressively, with due respect I cannot agree. Foreign affairs are your province and Security mine. This is a security matter.'

'More hangs on it than this man's immediate arrest.'

'Much more!' The sneer in Grauber's voice said as plainly as though he had spoken the words. 'The proof that this pretty mistress of yours has been harbouring a British spy.' Swing-ing round he cried to Szalasi:

*'Herr Major,* please bring in your men. We will search this palace from attic to cellar; and if we fail to get our man I'll drink the swine's blood out of that basin before you all.'

*'Herr Major!'* Ribbentrop's voice held cold fury, but there was just a quaver of panic underlying it. 'We are grateful for the help you have rendered. But this is now a matter between the *Herr Gruppenführer* and myself. Be pleased to withdraw your men, and take the French Captain and the Lieutenant of Police with you. I need hardly add that, if you wish to retain my goodwill, you will regard this affair as of the highest sec-recy.'

Fascinated, Gregory peered down at the two angry men who had squared up to one another in the hall below him—the German Foreign Minister, well-built, good-looking, suave, authoritative; the Gestapo chief, physically gorilla-like, his face a mask of malice, cunning and habitual cruelty, incredibly forceful in his determination not to be baulked of his prey. Upon the outcome of this battle of wills Gregory knew that his life, and probably Sabine's as well, now depended. But, temporarily at least, both of them had put the onus of decision on Szalasi.

The bulky Arrow-Cross leader looked desperately uncomfortable. Gregory had no doubt at all that his sympathies were with Grauber, who was obviously carrying out his duty; but Ribbentrop's prestige outweighed that of any Nazi other than Hitler, Goering and Himmler. After a moment's hesitation the Major said:

'*Herr Reichsaussenminister*. No one can dispute your ability to judge what is right in such a matter. You may rely on my discretion.'

With a quick bow, and another to Sabine, he made a sign to Puttony, who gave a hand to the almost comatose Cochefert, and the three of them left the room.

Gregory was suddenly conscious that his forehead was damp with perspiration. Stuffing the automatic back into his pocket, he pulled out his handkerchief to wipe his face. As he raised his hand, his elbow brushed against the leather surcoat of the armoured figure immediately behind which he was standing. Unseen by him in the darkness, it gave off a small cloud of dust. A moment later he felt a slight tickling in his nostrils.

Ignoring it, he continued to stare down into the hall, still anxious not to miss a single word, but fairly confident that Sabine had now spiked Grauber's guns. She had proved right in her contention that Ribbentrop would not allow the house to be searched; but, at the same time, she had landed both him and herself in an appalling mess. There could be no laughing off the fact that she had aided and concealed, and was presumably still concealing, a British secret agent; and that Ribbentrop had deliberately used his authority to prevent that agent's arrest. He might be able to stop Szalasi's mouth, but he could not stop Grauber's. What a story it would make;

and, perhaps, what a nail in his coffin if, next time he had done something to annoy Hitler, Himmler produced it with juicy trimmings as proof that the Foreign Minister was so under the thumb of his Hungarian mistress that he could no longer be trusted to act in the best interests of Germany and the *Partei*.

No sooner had the door of the vestibule closed upon Puttony than Grauber, made bold by the knowledge of the whip hand he held, put Gregory's thoughts into words. He no longer bothered even to refer to Sabine by her title. His chin thrust forward aggressively, he sneered:

'I had thought you cleverer, *Herr Reichsaussenminister*, than to suppose that by getting rid of the others you can get the better of me. The man Sallust is my personal enemy, and I mean to have him. This woman of yours has lied and cheated. She is a traitress and . . .'

'That is enough!' Ribbentrop exclaimed, going pale with anger.

'It is the truth!' Grauber retorted. 'First she led you to believe that Sallust was a Frenchman; yet all the time she knew he was English and, knowing that, she got him out of prison. Then she lied about having brought him back here, but we forced her to confess that she did. Lastly, she still swears that she has not hidden him in this house; yet we have proof that he cannot have left it. For less I have cut off women's breasts and chopped them up and made them swallow the pieces.'

'Stop!' shouted Ribbentrop. 'Stop. I forbid you to speak here of your vile practices.'

'Why should I not?' Grauber shrilled back. 'They are for the furtherance of the cause we both serve. But it seems you have forgotten that cause; so I must remind you of it.'

'I have forgotten nothing! I am as good a patriot and Party man as you!'

'That we must leave to be judged by my chief, *Herr* Himmler, when I report to him the way in which you have thwarted me.'

For the past few moments Gregory had been keeping his teeth tight clenched and a finger pressed hard on the bridge of his nose. The dust-like particles into which the soft leather of the ancient surcoat was slowly decaying were now causing acute irritation to his mucous membrane. He feared that at any moment he might give a violent sneeze. If he did he was bound to be discovered; yet he could not bear the thought of missing the denouement of this explosive altercation.

Ribbentrop suddenly seemed to get his temper under control, and said in a more pacific tone, 'Herr *Gruppenführer,* I sympathise with your feelings. But there are more ways than one in which we can serve our *Führer.* For his servants to quarrel among themselves is certainly not one; and subtlety often pays bigger dividends than force. I refrained from asking you to leave with the others because I have a proposal to . . .'

Gregory heard no more. To have lingered another minute would have been fatal. Now, with his nostrils clamped between finger and thumb, he ducked down below the level of the balustrade and swiftly fumbled his way out round the edge of the curtain. During the whole time he had remained hidden there no one had glanced up in his direction. Now he could only pray that the curtain's movement would not catch Grauber's eye and lead after all to a show-down in which he would have lost the advantage.

Hastening along on tip-toe, he managed to reach the far end of the corridor, then the explosive pressure in his head became too much. The awful sneeze, partly muffled by his grip on his nose, snorted and burbled; he choked and then began to cough. Dreading now that he must be heard, he grasped the handle of the nearest door, turned it and thrust the door open a few inches. The room was in darkness. Slipping inside he closed the door behind him and payed his debt to frustrated nature in an awful bout of gasping, sneezing, weeping, coughing, while the water streamed from his eyes.

It was a good five minutes before he had recovered sufficiently to feel safe in returning to his post of observation, then he had to pad softly back down the corridor and exercise great caution to shake the curtain as little as possible while squirming under it; so he reckoned that he had probably lost about seven minutes of the drama being enacted down in the hall.

As he approached, lower voices had already told him that the crisis was over, but it was not until he could again raise his head and peer out from behind the armour that he realised that Grauber had gone. Ribbentrop and Sabine were now sitting side by side on one of the sofas, and he was saying to her earnestly:

'You are a clever woman, Sabine. I have no fears that you will make a mess of things. By doing as I wish you can save yourself and render me a great service.'

'I know,' she replied. 'I do see that it is the only way in which I can save your face. But you can't expect me to like the idea of leaving everything.'

'Of course not. Neither do I like the thought of losing you. We can only hope that it will not be for very long.'

'I suppose it is the only thing to do?'

'The only thing. I shall have difficulty enough as it is to put over this explanation in the teeth of the report that Grauber will make to Himmler. As you had an affair with this man Sallust in the past, whatever your true motive in failing to tell us at once that you recognised him, the fact that you did not will make everyone believe you guilty of aiding an English spy. For that you would normally get the death penalty. You know the *Führer's* rages, and how he refuses to make the least allowance for other people's personal feelings. If I tried to protect you, he would break me; perhaps even accuse me of betraying our interests to the British myself. The utmost I dare do openly I have done already. The rest is up to you, if you wish to save your neck and ever see Budapest again. Can I rely on your promise to fall in with my proposal?'

She nodded. 'All right. I expect I'll manage to take care of myself, and it will certainly be exciting; but you must brief my very carefully before we start.'

'I will get everything for you in the morning—special passes from Horthy to prevent the Security Police from holding you up on your dash for the frontier, foreign currency and a permit to take your car out with you. About everything else I can advise you when we get to bed.'

'You mean to stay here the night, then?'

Smiling, he stood up, took her hand and pulled her to her feet. 'Why not? This may be the last chance we will get till the war is over.'

Without another word they came up the stairs and passed behind Gregory on their way to her room. When she reached it she pressed a switch which plunged the hall in darkness. For some while Gregory remained where he was, trying to extract all the meaning he could from their conversation.

The gist of it seemed to be that, as Ribbentrop was not powerful enough to protect Sabine, he was sending her abroad for the duration. By 'briefing' her, presumably she had meant advising her what line to take with her friends and servants before leaving the country. Her reluctance to do so was quite understandable; but—apart from the fact that her life might depend on it—nothing else could save Ribbentrop from being involved in a first-class political scandal. The only rather puzzling thing was that he had spoken of two special passes, and that she had used the plural when speaking of starting. It seemed to Gregory unlikely that Ribbentrop would be willing to connive at his escape, and almost as unlikely that, if Sabine were to leave Hungary for good, she would take her chauffeur with her; yet for whom, other than one of them, could the second pass be?

When at last he crept back to his room he was wondering again if his best chance did not lie in leaving the house, lying low with Levianski for several days, if the furrier would have him, then making a bid to reach the frontier.

On the other hand, it just might be that Sabine had, by some means, persuaded Ribbentrop to let him take him with her. Holding more promise, there was also her original plan for him to take her chauffeur's place. If that was still possible and the second pass was intended for the chauffeur, it was he who would reap the benefit of it.

One thing was certain: in an uneven battle Sabine had shown both courage and great skill. She had not lost her head for a single moment, and it was through no fault of hers that she had twice been caught out. She had not known that Cochefert had already blown Gregory's identity as Tavenier, or that her car had been followed by Puttony. Against ill luck and heavy odds she had stuck to her guns and, in the end, managed to come to some arrangement with Ribbentrop.

In the circumstances Gregory felt that he had no right to suppose that she might have left him out of her latest calculations; and he had promised her that he would not leave the house. That promise could hardly be considered as still binding after all that had happened during the past hour, and Sabine could not be in any way dependent on his help for getting across the frontier but, all the same, he decided to keep it.

The moon was still up and he undressed by its light, then slipped into bed. But he would rather have spent the night prowling the streets than between those soft sheets, for he knew that his life would not be safe until he was out of Budapest, and the strain of lying inactive was hard to bear.

It was not until morning that he dropped into a doze, and he was only fully woken by Pipi's tip-toeing in with his breakfast tray. On it there was a note from Sabine, which Pipi said had been passed on to him by Magda. The single line, scrawled on a fly-leaf torn from a book, read:

*Make no noise. Stay where you are until I come to you. S.*

To abide by her order he denied himself a bath, shaved and dressed with hardly a sound, then sat down in an armchair to wait for her. At a little after half-past-nine, still in a négligée, she came in to him.

'It's all right now,' she said with a smile. 'Ribb spent the night here. That's why I couldn't come up to you; and, Mary be praised, you didn't come down to me. I was terrified you would. He has just gone, and I've fixed everything; but it was touch and go last night.'

'I know,' he smiled back. 'I saw the whole party. I had hidden myself between the curtains and one of the suits of armour in the gallery. You certainly . . .'

'What!' She halted in her tracks, and her eyes grew round as saucers. 'D'you . . . d'you mean that you heard everything we said.'

'Not quite. Some dust got up my nose, and I had to creep away for about six or seven minutes to have a sneezing fit.'

'When . . . what was happening when you did that?'

'The smaller fry had gone. Ribb had been having one hell of a row with Grauber, but was just about to put some proposition to him.'

'You didn't hear then . . . what it was?'

'No, what was it?'

'Oh, simply an attempt to bribe him. But all those top Gestapo men have already made fortunes by threats and blackmail; so it didn't come off. What were we doing when you got back from your sneezing fit?'

'You and Ribb were alone. He was persuading you to leave the country for his sake and your own. That is damned hard on you. I'm more sorry than I can say to have been the cause of letting you in for this.'

She gave a heavy sigh. 'It is my own fault for having persuaded you to come back here with me.'

'Anyhow, you put up a marvellous fight. It was the most accursed luck that that fellow Puttony should have run into us just as we were leaving the police station. What else happened while I was not there to listen?'

'Oh nothing . . . nothing much. Ribb and Grauber went on wrangling. You must have heard everything that mattered; so there is no point in my repeating it all to you.'

'No. The thing I am anxious to hear is what do you propose I should do now?'

Taking a cigarette from the box beside his bed, she went over to him for a light, and said, 'I swore to Ribb that you really did leave the house soon after we got here, and said that you must have slipped past the Lieutenant while he was tele-phoning to Szalasi. Ribb believes that. At least I think he does. He wouldn't want you to be captured anyway because, if you were, my name would be dragged into it and involve him in the scandal he is so anxious to avoid. Anyway he is going to give a cooked-up version of the affair to the Regent, get him to issue an order to the Hungarian Security Police not to pursue the matter for the moment, and will get from him special passes ordering them not to prevent myself and my chauffeur leaving the country. But he told me that I can count only on temporary protection; so I must get out while the going is good. That means leaving tonight; and you, of course, will be my chauffeur.'

Gregory nodded. 'That looks like an easy get out for me, then.'

She shook her head. 'I'm afraid it may not prove as easy as it sounds. Grauber proved irreconcilable. He will be tele-phoning to Himmler to exert pressure on the Regent. That is why we must get across the frontier before a new order goes out for our arrest. In the meantime Grauber can raise quite a bunch of Gestapo men from the Villa Petoefer, and he has a lot of pull with the Arrow-Cross people. The last thing he said before he left was that he was convinced that you were still here, and that, dead or alive, he meant to get you; so he may try to intercept us.'

# 15

## Anxious Hours

Nothing could have given Gregory greater cause for alarm than the news that Grauber intended to take the law into his own hands. Swiftly he urged that they should start for the frontier at the earliest possible moment, so as to give the enemy the minimum of time in which to take measures that might prevent their leaving the city.

Sabine agreed in theory but was not very helpful in practice. She said that she could not leave without seeing her banker, her solicitor and her jeweller; moreover, as she was not returning to Berlin where she kept a separate wardrobe, but meant to pretend in front of the servants that she was, she must herself pack such clothes as she could take with her.

Gregory deplored the delay but was forced to submit to it; for Sabine pointed out that it would be madness to leave without the papers promised by Ribbentrop, and in order to collect them she had to lunch with him. That meant they would be unable, anyway, to start before mid-afternoon; so after some discussion they decided to put off their departure until early evening, as they would then gain the benefit of twilight, and there would be less likelihood of Grauber's people spotting that the driver of Sabine's car was Gregory dressed up in her chauffeur's uniform.

Again Gregory told her how distressed he was about bringing such trouble upon her and having disrupted her whole life, but she seemed to take the matter with commendable philosophy. Smiling a little wryly, she said that it could not be helped and that, if only they could keep clear of Grauber, she felt sure she would find compensations abroad for all she was being forced to give up. Then she promised to send Gregory something to read, and left him.

Pipi arrived ten minutes later with half a dozen English novels published in the '30s and a German paper printed in Vienna. While he made the bed and tidied the room, Gregory glanced through the paper.

During the past few days a great naval and air battle had been raging in the Solomons between the Americans and the

Japanese, and it was now admitted that the Americans had had the best of it.

There were further details about the death of the Duke of Kent, which had occurred on the previous Tuesday. His Royal Highness had been flying in a Sunderland to Iceland on R.A.F. duty when the aircraft had crashed with the loss of all but one of the fifteen men aboard her. Gregory had met the Duke on one occasion and found him charming; so he was able to form an idea of how greatly his loss would be felt by the Royal family.

Colossal battles involving millions of men were still raging in Russia. The Germans admitted withdrawals on the central front, and from the place-names mentioned it was clear that General Zhukov's recent counter-offensive had forced them back to positions 120 miles west of Moscow. But Von Bock's offensive across the Don was still making progress, the Germans claimed that their shock troops had broken through the outer defences of Stalingrad, and the threat to the city was now extremely grave.

As Gregory knew only too well, it was Stalingrad that mattered. No successes elsewhere could possibly compensate for its loss. Without it Russia's war economy must collapse, and that could lead to the loss of the war by the Allies, or, at best, a slogging match with no foreseeable end until half the cities in the world were destroyed and the whole of its population starving.

But he wondered now whether, even if he could get back to England safely and quickly, there would still be the time and the means to put his successful negotiations in Budapest to practical use. He had no doubt whatever about the soundness of his plan. If only the Hungarians could be induced to repudiate the Nazis and withdraw their army from the Russian front the Germans, in order to fill the gap, would within a week be compelled to raise the siege of Stalingrad.

First, though, the Hungarians quite reasonably required their guarantees. To secure them meant selling the plan, with all its postwar commitments, to both the Foreign Office and the State Department, then the British and American Chiefs-of-Staff Committees would have to be consulted on its military implications and, finally, the consent obtained of the War Cabinet and the President. It would mean every person involved in the High Direction of the War on both sides of the Atlantic being given a chance to have his say at one or more of innumerable committee meetings and the exchange of hundreds of 'Most Secret' cypher telegrams between Washington and London. With the best will in the world on the part of all concerned, a decision could not possibly be hoped for in less than a month.

And that was not the end of it. Given agreement, the operation against Hitler-held Europe, demanded by the Hungarians, would still have to be mounted. Even if tentative preparations were begun while the discussions were in progress, could an invasion be launched before the autumn gales rendered the risk entailed too great? Again, had we the forces available and, if we had, after Dieppe, would the Chiefs of Staff be prepared to gamble them in another cross-Channel assault?

There could now be no doubt that the Dieppe raid had proved a very costly failure. Apart from the destruction of a few coast defence installations, we had achieved nothing, whereas the enemy had sunk one of our destroyers, accounted for a number of our latest tanks and, worst of all, taken several thousands of our finest Canadian troops prisoner. Even so, those losses might yet pay a handsome long-term dividend by compelling Hitler to keep many divisions, which he would otherwise have sent to Russia, inactive along the European coast. For all Gregory knew, that had been the intention of the operation, and if the initial landings had succeeded, full-scale invasion would have followed. If so, the Chiefs of Staff had already shot their bolt as far as helping Russia was concerned; and, anyway, having alerted the Germans to the dangers of leaving their coast thinly defended was going to make any second attempt to land in force all the more difficult.

Gloomily Gregory decided that the Dieppe raid had probably queered his pitch. Even if Sir Pellinore could get the Hungarian plan adopted it looked as if the odds were all against the required fifteen divisions of Anglo-American troops being launched against the Continent before winter set in, and it now seemed very doubtful whether Stalingrad would be able to hold out until winter. However, he knew that speculating on such matters would get them no further. His job was to reach home as soon as he possibly could in order to submit his report to the people who took the big decisions.

When Pipi left the room, Gregory flung the paper aside and began to think of his own affairs. He and Sabine had got one

213

another into a pretty mess. But for her he would never have gone to the Arizona, and but for that it was very unlikely that he would have come face to face with Grauber. But for him she would never have acted against the interests of the Gestapo, and but for that she would not have been condemned to go into exile.

By bringing them together again Fate had played the very devil with his plans, and had stymied him each time he had tried to wriggle free. That was no fault of hers; it was his for having refrained from following his own judgment and acting with his usual ruthlessness.

He realised now that admiration for the fight she had put up the previous night had led him to act like a sentimental fool. He should not have waited to hear the outcome of Grauber's quarrel with Ribbentrop, or to say good-bye to her, but should have got out while the going was good. He was armed and had plenty of money on him. He should never have listened to her in the first place, after she had got him out of the police station, but gone off on his own. Under cover of darkness he could have got clear of the city at any hour of the night, and by now would have bribed some lorry-driver to give him a lift on the way to the frontier.

Getting up, he crossed to the window, and from behind a partly-drawn curtain, peered out. As he had half expected, a knife-grinder whom he had seen down below in the street when he had looked out earlier was still there. The man was not now even pretending to sharpen knives against his treadle wheel, or to secure custom from the palaces opposite, but was just leaning against his barrow smoking a cigarette. Obviously he was a Gestapo agent who had been sent to keep watch on that side of the Tuzulto Palace.

Returning to his armchair, Gregory began to wonder just how much pull Grauber had in Budapest, and decided that it was probably considerable. The order to the police that Ribbentrop meant to obtain from Admiral Horthy, that they should not interfere with Sabine, would not apply to him and at best it would make them no more than neutral while he was in her company. As long as he remained with her in her palace he would probably be safe; but she had to leave during the coming night at latest, and once out of it he must expect that Grauber would ignore the law and go to any lengths to get him. To attempt a break out on his own now, in daylight, would obviously be suicidal; so it seemed that there was no alternative but to wait and go with Sabine. There was just a chance that her plan might succeed, but he was far from happy about it.

He looked through the books Pipi had brought him with the idea of starting one to take his mind off his anxieties. On the jacket of one there was the picture of a slim dark girl pointing a small automatic at a man in a dinner-jacket. The girl had a faint resemblance to Sabine and Gregory's thoughts promptly turned from the picture to the lovely passionate girl who had jumped into his bed the night before.

With a smile he recalled the intensity of her fury when Ribbentrop's arrival had interrupted their love-making; although he knew that his own fury would have equalled hers had not the necessity for keeping his mind clear to cope with what might prove a new danger forced him to purge it of emotion. Until he actually had her in his arms he had forgotten the feel of the exceptionally satin-like quality of that lovely magnolia skin of hers; and that, although her arms and legs were strong, her torso had a yielding softness which gave the impression that except for her spine she had no bones between her shoulders and her lower limbs. All day they had been steadily stoking one another's fires of desire, and the moment her arms closed round his neck the check administered by his ill-fated meeting with Grauber at the Arizona had been wiped from his mind as though it had never occurred. The scent of her had gone like wine to his head and the dew of her mouth was like honey to his lips.

'What a night we would have had! Perhaps better even than our first,' he thought to himself with a sigh, 'if it hadn't been for Ribbentrop.'

He started three books but after a chapter or two of each found that their stories could not hold him. His mind was too occupied with anxiety about the coming bid to get out of Budapest. It was utterly infuriating to think that less than twenty-four hours earlier he could have left without the least trouble, whereas now, if things went wrong, less than another twenty-four hours would see him shanghaied over the frontier to Austria and being taken to pieces in a Gestapo torture chamber. The thought of the lovely young girl who had given him his passport at the S.O.E. Headquarters in London flickered through his mind. Diana; yes, that had been her name, and he had promised himself that he would bring her back the biggest tin of foie-gras he could find. No hope of that now.

Somehow he got through the morning and at half-past one Pipi brought him up lunch on a tray. He ate it slowly to kill time and, when Pipi had taken the tray away, lay down on the bed hoping that, as he expected to be up all night, he would be able to get a sleep. But sleep would not come. Thoughts of Grauber still plagued him.

It was certain that the *Gruppenführer* would be spending the day pulling every gun he had with the Hungarians. No doubt he would do his damnedest to get the Police to co-operate with him and, in spite of the Regent's order, hold up Sabine's car when she left in it. They would be loath to offend him, but might search the car on the pretext that they believed her to be helping a wanted criminal to escape by carrying him off in its boot. If they did hold the car up it was a certainty that his thin disguise as Sabine's chauffeur would never get past Grauber.

Even if the police refused their help there was still the Arrow-Cross. As they were Nazis and most of German or Austrian blood, their first loyalty was not to Admiral Horthy but to Hitler. Major Szalasi had funked offending Ribbentrop on the previous night but it had been plain where his real sympathies lay. He could keep a clean bill himself by not appearing personally in the business and afterwards denying that he had had any hand in it, yet give Grauber the loan of several troops of his young Jew-baiters to block the streets.

Last, but by no means least, there were Grauber's own thugs at the Villa Petoefer. They would stick at nothing, and even if one of them committed murder Grauber would only have to call on Berlin for enough pressure to be exerted to have the matter hushed up.

That he stood little risk of being murdered outright was Gregory's one small rag of comfort. If he was once recognised as Sabine's chauffeur, it would be the easiest thing in the world to shoot him from the pavement; but Grauber wanted him alive. There could be no doubt about that, and it would be a poor look-out for the Gestapo man who killed him, or even did him a serious injury, before he was under lock and key.

A little after four o'clock he was at last relieved from further harrowing day-dreams by Sabine's coming in to him. As he sat up with a jerk she made straight for the armchair, gave a sigh of tiredness from her exertions, threw herself into it and kicked off her shoes.

Slipping off the bed, he lit a cigarette for her and after a few puffs she reported that so far all had gone well. Ribbentrop had secured all the necessary papers for her and had explained to the Regent that she had fallen foul of the Gestapo, who might endeavour to have her and her chauffeur arrested on their way out of the country. Horthy had promised to give an order personally to his Chief of Police that she was not to be molested, and one of his secretaries had telephoned instructions to Zagreb that she, her man and her car were to be allowed across the frontier without being subjected to any formalities. But Ribbentrop had again warned her that she must not delay her departure beyond the coming night, as it was certain that Grauber would already have appealed to Berlin for help. By the morning at latest Himmler would be making a personal issue of it with the Regent that Tavenier must be caught and herself hauled in for questioning by the Gestapo.

She had given her solicitor a power of attorney to deal with her affairs and meet her liabilities during her absence, had taken out from her bank in cash all the money that she had immediately available—which amounted to about six hundred pounds—and had collected, to take with her, the most valuable of the Tuzolto family jewels.

'By Jove!' Gregory smiled down at her. 'You have had a day! No wonder you're tired. Was anything said about, er—your old friend Commandant Tavenier?'

She nodded. 'Ribb is no fool. I'm sure he believes that you are still here; and he probably guesses that I mean to take you out as my chauffeur. Anyhow, he is extremely anxious that you should not be caught, from fear of what the Gestapo boys might screw out of you. It is a hundred to one they would force you to say that I was an enemy agent and make it appear that he had been guilty of confiding secrets to me that only the inner ring of Nazis are supposed to know. He has told Admiral Horthy that you are one of his private operatives and he has special reasons for not wishing the Gestapo to know that; so the Police are being briefed to ignore any request that Grauber may make for help to catch you.'

'Well, that's some comfort. I suppose the next thing is to

fix things up with your chauffeur? I only hope to God he doesn't refuse to play.'

'I've already done that.' She gave a tired shrug. 'I had a talk with Mario first thing this morning. I had to in order to get his passport so that it could be specially visa'd.'

'Of course. I realise that. But do you mean that he has agreed to let me have it, and to hand over his uniform?'

'Yes. I felt sure he would. He was one of Kelemen's most trusted servants, and since his master's death he has transferred his allegiance to me. When I told him that helping you meant a great deal to me he agreed at once; and when he knew that it was the Germans we were planning to do in the eye he was absolutely delighted. I had great difficulty in persuading the old boy even to accept a present.'

'The old boy!' Gregory echoed in alarm. 'I'm not exactly in the junior subaltern class myself, but if you really think of him as old, I may have difficulty in passing for him, even in the distance.'

'He is older than you; but not all that much. It's only his hair's having gone grey early that makes me think of him as of Kelemen's generation. You needn't worry about that though. I mean to lightly powder your hair where it will show beneath the cap.' Picking up her bag, she took a packet of papers from it, picked one out, handed it to Gregory, and added 'Look, here is his passport. You had better keep it.'

Opening it quickly Gregory looked at the photograph. To his relief he saw that Sabine had been right. Mario had at least a superficial resemblance to himself. On close examination they could not possibly have been mistaken for one another, but that did not matter as Sabine had a special authorisation for passing the frontier with her chauffeur and they would not have to answer any awkward questions. The important thing was that both he and Mario were of the long-faced type, with straight noses and good chins; so, with the chauffeur's cap pulled well down, and seated behind the wheel of a car, Gregory felt that after dark there would be a good chance of the watchers, outside taking him for the Italian.

Having expressed his satisfaction, he said, 'Now, tell me, when you left the house did you see any suspicious types lurking about the courtyard entrance?'

'Yes. When I first went out, at about half-past ten, there was a man with a barrow of tomatoes; and hawkers don't come into these streets as a rule. When I got back, about midday, he had gone but a pavement artist had taken up his position opposite, and I've never known one choose that pitch before. I've been out and back twice since, and he is still there. There seemed to be one or two loungers farther down the street, too, who didn't quite fit into the usual scene.'

'I expected as much. This side of the palace is being watched as well; a knife grinder first thing this morning and later a crippled beggar who is selling matches. When you went out I take it you used your car. Did you drive yourself or have Mario drive you?'

'Mario drove me all three times. I wanted to keep my mind free to think about things, and not have to be bothered with parking.'

'Did anyone attempt to stop you?'

'Oh no, there was nothing of that sort.'

Gregory gave a sigh of relief. 'Thank God for that. It means they are far less likely to now they are used to seeing the car come out with you in it driven by Mario. You've made me much more confident about my chances of passing as him when twilight has fallen.'

'He is going over the car now—filling her up and seeing that she is in apple-pie order for a long run.'

'Good! My sweet, you think of everything. You've done a wonderful job.'

She smiled a little wanly and stood up. 'I've got to get you out somehow, and myself; otherwise, as soon as Grauber gets some extra backing from Berlin, it is going to be very unhealthy round here for both of us.'

'You're dead right about that.' He put an arm about her. 'But after your long day, you're all in, darling. Lie down and rest for a bit on the bed.'

Turning her head she gave him a quick kiss, but pulled away before he could return it. 'No. I still have to pack. And when I do next lie on your bed it is going to be for twenty-four hours without a break.'

Catching her arm he jerked her back, held her tightly to him for a moment and gave her a long fierce kiss. As he released her he laughed, 'So you shall, my pet; and that is an earnest of what I'll do to you. If you want a real rest we'd better shut ourselves up for a week as the Spanish peasants do on their honeymoons. I'm told they spend the last twenty-four hours sleeping.'

'Darling!' she gasped, when she could get her breath. 'I'm a fool to admit it, because as soon as we've left Hungary you'll be all I've got; but I'm crazy about you.'

Her words sobered him a little, but he did not show it. Giving her a swift pat on her small behind, he said, 'Get your packing done as quickly as you can, then come back to me. We must have a meal before we start, so let's have it together up here, and while we are eating we can fix up final details.'

She agreed and left him. He then made another attempt to settle down to one of the books. This time, by using considerable concentration, he managed to keep his mind on a novel by Gilbert Grankau called *Three Englishmen*. After he had been reading for about an hour and a half, Pipi came in carrying a chauffeur's topcoat and a suitcase containing the rest of Mario's uniform. Unpacking the case, he suggested that Gregory should see how the uniform fitted, then pack in the case such of the Baron's things as he wished to take with him.

The uniform proved a little tight across the shoulders and slack round the hips, but as he and Mario were much of a height it was otherwise not a bad fit. There was a tin of talcum powder in the bathroom, so he used some of it to make grey the hair above his ears. Then he went through the wardrobe and chest of drawers again, selected the most useful of the Baron's clothes and packed them into the suitcase.

He had only just finished when Pipi returned with cocktails, and ten minutes later Sabine, having changed her summer frock for a suit of light travelling tweeds, joined him. Now that she could relax, and her mind was no longer occupied with matters it was essential that she should see to, her spirits had fallen to a low ebb. She did not actually reproach Gregory for being the cause of a complete upheaval in her life, but it was clear that she was greatly worried and distressed at having to abandon a position which gave her security, interest and carefree pleasure for a very uncertain future. In the circumstances he could not do less than promise to take care of her, while thrusting into the back of his mind the infernally difficult problem of how he could manage to do so.

After a couple of Martinis she cheered up a little; then Pipi brought in their early dinner on a wheeled tray. She apologised for the meal being cold but said that the kitchen staff were still in ignorance of his presence in the house and had been told that she was dining out; so Magda and Pipi had had to scrounge food for them from the larder. Gregory refrained from remarking that, even so, it was a feast compared with anything that could have been got in a London hotel after three years of war, and did ample justice to the smoked ham, cold duck and foie-gras. A bottle of champagne followed by a good ration of very old *Baratsch* put good heart into them, and they were both feeling fairly optimistic when, soon after eight o'clock, they went downstairs to set out on their hazardous journey.

To assist the illusion that she was being driven out to dinner Sabine did not wear a hat, and had had her sable coat laid on the floor in the back of the car. Instead of it she put on over her tweeds an exotic cape of white ostrich feathers. For the same reason such luggage as they were taking had all been stowed in the boot, with the exception of a pigskin beauty box containing her jewels, which she was carrying herself and could be hidden under the rug she would have over her knees.

The garage was a part of the old stables occupying the whole of the left side of the courtyard, but it could be reached from the main block of the house by an interior passage. Pipi and Magda escorted them to it and Mario was already there giving a last loving polish to the bonnet of the Mercedes. Gregory had driven many cars so he had no doubts about his ability to handle it; but after thanking Mario for his help with the passport and uniform he got the Italian to give him a thorough run over its dashboard and the engine. Pipi meanwhile went out to reconnoitre the street and returned to say that it was as quiet as was usual at that hour. Gregory ran the engine for a few minutes to get it thoroughly warmed up. Sabine got into the back, the good-byes were said and 'good luck' called in low voices by the faithful servants. At Gregory's signal Mario pulled up the roller shutter at the exit end of the bay. With a gentle purr the car moved forward, turned and headed for the entrance to the courtyard.

It was a fine warm night. In the distance someone was playing a *tizmberlum* and the ping-a-ping-ping of its notes came clearly over the air. That and the voice of a woman calling a dog were the only sounds that disturbed the respectable evening hush of this rich residential quarter.

A light over the archway to the street showed that the pavement artist who had occupied a pitch opposite to it all day was now gone. As Gregory cleared the arch, out of the corner of his eye he caught a glimpse of a man on the near-side of the road tinkering with a motor-cycle. In Hungary, as in England, the unusual custom is followed of driving on the left of the road; so Sabine's car had its steering wheel on the right. Gregory was therefore on the side nearest to the motor-cyclist, and it was that window of the car which was lowered.

He was about to turn left, down the hill, but before he had time to look in that direction the man had grasped the handlebars of his machine and begun to waggle them. For a moment the beam of the headlight flickered wildly along the side of the Mercedes, then the man got it focused and Gregory's profile was caught in a blinding glare. Next second a tall blond man sprang out of the nearby telephone kiosk. Thrusting a whistle into his mouth, he blew a piercing blast.

## 16

## The Kidnappers

The balloon was up. Nothing could have shown more certainly that Gregory had been recognised. Tensing his muscles he swung the car round the corner. To his relief the way ahead was clear. He put his foot down on the accelerator. Cornering had carried his head out of the beam of light, but it now shone on the back of the car and its reflection in the windscreen momentarily dazzled him. Swinging round in her seat behind him Sabine swiftly pulled down the blind of the back window.

The dazzle ceased, but Gregory gave a mental groan. A hundred yards down the hill a big lorry was emerging from a side turning. He would have bet his last shilling that it had been lying in wait in the side street, and the whistle had been a signal to bring it on the scene. If he were right and its function was to block the road, at his present speed a head-on crash was inevitable. Taking his foot off the accelerator he put on the brake and for a few seconds kept his apprehensive gaze glued to the lorry. It turned neither to right nor left. Running straight across the road it brought up with a jerk, its fore-wheels coming to rest against the curb of the opposite pave-ment. The road was too narrow for him to pass behind the lorry, and he could not turn into the street from which it had come by mounting the pavement because a lamp-post barred the way.

There was only one thing for it. He must try the opposite direction. With a screech of tyres, he brought the car to a halt, threw the gear lever into reverse and began to back in a wild zig-zag up the hill. Owing to the narrowness of the street he could turn the car only by backing into the entrance of the courtyard from which he had just emerged. He had nearly made it when the man who had sprung out of the telephone kiosk came rushing at the car. Springing on to its footboard, he seized Gregory by the arm. Gregory tore his arm away. But the violent jerk upon it had wrenched the wheel round too far. There came a crash, a jolt and the car stopped dead. It had just missed clearing the nearest pillar of the arch-way. To back it further was now impossible, and it had not been backed far enough to make the three-quarter turn needed to drive it up the hill.

Gregory made a desperate grab at the gear lever, to pull it out of reverse so that he could run forward again. But the tall blond man was still on the footboard and again grasped his arm. As they strove together Gregory recognised him as one of the young Gestapo men who had come to collect Grauber from the police station on the previous night. It was he, Gregory realised now, who must have been the eyes of the ambush and in the glare of the motor-cycle headlight spot-ted that Mario had been replaced by the British Agent that the *Herr Gruppenführer* was after.

Drawing back his left fist Gregory smashed it into the Nazi's face. The man gave a yell, let go the arm to which he was clinging and slipped off the running board. For a moment Gregory again had both hands free. But it was too late now to put the car into gear and run her forward. Another car had pulled up only twenty feet away, sideways on, right in front of her bonnet.

As the Nazi staggered away, his hand held to his bleeding

nose, the helmeted motor-cyclist ran in, grasped the handle of the car door and dragged it open. As he did so several more men tumbled out of the car in front. Gregory saw that, if he remaining in the Mercedes, within a few moments he would be trapped there.

Sabine had already thrown open the back door on his side of the car and was scrambling out. Having got Gregory's door open, the motor-cyclist flung himself at him to drag him from his seat. But he had already swung round in a move to spring out himself. Shooting out his right foot he caught the man a good kick in the stomach. Clutching at his middle he gave a gasp and doubled up. As his helmeted head came forward Gregory kicked again and this time got him in the face. Still winded he could get out only a choking moan, then he fell over sideways.

Thrusting himself from the car, Gregory jumped across the prostrate body. Sabine was now twenty feet inside the archway. As she ran she was shouting at the top of her voice, 'Help! Police! Help!'

Gregory turned to follow her, but his path was barred by the blond Nazi whose nose he had flattened. Blood was streaming from it and tears were running from his eyes. Yet in spite of the injury he had received, he was still a formidable antagonist. He stood a good six feet two and had the shoulders of a professional boxer. As Gregory took a stride towards him he suddenly pulled from the top of his trousers a long rubber truncheon.

Gregory's hand instinctively went to the side pocket in which he was carrying his small automatic. A split second later it flashed into his mind that he dare not use it. If he shot one of these people it would give Grauber just the excuse he needed to insist on the Hungarian police taking immediate action. As things were, if he could get back to the house, he should still be safe for a few hours at least; but if the Nazis could say that he had killed, or near killed, a man, within a quarter of an hour the police would be on their way to arrest him. And, once back in prison, Grauber would see to it that he came out again only to be taken on a warrant of extradition to Germany. To go in unarmed against a young giant wielding a rubber truncheon was to ask for trouble, but Gregory had no alternative. Only by getting through the archway could he save himself, and the sound of running footsteps in his rear told him that at any moment the men who had arrived by car would be upon him from behind.

On a sudden impulse he resorted to a ruse which he hoped would give him a temporary advantage. In what almost amounted to one movement he grasped his chauffeur's cap by its peak and flung it from his head into the Nazis face. Hurling himself forward he followed it up with a blow aimed to land on the Nazi's chin while the cap momentarily blocked out his view of what was coming. Only two paces separated them. The trick should have worked but Sabine, in her haste to get out of the car, had dragged the car rug with her. It had dropped to the ground as she ran towards the archway. Gregory's right foot now caught in a fold of it. He tripped. His impetus was too great for him to save himself. His blow landed short, on the Nazi's chest, and with his feet still tangled in the rug, he went down hard on his knees.

Under the impact the tall thug staggered back. The cap had hit its target but as it fell from his face he saw Gregory kneeling in front of him. With a yell of joy at this chance to take vengeance for his crushed nose he raised the rubber truncheon on high. With a swish it came down in a knockout swipe directed at the top of Gregory's head. He had just time to jerk his head aside and throw up his left arm. The truncheon struck it with a dull thud. For a moment he thought the bone had been smashed. The pain was agonising.

The Nazi was raising his truncheon for a second stroke. In utter desperation Gregory flung his good arm round his opponent's legs and, head first, threw his weight against them. They seemed as firmly planted as stanchions, but suddenly they jerked in an attempt to break the grip, the heavy body above them rocked, toppled and came crashing to the ground.

Gregory staggered to his feet. His brief conflict with the blond giant had occupied no more than twenty seconds; yet that had been enough for the men from the car to close in. There were three of them. Before Gregory could kick his feet free from the car rug all three were striking or grabbing at him.

Sabine had halted in the middle of the courtyard. She was still shouting, 'Help! Police! Help!' On the opposite side of the street windows were being thrown up and heads appearing at them. People were calling to one another asking the cause of the commotion. Several passers-by had stopped and were forming the nucleus of a crowd out in the middle of the roadway. There were no police among them and Gregory felt certain that none would show up. Grauber's top man in Budapest would have fixed the local Police Chief or, if he was not amenable to pressure, each individual policeman would, as he went on duty, have been bribed or threatened sufficiently to keep him out of the Szinháy Utcza should he hear any trouble going on there.

But help was arriving from another quarter. Sabine's cries had brought her porter to the door of the lodge he occupied on the left-hand side of the archway. He was a big, bearded fellow, and emerged in his shirtsleeves with an S-shaped pipe he had been smoking, while listening to the radio, still dangling from his mouth. Sabine shouted something to him in Hungarian. He dashed back into his lodge to reappear a moment later without his pipe but armed with a stout wooden club.

Meanwhile Gregory was waging a hopeless battle. The blow from the truncheon on his left fore-arm had rendered it almost useless. With his right fist he continued to strike out at the blurred white faces that ringed him in. The blond Nazi had picked himself up, so had the motor-cyclist. It was now five to one. He managed to get his back against the body of the Mercedes, but he was struck, kicked, clawed and, within a few minutes, thrown to the ground.

It was at that moment that Sabine's porter entered the fray. Laying about him with his club, he fractured the arm of the motor-cyclist and broke the head of one of the other men. But, with his rubber truncheon, the tall Nazi caught him a blow on the side of the head that sent him reeling into the gutter. The other two men hauled Gregory to his feet and dragged him towards their car.

The driver had reversed it so that it now pointed up hill. Jamming on the brakes he got out, opened the rear door so that Gregory could be pushed inside, then ran forward to lend a hand in hauling him towards it. The porter was up again and battling with the tall Nazi. The club and truncheon smacked together like two short singlesticks, first to one side then to the other. Both men were well above average in weight and strength. The Hungarian was a lot older but the young Nazi had already had a severe handling. The odds looked about even until the German suddenly stepped back, ran in and kicked his antagonist in the crutch. With a roar like that of

226

a wounded bull, the porter fell to the ground, then lay there squirming.

Gregory was still fighting the men sent to kidnap him. Using his weight, he cast himself first in one direction, then in another. With his elbows he gave sudden savage jabs. Arching his back he splayed his feet wide apart. Every inch of the way he strove to trip, wind, or overthrow one of the three who were lugging him towards the car. He knew that if they once got him into it that would be the beginning of the end of him. Yet, strive as he might, panting and cursing, foot by foot they pulled and pushed him out into the road.

Suddenly he was hit a terrific blow in the small of the back. His feet lost their grip on the cobbles and he was pitched violently forward, dragging his captors with him. Next moment, one after another, they jerked him towards them, then let go their holds on his limbs and garments. In the same few seconds the whole group staggered apart under a deluge of water. Gregory found himself with his head actually inside the car and his hands on the bodywork to prevent his falling into it. But he was no longer held by hostile hands. Straightening himself, he swung about. Only then did he realise what had happened.

Pipi and Mario had a fire hose trained on Grauber's people. Aided by a footman and other servants who had come hurrying out in response to Sabine's cries, they had run out the hose, fixed it to the hydrant in the courtyard and were now using it as police do to break up crowds of rioters. Aimed for the centre of the group, the first smashing jet had struck Gregory; but as soon as the two men holding the nozzle of the hose had found its range they had directed it at the heads or legs of his attackers. Knocked headlong or swept off their feet they fell this way and that in the roadway. Bruised, drenched and blaspheming, as soon as they could they crawled for shelter behind their half-swamped car.

Rallying his remaining strength, Gregory came at a lurching run under the arch into the courtyard. Sabine caught him before he fell and supported him, gasping and near exhaustion, to the steps of the porter's lodge. Meanwhile the porter had picked himself up and, cursing like a trooper, had also staggered inside. Mario called to the footman to take his place helping to hold the nozzle of the hose, then sprinted out to the Mercedes. Jumping into the driver's seat, he ran her forward a few feet then backed her into the yard. The moment he had done so, the hose was turned off and a dozen willing hands swung-to the big wooden doors that closed the archway.

Five minutes later Gregory sat slumped in an armchair in the hall of the Palace. With Pipi's help Sabine had brought him there; and after telling him that she would be back in a few minutes, they had both left him. He was still a little bemused and felt one big ache all over; but he had been in such scraps often enough to know that he had not sustained any serious injury. For the moment there was nothing he could do, except thank his gods that the attempt to kidnap him had failed, and he was quite content to sit there while his pains gradually local-ised themselves.

When Sabine returned she was carrying a tray with hot water, bandages and bottles. As she set it down he muttered with a grin, 'This is history repeating itself. I hope it's not going to become a habit for me to get beaten up and you to play ministering angel every night.'

She smiled back a little wryly. 'If we are here for you to be beaten up tomorrow night, I'm afraid it will mean the end of both of us. But let's not talk about that for the moment. Do you think any of your bones are broken?'

'No, thank God. My left forearm is very badly bruised though. It got the full force of a blow from that blond brute's rubber truncheon. I think I'd better have it in a sling. I'm afraid my face is a bit of a mess. I've a nasty kick on the shin, and another on the thigh, and I've wrenched my little finger. Otherwise I'm all right.'

'We'll have to undress you to see to the bruises; so to start with I'll just clean up your face. That's a horrid cut on your lip, and you're going to have a whale of a black eye.'

The antiseptic stung but the eau-de-Cologne with which she bathed his temples freshened him up a lot. Halfway through he asked her for *Baratsch*. She brought him one from the tray of drinks that always stood in the hall. After he had swallowed a few gulps and she had completed her ministrations he felt considerably better.

Having helped herself to a brandy and soda, she said, 'I've thanked all the servants for their help, and they have gone back to their quarters; except for Pipi, Magda and Mario, who are waiting to hear what we mean to do now. But I must confess I haven't an idea how we are to get out of the trap we're in.'

'How about Admiral Horthy?' Gregory enquired. 'I gather Ribbentrop implied that he had secured the Regent's protection for you until he had to give way to pressure from Berlin. It might be worth telephoning to ask him to give you a police escort to see you clear of the city.'

She shook her head. 'There are several things against that. In the first place you can bet that via Grauber and his Chief of Police he knows all about us by now. To keep in with Ribb he promised to give me twenty-four hours to get across the frontier and to stop an immediate hue and cry after you. But he must be aware that Grauber will have telephoned to Himmler, and that by tomorrow morning at the latest he'll get a formal demand for our arrest; so the last thing he'll do is to compromise himself further by giving us his active help to get away.'

'I wasn't talking about us, but about you.'

'You implied that in what you said, and it is my second point. Even if he were willing to give official protection to a woman who is accused of sheltering a British Agent, he certainly would not tell his police to let her take with her out of the country a man whom the Gestapo are after. And we are in this thing together.'

Gregory leaned forward and took her hand. 'Darling, I beg you to be sensible. God knows, I've got you into enough trouble already! If there is any chance at all of your getting out on your own you must take it.'

'There is no chance of the Regent's providing me with an escort. I am convinced of that. And if there were I still wouldn't go without you; so please put that idea right out of your mind. Finally, even if I wanted to telephone the Regent I couldn't. The 'phone has been cut off.'

'Has it? When?'

'I imagine it was done to prevent us trying to get help, as soon as the attempt to kidnap you had started. Directly Pipi joined me in the courtyard and saw what was happening he ran in again to telephone the police. But the line was dead, and it still is.'

'Then there is no hope now of getting help of any kind from outside. Not that we could have got it anyhow, except by involving our friends. Still, we might have asked someone to hire or provide a car to meet us somewhere.'

'How would we have got to it?'

'By going out over the roofs and coming down through one of the other houses further up the street.'

'That would mean leaving our luggage behind.'

'I know. But I'm afraid it is the only chance of getting out left to us now. Even that may be closed if they have enough men to cordon off the whole block. But I didn't see any Arrow-Cross boys about. If Mario went ahead of us, dressed again in his uniform, anyone keeping watch would now take him for me. By acting as a red-herring he could clear the coast for a few minutes; then, unless they are very thick on the ground, we'd be able to slip through.'

Sabine was naturally most loath to leave all her clothes behind; but she agreed that it must be done, and Gregory cheered her a little by a suggestion which might enable her to secure them later. As the railway stations would be watched by Grauber's people their only means of reaching the frontier safely would be in a hired car; but there should be nothing to stop Pipi sending off the baggage by train in the morning, and they should have no difficulty in collecting it at Zagreb, as it would reach there before they did.

While they finished their drinks they discussed this new plan, and the dozen or so palaces that formed the block. At this time of year nearly all the families that lived in them during the winter would still be in the country; so the only inmates they were likely to encounter on coming down from a skylight were a porter or old servants who had been left in charge, and by leaving their illicit entry until after midnight the odds were that all of them would be sound asleep. In any case, it seemed wise to postpone this new attempt to get away until the early hours of the morning as by then, after a long and fruitless vigil, Grauber's men would no longer be so fully alert.

They eventually decided that, if Mario were willing to act as a decoy, he should get out through a palace three doors away down the hill which at present was empty and up for sale. If he was able to walk off unmolested, well and good; if he was spotted, it would draw the enemy off in that direction. Having given him a few minutes' start, the others would come out from a mansion near the top end of the row which was owned by an old Countess whose porter knew Sabine by sight; so he would not take them for burglars should they encounter him.

Five o'clock was fixed as the time for their attempt, as that would impose a whole night of growing weariness upon the waiting enemy, yet still leave an hour of darkness. It had two other advantages; they would not have to wait about for very long before a garage opened at which they could hire a car and, as it was still only a little after nine o'clock, they could get a good six hours in bed to store up new energy before again putting their fortune to a desperate hazard.

The three faithful servants were called in and the plan discussed with them. Mario agreed that the worst that was likely to happen to him if he was caught was that the Germans might give him a beating, and declared himself ready to take that risk. Magda then volunteered to aid the deception by accompanying him in some of her mistress's clothes; but her offer was gratefully declined because it was felt that if Mario was chased he would be able to run farther without her before being caught, and so maintain for longer the illusion that he was Gregory. They thought it most unlikely that the enemy would actually break into the palace, but Pipi announced his intention of staying up all night to keep watch. He said that he would call Magda in ample time to cook a good hot breakfast for them; and, later in the morning, take the luggage to the railway station.

Everything having been settled they all went upstairs to look out of the top windows and see what dispositions had been taken up by the enemy. The street in the front of the house now appeared to be deserted, but the gateway and the arch cut off from their view the nearer section of it; so it was probable that at least one watcher was lurking there, probably in the telephone kiosk. Down in the lower road behind the house a small car was standing stationary with its engine switched off. As there appeared to be no reason for its remaining there, they decided that it almost certainly contained one or more of Grauber's people; but the really comforting thing was there were no signs at all to suggest that the whole row of palaces had been cordoned off.

Pipi accompanied Gregory to his room, helped him to undress, ran a hot bath, then collected the chauffeur's uniform and said, 'Mario will need this to put on directly he gets up. I will look out some other clothes suitable for the *Herr Kommandant* to dress in tomorrow when I call him.'

Gregory thanked him for all he had done, then got into the bath and for twenty minutes eased his bruised limbs in the warm water. He was still drying himself when he heard Sabine, who had said she would come up to see to his hurts, enter the bedroom. She anointed his bruises, made a sling for his left arm, tucked him up in bed, then lightly kissed him good night and left him.

He put out the light at once, and lay for a little while staring up into the darkness, wondering far from happily where he would be at that hour the following night. If his luck held he should be well over the frontier into Yugoslavia; if not, he might be in hiding or, far worse, a prisoner. The previous night he had hardly slept at all, and during the past twenty-four hours he had been through a great deal; so he was very, very tired. Despite his anxieties, within ten minutes he was sound asleep, his last conscious thought having been that at least he would have six hours in a comfortable bed before he was called on to face new dangers.

In that he was wrong. Shortly after midnight Pipi burst into his room shouting, 'Wake up, *Herr Kommandant!* Wake up! The palace is on fire! Those devils are throwing fire bombs through the downstairs windows!'

# 17

# Trapped

One of the assets that Gregory had found most valuable in his dangerous work was his ability when woken suddenly to be almost instantly conscious of all the circumstances in which he had fallen asleep. In the present instance, before Pipi had finished shouting at him he had flung back the bedclothes and was tumbling out of bed.

'Fire bombs!' he echoed. 'Where? Have they broken through the gate into the courtyard?'

'No,' Pipi panted. 'They are at the back. They have thrown the bombs over the terrace into the big salon. I smelt smoke and found it coming from under the doorway. The room was full of it. I could see nothing; but while I was there another grenade crashed through the window and bounced along the floor. I slammed the door to and dashed upstairs.'

'Have you woken your mistress?'

'Yes, *Herr Kommandant*. I went to her first.'

'Good. Rouse the rest of the household, then get the fire hose going again. I'll be down as soon as I can get some clothes on.'

As Pipi ran from the room Gregory looked quickly about him. Mario's uniform had been taken away by Pipi and, owing to this unforeseen emergency, he had not brought up the suit which was to replace it. All the Baron's clothes that were use-able had been packed the previous evening; they were still in the suitcase that had been brought in from the car and left down in the vestibule. Pulling open the wardrobe, Gregory looked inside. All that was left there were a fur-trimmed Hussar's jacket, a silk dressing-gown, a carnival domino and a Chinese mandarin robe. Suddenly he remembered his own dinner-jacket suit. At the time of Ribbentrop's visit, fearing the house might be searched, he had hidden it in the unlit stove.

Hurrying into his underclothes, he pulled the suit from its hiding place. The hair oil had congealed into hideous stains on the satin lapels of the jacket, and it was crumpled to a rag; but that was of no importance at the moment. Within three minutes of Pipi's rousing him he was dressed, had snatched up his wallet and pistol, and was taking the stairs two at a time down to the next floor. Turning left along the broad corridor he ran into Sabine's room.

Unlike Gregory, when in a deep sleep she was difficult to wake. The light was on and she was sitting up in bed with her head lolling against its padded satin backboard. Evidently Pipi's reason for waking her had not penetrated to her brain, and immediately he had run from the room she had dropped off again.

With her dark hair framing her pale face, slim arms and one small firm breast exposed owing to the ribbon of her night-dress having slipped from her shoulder, she still looked a girl scarcely out of her teens. Her long black lashes made fans on her cheeks and her lips were a little parted. The sight of her, even in that hour of fresh peril, made Gregory catch his breath. Instead of calling to her, on a swift impulse he stooped and re-

233

woke her with a kiss on the mouth.

Her eyes flickered open. 'Oh, darling!' she sighed, and threw her arms round his neck.

Gently but swiftly he broke her hold, and said in a low urgent voice, 'My sweet, we're in trouble again. You must get up at once. That swine Grauber has set his thugs to burn down the house. Quick now!'

As he spoke he pulled back the bed-clothes. She gave a little shudder; then doubled up her fists and, like a child, began to rub the sleep from her eyes as she muttered, 'Oh, hell! Aren't we ever to have any peace?'

'Come along!' He took one of her arms and gave her a little shake. 'I tell you the house is on fire. For God's sake start getting yourself dressed.'

Swinging her long legs over the side of the bed, she got to her feet. Magda had left her underclothes laid out all ready for her on a nearby chair. She was fully awake now. Running to it she started to pull on her stockings.

Gregory left her and walked swiftly towards the windows. Both of them were French and led out on to the balcony. One was a little open , and he could now smell smoke coming from it. Opening it wide he stepped out on to the balcony. The moon was up, silvering the spires of the Parliament House across the river, and making the scene almost as bright as day.

As Pipi had said, Grauber's people were attacking the back of the palace. Seventy or eighty feet below, down in the road, near the small car that had been parked there earlier, there was now a big wagon. Grouped about it there were a score or more of figures, and Gregory grimly took in the fact that most of them were in the uniform of the Arrow-Cross. Then, after the first quick glance, his attention concentrated on the immediate foreground just below him. Two men had come up the steps cut in the steep slope. They were standing just beyond the iron gate, and could easily have forced it, but for some reason they had apparently decided not to break through on to the terrace. One was kneeling beside a square box and evidently fusing the grenades. The other had just taken one from him, and as Gregory watched, pitched it through a ground floor window.

Stepping back into the room, Gregory grabbed the first piece of furniture to hand. It happened to be the stool in front of Sabine's dressing table. Running out on to the balcony again he lifted it high above his head and hurled it down at the two men. Both ducked but one of its legs caught the kneeling man a glancing blow on the head and he toppled backwards. The other was holding another bomb ready to throw. He lobbed it up at Gregory. The bomb missed his head by inches, sailed over his shoulder through the open window, and fell with a dull thud in the room.

Swinging round, he ran towards it, hoping to snatch it up and throw it out again before it could explode. It was not a grenade, but a cylindrical tin cannister from one end of which sparks were sizzling. As he dived to grab it, there came a loud 'phut' and from the place where the sparks had been there shot out a jet of thick oily smoke. It was pointing towards him, so the smoke fountained up right into his face. Blinded and choking he staggered back, while Sabine let out a scream and ran to him, fearing that he had been seriously injured.

It was a good minute before he could get his breath and his eyes had ceased to water sufficiently to see again. Meanwhile the bomb had been vomiting forth its pitch and sulphur in a steady stream. For several feet around it there billowed a cloud of such denseness that it was no longer even possible to guess where it lay, and to have dived into the smoke again would have been to invite asphyxiation.

As they backed away still further a second bomb hurtled through the window and rolled under the bed. Gregory dropped to his hands and knees and strove to reach it. But again he was a few seconds too late. Before his groping hand could hit upon it the fuse ignited its contents. A moment later clouds of noisome smoke were coiling up in great spirals from under both sides of the bed and from behind its headboard.

By now the far end of the room was totally obscured. The electric light over the dressing table showed as no more than a faint blur in a pea-soup fog. In the centre of the room the smoke billowing out from under the bed hid all but its foot and, fearing that they would be cut off from the door, Gregory pushed Sabine round it. When rushing into the room he had left the door a little open; so a gentle draught from the window was causing the smoke to swirl and eddy inwards after them. With incredible swiftness wisps and fingers of it reached out from the two black central masses, while others now struck downwards from clouds of it that had hit and rolled along the ceiling. The eyes of both of them were smarting, their nostrils teasing and their throats full of acrid fumes. Sabine had had time to put on only her stockings, elastic belt, brassière and shoes; but it was impossible to remain there longer and Gregory thrust her towards the door.

'My jewels!' she gasped. 'My jewels!'

'Where are they?' he cried.

'In my beauty box. By the dressing table. I must . . .' A violent fit of coughing cut her short.

She had turned to go back for them, but he caught her by the arm. Although he was again choking and gasping he took a couple of paces forward. Then he halted and stepped back. The whole room was now filled with smoke. A few feet in it was so dense that he could no longer see the bed.

'No good!' he spluttered. 'No . . . no good. Suffocate in there . . . for . . . for certain.' Sabine had already stumbled from the room and was bent double in the corridor. Half-blinded again he staggered after her, pulling the door shut behind him with a bang. Gratefully they drew in the clean air; but it was several minutes before their eyes had stopped oozing tears and they had cleared their lungs sufficiently to breathe freely.

As soon as they were able they set off at a run along the broad corridor. At the stairhead they paused, still wheezing and weeping. The upper part of the hall was clear, but below, like mist upon a pond, strata of faint bluish haze were floating. It was coming from the back of the hall and under the stairs, filtering in beneath the doors of the big reception rooms that gave on to the terrace.

'My coat!' exclaimed Sabine. 'Holy Mary be praised! That's safe, anyway!' It was still lying on one of the settees where she had left it after Mario had brought it in from the car for her. They hurried down the stairs and as Gregory helped her into it, he remarked:

'By Jove, it's heavy.'

She nodded. 'Sables always are; but it's not only that. I've got a big flask of brandy in one of the pockets, and there's this.' Patting a bulging zip-up pocket in the lining, she went on, 'When I am travelling I always keep my passport and papers in here. There's less risk of losing them than in a handbag.'

Gregory wondered grimly if they would ever now have a chance to use their passports; but his mind was swiftly taken off speculations about the future by the doors of the vestibule being thrust open and Pipi appearing in them clasping the nozzle of the hose. Gregory ran forward to help him and Sabine quickly did up her fur coat to hide her semi-nakedness.

Several other servants appeared with coats pulled on over their night clothes. Between them, they ran out the long flat snake of canvas through the hall to the door of the saloon. They were all jabbering in Hungarian but, from their gestures as much as anything, Gregory gathered that a shout from Pipi would be relayed to a man in the courtyard who would turn on the water, and that as it spouted from the nozzle the footman was to throw open the door.

Gregory was a little dubious about the wisdom of opening the door, but a fire might be raging behind it; and, if that were the case, in doing so lay the only hope of saving the palace. In the event, his fears proved justified. The water rushed along inside the hose rounding it out in a matter of seconds, the footman flung open the saloon door, the jet of water erupted into the room; but, at the same instant, there welled from it a great convoluted cloud of stygian blackness that swiftly enveloped them all.

Coughing and cusing, they were forced to give way before it, while Gregory yelled, 'Shut the door! Shut the door!' But no one could now get near enough to do so. An order was passed for the water to be turned off, and the brass hose nozzle was thrown down on the floor, still emitting great gouts of water. Several of the men, Gregory among them, soaked handkerchiefs in it and tied them over their mouths and nostrils; but they were so blinded by the smoke now pouring out through the doorway that they still could not reach it.

The hall was filling rapidly and Sabine had retreated half way up the stairs. Joining her there, Gregory said quickly, 'Listen. It's clear that Grauber is trying to smoke us out. I suppose he hasn't yet got the O.K. to come in and get us, and fears that we'll manage to slip away if he fails to have us in his clutches within the next few hours. These bombs are the sort that troops use to make a smoke screen. They don't give out flames, so unless one sets a carpet or curtain smouldering there is very little risk of fire. If there had been a fire in the saloon we'd have seen the flames through the smoke. But the thing is that they'll go on chucking bombs in until the whole house is rendered untenable and we're driven from it; so if we're to get away at all we've got to make the attempt now.'

Sabine glanced down at her bare chest and said, 'I wish I had a few more clothes on. Still, fortunately it's a warm night; and if you say we've got to go now, we must.'

Gregory had caught a glimpse of Mario out in the vestibule. Choking and spluttering he made his way to it through the smoke and ran the chauffeur to earth just outside in the courtyard. Mario said that he was still willing to act as a decoy. They then told Pipi of their intentions and Gregory asked him to take charge. It was agreed that there was no point in making any further attempt to use the hose unless an outbreak of flame was seen, and that all the servants should be withdrawn to the fresh air of the courtyard until it become possible to re-enter the palace without risk of suffocation. Sabine kissed Magda on the cheek and held out her hand for Pipi to kiss, then the couple wished them luck and, accompanied by Mario, they headed for the clearer atmosphere at the top of the stairs.

Even on the first floor the lights were now made dim by a blue haze thicker than that seen in a night-club at four in the morning, and it was evident that the smoke up there would soon be as dense as it was on the ground floor. Thick wreaths of it were seeping from under the door of Sabine's bedroom and also from under that of another room, into which a bomb must have been thrown through the window.

Keeping their damped scarves and handkerchiefs pressed over the lower part of their faces, they went on up to the attics. Sabine led them into one which held a big water tank and a wooden ladder leading up to a glass sky-light. Before mounting it Gregory said to her and to Mario:

'Now, remember; we must stick to the middle of the line of roofs. If we get too near the edge our silhouettes will show up against the sky-line. Then they'll spot us and the game will be up. So keep low. If necessary, get down on your hands and knees and crawl. Sabine, you stick close behind me. Mario, you turn to the right as soon as you are through the sky-light. Good luck, and a thousand thanks again for the help you are giving us.'

When he reached the top of the ladder, he wrestled for a moment with the rusty lever of the sky-light; then he thrust it up and crawled out on to the roof. Sabine went up after him, her head on a level with his heels. When he had crouched there for a whole minute without moving she called impatiently:

'Go on! What are you waiting for?'

Instead of replying he gave only a low hiss to silence her, and waved backwards with his hand for her to remain where she was. Then he crawled a few feet across the roof, raised himself to a crouching position, sank down again, crawled back and thrust his feet over the edge of the sky-light with the obvious intention of descending to the attic.

Sabine gave way before him. When he was half way down the ladder he gently lowered the sky-light. As he reached the floor she asked in a voice still made hoarse from the smoke she had swallowed:

'What's the matter? What's wrong?'

For a moment he did not reply. Then he said quietly, 'I'm sorry, darling, but it's no good. Grauber's got one ahead of me. I might have guessed he would. He has either bludgeoned or bribed the caretakers in both the next-door houses to let him send men up to their roofs. On either side there are eight or ten of them just waiting for us to walk into their arms.'

To find their escape route blocked at the very outset was a wicked blow, and against such numbers there could be no possibility of forcing a passage. In deep despondency they made their way downstairs again.

On the last lap they narrowly escaped disaster. Down on the ground floor the atmosphere had become so laden with smoke particles that it was only just possible to see a hand held in front of the face. In the pitch black murk they lost their sense of direction, become separated and, for a few terrifying minutes, could find neither the doors nor one another. To regain contact they had to remove the damped covers from their mouths, so that they could shout, and the acrid fumes rasped their throats like red-hot sandpaper. By luck, a moment later, they stumbled into the vestibule, and from it were able to stagger out into the courtyard, but not before they were whooping as though their lungs would burst.

When they had recovered sufficiently they told Pipi how their plan for getting away over the roofs had been thwarted, and Gregory suggested that as a forlorn hope they should make another attempt to break out in the car. But Pipi shook his head.

'It would be hopeless, *Herr Kommandant*. Thinking you

safely gone old Hunyi, the porter, and I undid the gate a few
minutes ago and looked out. The street is blocked both ways
by lorries drawn across it and there are the best part of a
hundred Arrow-Cross men out there.'

'Did they make any move to rush the gate?' Gregory asked.

'No; they only laughed and jeered at us, and said that they
were waiting for the *gnädige Frau Baronin* and her Frenchman. And that if both of you did not come out soon, they
would have to take steps to make us all do so.'

'What about the police?' Sabine enquired hoarsely. 'Were
there none there?'

'No, *gnädige Frau Baronin*, I did not see any. But there were
a few firemen, and there is a fire engine farther down the
street. I suppose one of our neighbours telephoned for it, and
the Arrow-Cross men have refused to let it be brought up to
the palace.'

'That's about it,' Gregory agreed. 'I expect they have told
the firemen that they are using only smoke-bombs; so there
is no immediate danger of fire, and all they need do for the
present is to stand by.'

Sabine stamped her foot angrily. 'They have no right to
prevent the firemen coming in. One of these bombs may quite
well start a fire, and in that dense black smoke it might get
such a hold before anyone is aware of it that half the block
may be burnt down.'

'You ought to know by now the sort of pull these Fascist
organisations have,' Gregory could not resist remarking with
a trace of bitterness. 'In any country that wants to keep the
goodwill of Hitler they are allowed to break up the political
meetings of their opponents, and wreck the offices of newspapers that show a tendency to be Left-wing, while police
and firemen look the other way.'

She sighed. 'I suppose you're right, and that really I should
be thankful that they haven't broken in and wrecked everything in the place. What I don't understand, though, is why
they make no attempt to come in and drag you off to Grauber.'

'I do.' He replied quickly. 'There are still limits to what
these types can get away with in Hungary. Throwing smoke
bombs can be laughed off as showing disapproval of someone
they had been told is concealing an enemy agent; but the
Regent might get tough with them if they started taking it on
themselves to break into palaces and arrest people. And there

is more to it than that. Grauber hoped that his own thugs would catch us in their ambush. When they failed he went to Szalasi and asked for his help. I haven't a doubt that Szalasi replied more or less like this: 'No, thank you. I'm not making a deadly enemy of Ribbentrop by snatching his girl-friend and her chum for you; and he'd know that my boys wouldn't dare do a thing like that without my orders. But I tell you what I will do. I'll tip off one of my lieutenants that I'd like enough smoke bombs thrown into the palace to drive everyone out of it. Afterwards, it will be no concern of mine if there is a scrap in the street and, of course, you will have your boys outside mingling with the crowd. It will be up to them to nobble the two birds you're after as soon as they appear, but it should be easy money to do that once they are in the open, and to bring them along to you at the Villa Petoefer." '

'So that's the game slippery Szalasi is playing!' Sabine commented indignantly.

'That, or something very like it.'

'Since he was willing only to take such half-measures I wonder that Grauber didn't wait until tomorrow; because it's almost certain that by then he'll be able to get the full co-operation of the police.'

'I don't suppose he could have raised enough men of his own to man the roofs as well as the streets; so if he had waited till tomorrow, the odds are we should have got away. He did the wise thing in securing any help he could while the going was good.'

'If you're right about Szalasi, we may get away yet. When his young men have thrown all their bombs they are going to get bored with waiting about. They've driven us from the house but they seem to have overlooked the fact that we could spend the night here in the courtyard. It's not yet much after midnight. In another couple of hours they'll be thinking about their beds, and if they are not under Grauber's orders they'll pack up and go home. Say it is even three or four o'clock before they throw their hand in; we'll still have plenty of time before dawn to plan another attempt to break out, either over the roofs or wherever Grauber's men seem to be fewest.'

Inwardly Gregory groaned. Squeezing her arm, he said, 'No, darling: I'm afraid it's not going to be like that. Having rendered the palace untenable, their next act will be to do the same with the courtyard and the servants' quarters along either side of it. They must know that by now most of your household has been flushed out into the open, and it won't be long before they start on the job of forcing the lot of us out into the street.'

He had hardly finished speaking when the first tin canister came lolloping through the stone arch above the wooden double gates. It fell near one of the maidservants, who let out a scream, and next moment a spurt of the oily black smoke fountained up from it.

'Holy Mary!' Sabine muttered tearfully. 'What *are* we to do?'

'We've got to face it,' Gregory replied grimly. 'The game is up. I'm desperately sorry to have let you in for this—desperately sorry.'

'It's quite as much my fault,' she admitted huskily. 'If I hadn't persuaded you to come back here after I got you out of the police station; if I'd let you take a chance on your own last night as you wanted to; even if I'd listened to you this morning and agreed to make a break for it without delaying to get papers and things, we wouldn't have been trapped like this.'

He shrugged. 'It is no good considering might have beens, and all you did was to urge the course that you thought at the time would be best for us. But now we've got to resign ourselves to saying goodbye. The only chance of your getting out of this is for you to surrender yourself to the top Arrow-Cross boy and demand that he should take you straight to Szalasi. That should give him the feeling that he's one up on the Germans, so it's unlikely he'll refuse. Szalasi is going to be desperately embarrassed when you are handed over to him. The very last thing he wants is for Ribb to be able to pin it on him that it was he who scuppered you. All the odds are that he'll apologise for his boys and send you back here in a car. Then you must jump into the Mercedes and get Mario to drive you hell for leather to the frontier.'

'But what about you?'

'It is me that Grauber is really after, and there is nothing to be gained by my surrendering to Szalasi's boys. Ribb might be annoyed at my being caught, but he couldn't reasonably blame Szalasi for handing me over; so it's a certainty that he would hand me over, otherwise he'd make Grauber his enemy

242

for life. All I can do when the time comes is to attempt to shoot my way through, and hope for a chance to get away up some alley in the darkness.'

He tried to keep his voice light, but he knew now that he was really up against it. The odds against his being able to get the better of half-a-dozen Gestapo thugs, aided by scores of Arrow-Cross men, were fantastic. He could only hope that he would meet his end fighting and not get a knock on the head which would result in his being delivered alive into Grauber's hands.

That the time would soon come when he must take this last gamble with fate was apparent. While he and Sabine had been talking, four more smoke bombs had been pitched through the archway. Pipi had got the fire-hose going again and had succeeded in putting two of them out, but the others were belching their evil black smoke and it was obvious that the hose could not be switched quickly enough to douse all of the swift succession of them that were now coming down in the courtyard. The group of eight or ten servants were starting to cough and splutter, and casting anxious glances at their mistress.

Old Hunyi, the bearded porter, came hobbling up. He was still in pain from the kick he had received in the groin and leaning heavily on a thick stick; but he made an awkward bow to Sabine, and said in Hungarian:

'Gracious lady, if we remain here we shall soon all be suffocated. I beg that you will deign to accept the shelter of my lodge.'

She translated to Gregory who gave a sad shake of his head and replied in German, 'That would only be to put off the evil moment. From the street they can lob bombs through the windows of the lodge, and they will as soon as they have made the courtyard untenable. I'm afraid there is no possible way for us to keep out of their clutches.'

Hunyi considered for a moment. He understood German and now spoke in it. 'If we could find the trap door leading to the caves the *gnädige Frau Baronin* and the *Herr Kommandant* might get away by them.'

'The caves!' Gregory almost shouted. 'What caves?'

'The Buda hill is honeycombed with caves,' the elderly porter replied. 'There are lakes beneath our feet and many of the mineral springs rise in them. Legend has it that our forefathers took refuge down there when the Turks ravished the city in the fifteenth century.* Many of the old palaces have ways down into them; and I recall, when I was a boy and Pipi's father was Steward here, hearing him say that there was a way into them through a trapdoor in the cellars.'

For Gregory this possibility meant a chance of life and freedom, and for Sabine escape from the threatening attentions of the Gestapo. He did not attempt to keep the excitement out of his voice, as he cried:

'In the cellars! But where? Could you find it?'

Hunyi shook his head. 'No, *Herr Kommandant*. But Pipi might know where it is.'

Sabine called to Pipi to leave the hose to the footman and come over to them. Quickly they questioned him; but he could not help. He knew of the caves but had never heard his father speak of an entrance to them from the Tuzotlo palace.

Gregory's heart sank again. If it was there they should be able to find it. But since its existence was not even known to Pipi it would need careful looking for, and in the cellars of a large building like the palace such a search might take hours.

Rushing from place to place, their hasty conferences, and the wear and tear from constant fits of violent coughing made them feel as if the smoke bomb attack had been going on all night; but, in fact, it was less than half-an-hour since Pipi had given the first alarm, and there was a quarter of an hour still to go before it would be one o'clock. Given normal conditions, two or three hours should have proved enough to locate the trap-door. But conditions in the palace were not normal. The rooms on its main floors were now pitch black caverns, and Gregory knew that by this time enough smoke must have seeped down into the basement to asphyxiate anyone who remained there without a mask for more than ten or fifteen minutes.

Nevertheless, as it was that or death outside, and the yard was now becoming thick with smoke, Gregory determined to try it. The air was clearest near the gate; so most of the ser-

* At the end of 1944 Hungary, all too belatedly, repudiated her alliance with Germany and offered to surrender to the Soviet Union. In revenge Hitler ordered the destruction of the capital and, before the Russians arrived, the Germans shelled and bombed into ruins a great part of the beautiful palaces on Buda hill. But many thousands of Hungarians saved their lives by sheltering from the bombardment in the caves referred to here.

vants were now in a huddle by it, under the archway through which the smoke bombs were coming. Mario was among them. Gregory ran over to him and gasped:

'A pair of goggles! Have you a pair of goggles? I am going into the palace again.'

Mario nodded, and they ran together to the garage. At the back of it there was a motor-cycle that belonged to him. Snatching a pair of goggles from its handlebars he thrust them at Gregory and panted:

'One moment, I have others. If I can help I will come with you.' Turning to a box of spares he unearthed two older pairs, the elastics of which were stretched, but not too badly for them to be usable.

As they emerged from the garage, Pipi came running towards them. For the first time that night he was laughing. In his round blackened face his teeth flashed like those of a Negro. Behind him, by the wrist, he was dragging an old woman. For a moment he was seized with a coughing fit, then he spluttered out:

'I asked the other servants. This is old Ciská, our laundry woman. She knows where it is.'

'Thank God!' exclaimed Gregory. 'Quick! Give her one of those pairs of goggles, Mario.'

As she took them, Pipi snatched the other pair and said. 'She speaks only Hungarian; I will go with you to interpret.'

Mario shrugged. 'As you will. You know the cellars better than I do.'

Gregory turned to him. 'You can help in another way. God alone knows what it will be like in the caves. Anyway, we'll need torches, candles, matches. Please collect everything of that kind you can while we are gone.'

'We'll need a crowbar, too,' Pipi added. 'Not having been used for so long, it's certain the trap will be hard to get up.' As he spoke he ran into the machine shop and came out carrying a medium-sized jemmy.

Sabine was standing with Magda in an angle of the yard. Hurrying over to her, Gregory told her what he hoped to do, then rejoined the others. Parts of the yard were now two or three inches deep in water from the hose. In it they redamped the scarves and tied them afresh over their mouths and nostrils.

With Pipi leading and old Ciská following beside Gregory, they went through a passage at the back of the garage into the main block of the house. The smoke was dense, but troubled them much less now that they wore goggles. Pipi fumbled his way along a corridor and found the stairs to the basement. Down in it there was much less smoke, but enough to justify Gregory's fear that without a mask anyone would be driven from it within a quarter of an hour.

Pipi was snapping the lights on as he advanced and old Ciská kept mumbling to him in Hungarian. They walked in Indian file along several low stone-flagged passages, then came into a broader space along one side of which were trestles supporting a row of casks. There they halted, and after a moment Pipi turned to Gregory.

'She said it was in the beer-cellar and this is the beer-cellar. But now she says that, although it's nearly thirty years since she's been in this part of the basement, she's sure that the beer-cellar she remembers was not like this.'

'Probably she has confused it in her mind with a cellar that holds wine casks,' Gregory suggested. 'Is there one that does?'

'Yes, *Herr Kommandant*.'

'Then let's take her to it.'

For a moment Pipi was silent, then he burst out, 'St. Stephen's curse upon it! We cannot. The wine cellars are locked, and I keep the keys in my room upon the second floor. This scarf is not enough protection to go upstairs. I'd be suffocated before I could get back with them.'

'Perhaps we can break down the door. Anyway, let's go and see.'

With a despondent shake of the head Pipi turned about, and led them down a corridor at right angles to the one by which they had come to another open space. Giving a helpless shrug, he pointed to an ancient nail-studded door set in a low archway.

Gregory gave vent to a peculiarly blasphemous Italian oath that he used only in times of exceptional stress. The jemmy that Pipi was holding might have been a matchstick for all the good it would have been against such a door. Nothing short of dynamite would have burst its lock or forced it off its hinges.

The wave of evil fury that had rocked his mind was past in a moment. Swiftly he began to assess the chances of his being able to get Pipi's keys himself. It meant going up three flights of stairs—back stairs that were unknown to him—finding a room somewhere at the opposite end of the house to the one he had occupied—a room that he had never entered—then in pitch darkness locating solely from its description the right drawer in a bureau or writing table, and finally getting safely back to the cellar again.

'No,' he decided. Pipi was no coward and if he, knowing the house from cellar to attic, would not take such a gamble, it would be sheer lunacy for him, to attempt it. The sulphur-laden air would overcome him and he would be choking his life out before he could even find Pipi's room.

Yet, if they failed to locate the trap door, it could be only a matter of an hour or so and he would be choking his life out in his own blood outside in the street. Either way was going to be extremely painful, and he had an idea that asphyxiation would prove the more so; but it had the advantage that at least he would make sure of not falling alive into Grauber's hands. And, after all, there was always the chance that by some miracle he might succeed in getting the keys.

Old Ciská had been peering uncertainly round her through the bluish haze. Now she muttered something to Pipi. Turning to Gregory he exclaimed excitedly, 'She says this is it! That in the old days the beer cellar used to be here!'

The old crone was nodding her head up and down and pointing with a skinny finger to a wide embrasure about fifteen feet away between two great squat pillars that supported a vaulted arch. 'She says that's where the scantling used to run,' Pipi interpreted, 'and that the trap-door is in the corner by the left-hand pillar.'

Gregory was already staring in that direction; but instead of joy his face held a worried frown. In more recent years the embrasure had been used as a bin for empty bottles. Hundreds of them were stacked in it, six or eight deep and five feet high. To shift enough of them to get at the floor under any part of the stack was going to be a formidable task. In consternation he said, 'Ask her if she's certain—absolutely certain.'

Pipi put the question and, with a muffled cackle of laughter from behind her scarf, Ciská began to babble cheerfully. 'She should know, even after all these years. Béla the pantry-man had brought her there when she was a girl, given her too much beer and tossed her petticoats over her head. Afterwards they came there often. Once they had nearly been caught by the cellar-master. It was then Béla had shown her the trap-door. He had pulled it up and made her hide crouching on the steps underneath it until the old boy had gone. Soon after that Béla had been taken for the war, and there had been a child. The old Baroness had been very angry and sent her to live in the country. But there had been plenty of fine fellows there. None of them were such lusty chaps as Béla, though . . .'

Cutting her short, Pipi told Gregory that he felt sure the old woman knew what she was talking about.

'Come on then!' Gregory flund himself at the left-hand end of the great stack of bottles and began to throw them into the farthest corner. It was gruelling work and terribly exasperating; for no sooner had a space a foot or so deep been cleared at the side of the pillar than more bottles from the centre of the stack rolled down into it. Soon the pile of bottles and broken glass in the corner threatened to block the passage, so they had to start another pile against the cellar door. Smoke was still seeping down from above through all sorts of unsuspected crannies and the atmosphere was stifling.

Five, ten, fifteen minutes had slipped by since they had left the courtyard. They were still only halfway down the stack, and fresh avalanches set them back every few moments. Gregory began to despair of reaching the floor before they were exhausted. Old Ciská laboured manfully, but Pipi suddenly left them, so Gregory feared he had been forced to throw his hand in. But Pipi returned carrying a bundle of new laths that had been cut for him to bin away the year's making of *Baratsch*, and with these they succeeded in shoring up the bulk of the remaining bottles in the stack.

After that the work went easier, although Gregory was worried now that soon the courtyard would be getting so thick with smoke that Sabine would either faint from suffocation, or find herself compelled to break out with her servants into the street.

Sweating, half-blinded, and with throats like limekilns, they kept at it until the last dozen bottles in the corner where they were delving had been thrown aside. Gregory gave a grunt of relief and joy. They had uncovered a square stone slab with an iron ring in it.

Seizing the ring, he pulled with all this strength; but the stone would not yield. Pipi knelt down and jabbed fiercely with his jemmy at one end of it until the edge of the iron had entered the crack between the stones far enough to hold. Throwing his weight on the jemmy, he heaved. The stone lifted slightly. Another minute and they had it up. A draught of cold clean air hit them in the face. In great gulps they drew it down into their bursting, lacerated lungs.

For a few minutes they were too exhausted to do anything but crouch there, then Gregory said, 'Pipi, tell old Ciská that if I ever get back to Hungary I'll give her a pension for life. Take her up now, and bring down your mistress. And the torches and things Mario was going to collect for me.'

The wait for Sabine seemed interminable, but just bearable now that he had fresh air. When she arrived she was almost fainting, and being supported betwen Pipi and Mario. They said that except for Magda, who had remained with her mistress, all the other servants had found the smoke bearable no longer and gone out into the street.

The draught from the trapdoor speedily revived Sabine; but she drew back from its dark depths with an expression of horror. Mario handed Gregory a big torch and a canvas bag half full of other things. Gregory said to the two men, 'I'll never be able to repay you both for all you have done. Go up now and out into the street. When you are questioned tell everyone that your mistress and I decided that we would rather die in the palace than be handed over to the Gestapo: and that between us we swallowed the contents of a bottle of sleeping tablets.'

Switching on the torch, he shone it down in the cavity. Its beam showed a flight of crumbling stone steps that merged into darkness.

'I can't!' gasped Sabine. 'I can't! We don't know where it leads. We may never get out!'

'Courage, darling, courage!' Descending the first few steps, Gregory took her hand and drew her after him.

No sooner was her head below the level of the ground than Pipi and Mario shouted after them 'May God keep you! Good luck! Good luck!' then lowered the heavy stone into place.

They had escaped from the Gestapo and from Grauber; but, as the dank cold of the cave struck an instant chill into their bones, even Gregory's heart quailed at the thought of what now lay before them. This uncharted escape route must hold many perils. If the Goddess of Fortune should turn her back, they might die there in the darkness under Buda hill.

# 18

# In the Caves

The steps were only about eighteen inches wide, but they were steep and, as Gregory saw from the first flash of his torch, there were well over twenty of them. There was no rail to which to hold on either side. To the left a wall of rough hewn rock rose from them; to the right there was nothing—a sheer drop into unplumbed darkness. One stumble on those narrow stairs and, with nothing to clutch at, it would mean a headlong plunge into the gulf below.

Warily, Gregory tested every step before putting his weight on it. The staircase was far older than the palace above it and had probably been made many hundred, perhaps even a thousand, years ago. In the course of time earth tremors and gradual subsidence had caused some of the steps to crack and loose corners to fall away from them. It looked as if, at any moment, pressure upon one might cause an avalanche, which would send himself and Sabine cascading to the bottom.

Sabine tried to drive from her imagination a picture of both of them with bruised bodies and broken bones, half buried beneath a great pile of stones down on the still-unseen floor of the cave. That picture was swiftly succeeded by another. Perhaps the staircase had no ending; its bottom half might already have fallen away. If the gap were too big for them to dare jump down into the cave they would then be forced to retreat: to fight their way again through that searing, blinding smoke, and, after all, fall into the hands of their enemies. But worse. Most ghastly thought of all. Perhaps the stone flag above them was so heavy that they would not be able to lift it from below. In that case these crumbling steps would become a terrible prison from which there was no escape at all.

To steady herself, she had a hand on Gregory's shoulder. As terror flooded through her mind, her grip instinctively tightened. Then a flash of common sense told her that to press upon or encumber him would increase their danger. Exerting all her resolution, she took her hand away. Almost at once her courage was rewarded. With Gregory in front of her she could not see how far the beam of his torch penetrated, but it was now lighting the ground. Quickening his pace he stepped boldly down the last half-dozen steps, then turned, shone the torch on the lowest steps for her, and said:

'Well, we're over the first fence in having got safely down that lot.' His hoarse voice came back in a strange hollow echo, while the torch made their shadows huge and menacing on the rock wall beside them.

Taking a grip on herself, she followed the beam of the torch as he shone it up and down and round about. They were in a large tunnel. It was about twenty feet wide and so lofty that the cone of light did not reach the arched roof overhead. The stairway, the top of which was now hidden in the darkness, was no more than an excrescence on one of the walls of the tunnel, which appeared to be of the same dimensions in both directions. The floor was uneven but free of boulders though littered here and there with loose stones. It was quite dry and sloped slightly downwards in the same direction as the steps descended.

Gregory set down the canvas bag that Mario had given him and examined its contents. In it there was another, smaller, torch, three new candles and four partially used ones, a whole new packet of a dozen boxes of matches, a slab of chocolate and a three-quarters full bottle of orangeade.

He felt that Mario had done them well. If used sparingly there was enough lighting material there to keep them going for far longer than they should need to find a way out of the caverns. Yet that might take several hours; so the chocolate and the orange squash had been an excellent thought. The latter particularly was most welcome and their sore eyes lighted up at the sight of it. Each of them had a couple of mouthfuls there and then. It ran down their parched and lacerated throats like nectar, and made them feel once more like human beings instead of half-kippered demons just emerged from the sort of Hell invented by the early Christians to frighten their less intelligent enemies—and later depicted so admirably by the elder Breughel.

After savouring this unexpected and wonderful refreshment they instinctively turned downhill. Gregory carried the bag in one hand and the torch in the other. He held it pointed forward and a little down and, in order to save the battery, flashed it only at intervals frequent enough to ensure that they did not walk into some obstruction or fall into a crevasse. Sabine held his arm, and now that she was on firm ground she felt far less fearful of unknown dangers. They spoke little as their mouths were still dry and their throats sore from the agonising effects of the smoke they had swallowed.

As far as they could judge, the tunnel retained the same proportions; but its slope steepened. Gregory felt sure that it was following the contour of the Buda hill, and that they were coming down towards the level of the Danube. He hoped he was right, as he thought it almost certain that the long-dead people who had fashioned these caves, or at least adapted them for the use of humans during an emergency, would have seen to it that there were several entrances along the banks of the river. His belief that they were approaching water level was born out by the fact that, as the beam of the torch struck the floor ahead, the stones on it began to shine slightly. Then the ground underfoot became damp and, after another ten yards, the torch showed water.

Coming to a halt, Gregory waved the torch from side to side, then shone it into the impenetrable murk ahead. What they saw filled them with consternation. There was not a ripple on the water but it stretched from one side of the tunnel to the other and as far before them as the beam of light carried. Apparently, unless they were prepared to swim, it barred their further progress completely, and in its absolute stillness there was something vaguely menacing.

Gregory flicked the torch out. Instantly the darkness closed in upon them like a pall. His voice came with an unconcern he was far from feeling. 'This must be one of the underground lakes old Hunyi mentioned. We'd best turn back. There's certain to be a way round it.'

Swivelling about they set off up the hill. Knowing now that there was no bad break in the floor of the tunnel where a minor earthquake had caused a geological fault to open and become a crevasse, Gregory now flashed his torch from time to time on the walls on either side. Before they had gone far it lit a flight of stairs similar to those down which they had come. Halting again, he said:

'There must be a way out up there. It doesn't matter into whose cellar we come out. It's still the middle of the night and everyone will be asleep; so we should be able to walk out of the front door, or anyhow come out through one of the

252

ground-floor windows, without being challenged. Come on; up we go!'

Cautiously but quickly, shining the light on each step ahead of him, he made his way up the stairs, Sabine following close behind. When he reached the top he handed the torch to her; then, stooping his head forward, and bending his knees, he raised his shoulders until they were firmly braced against the square stone immediately above him. Clenching his fists he heaved, endeavouring to straighten himself. The stone slab did not lift. He made another effort, and another; but although he strained, holding his breath for a full minute, it would not yield a fraction of an inch.

Panting slightly, he relaxed and looked back at Sabine. 'Sorry. I'm afraid this one is stuck. Yours would have been too, if anyone had tried it from underneath before we loosened it with the jemmy. I expect most of those that haven't been used for half a century or more will be. But don't worry; we'll find one that isn't.'

With Sabine leading this time they made their way gingerly back down the long flight of stone stairs, then continued to retrace their steps up the slope. By flashing the torch along the walls now and again, in the next hundred yards they came upon two more flights of steps. The trap at the top of the first proved equally impossible to shift, but the second gave at the first heave.

Quickly, Gregory took the torch from Sabine and, keeping the heavy stone raised with one shoulder, shone the beam through the narrow opening across the floor of a cellar. Even as he did so he smelt smoke. Next moment the beam came to rest on a heap of broken glass and empty bottles. Failing to recognise the flight of steps down which they had first come, they had returned to the Tuzolto Palace.

For the time and effort wasted they at least had the consolation of knowing that if the worst came to the worst they could get out that way. That was, if they did not get lost and could again identify that particular stairway. As an aid to recognising it, when they were safely down they piled on the bottom step a little heap of loose stones.

Continuing on up the slope, they found that the tunnel soon began to narrow and lose height; then it took a curve and just round the bend they came upon another shorter flight of steps. Gregory ran up them while Sabine held the torch but, as he now half expected, the stone in the roof of the cave above the top step was stuck fast.

A little farther on the tunnel ended, and a few minutes' exploration showed that they had emerged into a large open space some eighty feet across and roughly oval in shape. Its ceiling was too lofty for the torch to pick up, and round the sides were openings to seven or eight other tunnels. Between two of these openings at the narrowest end of the oval the rock wall had been worked smooth, and about three feet up a large fan-shaped recess, roughly two feet deep, had been hollowed out in it.

As the light flickered over the recess Gregory noticed some ring-like marks upon the stone. Stepping nearer they made out the remains of an early wall fresco. The rings were haloes and below them could still be faintly seen the outline of the pointed faces of saints with huge flat almond-shaped eyes. Obviously it had once been an altar and the cavern used as a church, perhaps in the days when the infidel Turks were the masters of the city.

Somewhat to Gregory's surprise, Sabine bobbed before it, as though it were an altar in a still used church. Next moment she turned to him and said:

'Give me a candle, please: one of the whole ones. I want to light it to the Virgin.'

'Oh come!' he protested, as the echo of her voice died away. 'No religious rites have been performed here for centuries; and it's possible that later on we may need really badly the few candles we have.'

'I can't help that,' she retorted. 'Please give me one.'

'Sabine, be sensible. We simply can't afford to do this sort of thing. Down in this place candles are more precious than gold.'

'All the more reason we should donate one to the Holy Mother, and secure her protection,' came the swift response. 'You must give me one for her, Gregory! You must!'

Her voice had risen to an hysterical note; so, with considerable reluctance, Gregory got out from the bag one of their precious candles and a box of matches. Taking it from him she set it up in the embrasure, lit it, and knelt for a moment in prayer. Then, taking his arm, she said in a normal voice:

'I feel much happier now. Look at our shadows. Aren't they weird? Which way shall we try next?'

The lack of success with which they had so far met in endeavouring to force up stone flags in cellars decided Gregory that their best hope still lay in finding an entrance to the caves somewhere along the river bank; so they set off down the slope of a tunnel next to that from which they had emerged.

After ten minutes' walk they were brought to a halt; the tunnel ended as had the first, with its floor shelving into the underground lake. While going down the tunnel they had noticed several more stone stairways at its side, and on their way back Gregory went up three of these; but his efforts were wasted. It struck him now that probably very few of them any longer led into cellars that were in use. In the past five hundred years the great majority of the palaces above must have been rebuilt, and the replacement of timbered mansions by ones of stone would have required more solid foundations, so many of the old cellars would have been filled up with rubble and concrete.

On re-entering the big cavern they tried a tunnel on its opposite side. That led after only a hundred paces into another cavern, from which four or five lower tunnels fanned out. Afraid now of getting hopelessly lost they decided against exploring any of them, and, retracing their steps, turned into a third tunnel that had a downward slope. In another ten minutes they once again found themselves on the edge of the sinisterly still lake.

In walking up and down the three tunnels and exploring the two caverns Gregory reckoned that they must have walked a good three miles, and he saw from his watch that their explorations, together with the time expended in trying to force up flagstones, had occupied a little over two hours. Sabine had gamely refrained from complaining, but she was clearly tired, and was limping a little, as the rough rock floor of the cave was hard going in the thin-soled shoes she was wearing.

He was still convinced that if only they could get down to the river bank they would find a way out and it occurred to him that possibly the lake was shallow enough for them to wade through it.

When he told her his idea she murmured, 'Oh, God! Must we? If it wasn't for my fur coat, and that I've been using my limbs all this time, I'd be frozen already. I expect that water is icy.'

Stooping, he dabbled his hand in it, and replied, 'It's not too bad. And you needn't go in yet. I'll go ahead and find out how deep it is.'

'No, no!' She grabbed him by the arm. 'Don't leave me! Anything but that!'

'You'll be all right,' he soothed her. 'I promise you I won't take any silly risk, or go out of your sight.'

'But there may be a sudden drop in the bottom. You might be drowned.'

'There's no fear of that. You know I'm a good swimmer. At worst I'll get a thorough wetting.' As he spoke he set down the canvas bag, took two stumps of candle from it and, setting them up on a ledge of rock, lit them. When he had done, he added, 'There! Now I won't be leaving you in the dark, and if I do drop the torch I'll be able to see my way back to you. Should you need it the other torch is in the bag. Sit down and rest your poor feet for a bit. I won't be long.'

As she sank wearily down on the floor of the cave he waded cautiously out into the dark water. The slope was gradual and when he had progressed about twenty feet the water was still only midway up his thighs. A few steps farther on it began to get shallower, and he gave a cry of delight. The torch beam had picked up the opposite shore, and he was already more than halfway to it. Turning, he splashed his way back to Sabine.

'We'll make it easily,' he told her. 'Even if there is a hidden dip we can swim the last few yards; but it's very unlikely that we'll have to. We must try to keep your coat from getting wet through. Take it off and I'll carry it as a bundle on my head.'

Scrambling to her feet she slipped the coat off, giving a quick shiver as the cold air struck the flesh above and below her elastic belt. He put out the two bits of candle, returned them to the bag and took from it the smaller electric torch. Handing it to her, he said:

'You had better take this, just in case I drop the lot.' Then he rolled the bag up in her coat, put the bundle on his head and held it firmly there with his left hand. Side by side they went into the water. It proved no deeper the whole way across than he had found it on his reconnaissance. Within two minutes, and with Sabine's belt still dry, they were safely on the opposite shore. But in her near naked state the dank chill had made her teeth start to chatter; so as soon as Gregory had unrolled her coat he fished the flask of brandy from its pocket and made her take a couple of good swallows.

'That . . . that's better!' she spluttered. 'Thank goodness I've always made a habit of carrying cognac when I travel.'

As he helped her back into her coat she insisted that he too should have a pull and, seeing that the large flask was still nearly full, he gladly did so. Then they set out again. But they soon realised that they were not in the wide mouth of another cave, and after a dozen paces a flash of the torch showed them more water.

Thinking that they had landed on a curved promontory and that beyond it must lie a tunnel leading riverwards, they turned left and followed the water's edge. It was full of small irregular bays and creeks so its direction was difficult to guess, although in general it seemed to curve more to the left than right. Flashing the torch every few seconds they walked on for about ten minutes, then Gregory halted, shone it on a spur of rock, and exclaimed:

'Damn it! I could swear we passed that pointed bit before.'

Sabine agreed, and after they had gone a little farther they realised with dismay that they were on an island.

Striking inland confirmed their belief, as a bare twenty paces brought them to water again. They guessed the island to be about forty feet wide and about two hundred long and, by the one landmark they had identified, judged that they had walked about one and a half times round it. If they were right about that, having just recrossed it, the place where they now stood must roughly face the tunnel from which they had come. So they crossed the island yet again and, having again lit two of the candle stumps, Gregory set out on another reconnaissance, to see if he could locate the lake's further shore.

Before he had taken two steps he was knee deep in water. After a tentative third he drew back quickly, for if he had let his foot reach bottom he would have been in up to the waist. Sabine collected the bag and candles, and he tried at another spot some twenty feet further along. There the down-ward slope proved even steeper. For seven or eight minutes they wandered up and down, examining each little bay by the light of the torch, and Gregory trying out any that looked at all promising. But it was no use; evidently all along that side of the island there was deep water a few feet out.

Gregory was now beginning to become really worried, but

he endeavoured to keep the anxiety out of his voice as he said:
'I could do with a break. Let's sit down and have some of that
orange squash and chocolate. Maybe while we're resting some
new idea will come to us.'

But neither of them had any new ideas. Having put the torch
out to economise its battery, by the light of a single candle
they munched the chocolate and took a few swigs from the
squash bottle almost in silence. They had nearly finished the
modest ration they had allowed themselves when the unearthly
stillness was shattered by a loud 'plop.'

'Holy Mary! What . . . what's that?' Sabine gasped, throwing a terrified glance over her shoulder.

'Only a fish,' Gregory replied calmly.

'It . . . it might be an octopus,' she quavered. 'They are said
to live in subterranean caverns like this.'

'Nonsense,' he laughed. 'That's only in cheap fiction. The
sort of caves octopi inhabit are always among rocks beneath the surface of the sea. They never come up rivers; it is
unheard of to find them any distance from a coast. The sooner
you get that idea right out of your head the better, as we've
got to swim for it.'

'Swim for it?'

'Yes. There must be another side to this lake, and it can't be
far off. In a minute I'm going to strip and swim over to find it.
Then I'll come back for our clothes and things. I may have to
do two or three trips to get them all over dry, a few at a time
on my head. And on the last trip you'll come over with me.'

'No!' He could hear the shudder in her voice. 'No, darling;
I couldn't do it. I'd die of fright. Even if that thing we heard
isn't an octopus it may be a sort of shark or a sting-ray.'

'It is much more likely to have been a trout,' he protested,
'and crossing the deep bit of lake is our only way of getting
down to the river.'

'There's no guarantee that we'll find an exit from these
caves when we get there. It's only your own pet theory.'

To that he had to agree, but he pointed out that to find an
exit anywhere they must leave the island; so she would have to
go into the water again anyway.

'Of course,' she replied promptly. 'But it's one thing to wade
a few yards as we did before, and quite another to be attacked
by some awful monster when out of your depth and naked.

There's another thing. If we go back the way we came and all else fails, as a last restort we can climb up into the cellar of my palace tomorrow morning.'

Gregory knew that when people deliberately explored caves such as these they took with them balls of twine which they played out as they advanced; so that they could guide themselves back to their starting point. But the departure of Sabine and himself had been far too hurried for preparations of that kind. He had considerable doubts now if they would be able to find again the steps that led up to the Tuzolto cellars; but he refrained from voicing them and, as there was really as much chance of their finding an outlet in one direction as another, he gave way to her pleading that they should try their luck up hill again.

Crossing the island they splashed back through the shallow water. This time Gregory held the bag high, and Sabine threw the skirts of her fur coat over the back of her head to keep them from getting wet. She was now nearly weeping with fright and clung heavily to his arm. Her fears were not lessened when, instead of arriving at the entrance to a cave, the torch, which had gradually been getting dimmer, showed ahead a solid wall of rock.

Turning to the right they ploughed their way through the knee-deep water for thirty or forty feet then, to their relief, they came upon a high arched tunnel. Whether it was one of the three by which they had come down to the lake they could not tell, but thankfully they stepped back on to dry ground.

After another swig of brandy each, to help to drive the cold from their lower limbs, they set off up the gentle slope; but there was nothing they could do about their squelching shoes, and Sabine's limp was now beginning to hamper her. A sudden twist in the tunnel told them that it was not one of those they had traversed before; and, after they had covered two hundred yards, the big torch became so dim as to be almost useless. Evidently it had been used for several hours by Mario before he had handed it over. As Gregory took the smaller torch and switched it on, he prayed fervently that it would last longer. The candles and matches were a sheet anchor, but no more. If one moved at anything exceeding funeral pace with a candle the draught would blow it out. And they might have to cover a lot of ground yet before they found a way of escape from this nightmare labyrinth.

On and on they trudged up the incline. Now and then they passed a flight of stone steps, either set into or hacked out of one of the side walls. Three times, in desperation, Gregory made Sabine sit down while he climbed the steps and, with all his might, strove to prise up heavy flags set in the cave's ceiling; but he might as well have been trying to lift a mountain.

The tunnel they were in now was much longer than the others and had a gradual curve to the right. At last they came to its end. It opened into another cavern, but smaller and lower-ceilinged than either of those they had come upon earlier; and this had only two other tunnels leading from it.

'Take your choice!' Gregory offered with a lightness he was far from feeling. When they left the island he had decided that it was no longer any use for him to attempt to apply reasoning to the direction they took. It was now a case of the blind leading the blind. Their fate lay on the knees of the gods and either a Merciful Power would permit them to stumble on a way out or, after hours of agonised searching, sleep, more searching, hunger, more sleep, more searching, they would ultimately die of exhaustion.

'The right-hand one,' Sabine replied in a hoarse whisper.

With slow tired steps they went foward into it. The tunnel was not more than ten feet wide and eight feet high. After fifty yards it petered out in a dead end. Giving a shrug of resignation Gregory turned about. As he did so a beam of the torch swept in an arc across the floor of the cave. For a second it shone on a small white object. Swinging the beam idly back he lit up the white object again. Then he held it there. He could hardly believe his eyes. Sabine gave a sudden cry. She had seen it too. They were both staring down at a cigarette butt.

Gingerly he picked it up. It was a long butt. Whoever had smoked it had taken only a few puffs then thrown it away; and soon after it must have gone out. But it was fresh, that was the blessedly significant thing. If it had been lying on the ground there for more than a day or two it must have shown signs of damp. It meant that quite recently someone had been standing there in the cave smoking and, if they had done that, it was as good as certain that the entrance by which they had come in and gone out must be near at hand.

Now, trembling with excitement, they began to search.

There was no stairway on either side up to the low roof, and the beam of the torch, which easily reached it, showed the rugged rock ceiling to be unbroken. A moment later, as the beam swept the dead end of the cave, their hearts gave a bound. In one corner there was a small arched doorway so deeply recessed in the rock that they would never have noticed it had they not been looking for something of the kind. They ran towards, it, seized its iron ring handle, turned it back and forth and pulled upon it. But the little door was of thick ancient oak, firmly set into its surround of rock, and locked.

Sabine began to hammer on it with her fists and to shout for help, but Gregory drew her back and tried to quiet her by saying, 'It's no good doing that. Even if people come down here through that door now and then, you can be certain there is no one the other side of it to hear you at this hour.'

'But we must get through it! We must!' she cried hysterically. 'We might wander in these caves for days and never get so near escaping. If we don't get out this way we'll die here.'

Gregory knew that she might well prove right, and his own hopes of forcing the door were far from sanguine as he said, 'I'm going to try to blow the lock off. But for goodness sake don't count your chickens. A lock like this is a very different proposition to the flimsy sort of thing usual in modern flats, and I doubt if I'll be able to.'

From the ancient aspect of the door, he felt certain that its lock would be one of those great iron contraptions made in the middle ages; but as it was set in the wood on the far side of the door he could not even see it, or tell the position of its key-hole. His automatic was only a light one; so if the oak was more than a few inches thick the bullets might embed themselves in it without even reaching the lock and wrecking it so that its tongue could be pushed back.

After a moment he decided that the only chance lay in attempting to blow away a piece of the stone socket into which the tongue of the lock fitted. But that was going to be a tricky and dangerous operation; for the bullets would not bury themselves in the stone but ricochet off it and they, or bits of flying rock, might do him serious injury.

Handing the torch to Sabine, he emptied the canvas bag of its contents; then, holding the small automatic in his right hand, he put both inside it, wrapped it round them and with his left hand held the loose ends together over his wrist. The leather bottom of the bag and thick canvas now twisted in a wedge round his fist might, he hoped, be just enough protection to stop a small bullet smashing the bones of his hand should it ricochet back on to it. Having placed Sabine where she could shine the torch on to the tongue of the lock without being in the line of danger, he held the pistol close to it and fired three times through the canvas.

There came three spurts of flame and ear-splitting reports in quick succession. As the wisp of smoke cleared they peered eagerly forward. The trick had worked. A big splinter of stone two inches thick in the middle and eight inches long had been smashed off by the bullets on the far side of the tongue of the lock. One push and the heavy door swung open.

It gave on to a narrow flight of stone steps. Without pausing to collect the oddments scattered on the floor, they ran up them and found themselves in a low vaulted chamber. At one end of it there was an altar on which burned a small lamp. With hands outstretched Sabine staggered forward, threw herself on her knees before it and began to babble incoherently.

Gregory's ideas upon religion were by no means as orthodox as hers; but he was very far from being an agnostic and, although more slowly, he too went on his knees to render thanks for a merciful deliverance.

A few minutes later she was asserting her conviction that it was having devoted one of their precious candles to the Holy Mother, at the altar down in the cavern, which had caused Her to save them, and insisting that he should get the other candles in order that they too could be lit to Her glory; so he went down to fetch them.

On his return he found that Sabine had disappeared, and he was wondering a little anxiously where she could have got to when she emerged from the shadows at the far end of the crypt. She had just explored another stairway that led upward from it, to see if she could identify the church they were in, and had recognised it at once as the great Coronation Church on the top of Buda hill.

When he remarked that in that case he was surprised that the crypt was not larger, she said that it was not the main crypt and was probably part of a much older building. They decided that the cigarette butt they had found must have been left by some visitor who had been shown the entrance to the caves by a custodian, and had decided to light up there for a few quick puffs before coming back into the church.

While Sabine was lighting the remaining candles, Gregory looked at his watch and saw that it was just on five o'clock; so their ordeal in the caves had lasted over four hours. When she had done she said another prayer then, as she got up, turned to him with a smile:

'That's better! A quarter of an hour ago I was half dead from fatigue and terror. Now, I'm feeling a new woman. I wish I hadn't had to leave my jewels behind, and had a few more clothes on; but fortunately we have plenty of money.'

'Yes,' he agreed soberly. 'That's the one thing in our favour; and it may prove the means of our getting away in the long run. But I'm afraid you'll have to wait for a bit before you think of using any of it to buy more clothes.'

She frowned. 'Of course, it's Sunday morning, isn't it? For the moment I'd forgotten that.'

'Even if it were eleven o'clock on Monday you still wouldn't be able to go shopping.'

'Why not—at some little place where I wasn't known?'

For hours he had been seeing her only in semi-darkness; but now he was looking at her in the full light of six candles. He had known that she must have got dirty and untidy but he had been far from realising her true state. Her face and hands were still blackened with smoke, her eyes were blood-shot and red-rimmed, her hair was matted, her stockings were torn and her shoes were cut almost to ribbons. Apart from the fact that she was wearing a beautiful sable coat, she looked a veritable tramp.

He guessed that he must look equally grubby and villainous, as he said, 'Take a good look at me; then you can judge what you look like yourself. If you went into any shop as you are, they'd immediately jump to the conclusion that you had just stolen those sables.'

'Perhaps it's as well it is Sunday, then.' She gave a quick shrug. 'Anyway, my coat is covering enough for decency; and it will serve until we are safely out of Budapest.'

Gregory sighed. 'You're taking it for granted that we will be able to get out. Don't you see that as far as our appearance goes there would be no difference between a clothes shop and a garage. At the moment we look like a gangster and his moll who have just fought their way out of a shindy in some low night-dive—and my filthy dinner-jacket helps to create the picture. If we go anywhere in our present state and I produce a wad of money in an attempt to buy or hire a car, the people will think that we are a pair of thieves trying to make a getaway. They'll make some excuse to detain us then telephone the police.' He paused a second, then added unhappily:

'And that's not the worst. You've been wonderful, and I hate to have to say this, but it would be stupid to conceal from you what we are up against. Looking as we do, and with you in that ten thousand dollar coat, from the moment we step into the street we'll be liable to arrest on suspicion.'

# 19

# Gone to Earth

As Sabine stared at Gregory she realised that he was right. She might be smoke-begrimed and tousled, but his state was far worse. Within the past thirty-six hours he had been in two gruelling fights. Not only was his face blackened but he had several nasty cuts on it and the swelling round his left eye was now a bluish purple. Even that, and the filth on their hands and faces, would not have mattered if they had been dressed as gypsies or in shoddy old clothes. But his dinner-jacket, however stained, was still a dinner-jacket and, as he had said, it now made him look like a crook who had just had a beating up; while her sables, now that she appeared such a slut, positively demanded questions from the first policeman they met about how she had come by them.

'What . . . what are we to do then?' she stammered. 'I can't leave my coat behind.'

He raised a smile. 'No; as you've nothing else to put on you certainly can't. You'd be arrested for indecency if you did—quite apart from catching your death of cold. What we have to do is to avoid any patrolling policemen like the plague until we can get under cover with someone willing to help us. Do you know anyone you could trust—really trust—who does not live too far from here?'

After considering for a moment, she shook her head. 'I'm afraid not. You see, my affair with Ribb didn't exactly put my stock up with my old friends. As you must have gathered for yourself the Hungarian nobility are willing enough to use the Nazis as a buffer against Russia, but they don't like them; and, although the magnates have used me at times to get concessions for Hungary, most of them look on me as in the Nazi camp.'

'Yes, I appreciate that. And, anyway, it would be the devil of a job to think up a story to explain to strangers why I am with you. It was only a forlorn hope.'

'I've got it!' She snapped her fingers. 'Count László! His palace is only a few streets away, and he is a friend of both of us. He was with you when we met again, and knows that we've known one another for years. We will tell him that I've thrown Ribb over for you and that in revenge he's got the Gestapo to trump up some charge against us. Such a situation is just the thing to tickle the little hunchback's sense of humour; and I'm sure he will do everything he can to help us get away.'

It was, on the face of it, an inspiration, but there were snags to it of which Sabine was not aware. In the first place, Gregory hoped that Count László had taken his warning and left the city the day before; in the second, the last people he was willing to risk compromising were the members of the Committee. If one of them were arrested through him, the whole pro-Ally movement might be wrecked; so even if the Count was still in Budapest his palace would have been ruled out as a refuge. Having no intention of disclosing to Sabine the truth about his secret activities, Gregory gave as an objection to her suggestion another almost equally good reason.

'I'm sure you're right in thinking Count László would play; but unfortunately we daren't go to him. Within a few hours at most now, Grauber's appeal to Berlin will have forced the Regent to tell the Hungarian police to go after us. The first thing they'll do is to search the houses of people I'm known to have gone about with while in Budapest; and László is one of them. So we'd be caught there and he would probably be clapped into jail as well.'

'But you've forgotten our trump card. Pipi was going to tell the Arrow-Cross men that you and I refused to leave the palace and took an overdose rather than be driven out. By now everyone will believe we're dead. There will be no search for us, and we've nothing to fear except being taken up by the police as suspicious characters, and afterwards identified.'

He shook his head. 'You're wrong about that. Pipi's story was only to explain our non-appearance with your servants when they were finally driven out into the street. As we are supposed to have committed suicide, directly the smoke clears enough the police will go in to make a routine investigation. When they fail to find our bodies they'll know it was a trick, and assume that somehow we got out in disguise. So you see, as far as the police are concerned, we'll be very much alive again; and before long they'll be hunting high and low for us.'

'They are hardly likely to be after us yet. Couldn't we go to László's just for a wash and some fresh clothes? He might even let us have one of his cars.'

'It would be much sounder to go to someone with whom we could lie up for twenty-four hours. The fact you are feeling in such good form at the moment is due to reaction at having escaped from those terrifying caves. But after what you've been through it can't last. In an hour or two you'll be ready to do anything to get some sleep; and, frankly, I'm too done up to drive a car very far, even if we could get one.'

Sabine sighed. 'I ought to have realised that. And of course I'll be feeling the full effect of our night out before I'm much older. As a matter of fact I'd give a lot now for a good bed and unlimited time to sleep in it. The awful problem is . . .'

'I know,' Gregory cut her short. 'And I have one possible answer to it. It's an idea I've been nursing from the beginning; but it means going over to Pest, and I was hoping we might hit on some plan which would save us from having to cross the river, because there are always policemen on the bridges and passing quite close to one of them will be unavoidable. We'll make for Leon Levianski's.'

'Who in the world is he?'

'He's a Jewish merchant—a wholesale furrier who lives in the Kertész Utcza.'

'The man you told me about on Friday? The one whose name was given you in London as a safe contact?'

'That's the chap. He said that if I got into trouble he would do his best to help me out. Of course, when it comes to the point he may change his mind, or he may be away from home. Anyway, since you have no better idea, I think we had best head for the Kertész Utcza while the going's good. Otherwise we'll miss our chance of getting across one of the bridges while there is still some degree of darkness.'

'All right, then,' she agreed and, after a last bob to the altar, she walked quickly with him to the stairs that led up to the church.

Their hurried discussion about what they had better do had occupied only a few minutes, but getting out of the church took them considerably longer. They went from one door to another, but found them all locked; and they had to move round the vast empty building with caution for, even when walking on tiptoe, their footsteps on the ancient stones made whispering echoes that they feared might rouse some somnolent night-watchman. It was, too, getting towards the time when cleaners might arrive to prepare the church for early mass, or a priest appear to carry out some special devotion.

At length, in desperation, Sabine signed to Gregory to follow her to a low door she had noticed behind the organ. It opened at a touch and led, as she had expected, not to the street but to the vestment rooms and, farther on, to the priest's quarters.

Fearful that at any moment they might run into someone who would take them for thieves, and raise an alarm, they crept down several passages until they came to a side door. It was bolted and locked but had its key in it. Only a moment was needed to turn the key and draw the bolts, then they were out in a small courtyard.

While they were down in the crypt the first flush of dawn had come. Above them the stars were now paling in the sky, and with renewed anxiety they realised that it would soon be full daylight. There was a small archway in the north-west corner of the courtyard. Hurrying through it they found themselves in a side street. They turned left and a walk of a hundred yards brought them to the square, the east side of which was dominated by the front of the church. Its great bulk shut out the growing light from the east, so the ancient square was still in semi-darkness.

As they came stealthily round the corner into the dim deserted open space, a two-wheeled covered cart emerged from a turning opposite. Instead of proceeding through the square, its driver pulled up in front of a stone drinking trough.

'It's a market cart,' Sabine whispered. 'If only we could get its driver to take us across the bridge.'

'Market cart?' Gregory echoed. 'But today is Sunday. There wouldn't be a market on a Sunday.'

'Not of meat or fish; but some of the stalls open for a couple of hours to sell fresh vegetables and dairy produce.' As she spoke the horse began to drink from the trough. The elderly man who was driving the cart hitched the reins to a peg, climbed down and went into the nearby urinal.

'Now's our chance!' muttered Gregory, and on tiptoes they ran towards the cart. The horse stopped drinking and looked up but, evidently used to this early morning routine of being left there for a few minutes by its master, it did not move. Quickly and as quietly as possible Gregory gave Sabine a leg-up across the backboard of the cart, and followed her over it; then they crouched down under its hood. They did not see the driver return but, while they were still striving to quiet their hurried breathing after their dash to hide in the cart, it jolted into motion.

By peering between the flapping canvas curtains hanging from the back of the hood, Sabine was able to keep a check on the direction the cart was taking. It went at a quiet pace through the long *Parade Platz*, ambled down the hill below the Royal Palace and along the embankment, then across the Elizabeth Bridge.

Once over the bridge the cart had served their purpose. Soon afterwards, as it turned right on its way to the Market, it was held up for a minute by an early morning tram. Seizing the opportunity, they dropped quietly over its backboard, and hurried off down the nearest side turning that led away from the river.

There were now quite a few people about and had it been any day other than Sunday there would have been many more. Even as it was, several stared in open curiosity at the hurrying couple who were clad expensively yet looked as if they had just been dragged by the hair through a coal mine. Fortunately they had only three-quarters of a mile to go and two main boulevards to cross; so they succeeded in keeping well away from major crossroads where there were police, and arrived at the furrier's in the Kertész Utcza just as a nearby church clock was striking six.

A few yards from the entrance to the shop, a green painted door evidently led up to the flat above. Gregory pressed the bell beside it and, having heard it ring, they waited with such patience as they could muster while casting anxious glances up and down the street. Several minutes passed and no sound came from within the building so Gregory rang again. The shrill peal had hardly ceased when the door was opened.

To Gregory's relief it was Levianski himself who answered it. His dark curly hair showed no signs of rumpling, but he was clad in a blue silk dressing-gown and his eyes were a little bleary; so it was clear that they had roused him from sleep. As he took in Gregory's battered face his black eyes showed sudden fear and he made to close the door; but Gregory was too quick for him. Putting his foot in it, he said:

'Please don't shut us out. I'm Commandant Tavenier. We had a long talk together at the Café Mignon a little over a fortnight ago.'

Levianski slowly opened the door again, and nodded. 'Yes, I recognise you from your voice. I doubt if I would have otherwise. I thought you were a gangster who had just raided one of the night clubs and stolen those beautiful sables your companion is wearing—and that you had come here to try to force me to buy them.'

Gregory gave a wry grin. 'For the past half-hour that's the very thing we feared that a policeman would think, if we ran into one. But please let us come in.'

Instead of moving aside, the furrier said doubtfully, 'It is obvious that you have got yourself into serious trouble. Are the police after you?'

'No. At the moment they believe us both to be dead. In the course of an hour or two when they fail to find our bodies they will realise that we are not; but there is no possible way in which they could get any idea that we have come here.'

'Very well then.' Levianski stepped back for them to enter a narrow hall, shut the door behind them, and asked, 'What has happened that you should be in such a shocking state, and be in danger of arrest by the police?'

Gregory knew that within a few hours the story of the Arrow-Cross smoke-bomb attack on the Tuzolto palace would be all over Budapest, and that Levianski could hardly fail to identify Sabine as the Baroness; but he saw no point in telling the furrier more about himself than he had already, or of the parts that Ribbentrop and Grauber had played, so he said:

'The Vichy police agent here got on to me and in collaboration with the Gestapo asked the Hungarian police to pull me in. But as the Baroness Tuzolto is a very old friend of mine she used her influence with the Regent temporarily to spike the Nazi's guns, and gave me asylum in her palace. We meant to drive to the frontier last night but the Germans held up the car and tried to kidnap us. That's how I got so knocked about. Then they got the Arrow-Cross boys to try their hand at flushing us out with smoke bombs; but we got away through the caves that lie under Buda hill.'

Levianski nodded. 'And what do you plan to do now?'

'We have plenty of money on us and would like to buy a car to get away in. But we didn't dare to show ourselves at a garage in our present state; and, anyway, we are pretty well deadbeat. You were good enough to offer to help me, providing I didn't have the police on my track; so I've come to you. I was hoping that you would be willing to let us stay here for the day, so that we can get some sleep. Then if you could find us some second-hand clothes we'd be able to make a fresh start with a fair chance of reaching the frontier.'

Pinching his thick lower lip between his forefinger and thumb, the short square-shouldered Jew remained thoughtful for a minute, then he said, 'You seem to have got completely clear for the moment; but, all the same, to let you stay is a risk, and I have to think of my family. Please to stay here for a little, while I consult my wife.'

Having pulled out a straight-backed wooden chair from beside the hallstand for Sabine, he gave a jerky bow and hurried off up the stairs. There was no other chair, so Gregory closed his eyes and leaned against the wall. Although he had spent most of Friday night in bed, during the past forty-eight hours he had had little more than four hours' proper sleep, so he was very, very tired; and what they were to do should

Levianski refuse to let them stay there he could not think.

They were not kept waiting long, and when the furrier came downstairs again he was followed by a small, plump, bright-eyed woman of about thirty. She had hastily done her black hair up into a bun and put on a Persian lamb coat over her night-dress. He introduced her as his wife, and said:

'Huldah says the more trouble there is in the world the more we should try to help people who are in trouble; so you are welcome to stay here until you are well rested and can go on your way. But in a matter such as this we dare trust no one. We must take every precaution that your presence here does not become known to our employees or the neighbours; so we wish to conceal you from our two young sons. They are only six and eight, and children of that age cannot be trusted not to blurt out secrets. They might tell one of their little school-fellows, or the woman who comes in on week-days to help in the kitchen.'

Gregory nodded. 'I fully appreciate that; and we should not in the least mind remaining hidden if when we have slept you could bring some old clothes and cold food to us.'

'We will do that willingly; but we are worried about where to put you. In our apartment we have only four bedrooms: our own, that of the boys, that occupied by my wife's mother and one spare room.' Levianski paused and looked at Gregory. 'The attics on the third floor are all used for stock, and are visited regularly by my night-watchman; so if I made you up a bed on the floor of one of them you would have to be out of it by the time he comes on duty again this evening.'

Sabine looked up at him and said with a faint smile, 'Please don't let that worry you, Mr. Levianski. As the *Herr Kommandant* said just now, we are very old friends. Had it not been for the war we should have been married in nineteen-thirty-nine. As it is, we were married very quietly two days ago; so we shall be delighted to share a room.'

Little Mrs. Levianski's eyes went round with surprise and excitement at finding herself privy to the romance of a Baroness who was being hunted by the Gestapo, and she exclaimed, 'Oh, gracious lady, how tragic for you to find yourself in such straits on your honeymoon! We must put you in our room, which is much nicer; and we will do everything we can to make you forget your troubles.'

'No, Huldah, no!' The more practical Leon quickly shook his head. 'We will do all we can for our guests, yes; but how could we explain having given up our room to strangers? And we must lose no time. In half an hour or so the boys will be awake and, soon after, running about the apartment. By then our guests must be in the spare room and its door locked.'

'Come then, and quietly please,' Huldah gestured towards the stairway. 'I will show you your room and the bathroom. Forgive, gracious lady, that I lead the way.'

Having followed her upstairs, with Levianski bringing up the rear, they were shown a twelve feet square room with a vast double bed in it, and not far from it a bathroom. To an offer of food they declared that they were too tired to be hungry; and, after thanking the Levianski's most warmly, they shut themselves in to get cleaned up.

Both of them would have given a great deal to luxuriate in a hot bath—and it would not have been the first they had had together—but to make one with the gas geyser would have taken a quarter of an hour and, from fear of being discovered by the Levianski children, they dared not linger there too long. It was, after all, only their faces and hands which were so grimy. Having had a thorough wash and combed their hair, they tiptoed across the passage to the spare bedroom.

The big bed had as its principal covering one of those square goosefeather-stuffed pillow-eiderdowns beloved by Central Europeans. On it the Levianskis had laid out a clean suit of pyjamas and a flimsy night-dress. Sabine had already stripped. Picking up the night-dress she looked at it with a crooked smile, put it on, got into bed, and said:

'It was very kind of Mrs. Levianski to provide me with the bridal trimmings; but I'm far too tired to tease you into making me take them off.'

Gregory returned her crooked smile. 'At the moment I feel too old by a thousand years to care one way or the other.' Slipping on the pyjamas he got into the big bed beside her, and added, 'I never thought I'd break down on a honeymoon, but one lives and learns.'

She sighed. 'I never thought I'd break down on a honeymoon either. We've had the most filthy luck so far. But we'll make up for it before we are much older.'

Five minutes later they were both in the deep sleep of utter exhaustion.

It was more than twelve hours later when they were roused by a heavy knocking on the door, and on Sabine's calling a sleepy 'Come in' Leon Levianski entered carrying a well-laden tray. As he set it on the top of a chest of drawers that flanked the bedside, he said:

'I knocked on your door this afternoon when the children were out, but could get no reply. Now, Huldah has just put them to bed, and we thought you must be starving; so she first got this tray ready for me to bring up to you.'

Sabine murmured her thanks and quickly wriggled down to hide her bare shoulders under the bed-clothes; but Gregory sat up and said, 'I had no idea we had slept so long. We were hoping to get out of the city tonight but it seems we have slept away the chance to make any preparations.'

Levianski shook his head. 'It would have been foolish to rush matters and so increase the likelihood of your being caught. Much better stay here till tomorrow night. By then you will be fully recovered and far more capable of making a successful get-away.'

He was so obviously right that they did not attempt to argue the matter, but again thanked him for his most generous hospitality. With good appetites now, as soon as he had left them they set about the meal. Shuddering slightly, they covered the pickled herrings garnished with circles of onion with a plate; but the ample portions of cold goose and apricot compote washed down with a bottle of Bulls-blood of Badascony tasted as good as anything they could have got at the Ritz Grill of the Donau Palata.

When they had eaten, knowing that the children were in bed they crept across to the bathroom, and enjoyed a hot bath. Then, banishing the thought of the perils they must soon face again and, living only for the moment, they spent what they later agreed to be one of the never-to-be-forgotten-nights-in-a-life-time.

In the morning, although Huldah Levianski did not bring along their breakfast until her two boys had gone to kinder-garten, she found them fast asleep. She told them that she had sent her daily help, Rosa, out to do some shopping, so for the next hour they could use the bathroom without fear of discovery. Then she produced the morning papers and pointed out in them the accounts of the attack on the Tuzolto Palace.

The newspapers gave only a garbled version of the affair. It was stated that a rumour had got round that the Baroness had had staying in her palace the Commandant Tavenier, who had recently been received into Budapest society; and, believing him to be engaged in spreading propaganda in favour of the Allies, the Arrow-Cross had given a violent demonstration of their disapproval. Many windows of the palace had been smashed by smoke-bombs being thrown through them, and these had driven its inmates out into the street. The Baroness and her French friend had not been recognised; so it was believed that they must have disguised themselves before leaving in order to escape a rough handling by the young hooligans outside. No mention was made of the fight in the Arizona on Friday night, of Gregory's arrest or of the disturbance's having been inspired by the Germans. In two of the papers the accounts ended with an indignant denunciation of the Government's attitude in allowing the Arrow-Cross to carry out acts of violence against private property and citizens who had not been officially accused of any crime.

From this it was clear that the police had not yet issued a 'wanted' notice of Gregory and Sabine; but they felt sure that by this time Grauber would have forced the Regent's hand, and that the omission was a trick inspired by Grauber to lull them into a false sense of security while the whole police-force of Budapest was actually alerted to keep a sharp look out for them.

When they had discussed the reports of the affair with Huldah Levianski, and given her a more detailed account of their escape than they had done on their arrival, she raised the question of clothes and offered to go out and buy everything they needed.

They made a short list, and Sabine was able to reel off her measurements from memory, but Gregory's had to be taken from his much-soiled dinner-jacket suit. For two suits 'off the peg', ready-made underclothes, two dressing-gowns, toilet articles and a cheap suitcase to pack them in, Huldah reckoned that a thousand *pengoes* should prove ample; and Gregory having given her that sum she went off to shop for them while they spent a drowsy morning in bed.

Once when Gregory turned over and his body came in contact with Sabine's warm thigh, he thought for a second that he was back with Erika. Realisation that he was not came as a sudden shock, but he quickly put it from his mind and dozed off again.

It was half-past two before Huldah brought them their lunch, and she explained that she had had to wait until she could get rid of her two boys for the afternoon with a neighbour. While they were eating she brought in a second-hand suitcase and produced from it the purchases she had made for them. Then she said:

'Now you have clothes, Leon suggests that you should have dinner with us this evening; then I shall be able to give you a hot meal. My woman goes at six and I shall have the boys in bed by half-past-seven; so by eight o'clock the coast will be clear.'

'We should love to do that,' smiled Sabine, 'but isn't there a risk that one of the boys might be taken ill, or come along to you for something, and find us with you?'

'No. You must continue to be very careful about using the bathroom in the daytime, although Rosa is unlikely to come to this end of the apartment; but it wouldn't matter if one of the children found you with us this evening. We should simply say that you were two friends we had asked in to dinner.'

When Huldah had left them they saw no point in getting up and, even without the aid of some books she had brought them, they found no difficulty at all in whiling away the afternoon most pleasantly. Soon after seven they roused from a nap and started to dress. The clothes were a long way from being the type they would have chosen for themselves, and Sabine groaned at having to put on garments in such flamboyant taste; but Gregory pointed out that being so far removed from the creations in which people were used to seeing her made it much less probable that she would be recognised when she had to go out in them.

Levianski came for them at eight and took them along to a lounge which was over-full of modern furniture showing the same flamboyant taste that his wife displayed in clothes. There he introduced them to his mother-in-law, a Mrs. Klitzberg.

She was a very fat woman of about sixty with a sallow, wrinkled face and, although she was almost cringingly polite to Sabine, they could see that she did not at all approve of their presence. For that, Gregory did not blame her in the least, as it was very understandable that she should fear they would bring trouble on her daughter's family. In the hope of reassuring her a little, he remarked that now they had clothes they must not abuse the hospitality which had been so generously extended to them for a moment longer than was absolutely necessary.

Their host was pouring glasses of *Baratsch* for them. Looking up quickly, he said, 'I think you will have to remain here a few days yet; but it would be better if we put off discussing plans for you until after dinner.'

It was not an altogether happy meal. Huldah's anxiety to do her guests well had led her to give them too many courses and, as she and Leon refused to allow them to wait upon themselves, this resulted in the constant break up of conversation. Moreover, Mrs. Klitzberg remained covertly hostile, and Huldah persisted in calling Sabine 'gracious lady Baroness' although Sabine protested that she was now Madam Tavenier, and that she would prefer such friends as the Levianskis had proved themselves to be to call her by her Christian name. Leon alone of the three behaved naturally, and they wished that it had been possible for them to have dined with him without his womenfolk.

Soon after dinner Mrs. Klitzberg relieved them of her presence, and they tackled the subject which was uppermost in all their minds. Gregory opened the matter by asking Leon if he could buy them a reliable second-hand car.

'I could,' he replied, 'but I am doubtful if you would be wise to stick to your idea of trying to reach the frontier that way. In the first place, our one serious shortage here is petrol; and it is not easy to obtain even on the black market.'

'Oh, we'd be all right for that,' Sabine assured him. 'I was given a special allowance, and have more than enough coupons.'

He shrugged his broad shoulders. 'That is not the only thing. Owing to the petrol shortage there are far fewer cars on the roads these days, and they are hardly ever used for long journeys. It seems to me that you would run a great risk of being pulled up and questioned about where you obtained your petrol. Then, if your description has been circulated, it would be all up with you.'

Gregory pulled a long face. 'That hadn't occurred to me; but I'm afraid you are right.'

'How do you propose to get across the frontier if you can get to it?' his host asked.

'We have passports; but of course we wouldn't dare to use them now. I had intended to abandon the car in a wood and that in the middle of the night we should make our way across by stealth.'

Leon shook his dark, curly head. 'I feared as much, and the dangers you will encounter there are a lot greater than these others I have mentioned. Have you considered, too, the terrible demands that such a journey would make on a lady. I am told by friends of mine who know about such matters that the patrols not only keep watch on the frontier but also range for several miles in depth behind it. That means that from a long way back you would have to avoid all tracks, and so be faced with a most exhausting tramp through woods or across marshes. You would not dare to use a torch and might easily lose your way. Even if you succeeded in evading the Hungarian patrols, you might run into the Yugoslavs on the other side and be turned back.'

Gregory had crossed frontiers clandestinely before; so he knew, only too well, that Leon was not exaggerating the difficulties. Had he been on his own he would have backed himself to get through; but he realised now that during the past twenty-four hours his thoughts had been too distracted by more pleasant matters for him to give due weight to the handicap that having Sabine with him must prove. The abrupt awareness of what it would entail came as a very nasty shock. Now he was seized with a sudden fear that to do as he had planned would prove next to impossible.

# 20

# Journey into Trouble

With a sinking feeling Gregory faced up to the gulf that lay between crossing the frontier on foot and, as they had originally intended, in a car. It would mean a whole night of desperate strain and endeavour; perhaps more, as dawn might catch them before they were across, and that would mean having to lie up for the day. For hours they would have to crawl flat on their stomachs through scrub and along ditches; and if they were spotted they would have to run for their lives to the nearest cover. Sabine had plenty of courage, but she was just not the sort of girl that Girl Guide Captains are made from. Physically she was incapable of standing up to such a gruelling ordeal. Uneasily, he admitted:

'You're right. The dice will be loaded against us. But it seems there is no alternative.'

Leon leaned forward. 'You remember our first talk at the café? I mentioned to you then that Eichmann had already set up an office for so-called "Jewish Emigration" in Budapest. For us Jews that is the red light. We still pray that Hungary will protect us and that there will be no great persecution here. Most of us feel this to be so much our home that we prefer to take a chance on that, rather than give up everything and face a new life abroad almost penniless. But some, who have money or relatives in foreign countries, are already leaving from fear that the Nazis will force Admiral Horthy to abandon us to them. For those who wish to go it is not easy; because in wartime the Government will grant no exit permits, except in very special cases. In consequence, those who are leaving have to do so in secret. Some of them are doing as you suggest and attempting to cross the frontier at night. But for those who are rich enough there is an easier way. They are smuggled out in the big barges that go down the Danube to Turkey.'

'By Jove!' Gregory's eyes lit up. 'Do you mean that you could arrange for us to get out like that?'

'These barge masters are rapacious. It would cost you

two thousand five hundred *pengoes* each.'

'That is not much more than we should have to pay for a car.'

'No. If you agree then, I will see what I can do. But it will probably be several days before the people I approach would be able to find a barge that will take you, and is due to leave.'

'In that case, unless you know of anywhere else we can go, it will mean our continuing to accept your hospitality, and I feel that we have already trespassed . . .'

Holding up a plump hand, Leon cut him short. 'Please don't let that worry you. Huldah and I are glad to help. My mother-in-law may prove a little tiresome, but for our sake she will not breathe a word about your being here.'

'No, no!' Huldah put in. 'I am sorry that she was not more cordial to you at dinner. But you need not have the least fear that she will be indiscreet. From tomorrow, I have arranged for my little boys to stay for some days with my sister; so it is only of my woman, Rosa, that you will still have to be care-ful. If it were not for her you would be able to move freely about the apartment all the time. As it is you will have to spend the days in your bedroom, and keep very quiet there; but if you can put up with that. . . .'

They 'put up with that' without any grief or pain at all. In fact they greatly preferred it to having to sit in the lounge with Mrs. Klitzberg, or even the kind but gushing Huldah; and, as Gregory remarked, it was almost as if they were having the Spanish peasants' honeymoon of which they had talked— although it transpired that instead of a full week it lasted only five days.

Now and again thoughts of Erika drifted into Gregory's mind, but he came to dismiss them with angry resentment. He had been faithful to her for over two and half years, and he had never remained faithful to any other woman for more than six months. Her life before he had met her had been as hectic as his own and neither of them have ever subscribed to the 'one man for one woman' Christian ethic. He was still at the height of his manly vigour and for him to have suppressed it would have been, he decided, entirely against both the laws of nature and common sense.

During those days they emerged only to use the bathroom each morning, while Huldah sent her cleaning woman off on some errand, and in the evenings for a hot meal with the family; except for once after dinner on the second night, and then they ventured down into the street. Their reason was Sabine's anxiety about her jewels and her wish to get hold of them to take with her if she could.

The risk of telephoning from the Levianskis' flat was small, but there was just a chance that police had been installed in the Tuzolto palace and the call might be traced back; so Gregory accompanied her to a telephone kiosk some two hundred yards away. Her call was answered by Magda, who was able to assure her that the jewels were safe. But there was no possibility of getting them to her as, on the Monday morning, Pipi had lodged them at her bank, and it was certain that the bank would not let them be withdrawn again without her own signature. For her to call there herself would have been much too dangerous, and to have sent an order for their collection by anyone else might easily have led to their being traced; so she had to resign herself to leaving them behind.

However, with the large sum she had drawn in cash from her bank on the Saturday, and the considerable amount Gregory carried on him, even after paying for their transport down the Danube and their new clothes they still had over three hundred pounds between them; so they had no immediate anxieties about money.

It was on Thursday, after lunch, that Leon came to their room to say that he had unexpected good news for them. His friend had just let him know that the man of a Jewish couple who had planned to leave had been stricken with appendicitis; so the couple had had to cancel, leaving two places free on a barge that was sailing that night.

As they had few things to pack and there was ample room in their suitcase, it suddenly occurred to Gregory that he could, after all, take some *foie-gras* back to England; so he asked Leon to buy for him three of the biggest tins he could find.

That evening, after dinner, they sat about rather anxiously until eleven o'clock. When at last the time came to say good-bye Sabine handed a plain envelope to Huldah and said, 'in this is a message that I am particularly anxious should reach a friend of mine tomorrow evening, when we are safely on our

280

way. Will you please keep it and telephone it to her; but not till then.'

Actually in the envelope there was a slip of paper on which was written: *Etienne and I will never be able to repay you and Leon for your courage and kindness, but will you please buy something for your little boys with these,* and 'these' were two five-hundred *pengo* notes.

Leon took them as far as the Customs House and on a corner nearby handed them over to a small hook-nosed Jew, whom he recognised from a description that had been given him. The little man said quickly:

'It is unnecessary that we know one another's names. Just call me Ike. Please show me your money.'

Gregory produced his wallet, they exchanged a final hearty hand-clasp with Leon and then set off with Ike. For over half a mile they walked in silence, mostly in the shadow of tall dark warehouses and across seemingly endless railway sidings, until they came to a gate in a tall corrugated iron fence. There was a watchman on duty there, but at a word from Ike he let them through and they found themselves on the river-side near a row of towering grain elevators. Alongside the wharf lay a string of immensely long barges, at least three times the size of those in use on the Thames. A dim light was showing from the stern hatch of one of them. Following Ike, they scrambled aboard her and he called down the hatch, 'Szabó!'

A huge, untidy, hairy man lumbered up the ladder and greeted them in Hungarian. The Jew told Gregory to produce the passage money and he paid it over into the leg-of-mutton hand of the barge master. Szabó thumbed it through then peeled off notes to the value of a thousand *pengoes* and thrust them at Ike. With a quick grin the Jew pocketed them. Next moment, without a word, he had slipped back on to the wharf and was disappearing in the darkness.

Szabó spat and muttered in Hungarian. Sabine translated for Gregory. 'He says that little runt takes no risk and does nothing except guide passengers to the barge, yet he insists on a twenty per cent commission; and that all Jews are scum.'

'The Levianskis prove how wrong he is about that,' Gregory replied. 'But there are plenty of them like Ike, and it's his kind that gets the whole race into its troubles.'

Meanwhile Szabó had beckoned them to follow him, and

led the way below to quite a big cabin. It was clean with bright chintzes as curtains and covers and a row of brilliantly polished kitchen utensils hanging in one corner over a cooking stove. In a rocking chair a fat, jolly-faced woman of about forty was sitting knitting. She struggled to her feet and gave them a smile of welcome.

'This is my wife Yolande,' said Szabó, with a happy grin. 'She is the best cook on the whole Danube; so you are lucky to be travelling with us. My two hands, Dem and Zoltán, have cabins forward. They get a cut so you need not be afraid that they will split on you. Now, it is understood that we ask you no questions, but we must call you something. What shall it be?'

Again Sabine translated, and Gregory suggested, 'Joseph and Josephine.'

'So be it!' the big man nodded. 'And now a drink to a lucky voyage.'

Turning, he took a bottle of *Baratsch* and four glasses from a cupboard, then poured four generous rations. It was immature fiery stuff, but they drank the toast no less enthusiastically.

Their cabin was down a short passage. That too was clean, and more comfortable than they had expected. The bunks were one above the other and the springless mattresses in them much harder than the beds to which they had been accustomed; but each was quite wide enough to hold two people cuddled together, so they put the two mattresses one on top of the other in the lower bunk. As they undressed, although they had not yet sampled Yolande's cooking, they were already prepared to endorse Szabó's opinion that they were lucky to be travelling in his barge.

When they woke next morning the barge was in motion, although they would hardly have known it had it not been for the fast rippling of water against her sides. Having washed and dressed they went through to the big cabin. Yolande was there and cooked them a good breakfast of eggs and ham, but there was no tea or coffee, so they had to wash it down with light beer. She told them that there was nothing against their sitting on deck all day, except when the string of barges lay moored in a river-side town for the tug to refuel and the women of the crews to buy fresh provisions; and then they must remain under cover in case someone asked awkward questions.

When they had fed they went on deck and found big Szabó at the tiller. They had passed the large factory-covered island of Cespel in the early hours of the morning, and the flattish green plain now stretched away into the distance from both banks of the wide river. Their barge was the last of three being towed by a powerful tug, and Gregory estimated that she must be doing a good six knots.

Very soon they settled into a routine more peaceful than anything that either of them had ever experienced. Day after day, and night after night, the great barge ploughed almost noiselessly through the turgid green water. The only halts were those at the larger riverside towns, in which Yolande did her shopping. The current was with them and they covered anything from a hundred to a hundred and thirty miles a day. Yolande's cooking of unpretentious dishes was as good as her husband had promised, and neither of them was ever rude or surly.

Occasionally some scent, or sight or sound, reminded Gregory of Erika, but in this new world of blissful peace, England, the War, and Erika all seemed infinitely far away. It was a little difficult to realise that he was now on his way back to them and that, sometime, he would have to put his 'love-life'—as for lack of a better word he decided to term it—in order; but there was no hurry and no sense whatever in worrying about that yet.

On the fourth day they reached Belgrade. Gregory had contemplated leaving the barge there. He and Sabine both had passports visa'd for Yugoslavia, so a week earlier they would have met with no difficulty in catching the Orient Express and being twenty-four hours later safely in Switzerland. But the Germans were in control in Yugoslavia, so Grauber's writ ran there.

By now he would have ordered a look-out for them to be kept on every possible escape-route; so, although Gregory knew it to be his duty to get back to England by the quickest possible means, he had decided that to attempt going through Yugoslavia, with the risk of not getting home at all, was too big to be taken.

To remain in the barge all the way down to Turkey meant

at least a fortnight longer, but the risk while passing through enemy-held territory was almost negligible and when they did reach Turkey they would be in a neutral country; so in this case there was ample justification for a policy of hastening slowly.

Early on the morning of the 10th they came in sight of the great black rocks called the Iron Gates, which towered up on either side of the Danube and formed the frontier between Hungary and Rumania. For Gregory and Sabine this was the one real danger spot of their journey, but Szabó showed not the least uneasiness. He told them to pack all their belongings in their suitcase, then he set his crew of two to dig a hole amidships in the flat sea of grain that formed the cargo of the barge. After half an hour's hard shovelling Dem and Zoltán got down to a flooring of short wooden planks. The centre one was lifted to reveal a tiny room, no more than five feet square and four feet high. It was actually a large packing case, which had been put into postion on the bottom boards of the barge before the grain was loaded into her.

Sabine and Gregory climbed down into it with their suitcase, the plank was replaced, and eight feet of grain shovelled back on top of them. Their prison was unlit, only just large enough for them to sit side by side, and as silent as the grave. Their only danger of discovery lay in one of the customs officers striking the top of the little wood-walled room while he searched for contraband with his plunging rod; but the area of grain was so great compared with the surface of their roof, that this was very unlikely.

All the same, they spent an anxious and extremely uncomfortable four hours. It was dark as pitch, and soon very stuffy. Towards the end the air was almost unbreathable and they both had splitting headaches. Had either of them been alone he or she would have suffered from appalling claustrophobia. Even as it was they found difficulty in keeping out of their minds nightmare thoughts that Szabó and his crew might be arrested, which could lead to their dying from suffocation before they were found. It was with infinite relief that round about midday they heard the rasp of shovels above them, and soon afterwards were pulled up by willing hands, half-fainting, into the fresh air.

Once more they settled down to lazy untroubled days in the September sunshine. On the 15th they left the Danube at Cernavoda for the canal which enters the Black Sea at Mamaia, a few miles above the great Rumanian port of Constanta. There they again had to suffer a few hours' imprisonment in the big packing case while the Customs cleared the barges to proceed to Turkey, but it was such a routine business that the search was only perfunctory.

On the last three days of the journey the barge lost its charm for them. There were no longer pretty villages, wooded hills or lush water meadows with cattle peacefully grazing to be seen on either hand. Instead the stalwart tug drew the great lumbering barges through choppy seas, driven spray made the deck untenable and meals were no longer a joy to which to look forward.

Mentally as well as physically they both came gradually to realise that, without knowing it, they had been driven out of paradise. They were now only a day or two from Istanbul, and what was to happen then? Gregory had said nothing to Sabine about his future plans, and she was beginning to wonder anxiously what he meant to do about her. For his part, he needed no telling that Istanbul was no more than two days by air from London—and in his mind London was now synonymous with Erika.

He did not blame himself for his affaire with Sabine. Seeing the people they were and the way in which events had marched, it was hardly possible for them not to have become lovers. And, for a love affaire she was everything that any man could desire. But he certainly did not want her as a permanency.

Erika was the only woman he had ever wanted as a permanency; and he still wanted her that way. They had long since decided that when the war was over and she could get a divorce from Von Osterberg they would marry. Owing to Sir Pellinore's generosity they had already tentatively begun to look for a house in the country in which to settle down. Nothing must be allowed to interfere with that.

He felt reasonably confident that if Erika had to be told about Sabine she would be broadminded enough not to hold his lapse against him; but he had no intention of letting her know anything about it that could be avoided. In his view, people who unnecessarily gave pain to others, supposedly beloved by them, by pouring out mawkish confessions were guilty of the most cowardly self-indulgence. But Erika was certainly not the woman to countenance his having an intimate friendship with another woman. So something must be done about Sabine; and that 'something' could not be delayed much longer.

It was on the evening of the 18th, when they were actually entering Turkish waters, that he said to her, 'This has been a wonderful fortnight, and I'm sure we were right not to mar it by talking about the future. But you must have thought about it quite a bit, and we'll be in tomorrow morning. When we get ashore, what do you intend to do?'

Her dark eyes widened in surprise. 'What an extraordinary question! Naturally, I shall remain with you.'

'Of course—for the time being.' He endeavoured to keep his voice casual. 'But unfortunately I have to return to England —and as quickly as I can.'

She shrugged. 'Then you must take me with you.'

'That would be far from easy. You seem to forget that, as far as the British authorities are concerned, you are an enemy alien.'

For a moment Sabine considered, then her full red lips broke into a smile. 'There is one way we could easily get over that— if you cared to take it. You have only to marry me and automatically I shall acquire British citizenship.'

Gregory hoped that his face did not show his mental reaction to her suggestion. He was deeply attached to her and ready to go a very long way to spare her feelings; but, even had there been no question of Erika, he would certainly not have been prepared to pay the price of marriage for what, before the war, neither of them would have thought of as more than three weeks' lovely fun.

'Thanks for the implied compliment that you'd have me for keeps,' he smiled. 'But I fear it can't be done. You must know from the past that I'm not a marrying type of man.'

Next moment he could have bitten out his tongue. She had given him the perfect opening to reply, 'I'm sorry, my dear, but I am married already—or as good as'. He could then have explained his position to her and, although she might have been upset, she would have had no alternative but to accept it. As it was, he had now made it more difficult than ever to let her know that he had another mistress for whom he felt far more deeply than he did for her.

In blissful ignorance of his thoughts, she said. 'No; I was only drawing a bow at a venture. I didn't suppose you would want to marry. But if you mean to return to England you must take me with you.'

He made a wry grimace. 'It's all very well to say that. Naturally I should like to; but I don't see how it is to be done.'

'You'll find a way. You've got to!' Her voice suddenly became intensely earnest. 'You can't leave me here in Turkey. If I had been able to bring my jewels out of Hungary and sell them, at least I'd be independent. But I'm not. I've only enough money to last me for a month or two, and no means of getting any more till the war is over. I've earned my living before, and I can do it again. I don't mind that. But I must have some background—some security in case I am ill or get into difficulties. You say you love me; the least you can do is to provide that.'

'I'm most anxious to,' he replied; and he meant it. 'Fortunately I'm quite well off, and have ways in which I could get money to you wherever you are; but it is only fair to tell you that if I could get you back to England we wouldn't be able to live together. I am a serving officer, and it is certain that I shall be sent abroad again.'

She sighed. 'This bloody war! How damnable it is that the quarrels of governments should interfere with people's private lives. Still, we can't alter that; and I have to face the fact that I am now an outlaw from Hitler's Europe, Italy, France, Austria, in all of which I could have made a life with friends, are barred to me. I've never been to the United States or Scandinavia, so know no one in those countries. Where else can I go but England? Even if you have to be away a lot I'd still be in touch with you. And there is dear old Sir Pellinore. I feel sure that as an old friend of my father's he would act as a sort of guardian to me.'

For a moment Gregory had an awful vision of Sir Pellinore's sending Sabine up to live at Gwain Meads with Erika. That would put the cat among the pigeons with a vengeance. Swiftly banishing that shattering thought, he said:

'I'm sure he would do everything possible for you; but you'll find life in London pretty grim these days, what with the black-out, air raids, and everything rationed to a point where it is next to impossible to get a good meal or nylons. And we can't ignore the fact that as you are an enemy alien you would be liable to be interned.'

'I can't think that I should be,' she gave a quick shrug. 'After all, I am a refugee from Nazi persecution. There are hundreds of thousands of them in Britain and I gather that only a very small percentage are kept behind barbed wire. Owing to the highly secret missions you are sent on, you must be in touch with people who could arrange matters. You would only have to vouch for me and everything would be all right. As for war-time conditions, the air raids on London can't be anything like as bad as those I've been used to in Berlin, and I'd manage to put up with the other inconveniences.'

Gregory's suggestion about internment had been only a last ditch argument. He knew well enough that Sir Pellinore could save her from that, and he felt himself to be playing a mean part in opposing her going to England. All along he had realised that it was the logical solution to her future, and he had only hoped against hope that she might produce some other plan for herself when they reached Turkey. That she had not threatened to provide some very nasty headaches for him when they got to London, but that was little enough to set against the fact that by getting him out of prison she had saved him from Grauber and, as a result of that had herself been driven into exile. The very least he could do was to assist her to the best of his ability to establish herself in whichever country she chose to live for the remainder of the war. As that was England he must rely on skilful handling of the situation to prevent her meeting Erika; and as Erika rarely came to London that should not prove very difficult. Old Pellinore, if put in the picture at once, could be trusted to neutralise the only real danger ground, Carlton House Terrace, by giving orders that when one of them was there he was always 'out' to the other.

Seeing that he must accept a responsibility that for sometime he had regarded as almost inevitable, Gregory did so with a good grace. He told Sabine that he had given her the blackest side of the picture only because he was not one hundred per cent certain that he would be able to get a clearance for her with the Enemy Aliens Department, and did not want her to be disappointed if he could see little of her, or miserable in a London that, compared to Budapest, had been reduced by war to such dreary straits. Then he spent the last hour before he went to sleep in considering how he could best get her back to England with him.

Next morning they woke to find the barge tied up to a wharf, and learned that she had docked near the goods yard at Haidar Pacha, on the Scutari side of the Bosphorus. As they wished to leave Turkey openly—and entering it clandestinely would have made that more difficult—having taken warm leave of the Szabós they went ashore and surrendered themselves to the Dock Police, who took them to the Immigration Officer.

Gregory had his fake French passport as Commandant Tavenier, and Mario's Italian passport, while Sabine had her own as a Hungarian national; but now that they were in a neutral country he had decided against using any of these. He declared himself a British subject and, in order that their cases should be dealt with as one, continued the fiction that Sabine was his wife.

At his request he was allowed to telephone to the British Consulate, but could get no further than a minor official who proved anything but helpful, and would promise only that someone should be sent to take particulars of them some time during the day. That, since the Immigration Authorities would not release them until fully satisfied, meant that they would be held in the detention block for at least twenty-four hours, and Gregory had no intention of kicking his heels there that long.

As he had plenty of money he was able to make the interpreter a handsome present to arrange for a long-distance call to be put through for him to the British Ambassador in Ankara. There was a considerable delay and the call was taken by a secretary; but Gregory gambled on the Ambassador's knowing Sir Pellinore, at least by name, and said that he had a personal message from him for His Excellency. The trick worked, and Sir Hugh Knatchbull-Hugesson was brought to the line.

To him, in guarded terms, Gregory explained his situation, and requested His Excellency to telephone the Consul General, Istanbul, ordering him to give immediate aid, including the despatch of a Most Secret cypher telegram to London.

For the next few minutes there came over the wire a spate of questions about Sir Pellinore's appearance, background and habits; then, when the Ambassador had assured himself that Gregory really did know the elderly baronet personally, he agreed to do as he had been asked.

A little before midday a young man who appeared to be of Turkish extraction arrived from the British Consulate and accepted responsibility for them. When the formalities were completed he took them to a motor launch, and so across to the European side of the Bosphorus. On their way they had a lovely view of the Sultan Ahmed Mosque, Aya Sophia and the vast rambling old Palace set in the Seraglio Gardens. Then the launch turned into the Golden Horn and landed them at the steps below Pera. Half an hour later they were closeted with the Consul General.

Having received his instructions from the Ambassador, the Consul General asked no questions; but he put in hand for both of them documents which would enable them to leave Turkey, ordered seats to be obtained for them as early as possible on a plane going to Cyprus, and enquired about the secret cypher signal that Gregory wished to send.

He had already thought it out very carefully, so wrote it down without hesitation. It was addressed to Sir Pellinore, care of the Foreign Office, and ran:

*Mission one hundred per cent successful Stop Proceeding Cyprus immediately accompanied by representative carrying full terms Stop Please expedite air passage Cyprus-London for self and bearer of Hungarian Passport No. 476010 as matter of urgency Stop*

In that way he avoided having to give any lengthy explanation about Sabine, yet ensured that on the production of her own passport the Military authorities in Cyprus would make no difficulties about her accompanying him to London.

After changing some money with the Consul and thanking him for his assistance, they took a taxi to the Pera Palace, arriving at the famous hotel just in time for a late lunch. Although it was a Saturday afternoon, as the Mahomedan Sabbath is on a Friday all the shops were open; so after they had unpacked their few belongings they were able to go on a shopping expedition down the *Gran' Rue* and buy themselves some more suitable clothes. In the evening the Consul General's secretary telephoned to say that seats had been booked for them in a Turkish air liner that was leaving for Cyprus on Monday morning.

There had been no wireless on the barge and during the time they were in her such news as they had received of the war had been garbled and scanty; the only reliable item of interest was that two nights after they left Budapest the Hungarian capital had suffered its first air raid, although only a light one, from a few Soviet bombers. Having reached neutral territory, where unprejudiced accounts were available, Gregory had naturally taken the earliest opportunity to find out what had been going on, and during the day he had brought himself up to date.

The best news was that early in the month Rommel had launched an all-out attempt to penetrate to the Nile Delta, and that he had been repulsed with heavy losses by the new commander of the Eighth Army, General Sir Bernard Montgomery. But the British were still very much on the defensive, the Mediterranean was now an Axis lake, and the half-starved garrison of Malta continued, under almost non-stop bombing, to hold out only by the skin of its teeth.

The Japs had launched a powerful offensive in New Guinea, but the Australians there were showing their great fighting qualities and General Blamey had declared himself confident that they would be able to hold Port Moresby.

In Madagascar there had been indications that the Vichy French intended to sell out to the Japs, just as they had done in Indo-China; so, in order to ensure against the great island's becoming an Axis base, empire troops had recently landed there and taken over the whole of it.

During the first seventeen days of the month the R.A.F. had carried out no less than nine heavy raids on Germany, inflicting terrible damage on Bremen, Saarbrucken, Frankfurt, Dusseldorf and Essen, reducing the centres of all of them to flaming ruins.

Stalingrad still miraculously held out. Over a fortnight before, Von Bock had reached the Volga to the north of the city and during the past few days he had been making desperate efforts to reach it to the south. The Russians claimed that the Germans had already lost a million men in their endeavours to take the city, but their assault showed no signs of slackening. Yet the Russian defence was equally determined and it looked now as if there were a chance that they might be able to hold on until winter brought the German offensive to a standstill.

Gregory knew that it was now too late in the year to undertake the Anglo-American landing on the Continent for which the Hungarians had stipulated; but in another month or so the first snow would be falling in Russia. If Stalingrad could be held till then the Army defending it would get a respite until the late spring. That gave six months in which to conclude a secret treaty with the Hungarians and prepare a cross-Channel assault. It could be launched before conditions in Russia permitted the Germans to resume their offensive, Hungary brought over to the Allies and the whole position saved. The thought that, after all, his mission might lead to such magnificent results made him suddenly eager to get home.

Sunday they spent sightseeing, and went to bed wishing that they could spend more time in the fascinating city of the Sultans which, as Constantinople, and earlier Byzantium, had played so great a part in history. On Monday they flew down across Asiatic Turkey, landing in Cyprus in the late afternoon; but to Gregory's annoyance he learned that the Office of the Director of Transport had received no instructions about them.

From Cyprus the only means of proceeding to England was by R.A.F. aircraft, and places were so limited that many officers who had only a low priority had been waiting there for passages for several weeks. As Gregory had no official status he could not even get their names on the list; so he decided to see the Director in the morning and ask for another Most Secret cypher telegram to be sent. To his relief that proved unnecessary. During the night a signal came through from the Air Ministry giving them a sufficiently high priority to get them on an aircraft leaving on the 23rd.

Their flight over the Mediterranean was both dangerous and extremely uncomfortable. They were packed like sardines into the bomb bay of the aircraft, unable to see anything and scarcely able to move. For the greater part of the way the plane flew very high to avoid the attention of the enemy in those Axis dominated skies. That necessitated using oxygen masks and the discomfort seemed only a little less endurable than the violent acrobatics of the aircraft to escape attack when she came down at Malta to refuel.

As there was not half a loaf to be spared in the besieged island they had brought food with them, and while they ate it they watched an air battle almost above their heads. When the Luftwaffe squadron had been driven off they resumed their journey and after further hours of torture reached Gibraltar. There they got six hours of desperately needed sleep; then they were on their way again, still a prey to cramp and claustrophobia, as the aircraft carried them far over the Atlantic before curving in across south-western England to land them at Hurn in Hampshire.

Stiff and bleary-eyed they staggered from their prison to find that it was nine o'clock in the morning and that a Mr. Davis had been sent down overnight to meet them. Taking Gregory aside he explained that he was an official of M.I.5, and that as an enemy alien was being brought into England he had been instructed to attend to all formalities, then take them up to London.

A wash and breakfast revived them a little, then they set off with Mr. Davis in his car. For most of the way they slept, and the worst effects of their nightmare journey had passed off when, shortly before one o'clock, their escort put them down outside Sir Pellinore's mansion in Carlton House Terrace.

The door was answered by an elderly parlourmaid whom Gregory had not seen before; but she said that Sir Pellinore was expecting him and took them straight up to the library. The white-haired Baronet was seated behind his big desk. As Sabine walked into the room his bright blue eyes opened wide with surprise. Coming quickly to his feet, he smiled over her head at Gregory, and boomed;

'Delighted to see you back, dear boy. Delighted. But I er—I thought you were bringin' with you an Hungarian gentleman.'

'Surely you remember me?' Sabine smiled up at him.

'Why, bless my soul!' He stretched out a leg-of-mutton hand to her. 'You're my old friend Szenty's gel. Got mixed up with that scoundrel Gavin Fortescue in 1936, and Gregory, here, pulled you out. Of course I remember you.'

'I'm afraid I deceived you in my wire,' Gregory intervened quickly, with the object of tipping Sir Pellinore off that he did not wish to discuss his mission in front of Sabine. 'My reason for bringing Sabine with me was not the one that I gave. It's quite another story. Incidentally she has been married since you last met her, and is now the Baroness Tuzolto.'

'Well, well! No matter! I'm delighted to see you both. We'll have a glass of wine then you must tell me all about it.' Turning, Sir Pellinore took a stride towards the table on which drinks were always kept, but halted and added with a frown, 'Drat that new parlourwoman! As soon as Davis telephoned me to say that you were on your way I told her to have a magnum on the ice in here by half-past twelve. Suppose she is gettin' it now; but I'd best ring for her in case she's forgotten altogether.'

Returning to his desk, he pressed a bell on it, then resumed his seat and waved them to two elbow chairs facing him.

'Please sit down.' He smiled appreciatively at Sabine, and with a gallant gesture swept up one side of his fine cavalry moustache. 'So you're married, eh? Well, your husband's a mighty lucky feller. At least, he would be if he were here. Slipped by me for the moment that now you are in England you won't be able to get back to him until the war is over. And I fear that won't be for a year or two yet.'

With a wicked twinkle in her dark eyes, Sabine returned his smile. 'I lost my husband two years ago. For a time that made me very sad; but I decided it was just as well when Gregory turned up in Budapest again. As you know, we were in love with one another before the war. When we met again it was as though we had never parted. That was just as well too; as pretending to be married made it much easier for us to get away, and we had a lovely honeymoon on a barge all the way down the Danube.'

She had only just begun to speak when Gregory heard a faint noise behind them. A half-glance over his shoulder showed him that it was the parlourmaid coming in as quietly as a well-trained servant should, carrying the magnum of champagne in an ice bucket. Not having heard her, Sabine was continuing her gay revelation; and, as Gregory could hardly stop her, he could only hope that the woman would not take in the full significance of what she was saying.

Next moment he saw Sir Pellinore's face suddenly become frozen. For a second he thought that he, too, was concerned

294

about the maid's overhearing this wanton admission. The old man coughed loudly in a vain endeavour to drown Sabine's last sentence, then he half rose to his feet, his face a picture of consternation.

Swinging round, Gregory took in a tableau that made him gasp with dismay. The maid had her back turned. She had just set the heavy ice-bucket down on the table. Owing to its weight she had needed both hands to carry it, so had left the door open behind her. Framed in the doorway stood Erika. Her face showed that she had heard all that Sabine had said.

# 21

## Hell on the Home Front

Erika, white to the lips, remained standing in the doorway, as rigid as if she had suddenly been turned to stone. Gregory, his eyes wide and his mouth a little open, sat staring at her, his mind temporarily paralysed. Sabine looked from one to the other, guessed with a woman's swift intuition that she had unexpectedly been confronted with a rival, then riveted on Gregory a gaze in which surprise was mingled with anger. Sir Pellinore was the first to recover and he stepped into the breach.

With the bluff jovial manner that had tided over many an awkward situation, he boomed at Erika, 'Come in, my dear, come in. Done your shopping, eh? Here's Gregory, just back from Hungary; and the Baroness Tuposo. Daughter of a very old friend of mine. Baroness, allow me to introduce you to the Countess von Osterberg. Erika, we were just about to have a glass of wine. Glad you're in time to join us.'

In a hard voice that Gregory scarcely recognised, Erika replied, 'Thank you, but I'd rather not. I . . . I came up only to let you know that I shall not be in for lunch.' Then she turned on her heel and walked swiftly away. The parlourmaid, sensing that something was wrong, hurried out in her wake, closing the door behind her.

'Well, that's too bad! But a bigger share in the magnum for each of us, eh?' Sir Pellinore's determination to ride out the storm never faltered. Striding over to the table, he vented on the big bottle the intense annoyance he was concealing, by seizing it in a strangler's grip and wrenching out the cork in a single movement. As he poured the wine, Gregory joined him and took the first half-full silver tankard over to Sabine.

When the Baronet had filled his own tankard he lifted it and cried, 'Bottoms up! Come on, first round straight down the hatch! Just what you both need after your tiring journey!'

Automatically they obeyed him, and swallowing the long draught of fine wine almost immediately relaxed the tension they were feeling. Having refilled their tankards he again sat down at his desk and said, 'Now then; let's hear all about your adventures.'

Suppressing all mention of his secret negotiations, Gregory, aided from time to time by Sabine, gave an account of their meeting in Budapest, and all that had followed as a result of his running into Grauber. Lunch was announced when barely a third of the story had been told and they were sitting over coffee and liqueurs by the time it was finished. When they had done, Sir Pellinore looked across at Sabine, and said:

'Gregory owes his life to you. Not a doubt about that! And as I'm fool enough to be fond of the feller, I'm grateful. Shocking luck your being kicked out, though. No remedy for it, either. Now you're goin' to be stuck here in England for the duration have you formed any views yet of what you'd like to do with yourself?'

'I gathered from Gregory that there was some danger of my being interned,' she replied with a little grimace.

'No, no!' he hastened to assure her. 'You assisted a British agent to escape from the Nazis. That's quite sufficient to enable me to save you from any unpleasantness of that kind. But there's not much social life in Britain these days.'

She thanked him, and went on. 'Naturally, then, I should like to find some occupation. I am fluent in several languages so perhaps I could get work as a translator. It is only the prospect of the first few weeks that troubles me. I know no one in London but yourself and Gregory and, er . . .' she shot a meaning glance at Gregory '. . . he has already told me that his duties will keep him too busy to look after me. I'm afraid that quite on my own I shall find everything very strange and difficult.'

'Perish the thought, m'dear!' exclaimed Sir Pellinore gallantly. 'To cast you adrift would be no way to show our gratitude. Plenty of rooms in this great barrack of a house of mine. You're welcome to stay here until you can find a nice little place of your own. No hurry about that either. And don't worry your pretty head about money. I've more than I could spend in a dozen life times.'

Sabine gave a heavy sigh accompanied by a pale smile. 'Oh, if I might do that! You have no idea what a relief it would be to feel that I need not start life all alone for a while. I shall never be able to repay you.'

'Nonsense! The debt will still be all on our side. And now, after that frightful journey of yours, you must be dead beat. I'll get my housekeeper to take you up to the room she got ready for, er . . . Gregory's Hungarian friend. Bed's the place for you, m'dear, and twenty-four hours of it. Have a good sleep this afternoon. Dinner will be sent up to you. Then after you've had a good long night we'll talk again tomorrow. As a refugee you're entitled to some clothin' coupons. I'll have my secretary get them for you in the morning, and in the afternoon we'll go out together. Long time since I've had the fun of taking a pretty woman shoppin'.'

Desperately tired but much comforted by this concern for her well-being, Sabine agreed at once, and when she had been given into the care of the housekeeper the two men went up to the library. As soon as the door was closed Sir Pellinore said grumpily:

'Fine mess you've made of things!'

'Don't I know it!' Gregory muttered, flinging himself into a chair. 'But how the hell was I to know that Erika would be here?'

'You might have guessed. Knowin' you were on your way home I telephoned her yesterday to come down to meet you.'

'That was good of you; but I wish to God you hadn't.'

'And I wish that Hitler was dead in a ditch; but he isn't.'

'I wouldn't have had this happen for worlds.'

'It's your own fault. I'd have thought you were old enough to realise the wisdom of bein' off with the old love before bein' on with the new. It was downright wicked to spring this thing on poor Erika like that. If only you had tipped me off in your telegram I would never have brought her down from Gwaine Meads. You ought to be ashamed of yourself.'

'I am. But I had expected to have a little time in which to fix things decently.

Sir Pellinore shrugged his great shoulders. 'Well, what's done's done. Perhaps to have used the surgeon's knife may prove kinder to her in the long run.' His bright blue eyes took on a new ruminative expression and he went on, 'I must say, though, you're a wizard with the women. It's no mean feat to have taken Ribbentrop's mistress off him. And, by jove, this Toboso girl is something. She's a stunner.'

Gregory sighed. 'Yes, as brunettes go I've never seen her equal. Still, as far as I'm concerned, she's all yours if you want her.'

'Eh! What's that? If I were your age wild horses wouldn't hold me. But I don't want to die yet. If that wench took me on she'd kill me in a fortnight. Seriously, though, d'you mean that you're not in love with her?'

'No. For the past month I've been suffering from a glorious madness; but that's all there is to it. And unless I'm much mistaken it's the same with her. She hardly kicked at all when I told her that if I did bring her to England I'd be able to see very little of her. The only real love in my life has been, and still is, Erika.'

'God bless my soul! And you've cooked your goose with her. She thinks you've thrown her over for the Trombolo gel.'

'I'm afraid so.' Gregory agreed gloomily. Then he added, 'As Sabine is going to be your guest you had better get her name right. It's Tuzolto.'

'Oh, she must stay here. No question of that; and for as long as she likes. My offer was not made because I believed her to be your new girl-friend, but because she got you out of Grauber's clutches. And, of course, because I knew her father. But what else can Erika think? Damn it, man, she heard this shameless little hussy gaily admit that you'd been honeymoonin' together on the Danube.'

'I know. Erika arriving at that moment was the worst break I've had for years. Still, she has never pretended to be a saint herself, and she has a most generous nature. As soon as she gets back I mean to grovel, and . . .'

Sir Pellinore pulled an envelope from his pocket. 'She's not coming back. When we went down to lunch I found she had left this note for me on the table in the hall. Here, you'd better read it.'

Gregory took the single sheet of paper. On it Erika had scrawled in pencil.

*I am going straight back to Gwaine Meads. Please have my things sent after me. Tell Gregory that I do not wish to see him. If he follows me I shall leave the house at once for some place where he cannot find me.*

Throwing the paper down, Gregory stood up. 'Hell and damnation! She can't do this! She loves me. I'm certain of it; and I love her. Of course I shall go after her.'

'I wouldn't, if I were you.' Sir Pellinore shook his head. 'Not while she's in this state. Odds are she'll carry out her threat if you do. Poor gel's hit hard. That's clear. She'll be all right up at Gwaine Meads; but if you go chasin' her out of it she might do something rash. Don't want an inquest, do we?'

'God forbid! But I can't just leave things as they are. It would be wanton cruelty to allow her to go on believing for longer than I have to that I no longer love her.'

'You can say that in a letter. But keep it short. Just that, and that you want to throw yourself on her mercy as soon as she feels up to seein' you. Throw the ball to her. If she cares for you enough she'll come round when she's had a chance to simmer down.'

Gregory nodded. 'Better still, I'll send her a telegram. She'll get it on her arrival; and it may make tonight a little less miserable for her.'

'Good idea. Now, what about your sloe-eyed Susan. Shockin' waste of a good thing; but I'm afraid you'll have to kiss her good-bye if you hope to patch matters up with Erika.'

'You're right there. I'd meant to anyway. I'll go up and break it to her after dinner. I had intended to ask you for a bed, but I'd better not stay in the house while she's here. I'll telephone Rudd that I'm back and will be sleeping at Gloucester Road.'

'That's sound. You can dine here though. Then, after you've had your show-down with that lovely piece of wickedness upstairs, if there is anything left of you we'll have a talk about your mission.'

'I may as well tell you about it now.'

Sir Pellinore held up a big hand. 'No. You are overdue for a few hours' sleep. Write out that telegram to Erika. I'll send it off and telephone Rudd. Your usual room is ready for you. Go straight to bed. I'll have you called at half-past seven, in time for a bath, then we'll dine.'

When they met again Gregory was no less worried but, physically, his sleep and a hot bath had done him a lot of good. Over dinner their talk was mainly of the war, ranging in turn over the many far-flung battle fronts on which the Axis and the Allies were at death grips. Then, fortified by two glasses of Cockburn's 1912, Gregory went up to see Sabine.

He found her sitting up in bed clad in a nightdress of dark red chiffon that she had bought in Istanbul. She still had heavy shadows under her eyes as a result of their flight from Cyprus, but the colour of the chiffon set off her dark beauty to perfection. On his entering the room her expression hardened, and she said abruptly:

'Well, what have you to say?'

'Very little for myself,' he admitted, taking a chair beside her bed.

'That lovely blonde Countess is your mistress, isn't she?'

'Yes. And something more than that. We are engaged to be married as soon as she can get a divorce from her husband.'

'I seem to remember your telling me that you were not a marrying type.'

'That was true enough when we first met in 1936; but it seems the leopard can change his spots. Perhaps that's because I'm older now. Anyhow, for a long time past I've wanted to marry Erika von Osterberg, and I still do.'

'Why didn't you tell me that last night on the barge that you had someone in England?'

'I meant to. But, to be honest, I funked it. I was afraid that I would hurt you, and I'd hoped . . .'

'To let me down lightly, eh?' Sabine gave him a cynical smile. 'That was most considerate of you. And now, I take it, the chicken has come home to roost. How unfortunate for you that, being uninformed of your situation, and knowing dear old Sir Pellinore to be a man of the world, I should have

300

admitted to our having been lovers. That must have been a horrid shock to the Countess and, I fear, put an abrupt end to your engagement. Or have you made it up with her?'

'No,' Gregory replied dully. 'She has taken it very badly, and left a note in which she says she will refuse to see me.'

'Oh, my poor Gregory. I am so sorry for you.' Sabine's expression had suddenly changed and she was smiling at him.

'You . . . you mean that you don't mind?'

'Of course I mind. It is a terrible blow to my self-esteem that you should prefer any woman to myself. But I'll be honest about it. Love and attraction are two different things. I wasn't particularly attracted to my elderly husband; but I came to love him. On the other hand, you and I were terribly attracted to one another from the moment we met. We should count ourselves lucky that our feelings were mutual and that for two periods of several weeks we have been able to give full expression to them. It may not have been love, but we hit the high spots. That sort of thing can't last. It never does. But we've had it and should be grateful. After our talk that night on the barge, when you showed reluctance to bring me to England, I didn't suspect that there was someone else, but I did realise that we were pretty well through with one another I dug my toes in because at the time you were my only sheet anchor. Now dear Sir Pellinore has promised to take care of me that lets you out. I'll always have a soft spot for you, but I wouldn't want you for life any more than you want me. I'm terribly sorry if I've bitched things for you with your lovely blonde. I wouldn't have done it intentionally. But she's not exactly just out of the school-room, is she? So unless she is a very stupid woman I expect you'll be able to talk her into forgiving you. Anyhow, I hope so.'

Gregory stood up and smiled down on her. 'My dear, you've taken a great load off my mind. I would have hated to really hurt you. Thank goodness you know enough about life to see things in their true perspective. Thank you too for everything. Whatever happens I'll always be your devoted friend. If ever you need my help in any way, you have only to let me know and you can count upon it.'

Ten minutes later he was saying to Sir Pellinore, 'I had a suspicion that her feelings for me where just about the same as mine for her; but I didn't expect that she would behave with such generosity. To let me out without a word of reproach was damn decent of her.'

The corners of Sir Pellinore's eyes wrinkled up in quizzical humour. 'I must say, dear boy, there are times when I find your still youthful conceit most refreshing. High fliers like this pretty bird may enjoy coming down now and then to peck up a hearty breakfast from the lawn. But they live among the tree tops. You need never have feared that she might pine away in loneliness for you. She has only to show her plumage to have a Duke or millionaire industrialist in tow. Now, tell me about Budapest.'

Somewhat chastened, Gregory gave an account of his stay at Nagykáta with the Zapolyas, the formation of the Committee of Magnates and the final agreement to which that had led.

'Good show!' said Sir Pellinore when he had done. 'Jolly good show! That stuff you picked up from Sabine about the Nazis gamblin' everything on Stalingrad should prove very valuable. And by Jove, Gregory, you had something in your own plan! You were dead right. If we could have brought Hungary over to our side it would have saved Russia and altered the whole course of the war in our favour.'

Gregory frowned. 'You speak in the past tense. Does that mean that nothing can be done about it? I realise, of course, that landings on the Continent could not be made as late in the year as this, but if only Stalingrad holds out they would still pay us this magnificent dividend in the spring.'

'The Hungarians have stipulated for a force of fifteen divisions. There wouldn't be that number sufficiently trained to do the job.'

'Damn it all,' Gregory objected. 'It's two and a half years since Dunkirk. There has been an enormous intake during that time, armaments have been pouring out of the factories, and American forces have arrived here in their tens of thousands. If the new troops aren't capable of fighting yet they darned well ought to be. One doesn't win wars with an army that is content to sit indefinitely on its backside.'

Sir Pellinore considered for a moment, then he said, 'I take it you'll be reportin' back for duty at the War Cabinet Offices on Monday?'

'Yes, I suppose so. That is, unless Erika says I can go up to see her. Anyhow, I'll be back there early next week.'

'Then there's no reason why I shouldn't tell you what you're certain to learn in a few days' time. Within a month or so all our first line divisions will have left the country. Big show is being mounted now. Dead secret, of course; but you'll hear all about it when you get back to the War Room.'

'I don't understand. D'you mean that we really are going to do a cross-Channel operation? I should have thought that by the end of October the risk of bad weather would be far too great.'

'It would; and even earlier in the year I doubt if it could have succeeded. The Americans pressed it on us, particularly General Marshall. They maintained that a full-scale invasion of the Continent was the only way to draw pressure off the Russians. Right up to July they fought tooth and nail for it. At one time it looked as if we'd have to give way to 'em—at all events to the extent of seizing the Cherbourg peninsula and tryin' to hang on there through the winter. They more or less threatened that if we wouldn't play they'd go back on the agreed first principle for the grand strategy of the war— the defeat of Hitler before Japan—and send everything to the Pacific. That was the last thing we wanted. But our people didn't want a Continental landing either. They maintained that it would have been murder. I think they were right. The Yanks have plenty of guts, but are still children as far as modern war is concerned. We just couldn't make them understand the immense difficulties of landing great numbers of men and vast quantities of stores on enemy-held beaches against heavy opposition. But, thank God, Winston managed to argue them out of it and get his own pet plan adopted. It is, with or without the consent of the French, to occupy North Africa.'

Gregory looked a little dubious. 'I don't see how that is going to give very much help to the Russians.'

'Not immediately, but it will if they can hold out till the spring. The occupation of Morocco and Algeria is only the first phase. When the Anglo-American expeditionary force has consolidated it will drive east into Tunisia. Simultaneously the Eighth Army will launch an offensive through Libya, to the west. When they've joined up Malta will be relieved and the Mediterranean once more be open to British shippin'. It's estimated that we'll gain a million tons of shippin' through no longer having to send our convoys round the Cape. Then the real squeeze on Hitler will begin. With the sea and air superiority in the Med. regained, we'll be able to threaten the South of France, Corsica, Sardinia, Sicily, Italy, the Adriatic coast, and the Balkans all the way round to Turkey. He'll not dare to leave any part of that immensely long coast line unguarded. To garrison it adequately he'll be compelled to withdraw at least forty divisions and half his air force from Russia.

'I see. Yes; it certainly is a magnificent conception. But what are the odds on our pulling it off?'

'Fifty-fifty,' replied Sir Pellinore gravely. 'No more. It's an appalling gamble. If there is a leak and Hitler gets wind of our intentions he'll order his U-boat packs to intercept and make suicide attacks on our convoys on their way down. That could cost us thousands of our best troops before they even reached their first objectives. When they do land, if the French decide to resist, it'll be touch and go. Our forces will be a thousand miles from home, and with no air support except what the carriers and the one small air base at Gib. can give them. There can be no taking them off as there was at Dunkirk. If they fail to establish themselves ashore it will be a shambles.'

'Then what it really boils down to is that everything depends on the enemy's being kept in the dark about our intentions. Or at all events, as the cat can't be kept in the bag once our convoys are sighted passing through the Straits of Gib., our getting ashore before the Axis has time to take counter measures for our reception.'

'You've said it. Although after Gib. we shall naturally do our utmost to fool Hitler into believin' that we mean to land somewhere other than in French North Africa.'

That night, before going to bed, Gregory followed up his telegram to Erika with a letter. But with Sir Pellinore's advice in mind he kept it short: simply asserting that he loved her better than anyone in the world and begging her to let him come up to see her at Gwaine Meads.

Next day he put on his uniform and went to see Colonel Jacob. Sir Pellinore had said that he should inform the Colonel about his trip to Hungary, and the Colonel showed great interest in all he had to say; but, without giving any reason for it, he told Gregory that he did not think Allied Strategy for

1942-43 would permit of advantage being taken of his private negotiations with the Hungarian magnates.

On the Monday Gregory returned to the War Room. His colleagues there had been told that for the past two months he had been seconded for special duty and they were much too discreet to ask him any questions. So discreet were they in fact that although they brought him up to date with the situation none of them actually mentioned *Torch*, which was the code name that had been given to the North African expedition. All of them now knew about it, but they were not officially supposed to be in the secret of future operations; so they referred to it among themselves only obscurely.

However, in the course of the next few days, Sir Pellinore's assumption that Gregory would find himself in the picture was fully borne out. The movements of troops, air squadrons and shipping, which were all recorded in the War Room, told a story. Oblique references to this and that filled in gaps. Above all, the speculations on possible enemy reactions in certain circumstances, of highly placed visitors who had the entry to the War Room, left no room for doubt about the broad outline of the plan.

Anxiously he waited for every post, hoping to hear from Erika, but in vain. As by Wednesday he had still received no reply to his letter, he wrote again, declaring that his heart was broken and that only she could mend it by allowing him to go up and see her.

At last, on Saturday morning, Rudd brought him with his breakfast a letter addressed in her well-loved writing. Eagerly he tore it open, only to suffer grievous disappointment. It ran:

*From what I learned when I last saw you, I cannot believe that you have a heart worth patching up. But mine is truly broken, and with good reason. I thought that we had both long since finished sowing our wild oats, and were old enough to be faithful to one another. Anyway, I love you far too much to face a future racked with the thought that you may be secretly indulging in affaires with other women. Since there can now be no future for us I do not intend to submit to the additional pain of hearing you make excuses for your 'honeymoon on the Danube.' That it took place you cannot deny, for if you could you would already have done so. Should you come to Gwaine Meads you will drive me from it; so please at least spare me from having to make a new life among strangers. I hope in time to recover from the awful shock that was sprung upon me, and to be able to think again of the long happiness we had together. In the meantime I can do no more than wish you well.*

Bitterly, he realised that he was in a cleft stick. His only chance of altering her decision lay in his seeing and talking to her, but if he attempted to she might do as she threatened —and with Sir Pellinore's grim reference to 'an inquest' haunting his mind he dared not take that risk.

His decision to avoid Sabine had debarred him from visiting Carlton House Terrace or resuming his customary Sunday night suppers there; so he rang Sir Pellinore up and asked him to lunch at his Club. Wednesday was the earliest day the Baronet could manage and after the meal Gregory showed him Erika's letter. The old man was much distressed and offered to act as intermediary, but added that he was so heavily involved in matters connected with the war that he could not possibly give twenty-four hours to spending a night up at Gwaine Meads during the next ten days; so for the time being he could do no more than write to her.

Gregory gratefully accepted his offer, then enquired after the lovely cause of all the trouble. Sir Pellinore told him that Sabine was still at Carlton House Terrace, and as yet had taken no steps about finding a flat for herself; but she had got a job in which she had started the previous Monday. Apparently she had run into a pre-war friend who had introduced her to the Chancellor at the Moldavian* Embassy and, owing to her proficiency in languages, she had been taken on in the Chancellery there. As her alien status would have prevented her from working in any Government Department, and all commerce with Central Europe was at a standstill, this job in a neutral Embassy had seemed the very thing for her and she was delighted about it.

The following Monday morning Sir Pellinore rang up Gre-

---

* The Author is most averse to inventing fictitious States in his books; but the necessity for doing so in this instance will become clear as the story unfolds.

306

gory at the War Room to tell him that he had had a reply from Erika. But it contained no comfort for her distracted lover. She said that even if Sir Pellinore could manage a visit to Gwaine Meads during the course of the next fortnight she would not be able to bring herself to discuss the affair with him. Her mind was made up, she was doing her utmost to forget, and to reopen the matter could only cause her acute distress.

It was later that same morning, the 12th of October, that Gregory ran into his old friend of *Worcester* days, emerging from the Chiefs-of-Staff conference room at the far end of the basement.

'Hello!' he said. 'Been called in for consultation by the mighty? You are going up in the world.'

The airman grinned. 'No, they only meet down here at night when there's an air raid on. They've lent us their room because my little party has a global conference of its own on today. There's something rather awe-inspiring in the thought that the top boys who do our stuff overseas for us all flew in yesterday from places as far apart as Cairo. Washington, Delhi and Cape Town, to meet us round the table. But it was essential that we should get all the loose ends tied up.'

By now, although no definite reference was made to *Torch* outside the offices of the Planners, it was generally recognised that everyone in the basement knew about it; so Gregory raised an eyebrow and replied, 'You've left things pretty late, haven't you? I should have thought you planning boys would have handed your stuff to the staff of the Force Commander long before this, and been working things out for landings in Norway or Burma next summer.'

His friend shrugged. 'The STRATS and the FOPS are; and at the same time are arguing the respective merits of our going into Denmark, Holland, Cherbourg, Sardinia, Sumatra, the Kra Isthmus and lots of other places. But the little party to which I belong is operational as well; so we are in it up to the neck till the last minute. From the wars of the Ancients onward, every major operation has had to have its Cover Plan, and it's our responsibility to pull the wool over the eyes of the enemy. I don't mind telling you, it's quite a headache. We could easily make a mess of things, and if we do we'll have a hell of a lot to answer for.'

'I see. Then I don't envy that nice boss of yours. How d'you feel about your prospects?'

'It's difficult to say, because this is our first big show. I think they're pretty good. Of course, we are copying the Germans in putting out all sorts of false rumours, and everyone who's not in the show will be waving red cloaks like mad to draw the Nazi bull off in the wrong direction. But it's impossible to say if they'll fall for that. If they don't, it may lead to about the biggest disaster with which the British Army has ever met.'

Gregory nodded sympathetically. 'It must be worrying you out of your wits. Come along to the mess and have a drink. I'm sure you need one.'

Three days later he saw Sabine; but not to speak to. He had run into an old friend, a journalist who had become a war-correspondent, and as neither had anything on that night they agreed to dine together at the Café Royal. As they sat down in the restaurant he caught sight of Sabine only a few tables away. Her escort was a tall rather flamboyant-looking dark man, with a high bald forehead, flashing eyes and a bushy black moustache. On seeing Gregory she smiled and waved to him, and he waved back.

'Who is your lovely friend?' enquired the journalist.

Gregory told him, and added, 'It's really your job to know by sight everyone who matters. Does that cover the fellow she is with?'

'Oh yes. He is Colonel Vladan Kasdar, the Moldavian Military Attaché. Not a bad chap as they go; but I wish to goodness all these neutral military attachés could be made to take a running jump and drown themselves in the Thames.'

'Why do you wish that?' Gregory asked with a laugh.

'Because they are so damn dangerous. I'm on pretty good terms with one or two people in M.I.5, and they tell me that they have the Nazi spy system taped. If one is parachuted in or lands from a U-boat, they can nab him within twenty-four hours. So all the leaks that take place are through the neutral Embassies and Legations. Of course it's their job to collect as much information as they can for their own Governments and most of the Swiss, Swedes, Turks and the rest are our very good friends. But there are black sheep in every flock, and the Nazis pay big money for the real goods.'

'I see; and they get the stuff out in the Embassy bags.'

'That's it. The bags enjoy diplomatic privilege and are still immune from censorship; so it's easy enough for chaps like Kasdar to slip a private note in for someone who is working with them in their own capital, and within a few hours its contents have been passed on to Berlin.'

Gregory looked thoughtful, then he said, 'I wonder our Government doesn't put an embargo on the bags—anyhow for a week or so before big operations are to take place.'

'There would be one hell of a fuss if they did,' replied the journalist, 'but, all the same, I wish they would. And I have a personal interest in the matter at the moment. In your job you must know as well as I do that there's a big show pending. The northern ports are positively bursting with troops and shipping. Naturally people like myself are not told where they are off to or when; but it can't be long now because I've been told to stand by to go with them. And I don't mind taking normal risks, but I'm damned if I want to drown just because some Ruritanian type, like Kasdar, is anxious to earn a bit of extra cash to lavish on luscious little dishes of the kind he has with him now.'

The following day Gregory was not due to go on duty until the afternoon and, after breakfast, when he was straightening up the contents of a chest of drawers, he came upon the three big tins of *foie-gras* that Levianski had got for him in Budapest. He had intended one for Sir Pellinore, one for Erika and himself, and one for the girl in S.O.E. Since his return, during most of his off-duty hours, his mind had been too distraught with unhappy brooding to do anything about them; but it occurred to him now that a good way to fill in the morning would be to deliver the one for . . . yes, Diana was her name.

After a short wait he was shown into her office and presented his gift. She was naturally delighted, and said what a treat it would be for her step-father, whose passion for *foie-gras* had inspired her to suggest that Gregory should pose as a truffle merchant in Budapest. She then asked him how he had got on there.

He told her how the identity of Commandant Tavenier had unforeseeably landed him in the soup, and that he owed his escape to her private enterprise in having provided him with a safe contact in Levianski. He added that he had come home with what he believed to be a first class coup; but unfortunately he had had all his trouble for nothing, as the Government found themselves unable to take advantage of it.

'That is hard luck!' She looked down for a moment and her long lashes veiled her eyes as she added, 'I suppose they have their hands pretty full at the moment.'

'That's about it!' he agreed, 'and I expect you have too; so I mustn't keep you.' Then, as he stood up, he said on a sudden impulse. 'I suppose you wouldn't care to dine with me one night?'

The expression on her small aristocratic face remained non-committal and she replied quietly: 'That depends. Quite a lot of our men who have returned from doing jobs abroad ask me out to dinner. Many of them have been through a most appalling time, and they know that it will be only a week or two before they have to go off and risk their lives again. Some of them think that entitles them to expect me, or other girls in the office, to . . . er . . . play parlour games with them after dinner. I wish I could, because I feel terribly sorry for them. But . . .'

With a wry smile, Gregory checked her. 'In my case you've no need to worry about that. I'm head over heels in love with someone already; but I've made a ghastly mess of things so I'm feeling desperately unhappy. I'm afraid it's rather a back-handed compliment to anyone so young and lovely as your-self; but I was just hoping that you might be kind enough to come out with me for a chat, and so take my mind off my worries for an evening.'

Her face immediately radiated sweetness and compassion. 'But of course I will! How beastly for you. When shall it be? I'm afraid I can't make it tonight, but tomorrow if you like.'

'Thanks,' he smiled. 'I think your heart must be the same true gold as your hair. It's very gracious of you. Anyway, war or no war, at least I can promise you a good meal, with no strings attached.' They arranged that he should call for her at her office at six o'clock, and he left her rather wondering at himself, but glad that he had followed his impulse.

He took her to the Hungaria, knowing that, however scarce steaks, ducks, and Dover soles might be, his old friend Vecchi could always be relied on to provide them with a good main course, instead of the awful made-up dishes which were all that restaurants could now offer to the majority of their customers.

As they drank their cocktails he told her how untouched by the war Budapest still remained and what a good time he had had there until he had had to go to earth in a hurry. She remarked how much her mother and step-father had enjoyed their visits there before the war; and from that, to their mutual surprise, it emerged that her step-father was the airman on the Joint Planning Staff with whom Gregory had been in H.M.S. *Worcester*. That provided them with plenty to talk about through dinner; which was a good thing in view of the unwritten law that people employed in secret war organisations should never discuss war acitivities in public places.

After dinner they danced twice, then fell a little silent. During a pause longer than usual Diana powdered her acquiline nose—which with her oval face and good forehead made her look like a small edition of Queen Marie Antoinette— snapped her compact shut, and said:

'Now, tell me about this mess that you've got into with your girl-friend.'

He shook his head. 'I didn't take you out to bore you with my troubles.'

She had been chain-smoking American cigarettes, and lit another. 'Don't if you would rather not. But for some reason people who are older than I am often seem to find it helps to talk over their problems with me. I suppose that's really only because they have got it off their chests; but, anyway, I'm a good listener.'

'Be it on your own head, then,' Gregory smiled, and for the next twenty minutes she interrupted now and then only to ask him to give her a fuller picture of the backgrounds of Erika, Sabine and himself.

When he had done, she said, 'I think you were an awful fool not to have followed her to the country right away.'

'As I've told you, I was terrified of her going off on her own and doing something desperate.'

'I don't believe she would have for a moment. She's not a little thing just out of a convent, or a neurotic. You say she stood up to beatings by the Gestapo, and risked her life with you many times in Germany. Women who have the courage to do that never commit suicide. The worst that could happen

311

is that she would run out on you. But what does that matter? In your position you could get the Special Branch to trace her for you within a couple of days. Then you could go after her again. And if need be keep on chasing her until she does forgive you. That is the way to convince a woman that you really love her. How can she be expected to believe you do while you just sit here in London doing nothing about it?'

'I suppose there is something in that,' Gregory murmured a shade doubtfully.

'Something!' Diana repeated, looking at him from under her long lashes with a suggestion of contempt. 'Everything! Why, the poor woman doesn't even know yet that you didn't just go off the rails for fun, but got yourself into a position where you practically had to sleep with this Hungarian girl. Your Erika is a woman of the world, and if she has played tag with the Gestapo she must know that there are times when secret agents of both sexes have to do that sort of thing to save their lives. If she does love you it's unthinkable that she would have preferred you to keep your halo and be dead.'

Gregory looked across at the small, strong beautiful face opposite to him with sudden admiration. 'I hadn't thought of it that way. But, of course, you're right. I've been allowing my wretchedness to cloud my wits. Thank you a thousand times for letting in some daylight. I'll go up to Gwaine Meads just as soon as I can get a night off from the office.'

The next day was Sunday and, as Gregory was due for forty-eight hours' leave, he had no difficulty in arranging that he should take it from Monday morning. He reached Gwaine Meads soon after lunch and found Erika in her office, dealing as usual with the hospital accounts. She looked thin and ill and at once declared that she had no intention of discussing matters with him.

Imbued with an entirely new spirit since his evening with Diana, he thrust out his long jaw and said, 'Yes you will. Like it or not you are going to listen to me. But I can't say what I have to say where we may be overheard' Taking her top-coat from a hook on the door he held it for her and added, 'Come on. Put this on and come out into the garden. If you won't I'll carry you out as you are, then you'll catch your death of cold; so you had much better be sensible.'

'Very well.' Her splendid blue eyes above the high cheek

bones regarded him stonily. 'Since you insist. But I warn you that if you remain here afterwards I shall take an evening train to somewhere where you can't find me.'

He ignored her remark and they went out into the garden. It was October the 19th, and a cold wintry day; so not the happiest place in which to attempt a reconciliation. But he was now determined to beat down her defences, and as they began to walk up and down the lawn he plunged at once into his story. He did not attempt to excuse himself but gave a strictly factual account of the whole affair.

When he had finished she asked, 'Why didn't you come up here and tell me all this before?'

'God alone knows!' he exclaimed irritably. 'It was really old Pellinore. He put it into my head that if I drove you into solitude you might commit suicide. I was so desperately worried that I hadn't the sense to realise that you are much too well balanced to do anything like that.'

She gave him a quick look. 'I very nearly did the night I got back here. It would have been easy enough to get something from the dispensary. I had half a mind to, because I really felt that I'd come to the end of everything.'

'Praise be, you didn't! And if you love me that much surely —surely you can bring yourself to forget the wretched business?'

Suddenly she turned and grasped his arm. 'Oh, my dear. Now you've told me what really happened I can. But it was such a frightful shock. And from what she said it seemed impossible to believe that you had not fallen in love with her. As it is I can't even hate her any more. She saved your life, darling! She saved your life! What does anything else matter?'

Within a minute he had pulled her down a path into the nearest shrubbery and was kissing her fiercely while she wept with happiness at being once more in his arms.

Presently she said that she meant to try to put Sabine right out of her mind, as though she had no real existence, but that would not be possible if Gregory continued to be friends with her; so she wanted his solemn promise that in the future he would neither see nor write to her.

He gave it willingly, and fully restored her confidence in him by telling her that during the past three weeks he had deliberately avoided any meeting with Sabine, had seen her only once, and then not to speak to.

Soon afterwards they returned to the house and settled down comfortably in front of a warm fire. They had so much to say to one another that the afternoon sped by rapidly, and as there were no other guests staying in the house they were able to dine tête-à-tête in the little dining-room of the private wing. Gregory produced the *foie-gras* and told her about Diana. Erika was amused at his having taken the advice of a girl scarcely out of her teens, and pretended that she would find new cause for jealousy in this paragon who combined such wisdom with youth and beauty; but a minute later she added seriously that when she came to London she must meet Diana and thank her from the bottom of her heart for having sent him back to her.

It was shortly after the nine o'clock news that Gregory was called to the telephone. He was away for about five minutes and when he rejoined Erika every trace of his new happiness had disappeared.

'What is it, darling?' she asked anxiously. 'Don't tell me that you're been recalled to duty. That would be too awful.'

'No,' he said, in a somewhat bewildered way. 'No. That was Pellinore. At first I couldn't make out what he was talking about. But before he finished he made it plain enough. He rang up to tell me that Sabine Tuzolto has been arrested as a spy.'

Erika's blue eyes became round, her big generous mouth opened a little; then she suddenly sat back and gave way to peals of laughter.

'Stop that!' Gregory exclaimed angrily. 'This is no laughing matter.'

'Oh, but it is; it is!' Erika was half choking and tears of mirth were running down her cheeks. 'It is the funniest thing that has happened for years. You, my dear, Grauber's *bête noire,* the nightmare of the Gestapo, Britain's all-time high Secret Agent, you—of all people—have been fooled into bringing a Nazi spy into England and . . . and—cream of the jest—planting her in the house of the man who knows more than anyone outside the Cabinet about Britain's war secrets.'

'Very funny! Very funny indeed!' snapped Gregory. 'But may I remind you that this woman saved my life.'

Erika cast her eyes upward as though appealing to the gods against crass stupidity. 'Nonsense, you poor simpleton. Once they had decided how to make use of you your life was no longer in danger. This Hungarian tart did her big act because she was told to by Ribbentrop, and like a ninny you fell for it. Really, if there is a kindergarten for secret agents you ought to there for a refresher course.'

'You are wrong! Utterly wrong! The one thing had nothing whatever to do with the other. She got me out of Grauber's clutches without any prompting from anyone. It was only later, after they had found out about the way she had rescued me, and ordered her into exile on that account, that the question arose of her coming to England. And, damn it all, we don't even know yet if she is guilty. She may be the victim of some stupid mistake by M.I.5. Anyway, I owe her all the help I can give, and I'll have to catch the first train in the morning for London.'

Coming to her feet, Erika cried in a pleading voice, 'But darling! Only this afternoon you promised, promised faithfully, that you'd have no more to do with her.'

'I can't help that. Promises have to go by the board when a proven friend is in danger.'

Erika's eyes became hard as ice. 'All right! Go if you want to! If you do, it will be the clearest possible proof that you are still in love with her. And I'll not stand for that. It will be the end between us. Do you understand? The end! The end! The final, irrevocable end!'

## 22

## The Prisoner in the Tower

Gregory and Erika wrangled for an hour. They got no further. At length they went up to bed, Erika in tears and emotionally exhausted, Gregory bitterly resentful at what he considered to be her unwarrantable jealousy and lack of understanding. Instead of the joyous culmination of their reunion, which they had been happily anticipating until Sir Pellinore's telephone call, they slept in separate rooms.

In the morning Gregory decided on a last attempt to make her appreciate his point of view; but he found her door locked and she flatly refused to let him in.

Four hours later he was seated opposite Sir Pellinore in the library at Carlton House Terrace, learning the details of Sabine's arrest.

'Guilty?' boomed Sir Pellinore. 'Of course she's guilty! Must have bin comin' down here and snoopin' through my papers in the middle of the night. Anyhow, M.I.5. caught her with the goods on her.'

'What sort of goods?' inquired Gregory.

'Copies of some of the key letters in my correspondence with the Turks. As you must know, I made my first big money while on the board of a private bank that specialised in loans to the Near East. For a quarter of a century I've had a lot of pull in Turkey. And once we've opened up the Med. we hope to bring Johnny Turk in on our side. I've been sounding out the big shots there. Gettin' a line on who's for us and who's against us. That's the sort of thing the Nazis would give a lot to know.'

'Then why the hell didn't you keep it in your safe?' said Gregory angrily. 'It would have served you damn well right if it had got through to the enemy.'

'Ha! What's that?' The Baronet's blue eyes popped. 'I'm not accountable to you—or to any other young idiot who'd let a pretty woman twist him round her little finger. Safe's chock-a-block with more important stuff. Anyway, I don't expect my friends to, er . . . plant vipers in my bosom.'

If Gregory had not been so upset he would have laughed. As it was, he apologised. 'I'm terribly sorry. I shouldn't have said that. It has no bearing whatever on the case. But I'm half out of my wits with worry. After going through hell for the best part of a month, yesterday I got Erika to forgive me. Then you telephoned. When I told her that I must return to help Sabine, she blew up like a block-buster. Short of a miracle, I've now done myself in with her for good.'

'More fool you, then! Help Sabine, indeed! What help can you give her? Some thug in the Moldavian Embassy evidently

316

supplied her with a mini-camera and she's bin photographin' my documents. Seein' that she had only just arrived from Hungary, as soon as she got herself a job with the Moldavians M.I.5. were astute enough to keep tabs on her. Yesterday they intercepted her on her way to her office and politely invited her to show them the contents of her handbag. And there were the micro-films. You're a cleverer feller than I am, Gunga Din, if you can help her to laugh that off.'

'All right,' Gregory agreed reluctantly. 'Let's take it that she is guilty. That doesn't alter the fact that she saved me from being very slowly and very painfully done to death.'

'Yes, you loony! Saved you with her tongue in her cheek. Countin' on it that, if she could get you to bring her to England, owing to my friendship with her father I'd give her house room here.'

'No. You are being unjust to her in exactly the same way as Erika. Knowing that I was a British agent she risked her own position to save my bacon. She hadn't the faintest intention of leaving Ribbentrop until Grauber found her out and she was forced to go abroad.'

'You told me yourself that she hated the Russians' guts so much that she'd rather see the house-painter feller win than ourselves.'

'She would. She told me that the first day I talked to her, and she has been honest enough to make no pretence of having altered her views. Obviously that explains her conduct. She happened to meet some other pro-Nazis and discovered that through them she could put a spoke in the Russians' wheel. If you or I found ourselves stuck in Germany and were given the chance, wouldn't we do the same sort of thing to help Britain?'

'Um!' Sir Pellinore grunted. 'Suppose we should! Mark you, I like the gel. Enjoyed having her about the place with that nice scent she uses and her bangles clinkin'. After the way you've put it, I'm almost sorry for her. But she's made us look a fine pair of half-wits; and there is nothing we can do for her. The law must take its course.'

'All right; we'll agree that for the moment. But the least I can do is to let her know that she is not entirely friendless. You have quite enough pull to get me a permit to see her.'

'Maybe I have; but I wouldn't bet on it. Can't see why M.I.5

should let outsiders communicate with spies in prison. Not unless they can give a thunderin' good reason for wantin' to see the prisoner.'

'I can give one. I know more about Sabine than anyone in this country. Naturally they will want to get all the information out of her that they can. She is much more likly to spill the beans if they allow me to help with her interrogation.'

'Something in that. Very well, then. I'll give you a line to a friend of mine that they've nicknamed "Himmler". Not that he has anything in common with that Nazi horror who looks like a goofy toad. It's simply that he's the top boy for this sort of thing in M.I.5. If I'd been him I'd have jugged you for bringing that wench into the country; but he seemed to think you were too much of a fool to be dangerous.'

Gregory submitted to the irate Baronet's abuse without comment, and asked, 'What do you think she'll get?'

'How should I know? If this were the Continent her life wouldn't be worth a row of beans; but we're a lot of softies here. I doubt, though, if she'll get off with less than seven years; and for the duration, anyhow, it will be solitary confinement.'

'God, how awful for her!'

Sir Pellinore sighed. 'Yes. What a waste; lovely young creature like that. Another ruined life that Hitler has to answer for. Still, nothing we can do. We must get on with the war.'

When the letter was written Gregory took it straight round to the M.I.5. office, but he was told that the Colonel he wished to see was out and would not be in until the following morning. At nine o'clock next day he went again to the tall building that housed M.I.5. After a wait of half an hour he was taken up in a lift to the top floor and shown into a large bright office, where the man nicknamed 'Himmler' was seated behind a desk on which there was a row of different coloured telephones.

He was dressed as usual in civilian clothes, and was a big, powerful looking man with a full, ruddy face. His manner was courteous but he spoke very quickly. Having read Sir Pellinore's letter he fixed an unwavering gaze on Gregory through the tops of his bi-focals and said:

'I had intended to ask you to come to see me, in any case. Tell me all you know about this woman?'

318

Gregory complied, gave the full story of his trip to Budapest and offered his assistance as an interrogator. The Colonel asked a number of shrewd questions, then he said, 'I don't think it would be a good idea for you to see her yet. I'd prefer to see what my own people can get out of her first. They are very experienced at that sort of thing. But you may be able to help us later.' After a quick look at his engagement block, he added, 'Come back and see me again on Friday —three o'clock suit you?'

'Yes,' Gregory nodded. 'I can get away pretty well any time by swopping tours of duty with my colleagues in the War Room.' He hesitated a moment, then asked, 'What do you think they will give her?'

The big man shrugged. 'In peace time the maximum is ten years; but as we are at war she is liable to the death penalty. We have never shot a woman yet but we may do in this instance. Women agents are just as dangerous as men—if not more so. In the early days foreign women gave us a lot of trouble and they were allowed to get away with internment, or a prison sentence. But the Germans are behaving with complete callousness. They have done in any number of British and French women. As a matter of policy it might be a good thing to show for once that we can be equally tough. That would make some of the other women living here as refugees think twice about trying to ferret secrets out of serving officers. I am not saying I would advocate the death penalty myself; but it might come to that. Anyway, it is not for me to decide. That will be up to the Home Secretary.'

Gregory was about to ask where Sabine was being held, but the Colonel got abruptly to his feet. 'I'm afraid I can't spare you any more time now. I have an I.S.S.B. meeting at the War Office, and I've a number of papers to run through first. See you on Friday.'

His concern for Sabine now graver than ever, and frustrated in his attempt to see her, Gregory had no alternative but to take his leave. For the next two days there was nothing he could do, and in his off duty hours he brooded miserably upon the terrible situation that Sabine had got herself into, and the wrecking of his reconciliation with Erika.

Friday came at last, and after lunch Colonel 'Himmler' received him with his usual briskness. Coming to the point at once, he said:

'Glad to see you. My people haven't got very far; so I've decided to let you try your hand. She is in the Tower and I have here an authority for the Resident Governor to admit you to her. I also have here a list of questions to which I should particularly like answers. Study it carefully and memorise them. Your best chance is to cheer her up as much as you can by recalling pleasant times you had together, then work in these questions at intervals quite casually. I'd like you to report to me here some time before seven-thirty.'

Greatly relieved that Sabine had proved stubborn enough to justify his being called in to help in her interrogation, Gregory took the papers and promised to do his best. Outside he picked up a taxi, told its driver to take him to the Tower of London, and on the way there read through the list of questions. Most of them were to do with the Moldavian Embassy and seemed such straightforward ones he was a little surprised that Sabine had so far refused to answer them.

At the entrance to the precincts of the Tower he paid off his taxi. The sentry on the iron gate saluted him and a Yeoman Warder, wearing the flat black cap and picturesque red and black uniform dating from Tudor times, opened it to ask his business. He had not realised that the Tower was closed to the public, but the Yeoman told him that in wartime the only unofficial visitors allowed in were Service men who had made a special application to go round in one of the daily conducted tours, between either eleven and midday, or two-thirty and three-thirty in the afternoon. Gregory produced his letter for the Resident Governor and the Yeoman took him through to the little office where in peacetime the public buy their tickets of admission. There he signed a book and was issued with a temporary pass. Another 'Beefeater' then acted as his escort to the Governor's office.

First they walked down the slope to the twin towers that guard the entrance to the fortress proper, through the great arched gate between them and on to the bridge across the wide dry moat. Gregory glanced into it and quickly looked away again. In peacetime soldiers of the garrison played football down in it; but it was there, so he had been told, that on certain grim dawns spies caught during the war had been put up against the casement wall and executed by a firing squad.

A moment later they passed through a second great gateway, under the Byward Tower, and entered what seemed like a sunken road, as forty-foot walls rose on either side, almost shutting out the dim light of the late October afternoon.

From long habit, his Yeoman guide remarked, 'The river used to run here once, sir. That's why it's called Water Lane. The Normans built only the White Tower and the great Inner Wall on our left. It was Richard I, 1189-1199, who pushed the river back by dumping thousands of tons of earth here taken from widening the moat. The great Outer Wall on our right, with its five additional towers facing the river, was not completed till Edward I, 1272-1307.'

A hundred yards farther on Water Lane passed through an archway between the huge cylindrical Wakefield Tower and, on the river side, an oblong block as big as a small castle in itself, with smaller towers at each of its outer corners. This was called St. Thomas's Tower and held, perhaps more fascination for visitors than any other. Centrally beneath it ran a high vaulted tunnel which could be reached by a flight of steps down into a part of the moat. The Tower had been built to defend the tunnel, as until Victorian times it had been the entrance by river to the fortress, famous for centuries as Traitors' Gate.

After a glance at the great ten feet high double gates with their cross-bars of stout timber, Gregory turned with his guide towards the Inner Wall and accompanied him through it by yet another great gate which ran immediately under the Bloody Tower. As they walked up the steep slope on the far side of the gate he could now see the splendid cube of the White Tower to his right front. Unlike the other seventeen towers there was nothing in the least grim about William the Conqueror's original Palace-keep, yet its battlements and four domed turrets dwarfed all the rest into insignificance.

Turning away from it, his guide led him up a flight of steps set in a wall, to higher ground, and across an open space in which trees were growing, to a half-timbered Tudor building called 'The King's House'. Having rung the front door bell he handed Gregory over to another Yeoman Warder, who took his name, asked him to wait in a pleasantly furnished hall, and returned almost at once to say:

'Colonel Faviell will see you, sir. Please come this way.' The Yeoman then ushered him into a ground floor office.

Gregory produced his letter. As soon as the Governor had read it, he reached for his cap and said, 'That is clear enough. I'll take you across to her.'

As they left the house he went on, 'I don't mind telling you, this business has been quite a headache to us. The night of her arrest they put her in Brixton Prison, and why they couldn't have left her there, goodness knows. Perhaps the Government have some idea of making an example of her for propaganda purposes and feel that "Woman Spy Sentenced after Court Martial in the Tower" would ring a bigger bell with other young women who have an itch to do the Nazis' dirty work for them. Anyway, fathering her on us presented me with a tricky problem. You see, there hasn't been a woman prisoner in the Tower since the Lord knows when, and the question was where to put her.'

'Providing you imported a couple of wardresses to look after her, what would have been wrong with putting her in one of the ordinary cells?' Gregory asked.

The Colonel laughed. 'That's just it. There aren't any. People still think of the Tower as a State Prison; but it has long since ceased to be used for that purpose.'

'How about Baillie-Stewart; he was confined here?'

'Oh, Baillie-Stewart was confined in a first floor tower room in that building over there.' The Colonel pointed beyond the White Tower at a comparatively modern block in the north-east corner of the great quadrangle. 'It contains the Officers' Mess and sleeping quarters. Washing arrangements and so on ruled it out entirely as accommodation for a woman.'

'How did you solve your problem, then?'

'We put her in St. Thomas's Tower. Its interior was converted to modern needs as a residence for the Keeper of the Crown Jewels. There's a flying bridge from it over Water Lane to the Wakefield Tower where the Jewels are kept. I mean, were kept in peace-time. They were moved out of London for greater safety at the beginning of the war. General Sir George Younghusband was Keeper of the Jewels, but in April '41 a bomb was dropped nearby and the tower suffered a bit from the blast. In consequence, as there were no longer any jewels here to keep, Sir George decided to move out, and took most of his furniture with him. But there was enough left to furnish a few rooms, and no difficulty about making the place reasonably habitable.'

While they were talking, the Colonel had led Gregory back across the open space, down the steep slope and through the arch under the Bloody Tower. Crossing Water Lane, they went up some steps set sideways in the wall of St. Thomas's Tower that led to a narrow gallery immediately above the great pit in which lay Traitors' Gate. Some way along the gallery there was an ordinary front door. The Colonel rang the bell and a minute or two later it was answered by a muscular middle-aged woman in a dark uniform.

'This is Mrs. Sutton,' the Colonel said. 'She and her colleague, Mrs. Wright, have been lent to us from Brixton.' He then introduced Gregory and told her that he was to be left alone with the prisoner for as long as he wished.

Gregory thanked him and asked if he should report back when he had finished his interrogation, to which the Colonel replied, 'No. All you have to do is to hand back your temporary pass at the gate. That will check you out.'

The wardress conducted Gregory through into a lofty hall in one corner of which a short flight of stairs ran up to rooms on a higher floor. Crossing the hall she took a key from her pocket, unlocked a door, opened it for him, and said in a deep bass voice, 'When you want to be let out, sir, be good enough to ring.'

He stepped forward into a good-sized room. It had narrow mullioned windows at one end, some of which, owing to bomb blast, were boarded over. That, and the early darkness of the afternoon, shrouded it in deep twilight. Gregory could just make out that it was furnished only near the windows and the vague form of Sabine sitting with her feet up on a sofa. The wardress said from behind him:

'Gentleman to see you, ducks. Just what the doctor ordered to put an end to you sitting there brooding in the dark.'

Knowing the brutal treatment meted out by women guards to their prisoners in Nazi concentration camps, Gregory could not help contrasting with it the kindness in Mrs. Sutton's deep voice, and marvelling that she should show such forbearance to an enemy accused of inflicting grievous injury on her country. As the thought flashed through his mind, the wardress flicked on the light, shut the door and locked him in.

Next moment Sabine was on her feet, crying. 'Gregory! Gregory! Oh, how marvellous to see you! How clever of you to persuade them to let you visit me in this awful place.'

He took both her hands, smiled at her and pressed them, as he said, 'There wasn't anything very clever about it. I would have come sooner if I could; but the only line I had was offering to help interrogate you, and to begin with they thought the experts would get everything out of you that could be got without any help from me.'

She gave a contemptuous shrug. 'The people they sent tried wheedling and threatening by turns, but I knew that none of them dared lay a finger on me; so I just laughed at them. I stymied them from the beginning by quoting at them your Duke of Wellington. You know his famous dictum. "Never explain".'

'I felt pretty certain you wouldn't go to pieces,' he said seriously. 'But you being here is very far from anything to laugh about; and I hope you are going to explain to me, if not officially, anyhow off the record.'

'Yes. I owe you that.' She sat down and, as he took a chair beside her, went on, 'I didn't like making use of you; but I had no alternative if I was both to save you and keep from failing in what I regard as doing my best for my country.'

'When you persuaded me to bring you here, then, it was with the deliberate intention of spying for the Nazis?'

'Yes. It was the outcome of that night when Ribb spoilt our fun by turning up just after I had got into bed with you. During the awful wrangle that ensued with Grauber and the rest of them, I was driven into admitting the truth about how I really did first meet you, that through you I had met Sir Pellinore, and that he was an old friend of my father's.'

'I remember that.'

'But you didn't overhear what followed; because you were driven from your hiding place by a sneezing fit or something.'

'That's right. I missed five or six minutes of the row between Grauber and Ribb, and when I got back Grauber had gone.'

'Well, Ribb wouldn't be where he is if he hadn't a very quick mind. The moment he learned I was *persona grata* with Sir Pellinore, he realised that fact could be used to save him from Hitler's wrath. I mean if Himmler tried to do him dirt

324

by reporting to the *Führer* that his mistress had been aiding a British spy. If I could get you to plant me on Sir Pellinore, he would be able to say that I had been working for the Nazis all the time, and at great risk to myself had gone to England to carry on the good work.

'He tried his utmost to sell the idea to Grauber that there was far more to be gained by letting us escape to England than by cutting you up in little pieces and trying to have me put in a concentration camp. But Grauber wouldn't hear of it. He was obsessed with the idea of getting his own back on you. He went off still in a towering rage, vowing that he would stop at nothing to get you, and that if the Hungarian Police refused to co-operate he would demand that special pressure should be exerted on the Regent by Berlin.

'After all the admissions I had been forced to make, Ribb took it for granted I was concealing you somewhere in the house. As it was against his interests to give you up, when Grauber had gone I ceased to deny it. And I told him how we had planned for you to drive me across the frontier using Mario's passport. Ribb agreed that the plan offered the best chance for us to escape, and said that he could get the Regent to prevent any official attempt being made to stop us for twenty-four hours, but that any time after that Grauber might get the upper hand.

'Then he tackled me about working as a spy when I got to England. He said that apart from getting him out of the mess I had landed him in, and helping to defeat the Russians, it was in my own interests. If I wouldn't play, then there could never be any worthwhile future for me. I wouldn't be able to get my fortune out of Hungary, or ever go back there, or live anywhere in Hitler's Europe, after the war was over; and I'd be publicly branded as a traitor to my country. Whereas, if I could only get one really valuable war secret out of Sir Pellinore, and send it back to him, that would not only clear him with Hitler, but make me a privileged person in the Greater Reich for the rest of my life.'

Gregory nodded. 'It must have been just after you had agreed that I got back to my hiding place. I remember his saying that he would brief you next day, and wondering what he meant; but you told me afterwards that it was about getting across the frontier.'

'There was no need for him to do that; my passport and Mario's already carried special visas enabling us to cross any frontier controlled by the Reich without going through the usual formalities. I had to see him so that he could give me particulars of the people to contact in London, who would pass anything I could get hold of back to him.'

'So that's how it was. It was certainly a clever scheme—if it had come off.'

'But it hasn't. Where I slipped up, I don't know; but they caught me red-handed.' A sudden note of anxiety came into her voice. 'What will they do to me, Gregory? What will they do to me?'

'My dear, I don't know. You'll be tried *in camera*, and by a military court, I suppose. But let's not talk of that for the moment. Tell me about your contacts. I want to hear all you can tell me about the Moldavian Embassy.'

Sabine shook her head, 'No, my dear, no. I've told you my personal part in the story; and if you care to pass that on I've no objection. I see no reason why it should make my case worse. But I'm not giving away other people. As far as my activities since I've been in London are concerned, the Duke's dictum still stands: "Never explain".'

'That's all very well, but I'm afraid you've got to if I'm to help you.'

'Help me!' She made a little gesture of despair. 'I'm sure you want to. But with the best will in the world, how can you. Having brought me here must have made you to some extent suspect. I take it that they regard you as having been completely fooled by me; but now I've been caught anything you may say on my behalf could only make them doubt your veracity, and it wouldn't do me any good.'

He stood up and took her hand. 'I don't intend to say things but to do them.'

She looked up at him with a puzzled frown. 'Do? What can you do?'

'God knows! But no sentence they can inflict on you would be half as bad as what Grauber would have done to me if you hadn't saved me from him in Budapest. So I'll still owe you something if I can get you out of this. I mean to gamble everything on planning your escape.'

# 23

# Chivalry in Our Day

'Oh, Gregory!' Sabine came quickly to her feet. She laid her free hand on his shoulder and tears started to her eyes. 'How wonderful of you! But do you think it's really possible?'

He looked away from her, a shade uncomfortably. 'Honestly, I don't know. In some ways it should be easier to escape from a place like this than from a modern prison. In them they have all sorts of checking systems—cells that can be looked into at any hour of the day or night without the doors being opened, electric rays which if broken by anyone passing through them instantly set off alarm bells, and that sort of thing—whereas in the past they simply relied on big locks and thick bolts and bars. If this were an ordinary old fortress I'd back myself to get you out of it; but the trouble is, it's not. It's the size of a small town. To pull the wool over the wardresses' eyes and pinch the key to your room would be only a beginning. I'd still have three gates to get you through before we reached the street. At night they are locked, and as the Tower is now closed to the public any strange woman going through them during the daytime would be certain to be challenged. Perhaps it was wrong of me to rouse your hopes prematurely. I can only say that I mean to try.'

'I saw what a warren of towers and gates the place is when they brought me in here,' Sabine volunteered. Then she pointed to the windows. 'But there's nothing on that side. It overlooks an embankment and the river. Perhaps you could let me down with a rope?'

'That's a possibility,' he agreed. 'I've had no chance yet to make a detailed study of the place. We mustn't rush our fences, and I mean to pay you several visits so as to acquire a thorough knowledge of the set-up before deciding on a plan. That is why I want you to answer some questions about the Moldavians. I was specifically instructed to get out of you all I could about them, and if I go back empty-handed I may not be allowed to see you again.'

'In that case I'll try not to be too cagey. What exactly do they wish to know?'

He took out the list and handed it to her. Several of the questions were about members of the Embassy staff—what views they expressed on the course of the war, whether they appeared to be short of money, etc.; others were about frequent visitors to the Embassy; and others again about people not connected with it but with whom Sabine had been seen while she was being watched.

'These are the sort of things they have been asking me for the past three days,' Sabine commented. 'Some of the answers I don't know, but I could have answered most of them and only refrained because I thought it wiser to refuse to talk at all. As it is going to help I'll tell you all I can.'

For some minutes he took notes of the information with which she furnished him; then he asked, 'Was it to Colonel Kasdar that you actually gave your stuff?'

'None of the questions on the paper ask me definitely to incriminate anyone,' she protested, 'so why should you ask me to?'

'That last question was off the record, and I should have told you so. I have a very good reason for wanting to know which of the Moldavians it is who is acting as a Nazi agent, and you must trust me. I suggested Kasdar because he is the M.A. and I chanced to see you dining out with him. Am I right?'

'Yes, it was Vladan Kasdar. But he is a nice person; and I should hate to get him into trouble.'

'As he is sheltering behind diplomatic privilege the worst that could happen to him is that our F.O. should declare him *persona non grata*, and ask for him to be sent home. Anyway, you need lose no sleep about him, because now I know that he was your contact I mean to keep him in the clear. I shall cast suspicion on someone else: probably that nasty piece of work the Second Secretary Nichoŭlic. Now, I want you to write a line for me to Kasdar.'

'Must I?'

'Yes. After I have got you out of here—that is, if I can—without his aid there would be very little chance of your avoiding recapture.' As Gregory spoke he pushed along the table his fountain pen and a sheet of the paper he had been using to make notes. Then he told her that all he needed was a few lines addressed to Kasdar, saying that she had seen him that day and he was completely to be trusted.

When she had written them and passed the paper back, she remarked, 'How nice you look in uniform. I thought so that night I saw you in the Café Royal. What rank do those three rings on your arm give you?'

'Wing Commander.'

'That is *Colonel de l'Air*, isn't it?'

'Yes; though I'm a very phoney one, and have nothing to do with aircraft. It is simply that the system here, generally speaking, is that the rank one holds goes with the job one does. Mine is a Wing Commander's post; so, although I was temporarily seconded for special duty abroad, they kept on putting me up a rank a month until I reached it.'

Gregory asked her then how she was being treated.

She replied that the food was awful, and that she would give anything for some good warming wine to drink in the evenings as the fog which rose from the river most afternoons seemed to penetrate everywhere, and made her cold and miserable. But she had no legitimate complaints, and preferred being there to the one night she had spent in Brixton with its awful smell of cooked cabbage and disinfectant.

From his pocket he produced a box of pills, and said as he gave them to her. 'Hoping that I'd be allowed to see you, I had these made up yesterday. They'll do you no permanent harm, but if you take them according to the instructions on the box they will cause you to run a temperature. Take care that neither of the wardresses sees them and make a start tonight.'

'Of course, if you wish me to.' She raised her dark eyebrows. 'But what is the idea?'

'I want you to appear too ill to stand up to further interrogation for a few days. You see, even if I succeed in getting you out of the Tower that alone won't save you. The police would catch you and pop you back in again unless I can first arrange for you to go to some really safe hideout, or get you shipped off abroad. To make these sort of arrangements takes time. I am confident that M.I.5 won't send you to trial until they think they have got all they can out of you, but there is a limit to the spread-over that I can manage with the information you can give me. So this is a device for postponing our next talk till, say, Thursday. We had better not risk a longer interval than that in case a specialist is called in and tumbles to it that you have been doping yourself.'

A few minutes later, he congratulated her on the courage she had shown so far, urged her to keep it up, and rang the bell for Mrs. Sutton to let him out. When the wardress had done so he said to her:

'Now that I have been put on this case I'd like to get a full picture of the prisoner's surroundings and the routine she follows. I've no wish at all to interfere materially with your arrangements, but sometimes quite slight changes make them much more amenable to reason.'

Mrs. Sutton obliged at once. She reeled off the schedule for Sabine's day, then took him up the short flight of stairs leading up from the hall. Above was a servant's bedroom from which the furniture had not been removed and in it Sabine was locked up at nights. When they came down she conducted him over what must in normal times have been a spacious and charming flat. Now, most of its rooms were half-empty, with soot in the fireplaces and on the floors plaster brought down by the bomb blast. They then looked in on the room which was being used by the two wardresses as a bed-room; and lastly visited the kitchen in which the other ward-ress, a Mrs. Wright, had just started to prepare the evening meal.

Mrs. Wright had carroty hair and a freckled face. She was somewhat younger and a little taller than Mrs. Sutton but looked just as formidable. Gregory shook hands with her. He did not suggest any changes, said that he expected to be there again the following day, and took his departure.

Outside, there were no taxis to be had, so he took the Underground to St. James's Park, picked up one there and had himself driven to Boodle's. After an hour spent drinking with friends in his Club, he walked across the road to the M.I.5. building. Five minutes later he was making his report to 'Himmler'.

Having greatly intrigued the purposeful looking Colonel by giving him Sabine's version of Ribbentrop's plot for planting her on Sir Pellinore, Gregory doled out some of the information she had supplied about the Moldavians. After the past failures of his regular interrogators this was quite enough to encourage the Colonel to leave the interrogation in Gregory's hands, and even to press him to push on with it.

330

Gregory said that as he was due to go on night duty after dinner and would need a few hours' sleep in the morning, he would prefer not to go to the Tower again until the following afternoon. He added that he thought it would ease the wheels a bit further if he might provide the prisoner with some drink and, when he had a chance, collect for her some of her warmer clothes that she had left at Carlton House Terrace.

'Go down there whenever it suits you best, my dear fellow,' replied 'Himmler' cordially. 'You have made an excellent beginning. I'll telephone Colonel Faviell and tell him you are to be given access to the prisoner at whatever hours you like. As far as drink is concerned, there is no objection to your supplying her with a few bottles . . .' he laughed suddenly '. . . providing, of course, that you don't expect the "firm" to pay for it. I've no objection either to your taking her down some of her warmer clothes. Forgive me now. I still have a lot to do. Let me know how you get on.'

For several days past the Desert Air Force had been carrying out intensive attacks against Rommel's positions and communications; and, early in the morning, when Gregory and his colleagues were drowsing in the dimmed lights of the War Room, they were roused by the shrilling of one of the telephones. A signal had just come through that by the light of a brilliant full moon, General Montgomery had launched the Eighth Army from El Alamein in operation *Lightfoot,* the full-scale offensive which it had been planned should precede *Torch.*

Later that day, Saturday, October the 24th, after a good sleep, a bath and lunch, Gregory again went down to the Tower. To his considerable satisfaction the Governor informed him that the prisoner had been reported sick that morning. The doctor could not say exactly what was wrong with her. It was not 'flu but seemed to be a form of low fever. She was in no danger, anyhow for the moment, but in bed, of course, and might not be up to further interrogation for a day or two.

'Then I've had my journey for nothing,' said Gregory. 'Unless . . . yes, unless you will allow me to take the opportunity of going round the Tower. It is years since I've seen it properly, and . . .'

The Colonel was on his feet in an instant, exclaiming enthusiastically, 'But of course! I'll show you round myself!

Delighted to do so! Wonderful old place this! In normal times we get thousands of foreign visitors but it staggers me how few English people bother to come here. You would think being able to look at the Crown Jewels would be enough to induce them to visit us even if there were nothing else to see. But there are more things of interest in the Tower than there are in all the other historical buildings in London put together. It is the whole of English history from 1066. Before that even. We have still standing part of the original Roman wall built round ancient London, and in 885 repaired by Alfred the Great. It was in this house that Elizabeth was imprisoned before she became Queen, and Guy Fawkes was tried upstairs in the Council Chamber after the Gunpowder Plot. Come along and I'll show you.'

They inspected the State Axe and the site of the Block on Tower Hill, where so many noble heads had rolled. In the White Tower they visited the Chapel built by William the Conqueror—one of the most perfect examples of Norman architecture in England—and the wonderful collections of arms, armour and military trophies; then saw the instruments of torture in the basement, and the spot where the bones of the two murdered Princes in the Tower had been discovered in the time of Charles II. But the Bloody Tower was said to have been the actual scene of that crime, and of many others. In the stone walls of its chambers could still be seen the prayers and inscriptions cut so patiently by men and women who had made history and, mostly, left it only for the scaffold.

Coming out of the archway under it, the pit in which lay Traitors' Gate was immediately opposite them. Crossing Water Lane they halted by the guard rail which fenced off the broad flight of stairs up which Prisoners of State had come after landing from the barge that had brought them down the Thames.

'May I go down and look through to the far end of the tunnel?' Gregory asked innocently.

'By all means, if you like,' the Colonel replied. 'But it is blocked up. Has been ever since the Duke of Wellington had the moat drained when he was Governor here. So it comes to a dead end against the embankment, which is at the same level as this on the other side.'

Throwing a leg over the rail Gregory slipped down on to the

top step, ran quickly down the others and across the floor of the old moat to the gate. Its two halves were both formed from five thick horizontal beams, each held to the other by some twenty upright bars about six inches apart. The two central beams had slots holding a stout cross-bar which was secured by the biggest padlock Gregory had ever seen. From end to end it was a foot in length and its semicircular clasp was at least an inch in diameter.

The gate had no other fastenings at its top or bottom, but one glance was enough to show Gregory that the padlock would prove too much for him. To have filed through the hinged clasp would have taken hours and to blow the lock would have needed so big a charge that its explosion must be heard. Even if by bringing in a Bunsen burner he could have cut through the clasp fairly quickly there remained the question of whether he would be able to get the gate open; and there was no way in which he could test that before the event. Each side of it, he reckoned, must weigh something in the neighbourhood of a ton, and all the odds were that it had not been opened for years; so the great hinges would have rusted and made it impossible to shift.

He had no need to peer between the bars to see the end of the tunnel, as it was not flush with the farther wall of St. Thomas's Tower. The tunnel ran on for some twenty feet, forming another great pit similar to the one behind him; so daylight lit it from both ends. Its sides were formed by stone blocks each about two feet in height, and there were nine rows of them. The arch above the gate was filled by more beams with stout trellis works between them, and under the beam that ran parallel with the top beams of the gate there was a row of wicked iron spikes, so there could be no question of climbing over it.

Hiding his disappointment, Gregory rejoined the Governor, who then took him farther than he had yet been along Water Lane and through a gate in the Outer Wall that led on to the tree-lined embankment—which stretched unbroken from the western to the eastern end of the fortress. Along its whole length, pointing out over the river, were a long line of artillery pieces of all ages, and they went over for a closer look at some of the more interesting ones.

Gregory noted that there had been a sentry on the gate

through which they had come. The gate was only about fifty yards east of St. Thomas's Tower, and he soon saw that two other sentries were stationed one at each end of the embankment. When he and the Colonel came opposite to the Tower, while they were examining the cannons he stole several quick looks up at it.

The central windows, which he judged to be those of the hall and the rooms on either side of it—in one of which he had seen Sabine—were immediately above the pit in which lay the dead end of the tunnel. It was a drop of fifty feet, and even if he could lower her and himself they would then be in the eighteen feet deep pit instead of on the embankment. As her bedroom was on the other side of the tower and looked out on Water Lane, it would be pointless to come down from the window there. By swinging like a pendulum on a rope from the window of the room in which he had seen her, it might be possible to land on the embankment instead of in the pit, or the attempt might be made from a window of one of the flanking tower rooms—if he could get her to it. But even then it would mean a drop of thirty feet and take at least ten minutes for the two of them to accomplish. It was the thought of the time factor which made him rule it out. With one sentry within fifty yards, and two others walking their beats with an uninterrupted view of the tower, it was almost a certainty that they would be spotted. More out of curiosity than anything else he asked the Governor:

'Are the sentries here issued with ball cartridge?'

Colonel Faviell laughed. 'Good gracious, no! We've had plenty of air raids, but at least we have no cause to fear a sea-borne assault by the enemy. There is little point in their being here really, now the Jewels have gone; but it is tradition that we should have them, and tradition dies hard.'

In spite of this reassuring reply, Gregory still felt that the odds on being caught, if they came down from a window, were so big that as an escape route it was not worth further consideration. They returned to the King's House, where the Governor gave him tea; then, having thanked him for a most interesting afternoon, Gregory made his way back to the West End.

Next morning he rang up the Tower to confirm that Sabine was still too ill for her interrogation to be continued, and asked that when she was better he should be notified by a message to the War Room; then he telephoned M.I.5 to inform Colonel 'Himmler' of the situation. After that, as it was a Sunday, he rang up Sir Pellinore to suggest that since Sabine was no longer his guest they should resume their Sunday night suppers, and the Baronet said he would be pleased to see him.

At Carlton House Terrace that evening, as soon as Gregory had been provided with a glass of sherry, he told his host of his visit to Sabine, and that she had sent a message conveying her most abject apologies for her shocking abuse of Sir Pellinore's hospitality and her hope that, as she had been inspired by patriotic motives, he would not think too badly of her.

'Queerest apology I've ever had,' grunted Sir Pellinore. 'And I don't want any more like it. Still, shows the wench has good manners. That's more than many young people have these days. Can't help bein' sorry for her, in a way. Confounded nuisance though. You and I are bound to be dragged in at her court martial, and made to look a pair of fools. Fine kettle of fish your idiocy has landed us in.'

Gregory gave the 'soft answer that turneth away wrath' and changed the subject.

During the meal their talk, as usual, ranged over the battle-fronts. The previous Sunday night Lancasters had carried out a terrific raid on Le Creusot, practically eliminating the great munition works there that French collaborators had been running at full blast for the benefit of the Germans. The Admiralty had announced a great increase in the strength of our Fleet, the two great new battleships *Anson* and *Howe* now being in commission, and that since the beginning of the war we had accounted for no less than 530 enemy submarines. The Germans were still hurling their troops against Stalingrad but the attacks showed signs of weakening. Moscow claimed that some of the German divisions had lost up to seventy per cent of their effectives; and it did really begin to look as if the all-important city on the Volga would succeed in holding out through the winter. On the past two nights the R.A.F. had bombed Genoa, causing great havoc among wharfs and shipping. As the port was Rommel's principal supply base, these actions were clearly designed to assist operations in North Africa; and General Montgomery's offensive had started well,

335

some points in the enemy's main defences having been penetrated.

They took their port up to the library, and when they had settled down there Gregory told Sir Pellinore the story, as disclosed by Sabine, of her plot with Ribbentrop. The older man listened with the greatest interest, then exclaimed:

'Strap me! What a lot these Nazis are! Just think of Anthony Eden, sayin' he had a mistress, lettin' her shield a German spy, then go as a spy with him to the Fatherland in the hope of making John Anderson look a fool in front of Churchill. Berchtesgaden must be a regular thieves' kitchen. It's the gel who's got the raw end of the deal, though. And it's worse for her than it would be for a man. Prison plays the very devil with women's looks. She'll be prematurely old and no good for anything by the time she comes out.'

'That won't be the case if I can help it.'

'Eh? What d'you mean by that?'

'I'm planning her escape.'

The Baronet's blue eyes bulged. 'You're joking!'

'I'm not. I was never more serious in my life.'

'Then you're crazy. You don't know what you're talkin' about.'

'I tell you I am planning her escape. And what is more I need your help.'

Sir Pellinore sprang to his feet. 'God in Heaven, man! Is it likely! You're drunk! Barmy! Off your rocker!'

'I'm as sane as you are.'

'Then you're pulling me leg, and I don't like it. I can take a joke, but this has gone far enough.'

'It has hardly started yet,' Gregory replied calmly. 'I assure you that I am in deadly earnest. I mean to do my damnedest to get Sabine out.'

'But damn it all! You can't have realised the implications. To make such an attempt would be treason.'

'I know that; but I hope to escape being tried for it.'

'You would be, if you were caught. And you will be. You can't get prisoners out of a place like the Tower. It's not some tin-pot little concentration camp.'

'I know.' Suddenly Gregory smiled. 'Yesterday afternoon the Resident Governor kindly took me all over it.'

'My God, you must be made of solid gall! All the same, if

you had reconnoitred the place for a month you wouldn't be any better off. To make such an attempt would be madness. It couldn't possibly succeed.'

'Probably you are right. But that remains to be seen. I am simply telling you that I mean to have a crack at it.'

Sir Pellinore sat down again, and tried sweet reason:

'Now look here, Gregory. You really must try to get your feet down on the earth. Naturally, havin' had an affaire with this young woman you're very distressed about her. I understand that. You'd be a cad if you weren't. But she is accused of having aided the enemy, and if you try to help her to escape you'll be betraying your own country.'

'I admit that it may look like that. But, after all, she is no longer a danger to us; and if she did get away she has no information of importance she could take with her.'

'That's true; but it wouldn't make your case any better.'

'Not if I'm caught; but I hope I won't be.'

'My dear boy, you positively must not take this risk. Your having been in love with the gel is no justification for it. You are not yourself. Your mind is being unduly influenced by your feelin's for her.'

'You are quite wrong about that,' Gregory sighed. 'It is Erika I am in love with. As I told you when I was last here, I have queered my pitch with her through insisting that I must do what I can for Sabine. But please put it right out of your mind that my intentions in this matter are dictated by sentiment. To use an outmoded phrase, it is "an affair of honour" or, if you prefer a more modern one, it boils down to "cutlet for cutlet".'

Sir Pellinore nodded morosely. 'You mean that because she got you out of clink in Budapest you feel that it's up to you to get her out of clink here. Sound enough reasoning in its day, but not accordin' to modern ideas. The age of chivalry is past.'

'More's the pity. Anyhow, I am going to attempt a damsel-rescuing act, and you are going to help me.'

'By God, I'm not!' Sir Pellinore was on his feet again. 'If you are berserk enough to try this thing I can't stop you. But I'll not touch it. No, not with a barge pole!'

'Yes, you will. I'm not asking you to hold the ladder, or anything of that sort. In fact, I'll take special pains to ensure that you are not involved; but you have got to pull some strings to clear the way for me, and get me some highly secret information.'

'I'll see you in hell first!'

'There is no need to be rude.' The more violently agitated the handsome old man became the more quietly determined his lean-faced junior seemed to become. Holding up a protesting hand, he went on. 'Do please sit down again and take it easy. Like it or not, you are going to listen to me for ten minutes while I tell you the basis of the plan I've formed, and what I want you to do.'

Sir Pellinore would not sit down. He poured himself another dock glass of port, tossed it straight off, and began to stride restlessly up and down the room. Like an active volcano, while listening to Gregory he occasionally rumbled protests:

'Impossible! Hell's Bells, you can't be serious! They wouldn't tell me that; why should they? You'd be playin' with dynamite. No, no; you'd never pull it off! This is the maddest scheme I've ever heard of. They'd never stand for it! But just think of the risk! It'll be the finish of you. Finish of me too, like as not. The very thought of the gamble we'd be takin' makes me shudder.' Yet gradually his objections became less vehement, and at length he said:

'God alone knows what will come of this. Still; suppose I must do as you wish. That wench is mighty lucky to have a man of your calibre feel under an obligation to her. Odds still are though that she'll spend the next seven years in prison. If she does it'll be because you've failed. Can't say I'd lose much sleep over that as far as she's concerned; but if you really make a mess of things they might hang you.'

'If I do they may hang her too—or shoot her; which comes to the same thing. The French shot Mata Hari in the last war, and the Germans Nurse Cavell. This time the Boche are just butchering out of hand any of our women agents whom they catch connected with the resistance; and your friend at M.I.5 seems to think the Home Office are taking the view that we are overdue in staging a few reprisals.'

'The devil they are!' Sir Pellinore halted in his tracks. 'If that's the case your urge to play knight errant is much more justifiable. But the way you propose to set about it sends cold shivers down my spine. 'I'll do what you want, but I greatly fear we'll both have cause to rue it.'

They talked on for another hour. With great reluctance Sir Pellinore gave Gregory some of the secret information for which he asked, and promised to do his best to get for him the still more secret particulars, knowledge of which was essential to the success of his plan.

A little before eleven Gregory walked across the Park to do his tour of duty in the War Room. The officers on the staff there were under no obligation to maintain secrecy about where they were employed and habitually used the official paper for their correspondence; so during the night, on a sheet of the blue vellum headed 'Offices of the War Cabinet', he wrote a note to Colonel Kasdar. It ran:

*I have visited the Baroness Tuzolto in prison and she gave me a message for you. In the circumstances I feel that it would be inadvisable for me to call at your Embassy or for us to be seen together in any public place. I should therefore be glad if you would call upon me this evening any time between six o'clock and midnight at my private address—272 Gloucester Road, S.W.7.*

In the morning, on his way home, he dropped the letter in at the Moldavian Embassy.

That evening he described to Rudd the man he was expecting and told him that if anyone else called he was 'not at home'. Then he shook a cocktail, which he hoped his visitor would arrive to share with him, and sat down to wait with far from easy feelings. It was, he knew, quite on the cards that, fearing a trap, the Moldavian Military Attaché might not come; and, if he did, great subtlety and tact would be required to win him over. Sir Pellinore had been difficult enough; Colonel Kasdar might well prove more so, and if he could not be induced to play, the plan that Gregory had evolved would prove unworkable.

Half-past six came, seven, half-past and eight. Gloomily Gregory sat down to a cold meal that could easily be pushed aside. In twenty minutes he had finished it. Nine o'clock struck, and he began to fear that Kadar did not mean to come; but at a quarter-past, footsteps sounded outside on the landing and Rudd showed in the tall, dark Colonel.

Gregory greeted him cordially, mixed him a whisky and

soda and said, 'I expect the Baroness will have told you that it was I who brought her from Budapest to England.'

'Yes, so,' the Moldavian replied. 'Der Café Royal we dine at, ja. There she haf you point out to me.'

'Fine. Your having the low-down about me already should ease the wheels between us quite a lot.'

'Excuse, please, my English am not var good.'

'If you would prefer, we will talk in French or German,' Gregory suggested. 'I am quite fluent in both.'

The Colonel's swarthy face lit up with a smile. 'Let us use German, then,' he said in that language. 'For us Moldavians it is our second tongue.'

'By all means,' Gregory smiled back. 'What I was saying was, that since the Baroness has told you that we serve the same interests, that will make it much easier for us to understand one another without beating about the bush.'

'She did not say that.' A swift glint of suspicion showed in the Moldavian's yellow-flecked eyes. 'She led me to suppose that when she met you in Budapest you were there on a secret mission for the British.'

'That is true. But didn't she also tell you that my sympathies are Fascist, and . . .' Gregory added the lie unblushingly '. . . that before the war I had many friends among the high-up Nazis?'

'She told me only that you are strongly anti-Communist, and remarked what a pity it was that in this war you, and many Englishmen like you, are on the wrong side.'

'Then she at least made it clear to you that we hold views in common.'

'I am a neutral,' the Colonel replied warily. 'I have given you no reason to suppose that I am a pro-Nazi.' Then he glanced nervously round the room.

'You don't have to,' Gregory's retort was swift. 'I know you to be. The Baroness has named you as her contact with the Nazis. And you have no need to be afraid there is a microphone in the room. You can search for it if you like.'

The Moldavian did not accept the offer, but said in a low voice, 'So the little Sabine said that, did she? I feared that might be the case when I got your letter. If then, as you say, you are a friend, is it that you have sent for me to tip me off that the Foreign Office will be asking my Government to re-call me?'

'No. She told only me. No one else knows; so you are in no danger of being had up on the mat by your Ambassador for unneutral activities. In fact, I am going to make certain that no suspicion attaches to you by reporting that Sabine said it was to your Second Secretary, Mr. Nichoŭlic, that she turned in her stuff.'

'Wing-Commander, you place me in your debt. But I am at a loss to understand . . .'

'Have I not said that I, also, am an admirer of the Nazis. I had the honour to enjoy the friendship of *Reichsmarschall* Goering.'

'Indeed! I, too, know him; but only slightly. I was once asked to shoot at Karinhall, when I was Assistant Military Attaché in Berlin.'

Gregory jumped at the chance to consolidate his position. He had once spent a night at Karinhall and, while refraining from disclosing the very exceptional circumstances of his visit, he at once began to dilate on the beauties of Goering's imposing home. When they had discussed it and its owner for some minutes, Kasdar said:

'In your letter to me, Wing Commander, you said that you had a message for me from Sabine.'

'Yes; here it is.' Gregory took the note from his pocket and passed it over. When the Moldavian had read it he stroked his fine black moustache thoughtfully and remarked:

'The conversation we have already had naturally inclines me to feel at ease with you, and I am glad to have the Baron-ess's confirmation that I may be so. However, the very fact that she did write it and that you asked me to come here indicates that you have something more to say to me.'

Gregory nodded. 'You are right about that. And I will be frank. I am not proposing to mask your activities by throw-ing suspicion on Nichoŭlic solely because I would rather see Russia defeated than Germany. It is because I am contemplat-ing an undertaking in which I need help; and the sort of help I require can be given to me only by someone like yourself, who is actually in touch with the Germans.'

'What is this undertaking?' asked the Colonel cautiously.

'It is to rescue Sabine from her prison.'

The bulky Moldavian sat up in his chair with a jerk. 'But is that possible? It must be far from easy to get an ordinary prisoner out of a modern prison, and I imagine she is particularly carefully guarded.'

'She is not in a modern prison. She is in the Tower of London. Mind you, it may prove every bit as difficult to get her out of there. I am by no means sure that I can yet; but I mean to try. I have managed to escape myself from several prisons and prison camps; so I know quite a lot about that sort of thing, and this time I have the advantage of being outside the fence. You see, I am assisting in her interrogation. that enables me to see her at any time I like and, without being suspected, concert arrangements with her or, if desirable, take in to her some form of disguise.'

Kasdar drew heavily on his cigarette. 'As it was you who brought her into England, I was much surprised to learn that they had allowed you to see her. It was clever of you to get yourself called in on her interrogation. But I fear I cannot aid you in helping her to escape. Much as I should like to do so, I am not prepared to take that risk. If I were caught it could be ruled that I had exceeded the limits of diplomatic privilege. Then I would find myself in a British prison.'

'I am not asking your help to get her out of the Tower,' Gregory said quickly. 'It is getting her to some place of safety afterwards that would prove too much for me alone. There would be no sense in rescuing her if she was likely to be caught again within twenty-four hours; and she almost certainly would be if she remained in London.'

'That is true. What are your proposals to meet this situation?'

'I have none; because I don't know how the German system works for smuggling people in and out of this country. But I take it you do, or could find out.'

Instead of replying, the Moldavian asked a question. 'Tell me, Wing Commander, what lies behind all this? The risk to yourself is immense. If you are caught you will be cashiered and receive a prison sentence long enough to ruin your whole life. I cannot believe that you would lay yourself open to such a terrible penalty solely because you are a friend of *Reichsmarschall* Goering and would prefer a Fascist dominated Europe to a Communist one.'

'Of course not!' Gregory had been ready for this. 'That is one reason; but I have two others which weigh much more with me. The second is that I am in love with Sabine. Circumstances dictated that once having got her to London I should refrain from going about with her for a while. But —perhaps she told you this—in Budapest we became lovers, and all through our long journey to London we lived as man and wife.'

'Yes; she told me that.'

'You will understand, then, that the thought of her in prison is torture to me. Desperation at the knowledge that she will be left there for years to rot, unless I can restore her to freedom, drives me to this act. Even if I cannot reap the reward for saving her, I owe it to her for the happiness she has given me.'

He paused a moment, then went on, 'My third reason is an entirely selfish one. I am convinced that Herr Hitler will win this war. I hope it will end in the utter destruction of the Russians and a compromise between Britain and Germany. But it may not. Churchill is incredibly pig-headed. He is the sort of man who will refuse to recognise when we are beaten. To bring an end to hostilities Herr Hitler may be compelled to land troops here and subdue Britain by force of arms. That would mean years of great misery for the population. All my life I have lived well. I hate poverty, indifferent food and discomfort. I was well thought of by the Nazis before the war. If I can put myself definitely on the right side by doing them some signal service—such as restoring Ribbentrop's beautiful mistress to him—I should be made a member of the *Parti*, and rewarded with some responsible position under the occupation Government. They might even make me a *Gauleiter*, or something of that sort. You see, I am being completely frank with you.'

'Admirable, admirable,' purred the tall Moldavian. 'You and I are birds of a feather, Wing Commander; sensible people who know which side our bread is buttered.'

After his great effort Gregory gave a silent sigh of relief. He felt confident now that he had really won his visitor's confidence, and got him exactly where he wanted him. Next moment he suffered bitter disillusion.

Finishing his whisky. Kasdar said, 'I envy you the joy you

had of the little Baroness. I had aspirations in that direction myself. But I lack your altruism in being prepared to run risks for her only to hand her over to Herr Ribbentrop. As for your ambitions, I find them most laudable; but they are no affair of mine. She has had the bad luck to get caught, and as far as I am concerned that is the end of the matter. The co-operation which you ask might well bring about the ruin of my career; and nothing would induce me to play ducks and drakes with that. I repeat—nothing.'

## 24

## Playing With Dynamite

The Moldavian stood up to leave. Gregory stood up too, but instead of turning towards the door he picked up the whisky bottle and said in a casual voice:

'You might as well have the other half before you go.'

Without waiting for a reply he began to pour out. While he did so his brain was working with the speed of a dynamo. If he could not, here and now, secure the Colonel's promise to help him he might not get another chance. Knowing what he intended to attempt Kasdar might consider it dangerous to have anything further to do with him.

He could, of course, try blackmail—threaten to have Sabine tell the truth about the Colonel's having been her contact instead of saying that it was Nichoŭlic—but he had a feeling that would not come off. Gregory was a shrewd judge of character. In his secret work he had to be, for there were times when a mistake in assessing trustworthiness could have cost him his life. In the past half-hour he had summed up Kasdar and would have reported on him as:—

'A typical Balkan soldier of good family. Not very clever, but brave, proud, ambitious, honest according to his lights, and likely to be very touchy about anything reflecting on a somewhat outmoded code of honour that was held by his class.'

His acting, although a neutral, as a Nazi Agent could no more be held against him than it could against Gregory that he, in the previous year, had gone as a spy to Russia, although that country was Britain's ally. The great majority of upper and middle class Central Europeans, having for the past twenty years lived under the menace of their countries being overrun by the Soviets, had seen their only protection in entering the Fascist and Nazi camps; so it was natural that most of the Moldavians were hoping that Germany would win the war. It was that, no doubt, rather than payment for information received, which had led Kasdar to help the Nazis. In fact, if he were well-off—and most military attachés were chosen from among the richer officers of their armies—he might strongly resent an offer of money from either side. The odds were still greater that he would resent an attempt to blackmail him. It was liable to arouse in him all the primitive instincts of his type—anger, courage and defiance. The only hope was to handle him with velvet gloves and to titillate his ambition.

As he sat down again, Gregory said with a smile, ' "Nothing" is an all-embracing word. I hardly think you would stick to it if, in exchange for your co-operation, I were in a position to make you President of Moldavia or, say, Chief of the Moldavian General Staff.'

Kasdar gave a deep laugh. 'But, my friend, you are not.'

'True. Yet you give as your reason for refusing your help fear of ruining your career. Hasn't it occurred to you that I might be able to assist you in it?'

'I do not see how.'

'Just now, when I spoke of my wish to gain for myself a privileged position, should the Germans ever occupy this country, you remarked that we were birds of a feather. If you really meant that you must have been thinking on the same lines. Moldavia, we both know, is at Herr Hitler's mercy. He has allowed it to remain isolated and neutral only because it suits him to do so; just as is the case with Switzerland. When the war is over and he re-makes Europe he will either absorb Moldavia, or at least see that it is run by a puppet government under Nazi direction. When that day comes, it will be the officers who have shown their Nazi sympathies during the war who will be certain of rapid promotion, and the better they have served Germany the higher the posts to which they will be appointed.'

'Naturally. And I admit that it is with just such a future in mind that I serve the Germans.'

'Well, I could enable you to serve them better. As you know, I work in the Offices of the War Cabinet.'

Kasdar's eyes opened wide and he suddenly sat forward. 'You . . . you mean that you would supply me with valuable information.'

Gregory nodded. 'By doing so I should be securing my future as well as helping yours. But I shall be taking a far greater risk than you will; so I want part payment in advance. You may think it quixotic of me to wish to save Sabine for Herr Ribbentrop, but I love her, and there it is. My price is that if I can get her out of the Tower you should get her safely out of the country.'

'That is easier said than done.'

'I feel confident you could arrange it. To fly her out would, I imagine, be impossible. But she could be picked up by a U-boat from some lonely spot on the coast.'

'I cannot see the Germans risking one of their U-boats for such a purpose—unless, that is, we could first get her to Eire. I gather that they look in fairly frequently at secret rendezvous along the southwest coast. As Eire is neutral, simply to get her there would be enough. It could then be left to the German Embassy in Dublin to make further arrangements for her.'

'Yes, she would be safe from recapture in Eire, but how would you get her there? Remember, she would not have a passport.'

'I could get a Moldavian passport faked up for her.'

'No good.' Gregory shook his head 'If I get her out of the Tower it will be known by eight o'clock that following morning. M.I.5's security network is extremely efficient. Within half an hour officials at every port in Britain will be on the look-out for her. There aren't a great number of Moldavians here, and as she is known to have been turning her stuff in to the Moldavian Embassy, anyone attempting to leave on a Moldavian passport is certain to be subjected to special scrutiny. No disguise, however excellent, could possibly stand up to it. They would get her for certain.'

'I fear you are right.'

'Surely you have other recourses, or by secret cypher telegram to Germany could have them made available to you. I know that M.I.5 has succeeded in clearing the country of active German agents but among the enormous number of refugees who settled in Britain before the war, and kept on coming in right up to the time of Dunkirk, there must be a number of Nazi sympathisers who are listed and could be made use of at a pinch. If Sabine is to be got to Eire she will need places to lie hidden in for a few days until the hunt slackens off, then a small boat and a crew that will ask no questions to run her across from some little fishing village in Wales. If you cannot manage such requirements, I've no doubt Berlin could provide them for you.'

Kasdar waved the suggestion away. 'You are wrong, my friend, and I will tell you why. The Germans have three separate secret services. First that of the Abwehr the original Military Intelligence Branch, run by Admiral Canaris, Second, and now far bigger, that built up by Heydrich as the ears and eyes of the Nazi Party, which operates as a Department of the Gestapo, under Himmler. Third, a quite small organisation run as a private intelligence service by Herr Ribbentrop, whose sources are confined to diplomatic channels. Not only are all three independent, but the jealousy of their Chiefs is such that none of them would lift a finger to help an agent of one of the others. It is possible that the Gestapo have the sort of facilities here that you suggest, but I doubt if the Abwehr have, and I am quite certain that Ribbentrop's private system has nothing of the kind—and, of course, it is with this last that Sabine and myself are associated.'

The statement confirmed what Gregory had supposed to be the situation; so he said: 'In that case we are thrown back on our own resources. I am in no position to hide Sabine with anybody even for a night, much less find a crew to take her across the Irish Channel. Could you not secure the help of some of the Moldavians who are living in the country? It should be possible to buy a boat and perhaps you could get hold of some Moldavian seamen to man it?'

After considering for a moment, the Colonel replied, 'As you must be aware, we Moldavians are not a seafaring people. Most of the ships we owned were cargo vessels trading in the Mediterranean. Since the war they have been chartered to the

347

Axis. A few, of course, were on the oceans, and those that have not been sunk are under charter to the Allies; but there are never more than a handful of Moldavian sailors in British ports. The only ones actually resident here, as far as I know, are the crews of our tugs.'

'Tugs!' repeated Gregory quickly. 'How do you come to have tugs here?'

'We had four on order in British shipyards when the war broke out. Normally, when completed they would have been sent round by the Black Sea to us for work on the Danube. Two were actually about to sail and the British made a move to commandeer them. But we resisted it, and a compromise was reached by which it was agreed that we should supply crews for them and they should fly the Moldavian flag, but be chartered by the Ministry of Shipping for the duration. They are powerful vessels so suitable for coastal work, and are employed in bringing strings of coal barges down from New-castle to London. One has been sunk but three are still in service.'

Gregory leaned forward with sudden excitement. 'I believe this might be the solution to our problem. The essence of success is to get Sabine away quickly. Once the hunt is on police all over Britain will be holding up cars to check the people in them. That's why I don't like the idea of taking her right across England. We would probably have to make two bites at the cherry; and we'd certainly not be able to get her away to sea the same night. On the other hand, a car could run her down to the Kent or Essex coast before her escape had been discovered, and if one of your tugs could pick her up she would be pretty well in the clear.'

'You speak of my tugs. But they are charted by the British Government.'

'I know; but you say they are manned by Moldavian crews. Therefore the real points at issue are: —could you induce who-ever in the Moldavian Embassy is responsible for these tugs to order the Captain of one of them to take her across to the Continent and, on receiving such an order, would he and his crew obey it?'

'It is I who am responsible. Apart from a few gunboats on the Danube, Moldavia has no navy; so her Military Attachés include in their duties such very occasional naval matters as arise. Since the tugs were built to the order of my Government and not to that of a private company, it was decided that it was more suitable that I should arrange about their charter, rather than our Commercial Attaché. As for obeying, yes, I think so. They are simple seamen, and in a matter like this there is some compensation to be gained from Moldavia's being a rather backward country. Her lower orders are patriotic, so willing to take risks for her, and they are still accustomed to accept without question orders from highly placed men of their own nationality, such as myself.'

'All this sounds almost too good to be true.'

'One moment, please.' The Colonel raised his hand. 'I was about to add that living in Britain for so long will certainly have made many of them pro-Ally. Some of them, too, have married English girls, and perhaps intend to make their homes here for good. So although they are by nature patriotic and well disciplined, some of them would obey only with reluctance. And there is always the chance that, rather than leave England, one of them would betray our intentions.'

'I appreciate that; but there is also the other side of the picture. For over three years all of them have been cut off from their homeland. Some of them must be cursing the war which keeps them in compulsory exile and looks as if it will never end. I have no doubt that there are quite a number who would give anything for a chance to get back to their wives and families. Couldn't you sound the Captains? Find out which of them is eager to get home. Then set him to sound the men of all the crews. As soon as he had reported to you, you could order a reshuffling of crews, so that all the pro-home birds are concentrated in one tug. Get the idea?'

'I do; and it is a good one. But to do as you suggest would take some time.'

'True; but there is no immediate urgency. I think I can drag out Sabine's interrogation until early November.'

'In that case, yes; I think I could arrange things. There remains, though, the problem of detaching the chosen tug from its normal service.'

'That should not be difficult. At the appropriate time, either on her run up to Newcastle or down to London, somewhere between Clacton and the Nore, she would develop engine trouble and would have to put in to one of the small yacht

349

harbours—either Brightlingsea or Burnham-on-Crouch.
While her string of barges lay safe at anchor, her engineer
would be tinkering with her engine, perhaps for two or three
days, until he got the O.K. from you. Then that evening she
would put to sea, without her barges, for a trial, pick up Sabine
in the early hours a few miles along the coast and, of course,
never come back.'

'A brilliant conception,' murmured the Colonel, stroking
his moustache. 'Yes, a brilliant conception. I really believe
this might be done. But let us talk now of another matter. May
I take it that in exchange for my help you are ready to give
me the date and the objective of this great operation that is
now being mounted in your Northern Ports?'

His question was a facer. Gregory had known that it must
arise ultimately, but he had no intention of going so far so
soon; so he temporised, by saying 'Then you know about that?'

'Naturally. There are Moldavians living in every city in
Britain. They are not spies, but the more responsible of them
regard it as their duty to keep their eyes open and to pass on
to their Embassy anything of interest they may see. It would
be childish to expect no one to notice the hundreds of ships
that are being concentrated in the Clyde and the masses of
troops that are almost bursting out of the transit camps that
have been constructed in that area.'

Gregory smiled. 'Yes, even the best security measures could
not conceal from anyone in your position that a big show is
impending. But I can tell you neither its D-Day nor its objective. You see, I am not on the Joint Planning Staff; I only work
in the Map Room.'

Kasdar's face suddenly hardened. 'I trust you have not been
trifling with me. There are big risks attached to getting Sabine
out of this country, and I am not prepared to take them unless
you can give me something really worth while.'

'I hope to. Security inside the Cabinet Offices is bound to
loosen up as D-Day approaches. As soon as I can get anything definite I will pass it on to you.'

'That is not good enough. Even in sounding these tug Captains I shall run some risk of betrayal. If the matter is to be
proceeded with at all such preliminaries should be got on with
right away. But I will not risk so much as an eyelash unless

you are prepared to give me here and now some evidence of your good faith.'

'Very well. At least I am certain of this much. It is to be an Anglo-American operation and the Commander-in-Chief is to be the American, General Eisenhower. The Task Force Commanders will be Generals Patton and Mark Clark and the G.O.C. British troops General Sir Kenneth Anderson.'

'Good. What you tell me is of great interest. We heard a rumour that this General Eisenhower had been appointed C-in-C; yet we could not believe it, because until recently he was only a Major General, and can have had little experience of war.'

Gregory shrugged. 'None of the Americans has; but he was their chief Planner, and is General Marshall's blue-eyed boy.'

'That explains the matter,' Kasdar nodded, and went on briskly. 'Now tell me about the Order of Battle of this expeditionary force.'

'I don't know it,' Gregory spread out his hands. 'But I may be able to get it for you in a few days' time.'

'That, and the date of D-Day and the objective. All these I must have if to do as you wish is to be worth my while.'

'I will do my best; and I have already given you something for nothing. It is up to you now to investigate the situation and, if possible, to arrange for one of the tugs to be available on the Essex coast early in November. I suggest that you come here again at the same hour on Saturday next. That is, the 31st; by then both of us should be in a position to say whether we are able or unable to carry out our sides of the deal.'

The Moldavian agreed and left soon afterwards. When he had gone Gregory mixed himself another very stiff whisky and soda. In one way the interview had terminated far better than he had thought at all likely. They had actually agreed on a possible means of getting Sabine out of the country, and without the dangers and delays incumbent on transporting her to Eire. But he had had to pass on some of the secret information that he had extracted from Sir Pellinore the previous night. He could not think that the Germans were going to derive any important benefit from learning the names of the principal Commanders of the expedition; but, all the same, that had been graded 'Most Secret', and the knowledge that, owing to him, it would shortly be known in Berlin made him gulp the whisky down more quickly.

How he was to keep the ball rolling on Saturday was a matter that he did not yet care to think about. It was clear now that Kasdar was not prepared to go through with the business unless he received his pound of flesh; and to give it to him without one drop of good red blood seemed practically impossible. It could be done only by positively split-second timing. That meant, Gregory knew, that during the final preparations for Sabine's rescue he would be walking on eggshells; and he knew too that if he went through them he would deserve to be shot.

It was not until Thursday that he saw Sabine again. In accordance with their arrangement, she had used the pills he had left with her to keep herself in a state of low fever for the past five days, but was now reported well again. With him he took to the Tower some warmer clothes for her, which included a black turtle-neck sweater, black slacks and a black coat, and three bottles of port wine.

He unpacked the suitcase in which he had brought these items in front of Mrs. Sutton, gave the wine into her charge and said, 'I have had to pay for this myself, but I'm hoping that it may help to loosen up our prisoner's tongue. What I want you to do is to give her a bottle each evening after she has had her meal and let her drink as much as she likes. At the end of the week I mean to pay her some evening visits, and if she has been knocking back the port for an hour or two before I put in an appearance I may get something really worth while out of her.'

'Very good, sir.' Mrs. Sutton accepted his instructions and remarked: 'I bet the Nazis would find a less expensive way to make her talk.' Then she added with a laugh, 'A drop of anything good is so hard to come by these days, it almost makes me wish I were in her shoes.'

Gregory laughed too, and, taking the clothes, went in to see Sabine. He told her nothing about his talk with Kasdar and only, to keep her spirits up, that although he had as yet not been able to formulate any definite plan for getting her out, he had various ideas on the subject and was determined to make the attempt when he had decided which offered the best prospect of success.

First thing next morning he went to the M.I.5 office and made his report, disclosing some more of the information that he had received from Sabine on his first visit, and adding that he felt almost certain now that Nichoŭlic had been her contact at the Moldavian Embassy.

'You are doing very well,' said Colonel 'Himmler' briskly. 'Stick to it. Try to get us confirmation about Nichoŭlic; so that we can ask the F.O. to require his removal. I have a lot to do. You must excuse me now. I'll be seeing you.'

As Gregory was on afternoon duty in the War Room, he went straight down to the Tower, and he spent the best part of two hours with Sabine. He told her that in order to prolong the interrogation it was necessary to break new ground, and suggested that although she had refused to tell him about her visits to Berchtesgaden when they were in Budapest, she should do so now.

At first she showed reluctance, but Gregory told her that her only chance of freedom lay in providing him with material for feeding M.I.5; so that no arrangements to bring her to trial would be made for at least another week and that, as it would be checked up, should she tell a lot of lies the interrogation would be called off and her trial brought forward. He added that, since she was convinced that Hitler would win the war, nothing she could say about him and his entourage was really going to cut very much ice.

Persuaded by these arguments she gave him some most intriguing data about Hitler's private life and those of the people round him. By twelve o'clock they were through, so Gregory was in time to catch Colonel 'Himmler' in St. James's Street before he went out to lunch.

He reported that Sabine had now definitely admitted Nichoŭlic to be her contact, upon which the Colonel beamed through his bi-focals and said, 'Well done, you've been a great help to us. Now I can tell the Provost-Marshal's people to go ahead and arrange about her trial. You'll be wanted as a witness, of course.'

'I wonder if it wouldn't be worth while to postpone her trial for a bit,' Gregory suggested tentatively. 'It is nothing to do with me, but this morning I got her talking about the top

Nazis. As Ribbentrop's mistress she knew them all personally, you know. I found the low-down she was giving me fascinating, and I'm sure I could get a lot more out of her. Still, perhaps that sort of thing isn't of much value?'

It was a critical moment. If his proposal were rejected he would have to fall back on Sabine's taking more of the temperature raising pills he had given her as a means of postponing her trial and, far worse, he might find it difficult to pay more than another one or two visits to her on the excuse of tying up loose ends. However, he felt on fairly safe ground and almost at once the Colonel gave the sort of answer he had expected.

'That kind of material is of no value to me, but it would be of great interest to the branch of the firm that operates abroad. I'll have a word with them and one of their people will get in touch with you at the Cabinet Offices.'

Greatly relieved, Gregory walked across the Park to lunch in the basement mess at the end of the corridor in which the War Room lay, then went on duty. That evening one of the Royal Marine orderlies came in to say that there was an officer outside who wished to see him. Out in the corridor he found a small grey-haired Major who introduced himself and said in a naturally low voice, 'I've come to talk to you about the prisoner in the Tower.'

As there was no waiting-room Gregory took him down a side passage and into one of the emergency bedrooms always kept in readiness for members of the War Cabinet—it happened to be Mr. Attlee's. It was furnished simply with an iron bed, washstand, small table for use as a desk, scrambler telephone and two hard chairs. They sat on the bed talking for a few minutes then the Major moved to the table and took notes of Sabine's disclosures. When they had finished, he said:

'This stuff may come in very handy some time or other. Please get from her all you can; particularly about any of the top Generals she happens to know, but even the names and peculiarities of Hitler's servants might prove useful. The Chief of my branch is rather against people coming to our office; so I'll come to see you here again, if you don't mind. What times suit you best?'

'My duty hours vary,' Gregory replied. 'But I am supplying her with drink, as I find that she is much more forthcoming

354

when she has had a few; and to take the best advantage of that I mean to arrange my shifts for some days now so that I can see her after dinner in the evening. That means I'll be here all day, most days; but it would be best if you ring me up just to make certain I am here.'

'All right. I'll do that. There is no point in my coming to see you every day. I'll give you a ring on Monday, and come in to collect all the dope you have managed to get by then.'

After dinner that night Gregory went to see Sir Pellinore. The meeting was not a happy one. Gregory reported the progress he had made to date, then flatly refused the Baronet's pleas that he should give up his plan. Seeing that nothing would move him, Sir Pellinore, being a man of his word, divulged, albeit with great reluctance and misgiving, the 'Most Secret' information that he had secured for him.

On Saturday afternoon good news came through from the Western Desert. For the past week the Eighth Army and the Afrika Corps had been engaged in a tremendous slogging match at El Alamein. Many tanks had been destroyed on both sides and the British had taken a considerable number of prisoners; but so far General Montgomery had failed to dislodge Rommel from his main positions. Now it was reported that another all-out attack had been launched that morning and definite breaches had been made in the German defences.

At six o'clock Gregory went down to the Tower and spent an hour with Sabine, questioning her about Hitler's principal Military advisers, their habits, vices and personal backgrounds. At seven Mrs. Sutton brought her in her evening meal; so he left her. Out in the hall he said to the wardress:

'I can't stay tonight, but tomorrow evening I mean to pay her a late visit. How is the supply of port going?'

The wardress went to the cupboard and showed him that there was one bottle left. He said with a smile, 'I could do with a drink, although it is hardly the hour for port. Let's open it and have one. I'll bring some more down tomorrow. You'll join me, won't you?'

Nothing loath, she fetched a corkscrew and glasses. They had two goes apiece; then he went out into the chill raw misty night, and took the Underground down to Gloucester Road.

After Rudd had served him with a meal he spent a worrying half-hour, obsessed with the fear that Kasdar might have got cold feet and not turn up after all. He had by now thoroughly examined every possibility for getting Sabine out of the Tower and made up his mind how he meant to attempt it; but if the Moldavian let him down his own plan would have been made for nothing.

His fears proved groundless. Soon after nine, with a sigh of thankfulness, he heard the heavy footfalls outside on the landing and Rudd showed in the big black-moustached Colonel.

The Moldavian was in an excellent humour and, as soon as Gregory had mixed him a drink, opened up their business. One of the tugs was at sea and the other two at Newcastle, so he had gone up there to see their Captains; and he had been lucky. The father of one of them had recently died and he had inherited a very pleasant property in Moldavia, so he was anxious to get home to enjoy it. He had sounded his crew and found that for the chance of getting back to their own country all but one of them were also willing to accept some risk of being caught by the British while making a break across the North Sea. His tug with its tow of barges should be off Harwich, on the way down to London, on November the 2nd, and he could fake engine trouble which would enable him to lie up at Burnham-on-Crouch for, anyhow, two or three days.

Kasdar had then taken the tug Captain down to Burnham and they had hired a car to explore the neighbourhood. A lonely inlet a few miles away, which could easily be identified, had been settled upon as the point of embarkation. The wording of an innocent sounding telegram had been agreed, which Kasdar was to send to the Captain at Burnham on the afternoon preceding the escape. That night he would have his tug lying off the inlet, and should he be challenged by naval craft he would say that, having taken her out for a trial that evening, she had broken down again. From two o'clock in the morning he would have a boat inshore ready to pick up his passenger.

Gregory was delighted. He felt that had he handled the job himself he could not have done it more efficiently; but now he was faced with the awful moment when he must make payment in advance or Kadar would call the whole thing off.

Already the Colonel was saying eagerly, 'And now, my friend, don't keep me in suspense. When is D-Day and where is this great seaborne expedition to make its landing?'

On the previous night Gregory had secured both those major secrets; and numerous others, from Sir Pellinore, but he did not mean to pass on much of his material yet. He shook his head. 'Only the very top boys and the Joint Planning Staff know that as yet, and they are being as tight as clams. But in the meantime . . .'

'Come!' Kasdar broke in angrily. 'I will not be trifled with. Either you . . .'

In turn, Gregory cut him short. 'Don't be so damned impatient! I am working on three separate people, all of whom could tell us what we want to know; but I dare not ask any of them outright. You have got to give me another day or two to get the high-spots. In the meantime here is something pretty good. The code-word for the operation is *Torch*, the naval commander of the expedition is Admiral Sir Bertram Ramsey—the chap who organised the evacuation from Dunkirk—and the convoys sail tonight.'

'Tonight!' Kasdar came swiftly to his feet. 'That is certainly something worth knowing. But, if so, D-Day cannot be far off. Only three or four days, perhaps.'

'Longer, I think. Don't count on this. It is only an idea I got from something I overheard, and I may be wrong. But I gained the impression that this is a second and much more powerful expedition to take Dakar. If so, D-Day is still ten days off, at least.'

The Moldavian swallowed the rest of his drink, and said hurriedly, 'I must go and get this in code for the other side. But it is not enough, you know, to induce me to handle the Sabine business. I want the date and place before I will do that. When is the earliest you can hope to get them?'

'I may do so any time. As soon as I have anything worthwhile I'll telephone you to fix another meeting.'

When Kasdar had gone, Gregory found that he was sweating. He strove to reassure himself by reasoning that the code-word *Torch* had now served its purpose. For months past, in an ever-increasing circle, more and more people in the Ministries and Service formations had had to be appraised of its meaning, so that thousands of officers, civil servants, typists and clerks, Captains of merchant ships, dock and railway officials, all now knew it to apply to the great offensive operation planned by the Allies for 1942; and therefore from some few of those thousands it must have already leaked to Eire and so through to the Germans. He knew too that the slowest vessels had started as early as October the 22nd and that the bulk of the troops had sailed on the 26th. It was only the last flotillas of the great armada that were to sail that night; so he was able to argue that the expedition's departure could not have been concealed from men like Kasdar for more than another twelve hours. In the morning Glasgow and Liverpool would wake to learn that Clydeside and Merseyside had overnight become empty of shipping. Neutrals resident in those cities would unquestionably telephone that news to their Embassies in London.

Yet he hardly slept from worry and a succession of nightmares about appalling catastrophes which just might result from his personal action. The worst was the convoys being torpedoed; although once they had sailed they stood that risk anyhow, and if they had been going to Dakar they would have passed hundreds of miles outside the Straits of Gibraltar, which was the worst danger spot; so the red herring he had thrown out might help to minimise the risk they ran.

On Sunday morning there was again good news from El Alamein. A British thrust to the north had cut off a large pocket of Germans on the coast; but knowing that the *Torch* convoys had sailed everybody in the War Cabinet Offices was now anxious and restless.

Instead of supping with Sir Pellinore, at nine o'clock that night Gregory arrived at the Tower. The red-headed Mrs. Wright was on duty and, taking three bottles of port from his attaché case, he suggested that she might like to have a drink with him before he went in to start his interrogation. Like her colleague, she displayed no reluctance, and while they were having it she remarked:

'You won't have long with her tonight, sir, unless you've got the countersign. The gates are shut at ten, and no one's allowed in or out after that, unless they have.'

Having thanked her for the information, he went across to the Governor's office, explained that he wished to spend at least an hour with the prisoner, and was given the countersign for the night, which would allow him to pass out of the wicket gate up till twelve o'clock. But he was warned that unless he was out by that hour he would be locked in till morning.

On returning to St. Thomas's Tower he found that Mrs. Sutton had just come in from an evening off. It was about twenty to ten and she asked him if he had ever seen the Ceremony of the Keys. As he had not, and it was due to take place in only a little over ten minutes' time down in Water Lane, just below the front door, she suggested that he should wait to see it before going in to the prisoner.

They had another drink all round, then went out on to the stone gallery above the pit in which lay Traitors' Gate. At 9.53 the Chief Warder, an ancient lantern in hand, joined the Escort of Troops awaiting him in the archway under the Bloody Tower, upon which Gregory and the two wardresses were looking down. Carrying the Keys, the Chief Warder proceeded in turn to the West Gate, the Middle and the Byward Towers. At each, as he locked the gates, the escort presented arms. The party then returned to the archway of the Bloody Tower where it was halted by the sentry with the challenge, 'Who goes there?' The Chief Warder replied, 'The Keys.' The sentry demanded, 'Whose Keys?' The Chief Warder replied, 'King George's Keys.' Upon which the sentry cried, 'Advance King George's Keys. All's well!' And so concluded the ceremony.

'Really romantic, isn't it?' commented Mrs. Wright. 'And just to think it's been done the same night after night for nearly seven hundred years.'

Gregory spent his hour with Sabine, extracting more information from her about Hitler's habits and those of his favourites. He was out of the Tower by eleven-twenty and spent a somewhat better night owing to the comforting thought that the build-up for Sabine's escape was proceeding well.

Next morning, at the Cabinet Offices, the little grey-haired Major telephoned, then came to see him about midday; and he was able to assuage his troubled conscience a little with the thought that he was, at least, the means of providing a mass of high level intelligence data which it would otherwise have been extremely difficult to obtain.

But Kasdar again loomed dark and sinister in his thoughts. He dared not hold out too long on the Moldavian, otherwise all that he had yet done would go for nothing. Steeling himself to it he rang up from a call-box outside on Clive Steps, and asked the Colonel to come down to Gloucester Road that night at eight o'clock.

Kasdar was punctual to the minute. Striving to make his voice sound natural, Gregory said to him, 'I've got it for you, as I promised. D-Day is Monday, November the 9th.'

'*Kolossal!*' cried the Moldavian, almost quivering with excitement. 'Now we have really got somewhere. And the objective?'

Gregory shook his head. 'I am still stymied on that.'

'But the one loses nine-tenths of its value without the other.'

'I know. But I can't help it. I'll get it for you within the next twenty-four hours. And listen! I've got for you the British Order of Battle.'

'You have!'

'Yes.' Gregory produced from his pocket a list of the Divisions and Brigade Groups that were taking part in the operation. He had compiled it without aid, simply by using his knowledge obtained in the War Room of the formations which had been moved to ports. He had not dared to fake it, as he felt sure that any Military Attaché would already have a shrewd idea of the best trained, fully equipped formations available, and would probably have had his civilian informants identify by their arm flashes those which during the past fortnight had moved up to the North.

After a glance down the list, Kasdar exclaimed, 'This is good! You have done well, my friend! But not well enough. The objective is all important. When can you let me have it?'

'Tomorrow, I hope. Anyhow by Wednesday. And that is the day for which I have planned Sabine's escape. I mean that night. May I count on you to send a telegram giving the word to your tug Captain on the afternoon of Wednesday the 4th?'

'Providing that you have by then given me the objective.'

'I understand that; but we cannot afford to postpone our preparations. You are in a position to refuse your aid at any moment, should I fail you. But the preparations must be made. On Wednesday, after lunch, at half-past two, I wish you to be at the blitzed entrance to St. Thomas's Hospital, on the south side of Westminster Bridge. I will be waiting for you there. By then, if I haven't given it you before, I'll be able to tell you the objective. But, Wednesday we must definitely meet in order to reconnoitre the approach by water to the Tower, and lower down the river; so that you can decide where you will have your car waiting to pick Sabine up that night.'

After a moment's hesitation, Kasdar agreed. 'All right then. Wednesday, two-thirty, outside the hospital, on the far side of the bridge.'

Having got rid of the Moldavian, Gregory went along by Underground to the Tower, arriving there about half-past nine. He went straight to the Governor's Office to get the countersign, then again gave the two wardresses a glass of port and watched the Ceremony of the Keys with them. Soon after ten he was locked in with Sabine.

He talked to her until a quarter to twelve; then Mrs. Sutton came to the door to warn him that it was time for him to leave. He said he must have another five minutes, and when he came out he was cursing audibly at having had to terminate prematurely a most promising session of his interrogation. It was only by running for it through the dark rain-misted night that he managed to get to the wicket gate in time to save himself from being locked in.

First thing on Tuesday morning, having decided that it would be as well to let Colonel 'Himmler' know how the interrogation was going, he called at the M.I.5 office. That bustling and cheerful officer listened to his report with interest, then said:

'It will take a few days to arrange for her trial, but I see no reason now why it shouldn't be started next week.'

Gregory nodded. 'After another two long late sessions I reckon I'll have sucked her dry; so I should be able to make my final report to your little Major friend on Thursday. In any case I'll be through well before the weekend.'

Having thus ensured against any sudden interference with his plans by M.I.5 during the next forty-eight hours, he walked across the Park to his office. There he learned that the El Alamein battle was still raging furiously. The Germans claimed that Rommel was winning the tank battle but the signals from General Alexander contradicted that, and in the southern sector our infantry had made an important advance, taking many prisoners.

Everyone realised that a great deal hung on the outcome of the battle, but both victories and defeats in the Western Desert were no new thing; so, from the Chiefs of Staff down to the most junior Major, the whole personnel of the Fortress Basement had their thoughts on the Atlantic.

As super security the position of the Convoys was not even marked up on the map in the War Room; it was known only that they had taken a wide sweep out into the ocean so as to be outside the range of the Fockewulf aircraft that the Germans used to spot for their U-boat packs. But it was also known that a concentration of no less than forty U-boats was lying off the Canary Islands; and the Convoys had to go through the Straits of Gibraltar. Still worse, for some reason that even the sailors seemed unable to explain, they would have to spend no less than forty-eight hours milling round outside the Straits while they were regrouped into new formations for the assault. From the present position of the U-boats it looked as if the Dakar cover story had got through; but when those hundreds of ships had to become more or less stationary, circling round one another for two days and nights at no great distance from the Straits, it seemed almost impossible for them to remain undiscovered, and that the U-boats would not come racing north to deal death and destruction among them.

There was, too, another cause for acute anxiety. The original British plan had been to throw everything into the Mediterranean, for three landings at Oran, Algiers and Philippeville, but the Americans had baulked at the idea, fearing that if the Germans came down through Spain the whole expedition might be cut off and bottled up in North Africa.

To ensure keeping open a supply line to it they had pressed for the major landing to be made at Casablanca, on the Atlantic coast, and only a minor one at Oran. The British had argued stubbornly for landings at Algiers and Philippeville, because the prime object of the operation was to get into Tunisia as rapidly as possible and join up with the Eighth Army advancing from the East; and Philippeville was five hundred miles nearer to the Tunisian border than Oran. But the best that could be got was a reluctant consent by the Americans to a landing at Algiers, and they also continued to insist on one at Casablanca.

The decision to abandon the Philippeville landing was to prove an error of the first magnitude, as it resulted in the

Germans being able to get strong forces into Tunisia before the Allies could do so, and a most costly campaign of many months' duration before the enemy were finally thrown out. But the matter which was causing such anxiety at the moment was the Casablanca landing. Being on the Atlantic coast the seas on its beaches were much rougher. On average there was only one really calm day per month, and on four out of every five the giant rollers were so high that they would make it impossible for the assault craft of the separate expedition, which was on its way over direct from the United States, to be beached without being battered to pieces.

Down in the Fortress Basement there was now nothing that anyone could do but await results, and there were still five days to go. The strain was almost unbearable, and like his colleagues Gregory could not help being affected by it; so he was glad when his tour of duty was up and he could concentrate solely on his own intensely harrowing problems.

That night he again reached the Tower at nine-thirty, secured the countersign from the Governor's Office, stood the two wardresses a glass of port, and went in to see Sabine. She had frequently begged him to tell her how he was progressing with his plans for her escape, but he had refused to do so from fear that as the time drew near she might arouse the suspicions of the wardresses by showing signs of excitement. He therefore followed what had become his established routine of questioning her about leading Nazi personalities.

At ten to twelve Mrs. Wright unlocked the door to tell him that his time was up. As on the previous night he said impatiently that he must have a few more minutes. At five to twelve she came in again; so muttering angrily he began to get his papers together, but he appeared to have difficulty with the lock of his attaché case and it was close on midnight when he hurried out.

He ran the last hundred yards to the wicket entrance but, as he had planned, by the time he reached it the gate was closed. He saw the officer of the guard, but the regulations were positive. No exception could be made for him and he must remain within the precincts of the Tower for the night.

Retracing his steps to St. Thomas's Tower he rang the front door bell and with a crestfallen expression explained to Mrs. Wright what had happened. Then he put a brighter face on

363

the matter and said philosophically:

'Anyhow, it will enable me to resume my interrogation for a while; and I can sleep on the sofa in the room that the prisoner occupies in the daytime.'

Sabine had been taken up to her bedroom, but she had not yet undressed and was brought down again. For about three-quarters of an hour he put further questions to her, then he rang for Mrs. Wright. After Sabine had been taken away, the yawning wardress helped him to make up a shake-down with cushions, newspapers, a rug and his great-coat on top of them; but when she had left him he got up.

Going to one of the mullion windows that had not been boarded over, he drew aside a corner of the curtain and peered out through its small diamond panes, hoping to find out how frequently the sentries left their boxes to walk their beats. The blackout, which so often in the war had proved his best friend, would, he knew, once again do so in his attempt to get Sabine away; but now it defeated him. Not a glimmer of light broke the sombre pattern of black outside, and gusty rain further reduced visibility. With difficulty he made out the line of the embankment, but he could only guess at the positions of the cannon along it, and nearer in there seemed little chance of picking up from above a moving figure against the dense blackness of the foreground.

After straining his eyes for twenty minutes he gave it up, and praying that he would be favoured the following night with similar conditions, made the best he could of his far from comfortable couch.

In the morning, knowing that the Tower gates were opened at six o'clock he rose early, and by seven was back at Gloucester Road. This was November the 4th, his D-Day, and he had much to do on it; so he had arranged to take it as his weekly clear twenty-four hours off from the War Room.

Having bathed and had his breakfast in a dressing-gown, he rang up several boat yards along the Thames above London, enquiring if they had a motor launch for hire. At this time of the year most boats were laid up for the winter, but his fourth call was to a firm at Kew, which had one available and said that it could be ready for him by midday. Then he snatched the best part of two hours in bed.

On getting up he dressed in civilian clothes, hunted out a

fishing rod that he had not used for years, threw a few things into an old suitcase, then, taking Rudd with him, took a taxi down to Kew. The manager of the yard expressed surprise that anyone should want to hire a launch for a week in November; but Gregory told him, with some truth, that he was a chair-borne airman whose lot it was to work month in, month out, in a stuffy basement; so even if it rained cats and dogs it would not spoil for him the joy of a week's fishing.

The man warned him that the daily allocation of petrol he was allowed to give under rationing was small, so it would not take him very far; but Gregory took delivery there and then of his seven days' quota, which was ample for his purpose. Having paid the deposit they went aboard; Rudd, who had been brought only to jump ashore with the painter when the time came to tie-up, was in the bow, and Gregory at the wheel.

During the run down river he put the launch through her paces to make sure that her engine was not likely to break down, and soon after two o'clock they tied up at the landing stage fifty yards below the County Hall. By this short expedition Gregory had not compromised his faithful henchman, and he had no intention of doing so. He now told him to walk through to Waterloo Station and take the Underground home, then he himself walked the short distance to the south end of Westminster Bridge, where he took up a position near the blitzed entrance to St. Thomas's Hospital.

He had not long to wait before Kásdar arrived in a taxi. When the Moldavian had paid off the cab he gave Gregory a sullen stare and asked, 'Did you know about the diplomatic bags?'

'What about them?' Gregory replied innocently.

'Why, that they had been stopped. We were notified of it only this morning. The Foreign Office informed us with regret that His Majesty's Government had instructed the G.P.O. to hold all bags delivered after midnight on Tuesday, and that none will be forwarded until further notice. Never before has such a step been taken. It is an outrage against International convention.'

'Really!' Gregory raised his eyebrows. 'I've no contact with the Foreign Office, and it is news to me.'

'But do you realise what this means? My message giving the date of D-Day and the Order of Battle are held up. They will not now be passed on to Berlin until after the expedition has reached its destination. I thought perhaps . . .'

'What! That I had double-crossed you? Don't be a fool; I have too much at stake.' As Gregory spoke he was feeling immense relief. He considered the Foreign Office to be reprehensibly soft in its treatment of neutrals and had feared that grounds might be put forward for postponing the measure at the last moment. Now he knew that his fears had been groundless and his timing all right; so he was over that hurdle.

With a shrug of his broad shoulders, the Colonel said more affably, 'Fortunately all is not yet lost. If you succeed in rescuing Sabine, she will act as our courier.'

Gregory heard the suggestion with grim satisfaction. That was just what he had been planning for all along. He need now no longer fear that, when Kasdar had got all the information he could out of him, he would double-cross him and fail to keep his side of the bargain. For his own ends now, he had to get Sabine out of the country. But in her case too there was this nightmare problem of exact timing.

'The objective?' Kasdar shot at him suddenly. 'I take it you have now found out about that?'

'Yes, and I will give it you within the next quarter of an hour. This is no place to talk about it. Come along with me.'

Crossing the road they walked almost in silence through York Street and down to the landing stage where the launch was tied up. Going aboard they entered her tiny cabin, then Gregory produced a piece of paper from his pocket. On it was a rough sketch map of the western half of the Mediterranean with arrows to indicate landings place. Handing it over, he said, 'There you are.'

After one glance the Moldavian exclaimed, 'Then it is not Dakar! That is surprising. We have had it from several sources that it was.'

'I thought so too,' Gregory agreed. 'But you will remember I warned you that it was only an idea of mine; and I was wrong. Now I've done my part it is up to you to do yours. Let's go ashore and send that telegram.'

Kasdar raised no objection so they walked the short distance to Waterloo Station and from the Post Office there despatched the agreed message to the tug-boat Captain at Burnham. As they walked back to the landing stage, the Moldavian said in a low voice:

'It is just as well that this embargo on the diplomatic bags was not put on earlier. I was, anyhow, able to get through to the other side news of our intentions, and receive back the special recognition marks for our tug to display as soon as she is clear of British controlled waters. Otherwise she might have had the ill-luck to be sunk by the Luftwaffe or a German E-boat.'

When they were back in the launch Kasdar untied the painter and Gregory nosed her out. A quarter of an hour later, moving at a slow speed, they came opposite the Tower of London. Then Gregory said:

'You see the big block nearly in the centre of the Outer Wall. That is St. Thomas's Tower and Sabine is in it. However dark it is tonight you will still be able to identify it because the two turrets at its extremities will stand out against the sky-line. I want you to bring this launch in under the embankment as nearly as possible halfway between the two turrets at a quarter to eleven. If Sabine and I are not on the embankment ready to come off at once, take the launch to the other side of the river and tie up there; then come over again at a quarter to twelve. If we are not there repeat the process at a quarter to one and at a quarter to two. If we have still not appeared, you will know then that I have failed, and the job is off. Is that clear?'

'Perfectly. But what of the tide?'

'I have checked that. At low there are a few yards of imported sand beach on which children play in the day time. At high you would be able to get her right up to the river wall. Tonight will be fairly favourable. You should be able to get right in at ten forty-five, but it will already be on the ebb. Later we would have to drop in the shallows and wade out to you. In case we have to do that there is a suitcase in the cabin with dry slacks, socks and shoes in it for Sabine and myself.'

'You intend, then, to come too?'

Gregory shrugged. 'What the hell else can I do? There will be no disguising the fact that it was I who arranged her escape. I have got to disappear. If I remained in this country the police would get me within a week. And the charge would be treason. No! I'll have burnt my boats; so the only thing I can

367

do is go over lock, stock and barrel to the Nazis.'

'Don't look so despondent about it.' Kasdar clapped him on the shoulder. 'Personally, I envy you your luck in getting out of this benighted country. And, after all, there is the little Sabine. She will owe you much. Perhaps she will console you in your exile instead of going back to Ribbentrop.'

'I will confess,' Gregory admitted with a half-smile, 'that possibility had not altogether escaped me.'

Meanwhile the launch had passed under Tower Bridge. For another two miles Gregory kept her headed down-stream, then he brought her in close to the north bank, and said, 'I thought we might find a suitable place to land somewhere along here on the Poplar water-front.'

Between the entrance to the Limehouse Cut Canal and the West India Docks there were stairs every hundred yards or so. Tying the launch up at one of them, they went ashore. At the near end of a street called Ropemaker's Fields they found a suitable place to park a car. So it was decided that early that evening Kasdar should drive down there with his chauffeur. Then, having made certain that the man knew how to find the spot again, the chauffeur should bring the car down himself to arrive a little before eleven o'clock and wait there with it, if need be until a quarter-past two.

This settled, they returned to the launch, and headed back up river. On the return journey Gregory made his companion take the wheel and controls, so that he should get some practice in handling her. After tying up again at the stairs below County Hall, they ran over their plan again to make certain that they fully understood one another; then they clambered ashore, walked to the nearest street corner, shook hands and separated, Gregory making for the Waterloo Underground. Soon after five he was back at Gloucester Road, and a quarter of an hour later in bed sound asleep.

Rudd roused him at half-past seven, and reported that soon after six the 'foreign gentleman' had rung up and left a message. It was that 'the sailor had telephoned to acknowledge receipt of the telegram'. This news heartened Gregory considerably, and he felt that he was lucky in having anyone so efficient as Kasdar to work with him. That the Moldavian might fail him that night he now had little fear; and as the creek near Burnham, off which the tug was to lie, was not

368

much over forty miles from Poplar, he reckoned that, if his own part of the job went without a hitch, Sabine should be aboard her soon after midnight.

He had a bath and got into uniform; then, as he had had no lunch, he ate a very hearty dinner. After it, he packed into the bottom of a suitcase a short electrically driven saw with a blade of tungsten steel and a battery he had attached to it by a yard of flex, some spare blades, a mallet muffled at one end with a cloth pad, a dozen ten-inch steel spikes, and two belts, with quick release buckles, attached to one another by fifteen feet of thin wire-cored rope. Over these he laid a rug, a dressing-gown, and pyjamas, packing among them three more bottles of port.

When he had put on his great-coat he told Rudd that he was going on a dangerous expedition and did not expect to be back for some time. Rudd pleaded to be taken with him, but he said that was not possible, and with his old friend's 'Well! All the luck, sir; and a safe return' ringing in his ears, he went out into the blackout to play the last desperate hazard.

## 25

## The Final Hazard

It was again dark and misting with rain. At Gloucester Road station an old newsvendor was shouting, 'Speshul Edition! Speshul Edition!' Gregory joined the little crowd eagerly reaching out for the man's papers, and bought one. It had a banner headline GREAT DESERT VICTORY.

A special communiqué had been received in London that evening from General Sir Harold Alexander. After twelve days and nights of desperate fighting, Rommel's army had broken and was now in full retreat. His disordered columns were being relentlessly pursued by Montgomery's troops, and ceaselessly strafed by Coningham's Desert Air Force. Nine thousand prisoners had been taken, two hundred and sixty tanks and two hundred and seventy guns captured or destroyed. General von Stumme was among the dead and General von Thoma among the prisoners. This was no limited success but a victory of the first magnitude, which would make the words 'El Alamein' and 'Eighth Army' live in history.

To Gregory this splendid news meant even more than it could have to the people with whom he was sitting in the cold and gloomy underground train, for he knew that this was only the first phase of the great overall plan. Would the second prove equally successful? By now the armada must be off the Straits of Gibraltar. For the next two days they would be carrying out their perilous regrouping, then on Friday night, with all lights out, they would be steaming in an endless column at full speed through the narrows. By Saturday afternoon they would be within range of General Kesselring's powerful Air Force based on Sicily; so might be subjected to ferocious aerial bombardment. Would they, in the dawn on Sunday morning—the 8th and the true D-Day—succeed in getting ashore, or would they instead have become victims of terrible disaster?

When he came out of Mark Lane Station he found the night even more murky; for down there by the river, as was often the case in November, the atmosphere was laden with fog. Thanking his gods that conditions were so ideal for his purpose, and flashing his torch now and then, he made his way across Tower Hill to the gateway of the Fortress.

When he had signed himself in, he went to the Governor's Office. There, he stated his intention of remaining in the Tower for the night, on the grounds that having had to do so the previous night had enabled him to prolong his interrogation and extract valuable information from the prisoner, owing to the fact that she had become tired out and been no longer able to stand up to the pressure he put upon her. No objection was raised and at a quarter to ten Mrs. Sutton let him in to St. Thomas's Tower.

She had heard the news of the desert victory, and was full of it. After they had discussed it for a few minutes, he told her that he meant to stay the night, and had brought a few things to make himself more comfortable. Unlocking his suitcase, he gave her a glimpse of his pyjamas and dressing-gown; then he asked, 'How is the port situation?'

'We're nearly out, sir,' she replied in her deep voice. 'She's

370

got the last bottle in there now; and judging by what she usually drinks it must be nearly empty.'

Gregory had expected that, as he had carefully budgeted for it. Unpacking the three bottles he had brought in the suitcase and standing them on the hall table, he said, 'It's just as well I brought a new supply then. Call Mrs. Wright and we'll have our evening ration before I go in to her.'

The red-headed wardress joined them at Mrs. Sutton's call, with three glasses and a corkscrew. Gregory took the corkscrew from her, tore the capsule off one of the bottles, pulled the cork and poured out the wine. As they took up their glasses he said cheerfully:

'We'll have a double ration tonight to celebrate the victory. First one to the Eighth Army and the final defeat of Rommel. Straight down the hatch; no heel taps. Here we go!'

They all raised their glasses. He had his to his lips and tilted back his head. But suddenly he set it down again untasted, explaining his act by whipping out his handkerchief and sneezing into it. The two women had already emptied their glasses.

For a moment they both stood quite still. Then their eyes began to bulge. Mrs. Wright dropped her glass, staggered and clutched at the table. Mrs. Sutton was made of sterner stuff. Her eyes glaring accusation, she let out a strangled gasp, turned, and lurched towards the telephone.

In an instant Gregory was round the table. Grasping her by the shoulders he swung her about and pushed her down into a chair. Mrs. Wright groaned and fell to the floor. Mrs. Sutton heaved herself up, reeled sideways and collapsed beside her. Both of them moved their limbs feebly for a few moments then lapsed into unconsciousness. Gregory had doctored the bottle with knock-out drops, recorked it and replaced the capsule. The Mickey Finn he had given them had done its work perfectly.

Taking Mrs. Sutton's keys he unlocked Sabine's door and called to her. 'This is it! I've dealt with the two good women who have been looking after you. Come out and give me a hand with them.'

'Oh, Gregory!' she cried. 'Can it really be true?' Then, her dark eyes bright with excitement, she ran out to him.

Between them they carried the two stalwart wardresses into

371

their bedroom and laid them on their beds. When they had done so she said:

'I'll never forget what you're doing for me! Never! Never! But what about yourself? These two women must know it was you who knocked them out. You won't possibly be able to cover up the fact that it was you who enabled me to escape. Oh, my dear! My dear! What will become of you?'

He made a rather hopeless gesture. 'I'm done for—anyhow as Wing Commander Gregory Sallust. That is not too high a price to pay, though, for your having saved me from Grauber. I learned that it was quite on the cards they would shoot you, and I couldn't possibly let that happen. Colonel Kasdar is to pick you up outside, and it is hoped to ship you across to the Continent tonight. I had thought of coming with you. But I've changed my mind. Damn it all, I am an Englishman! I'd be utterly miserable living over there like a ticket of leave man— by permission of the Nazis—because I'd saved you. Somehow I'll managed to disappear. Fortunately I've got plenty of money. I think I'll try to get to Ireland and start a little war of my own. The U-boats put in at places on the south-west coast from time to time. I don't doubt I could ferret out one of the secret landing places where their crews come ashore at night. To ambush some of the murdering swine who drown men, women and children indiscriminately would give me quite a lot of satisfaction.'

Breaking off, he handed her the key to her bedroom, and said in a brisker voice: 'But we mustn't waste time talking. Go up and change into those black clothes I brought you. See that there is nothing light about you that will show. You'll need both hands to climb, so don't encumber yourself with a handbag. Put your lipstick and toothbrush in the pockets of your coat. Get back here as quickly as you can.'

When she had left him he tore a sheet into strips and secured the two wardresses' hands and feet, then tied them to their beds. He knew that they would be out for about two hours but, in order to postpone discovery of the escape as long as possible, he took their two pillow-cases, ripped a hole in the bottom of each, then pulled them over their heads; so that, while there was no danger of their suffocating, when they did come round their shouts would be muffled and it would be impossible for them to be heard outside the building.

Closing the door of their room behind him he walked down the corridor back to the hall. As he entered it his heart missed a beat. He halted in his tracks. A cold perspiration broke out on his forehead. Sabine lay there on the floor. She was as limp and motionless as if she were dead.

Almost at the same instant as his glance fell upon her he realised what must have happened. In passing through the hall she had noticed his untouched glass of port still standing on the table. Prompted, no doubt, by the thought that a drink would help key her up to face the uncertainties of the next half hour, and in her excitement failing to associate the port with the two unconscious wardresses, she had, on an impulse, tossed the drink down. She had knocked herself out with a Mickey Finn.

Up till now everything had gone like clockwork, but her act had stopped the clock dead. And everything hung on timing. The die had been cast. There could be no going back. Gregory knew that if he could not get her out that night, she would have to take her medicine—even if it came to being shot. As for himself, the thought of the situation in which he had landed himself to no purpose made him seethe with rage. It struck him that this was just the sort of unforeseeable happening that so often ruined the plans of murderers.

As he stood staring at her twisted body, he fought to make his brain work calmly. Should he leave her there and quit, or was it still possible to retrieve the situation? He had counted on her to act as his look-out. He had meant her to climb an eighteen-foot wall and wriggle across sixty feet of open ground on her tummy. To carry her the whole way would add enormously to the risk of their being seen, and he doubted his physical ability to do it. Yet so much hung upon his rescuing her. And finding himself up against some unforeseen difficulty had never yet made him throw his hand in.

With sudden resolution he ran forward, snatched up the key that had fallen from her hand, grabbed her wrist and pulled her arm round his neck. Then, with a fireman's lift, he carried her up the short flight of stairs to her room.

Having got her into it and on to the bed, he ripped off her outer clothes, hunted round till he found the black slacks and turtle necked sweater, and thrust her flopping limbs into them. Deciding that cold or no cold she would have to go without a coat because its flapping skirts might get in his way, he carried her down to the front door. Leaving her there, he went back for his suitcase. When he had fetched it, he opened the door quietly and looked out.

From where he stood he could make out the silhouette of the Bloody Tower opposite, and the top of the Inner Wall running west from it, but down below was a grey foggy darkness that would have hidden anyone standing there. He listened for a long moment. Hearing no sound of footfalls, he left the door on the latch and went out on to the stone-walled balcony. Walking at a normal pace along it, he went down the steps at its end into Water Lane. After having strained his eyes, peering first one way then the other into the murk, he coughed loudly to draw attention to himself. No challenge came. The place was deserted.

Turning, he ran back up the steps. His rubber soled shoes made his quick movement almost soundless. Dragging Sabine and lifting his suitcase out on to the gallery he shut the door firmly. Again he got her into a fireman's lift across his shoulders, picked up the suitcase with his free hand, and at a shambling run carried them down into the roadway.

For all Sabine's slim figure, her dead weight was considerable. By the time he got her to the railing in front of the steps leading down to Traitors' Gate, he was panting like a grampus, and sweating profusely. Unceremoniously he bundled her over on to the top step, then followed with the suitcase. The pit was a canyon of utter blackness and, as he staggered down the steps with her limbs dangling about him, he knew that he was now out of danger for the moment.

At an easier pace he crossed the stone floor of the old entrance to the moat and so pitch dark was it that he walked right into the great gate before he saw it. Lowering Sabine he undid his suitcase then glanced at the luminous dial of his wristwatch. It was twenty-past ten. He had lost only ten minutes through having to dress Sabine. If things went well, and his strength did not fail him, he might yet get her on to the embankment by a quarter to eleven.

Not daring to use his torch, he felt for the saw, switched on the battery, and set to work on cutting through one of the iron bars of the gate between its two lower horizontal beams. The bars were square and about an inch thick, but very old and partially rusted through; so, if he had not been afraid of discovery, he could have made short work of them. As it was, every other minute he had to switch off and pause to listen, in case someone passed above and heard the buzzing of the saw. Once he caught the sound of voices, and remained dead still for three minutes by his watch, to ensure that whoever it was had passed well out of earshot.

The two cuts to get out the lower section of the first bar took him sixteen minutes. As he had to cut out two more before there would be an opening large enough to crawl through, he knew already that he had been unduly optimistic in hoping to get Sabine to the launch on its first run in. But his experience with the first bar made his work on the other two considerably quicker.

Grimly, he alternately worked away with his saw and paused to listen. At last the job was done. After wrenching out the third bar he looked at his watch. It was two minutes to eleven. Raising Sabine he pushed her through the two-foot square hole he had made. Then he repacked his suitcase, crawled through himself and pulled it after him.

He now had ample time, so he sat with his back against the gate resting for a couple of minutes. Getting to his feet again, he carried Sabine through the tunnel to the far end of the pit in which it terminated. It was somewhat lighter there, as it was not surrounded with high walls, and had only the grim façade of St. Thomas's Tower on its north side; but the shroud of darkness and fog was still sufficient to hide a person down in it, providing they kept still, from anyone looking down from above.

Having fetched his suitcase, Gregory got from it the ten-inch steel spikes and the mallet with the padded top. To his relief he found no difficulty in driving the spikes firmly into the crevices between the two-foot deep blocks of stone that formed the side-walls of the pit, and the mallet having been muffled its strokes made little noise. But when he had to stand on the lower spikes to drive in others higher up, it was a precarious business.

As he took his time over it, fourteen minutes elapsed before he reached the top. The stone parapet shelved outward and, leaning his arms on it, he peered about in all directions. There was no sign of movement and he could just make out a few of the nearest old cannons, some sixty feet away.

Descending to the pit, he looked at his watch. It was sixteen minutes past eleven. There was still nearly half an hour to go, and to wait about on the embankment would be to court disaster. For the final stage he reckoned ten minutes should be easily sufficient, so for the next nineteen they must remain where they were, in the pit.

A dank chill pervaded the old moat, making it bitterly cold down there. Gregory got out his flask and took two long swigs of brandy; but he did not dare to force any down Sabine's throat. To do so might now have brought her round but made her vomit; and he knew that he stood a better chance with a limp body than one half-conscious, moaning and racked with pain.

The minutes dragged interminably, and now that he had time to think he was plagued with fresh fears. Had he made it absolutely plain to Kasdar that if they were not on the embankment at a quarter to eleven he was to return at a quarter to twelve? Had Kasdar, after not finding them at the rendezvous the first time, been seized with the idea that they must have been caught, that the guards would now be on the alert, and that he might be caught too if he risked bringing the launch in again? As there had been no alarm or shouting out on the embankment during the past hour the launch must have remained undetected on its first run in; but would it be so lucky next time?

At last the gruelling wait was over. Taking the two belts out of the suitcase, Gregory fastened one round Sabine's waist and the other round his own. He had brought them only for the purpose of lowering her over the twelve foot deep embankment to the launch. Now, he thanked his stars he had thought of that, for without them and the rope which joined them it would have been utterly impossible to get her up the ladder of steel spikes.

Suddenly, when he was already half way up it, he was struck by an appalling snag. The rope was only fifteen feet long and the wall eighteen feet high. Before he got to the top he would find himself anchored by her weight and unable to proceed farther. Coming down again, he stared at her still motionless body, frantically racking his wits for a way to overcome this apparently insurmountable obstacle to getting her to the top.

A moment, and he had it. Undoing his own belt he slipped it over his arm, went up again to within three feet of the top, hooked the belt over one of the spikes and, after another cautious look round, climbed out over the edge. By reaching down he was now able to grasp the belt and haul upon it.

Lying on his stomach, he took the strain. She had been heavy enough while he was carrying her, but now she seemed to weigh a ton. As soon as she was off the ground he edged along a couple of feet to get her clear of the spikes; then he strove to haul her up.

The strain on his wrists and arms was agonising. He could only manage to hoist her a few inches at a time. Sweat poured off him. The thin rope bit into his fingers. Once, when she was two-thirds of the way up, it slipped. Like a red-hot iron it seared into the flesh of his hands. He could have screamed from the pain. Clenching his teeth and shutting his eyes, he managed to check the slipping rope and hang on. Another two minutes of almost superhuman effort and he was able to grab the belt round her waist with his right hand. For a few moments he lay there panting. Then in one great heave, he dragged her up beside him.

It had taken longer than he had allowed to get her up out of the pit. There was now not a moment to be lost. One quick look round and, still gasping for breath, he pulled her across his shoulders. Lurching to his feet he staggered with her at a stumbling run towards the river. Half-blinded by sweat he reached the railing. Lowering her beside one of the cannons, he dashed the sweat from his eyes and peered down at the black fog-misted water. To his unutterable thankfulness he saw the dark bulk of the launch just nosing her way in.

In a hoarse whisper he hailed her. A low answering hail came back. Apprehensively he glanced over his shoulder, but no movement broke the surrounding gloom. The tide was ebbing fast. The nose of the launch grounded three feet out from the embankment wall; but it was near enough. He hoisted Sabine's limp body on to the rail. Then he leaned over and said in a voice just loud enough for Kasdar to hear him:

'She is unconscious. By mistake she took some dope that knocked her out. But that was over an hour and a half ago. Water in the face and a hard slapping ought to bring her round pretty soon now.'

377

As he finished speaking he grasped the rope again in his lacerated hands, and tipped her over. Lowering her was renewed torture, and he could feel the blood oozing between his fingers. But a man that Kasdar had brought with him was standing in the bow. He caught Sabine by her dangling ankles, drew her towards him, seized her round the waist, and took the strain. With a moan of relief, Gregory let go the rope.

At that instant the silence was shattered by a challenge, 'Halt! Who goes there?'

Gregory swung round. Only a dozen yards away a figure had suddenly emerged from the fog and was rushing upon him.

'Jump for it!' shouted Kasdar. 'Jump for it!'

But momentarily Gregory seemed paralysed. Within a matter of seconds the sentry was upon him, yelling, 'Hands up! Hands up! Stay where you are, or it'll be the worse for you!'

Coming to life Gregory sprang at him and seized his rifle. As they struggled for the weapon their voices mingled in new shouts. Gregory was calling to Kasdar:

'Get her away! Her life depends on it! Never mind me! Get her away!' while the sentry was bellowing:

'Turn out the guard! Turn out the guard!'

Already the other two sentries had heard the commotion. Their nail-studded boots rang upon the roadway as they raced to the scene, and both of them were echoing their comrade's shouts:

'Guard, turn out! Turn out the guard!'

Another minute and Gregory was the centre of a mêlée in which all three men, although hampered by their rifles, were trying to seize him. He caught a glimpse of the launch disappearing in the darkness. Then one of the soldiers reversed his rifle and struck at him with its butt. The heavy blow caught him on the shoulder. His knees buckled and he fell backwards. His head struck the iron wheel of the cannon behind him, and he went out like a light.

# Epilogue

On the morning of Thursday, November 12th, Sir Pellinore was sitting at his desk in his big library. At a little after midday Erika joined him there. She had only just arrived from Gwaine Meads, as the result of a letter she had received from him that morning. Her rich gold hair was as smoothly done, and her fine face as carefully made up, as usual, but there were deep shadows between her high cheekbones and pansy-blue eyes; and, whereas she habitually carried herself with distinction, there was now a despondent droop about her shoulders.

Coming to his feet, Sir Pellinore boomed, 'Delighted to see you, my dear. Got your telegram an hour ago. But you needn't have bothered to send one. You're always welcome here. You know that.'

As she thanked him she stood on tiptoe to kiss his cheek. Then he held a chair for her and went on, 'Bad business this, about Gregory; but I thought you ought to know.'

'It's terrible!' she said. 'Terrible! I think that woman must have Satanic powers, and have cast a spell on him. But witch or not, I could cheerfully murder her.'

'Oh, I don't know.' Sir Pellinore sat down again, leaned back and tapped the tips of his fingers together. 'She wasn't really to blame for this business. Gregory was determined to get her out even before he'd been down to the Tower to see her. You could hardly expect her to refuse the offer.'

'Why didn't you stop him?'

'I tried to. But you must know what he's like when he's got the bit between his teeth.'

'Is he badly injured?'

'Troops gave him a pretty rough handling. One of them broke his collar bone with a rifle butt, and he cracked the back of his head open fallin' against an old cannon. But he wasn't looking too bad when I went down to see him in the prison hospital yesterday.'

'What will they do to him?'

Sir Pellinore pulled a long face. 'The charge for assistin' an enemy agent to escape is treason. At the worst that could mean death. But it may not come to that in view of the services he has rendered to his country.'

Seeing that Erika's lower lip had begun to tremble, he leant forward quickly. 'Don't take too black a view! No good doin' that. Let's talk of something more cheerful. This North Africa show has been a wonderful success. Little short of a miracle. Off Casablanca the night before the weather was most unpromisin'. But whatever the Americans' faults they've plenty of guts. Their Admiral decided to go in, and God calmed the waters for them. Our end, too, went without a hitch. Just think of it! All those hundreds of ships, and nearly a hundred thousand troops, conveyed over a thousand miles of ocean without the loss of a single life.'

Erika nodded. 'Yes, it's almost unbelievable.'

'I happen to know the inside story of how the job was done,' Sir Pellinore went on, 'and it's fascinatin'. Positively fascinatin'. As everyone knows, from Marlborough to Hitler, a good Cover Plan has always been half the battle. To start with, by putting rumours out among the neutrals, and that sort of thing, our people persuaded the German Intelligence to believe that the convoys were heading for Dakar. But, of course, that couldn't hold once they'd passed through the Straits of Gib., so we tried to fox them that we meant to relieve Malta and invade Sicily. Not easy that.

'Stuff that's come into our hands shows that right up to the Friday Kesselring was convinced that we meant to go into North Africa. He had his Air Force based on Sicily all ready to strike. If he had struck on the Saturday afternoon we must have lost scores of ships and thousands of men. But he didn't. That night he had positive information from his boss, Goering, that the convoys would sail past southern Sicily and make their landings on the east coast of the island. He decided not to risk a single aircraft in a long range attack.

'Instead he made his fellers spend the whole of Saturday tinkerin' up aircraft that had been damaged or were out of commission. He gave orders that every plane that could be made to fly should go up on Sunday afternoon. He'd worked it out that our convoys would then be goin' through the narrows between the tip of Sicily and Cape Bon. If they had it would have been a massacre. But they didn't. On Saturday evening they sailed past Oran and Algiers, to keep him thinkin' that he was right and would make his killing. Then, after dark, they turned back. Early on Sunday morning they went in to their true objectives, and left the enemy flat.'

Again Erika nodded. 'I see,' she said without a smile. 'That was ... What a clever thing to do.'

Sir Pellinore stroked up his white moustache, and remarked a shade reproachfully, 'You don't seem particularly interested, m'dear.'

'Of course I am!' she murmured. 'It was a wonderful idea.' Then she burst out: 'But how can you expect me to think of anything but Gregory? From the moment I had your letter, telling me how he had helped that woman to escape, and of his awful intrigue with the Moldavian Colonel, I've been able to think of nothing else. It's horrifying, terrible, to think what they may do to him.'

The old man raised his bushy eyebrows. 'Naturally you are upset. Knew you would be. You're much too nice a gel not to be sorry for an old friend who's made a mucker. But I understood from him after you last saw him that you had broken with him entirely. Does this mean that you still love him?'

'Love him!' she cried. 'He is more to me than my life! I don't care what he's done! For him to have played the traitor seems utterly inconceivable. But if he has, I don't care. I came down on the first train to beg you to arrange for me to be allowed to see him. He's ill; not only physically but mentally. He must be if this awful charge is true. I mean to tell him that I am still his, now and for always; and that if he is sent to prison I'll wait for him till he comes out.'

She burst into tears. Sir Pellinore stood up, came round from behind his desk and laid a hand on her shoulder. 'Don't cry, my dear. Everything is going to be all right. Afraid I've led you up the garden path a bit. But I had to. Seemed to me that provokin' you into a first-class emotional crisis was the best way to make you put the past behind you and think only of the future.'

Erika drew in a sharp breath. 'Do you ... do you mean that he won't be sent to prison?'

'He's been in prison for the past week,' Sir Pellinore smiled, 'but they're letting him out. Now, dry your tears, m'dear, and

I'll tell you the inner inside story of the great show I was telling you about just now.'

While Erika dabbed at her eyes with her handkerchief the Baronet went back to his chair, and began:

'After Gregory had decided that come hell or high water he meant to get the little Baroness out, he evolved a plan for doing the job which entailed giving away to the enemy some of our secrets. I didn't like it. Damnably risky. Might have caused a ghastly mess if things had gone wrong. Still, seein' that he was determined to get her out anyhow, and this scheme offered the only chance of saving him from landin' himself in prison, I reluctantly agreed to help.

'Getting her out of the Tower could be fixed. It was, and by me; but not till the very last day, and then only to a limited extent. One indiscretion could have blown the whole works. With the approval of the people at the top I roped in a friend of mine, a Colonel in M.I.5. He fixed things with the Governor of the Tower and the Officer of the Guard for the night. The sentries were given orders to watch for the launch. They were to make certain that the woman got away in it, then run in and grab the man. They were told nothing else.

'Unfortunately Gregory put up too realistic a fight and got hurt. Anyhow he would have been arrested and clapped into jail. He had to be, and everything else about the escape had to be one hundred per cent genuine. Otherwise the Baroness might have suspected that things weren't quite what they looked, or through a leak it might somehow or other have got through to the Germans that her escape was a put-up job. It was in order that the Moldavians should continue to be hoaxed that we've kept Gregory in the hospital at Brixton Prison. There was no avoidin' dopin' the two wardresses, but they are both being given a month's leave on full pay. And although a few people may wonder why Gregory is allowed to go free, no one except a little handful of us will ever know the whole truth.

'But gettin' her out of the Tower was only half the job; and the easier half, at that. She had to be got out of the country. Not to Ireland or South America, but straight back to the Continent. And on a date that couldn't be altered. That's where Gregory excelled himself. He got hold of this Moldavian Colonel—feller called Karbar, or some such outlandish name.

382

Pretended he was potty about the Baroness and asked this feller's help. It transpired that Karsar could put her across in a Moldavian sea-going tug; and, of course, we could fix the Navy to let it through their patrols. But he wouldn't play without some inducement. We'd expected that. It was to feed him that I got for Gregory those tit-bits of true information. God Almighty, what a game it was. My hair's white already but it's a marvel the lot didn't drop out. Every move depended on perfect timing, and the worry of it nearly drove me to drink. Still, we managed to block the most important bits by stopping the diplomatic bags from November the 4th. That was all part of the plan. It forced Kabbar to use the Baroness as a courier. You see, as she was in the lock-up we couldn't give her the stuff to take out with her. It had to be passed to her by this old friend of hers, the Moldavian; otherwise she would have smelt a rat.'

Sir Pellinore paused for a moment and Erika said, 'But I don't understand. You say this was true information that Gregory was giving to the Moldavian. Why did you want her to take it out?'

Sitting back, the old man gave a great guffaw of laughter. 'My dear, that was the cream of the jest. The German Intelligence take a lot of foolin'. I believe our people did a grand job; but the only way to clinch the deal was to land a red-hot tip on Hitler personally. The Baroness tricked Gregory into bringing her here to spy for the Nazis. He tricked her by making her take out the stuff.

'The neutrals aren't all pro-Germans by a long chalk. We have plenty of them working for us, and we know quite a bit about what takes place on the other side. Yesterday we learned what happened last week. By the morning of the 6th the Baroness was back with her old pal Ribbentrop. He put her stuff slap on the house-painter's desk. Hitler told Goering to get on to Kesselring and order the all-out attack for Sunday afternoon. The information Gregory gave Kasbar was dead right—except that to fit the Cover Plan he told him that D-Day was on the 9th instead of the 8th. Then he sold him the Cover Plan about our going into Sicily for the Baroness to take back to Berlin. It's the greatest coup he's ever pulled off.'

Erika was now crying with joy. Running round the big table-desk she threw her arms about Sir Pellinore's neck, kissed him again and again, and stammered out her relief and happiness.

'Steady on, m'dear,' he said after a moment, 'or you'll have me trying' to take you off Gregory yet. It's time we had a glass of wine. You look as though you could do with a tonic.' Leaning forward, he pressed the bell on his desk twice.

Two minutes later the door opened. The elderly housemaid came in carrying a magnum of Louis Roederer '28 in an ice bucket. Behind her, framed in the doorway, stood Gregory. His head was bandaged, his left arm was in a sling, and he was pale from loss of blood; but he was smiling.

He was looking at Erika and she at him. No words were needed. All the love they felt for one another was in their eyes.

Sir Pellinore too was smiling. Brushing up his white moustache he murmured to himself, 'The greatest coup he has ever pulled off; and I haven't pulled off a bad one myself.'